Excluded

CATHERINE MARSHALL

© Catherine Marshall

Catherine Marshall has asserted her rights under the Copyright, Design and Patents Act, 1988, to be identified as the author of this work.

This edition published by Sharpe Books in 2019.

CONTENTS

One
Two
Three
Four
Five
Six
Seven
Eight
Nine
Ten
Eleven
Twelve
Thirteen
Fourteen
Fifteen

*' ... we but teach
Bloody instructions, which, being taught, return,
To plague the inventor; this even-handed justice
Commends the ingredients of our poison'd chalice
To our own lips.'*

William Shakespeare

'Children now love luxury. They have bad manners and contempt for authority. They show disrespect for the elders and love chatter in the place of exercise; children are now tyrants, not servants of their households.'

Socrates, 2500 years ago

'Use your head. Teach.'

Government recruitment slogan.

Donna leaned in to the mirror above the chest of drawers and drew a thick black line along the upper eyelashes of her right eye. Spig, lying on her bed fiddling with her radio, glanced up at her. "He's not gonna look twice at you if he thinks you're a tart."

"Shut up." She drew the corresponding line along her lower lashes. "I don't look like a tart." Her confidence, never robust at the best of times, wavered. "I don't, do I?"

"'Course you don't." He went too far, sometimes, he knew that. She was so much more fragile than other girls. Than other girls he knew, anyway. Which maybe wasn't saying much. "You'll look great. If he doesn't want you, I'll have you myself."

"You won't, you know."

He grinned. They'd been friends for years, even since he'd first come here when social services had found out his mum was off her head. When her girlfriends let Donna down, as they often did, or his mates got annoying, as they often did, he and Donna turned to each other. She had turned to him tonight, wanting her ego boosting before her night out, needing someone to be there for her in case it all went wrong. They both knew they would never admit any of this to each other in a million years. He said, "What d'you see in him, anyway?"

"Oh, he's just ... " She was never able to find the words, concentrated instead on her other eye. "Special," she finished, straightening to approve her work.

Spig said nothing. He was pretty sure no one had ever thought him special. He'd give anything for someone nice, someone sweet like Donna, to think he was special. She could be a bit flaky, though, Donna. Bit intense sometimes. But then so could he. They were entitled to be intense and flaky, weren't they, the lives they'd been blessed with. He imagined the fairies at the christening from Sleeping Beauty when he and Donna had been born, granting them feckless parents and poverty and no hope. It hadn't bothered him when he was younger. He hadn't known any different. But lately he'd seen for himself how the world worked for other people. How much easier it was for them. It had been about the same time they'd told him he had an anger problem at school.

"Close your eyes," she said.

He obeyed, realised he couldn't fiddle with the radio with his eyes closed, and sighed heavily.

"I won't be long," she said.

He settled himself into her soft and grubby sheets, listening to her undress and dress again. After a minute or two, getting bored, he half-opened one eye to glimpse her flat little breasts, her concave stomach with its pierced navel. "Did that hurt?" he said.

She shrieked and threw her t-shirt over his face. It smelled of her, though he couldn't define it. Minty, was that it? Flowery minty? He started to laugh.

"What? Why are you laughing?"

"Just trying to decide what you smell like."

"Shut up*!" A few more shuffling noises, drawers opening and closing, a silence. Then she said, "You can open your eyes now."*

She had her hair scrunched and messy, wore a white sleeveless slash-neck top, a red skirt which showed her knees, silly strappy shoes she wouldn't be able to walk anywhere in. He swallowed. She did look great, and he did want to have her himself. The desperation in her eyes was more than he could bear.

"You look fantastic," he said quietly. She was fantastic, daft and funny and full of life, no idea how pretty and sexy she was. He knew he was a long way from being the only one who thought so.

Donna smiled. "I'm starting to feel a bit excited now," she confessed.

"Well you go, you go and have a good time, and don't worry about me sitting in the street throwing stones at cars all on my own."

She laughed. "You'll be getting pissed in the park."

She was right. He had to hand it to her. Getting pissed in the park was about all he was good for.

One

He had been released hours ago. Hours, after years. Sprung into a grey morning's crash and lumber of traffic, the haste of passers-by. The drizzle. Dean had steadied himself, waiting, motionless, for this outside world to take shape around him.

He'd expected ... he didn't know what. Relief. Exhilaration. Something. But cast loose again into the brashness of ordinary life he floundered and was, for the most fleeting of moments, helpless. A newborn still half-blind with birth.

Fuck, he'd thought, panicked. Then remembered where he was and relaxed. It was all right. He didn't have to guard his back. No one out here was watching him, watching for the chink, waiting to pounce. It was what freedom was, wasn't it?

The day shifted like a kaleidoscope into focus. He'd shaken himself and moved on.

He had walked fast, keeping pace with the pulse of the city. Buses, vans shuddered past. Streets lined with an endless irrelevance of shops - classy, chainstore, cheap and nasty. He'd slowed outside a pub, always thought it'd be his first call. But not yet. Not yet.

People to see, business to attend to. He hadn't been idle, these last months. Putting the feelers out in preparation. Dues to collect. There came a rhythm to his stride as he pounded on, afraid to stop for the city wasn't his city, he'd been uneasy in it all his life, coming from where he did. You couldn't trust the city. Look at someone the wrong way and your face'd be in a wall. Fight back and you were banged up. He was off-kilter enough as it was, staggering like a drunk in his head. Couldn't quite get a grip.

A mile or so south of the centre, arterial roads loud with heavier traffic. He'd been here maybe twice in his life, both times bricking it, expecting to get shot, knifed, glassed in the face. It was as it had always been, a deserted concrete wasteland of burned-out cars and boarded windows, a sci-fi landscape from some depressing tv series about a futuristic

Britain. Not his territory. Nowhere near. But the months he'd spent keeping his mouth shut and looking the other way pushed him on. He found the address.

Business attended to, time to go home. He sat in the car park of the first service station he'd come to, in the car he'd just called in debts to acquire, with a can of Stella and an egg and bacon sandwich, tension easing out of him. He didn't want to be there before dark, he couldn't be sure anyone knew he was out today. Couldn't be sure anyone would even remember him. They could all have left the country, for all he knew. Except they didn't, his people. Ever. Didn't leave the country, or the valley, or even the streets they'd been born on.

The same streets they died on.

If it'd been one of his people he was after, it'd be a piece of piss.

He drove, getting his bearings again, getting the feel of the wheel again and liking it. The last rays of evening sun sliced the cloud, tingeing the hills around him gold and the euphoria he'd been waiting for all day rippled through him.

Home.

He drove, squandering petrol, rubber, time. The sun had set, the lights of the mill towns glittering in the dark as he tried to block out the suspicion that home was going to be nothing more than a location. The familiarity of quarry scarred hills and a bust-up old council estate might be all he had to look forward to. He told himself it didn't matter. He wasn't planning on being there long.

Barely a mile to go and midnight not so far off. His instincts kicked in before his brain did, for he was sweating suddenly, breathless with the memory of death. Its impact blinded him for a moment, the sound of car horns and smashing glass and screaming in his ears as vivid as it had been then. He slewed off the road, breathing hard. You didn't forget. Something like that, you never forget. *Shit*. He could still see it now, the mangled mess of the car and the broken body, the spillage of windscreen and brain matter across the carriageway. His heart was pounding.

A car slowed, a voice called – "You all right, mate?" He

raised a hand in assurance, in thanks, and the car passed by. He took a breath, the sweat cold now on his skin. Pulled himself together. Drove on.

As no one moved away, so nothing changed. A new retail park, a kebab shop he didn't recall, the mill converted now into flash apartments, but the town was still bleak, pitted with the shells of failing industries, rows of back to back terraces strung between the low, littered main road and the higher avenues and crescents perched at the edge of moorland. The Victorian grammar school, grand and self-satisfied with its sweeping views across the valley, the concrete sixties comp he'd once attended himself, sunk into the boggy depths. He turned the car off the road, away from the lane leading to farmland and tacky barn conversions, and rolled down into the estate.

He parked on the empty track at the back of the furthest row of houses, an alley of wheelie bins and chip papers, an abandoned mattress and an upturned supermarket trolley. The fence dividing the by turns neat and neglected gardens from the alley was rotting in places, kicked away in others. Locating the stretch of fencing he wanted, he stood on a crate and vaulted soundlessly into the soil and hydrangeas below.

Lights ablaze in the kitchen, he kept to the shadows, though he could detect no movement from inside the house. He crept closer. The kitchen was empty. Gently depressing the handle, he felt the catch give, the door open a crack. He stepped silently inside. The door into the back room stood open, displaying the detritus of beer cans and take-away pizza boxes, the television blaring with some sort of bizarre late-night chat show.

And there, on the sofa, entirely oblivious to him, was the boy.

Two

It was interesting, Stephen thought, how wrong you could be. Take the woman sitting on the red sofa at right angles to his blue one and speaking authoritatively to camera. She was Deborah McGillis, the blonde, thirtysomething anchor woman of *News North West* and known to the nation – or at least the north-west corner of it – or at least those who sat in front of regional news programmes when they arrived home from work - as incisive and icily professional and, well, scary, quite frankly. In the flesh it turned out she had bitten finger-nails and a fruity laugh and a flirty knowingness in her eyes which, given the projected incisiveness and icy professionalism, were actually very sexy. Intrigued, and quelling his own nerves, Stephen watched her while she talked.

"Tomorrow morning children across the country will be beginning their new school year, none more nervous than year 7 as they leave behind the security of primary school for the strange and sometimes very frightening world of secondary. Tonight we're taking a look at what, in the current educational climate, secondary schools are offering our eleven year olds. Are our schools still a safe place for our children to be? And with GCSE results rising year after year, what are parents to make of accusations of dumbing down? We have with us in the studio Stephen Lord, head of Rapton Community High School in Lancashire. Stephen, what is your response to the argument that schools today are failing to provide their pupils with a safe environment in which to learn and failing to give them worthwhile qualifications at the end of it?"

Stephen gave her his polite-yet-assertive smile. "Well firstly I take issue with anyone who suggests that schools and exam boards are 'dumbing down'. Not least because it under-mines the achievement of hundreds of thousands of bright, hard-working pupils. How can we expect even our most motivated students to stay focused if we're telling them that the As and A*s they come out with are worthless? It does them, and us, an enormous disservice. "

"But is it true? The bottom line is *are* GCSEs easier than the O Levels you and I would have taken twenty or thirty years ago?"

"They are different," he admitted. "Most subjects now include coursework, and the whole way we approach subjects has changed, quite considerably in some cases. That doesn't make them easier. I think what's at work here is the national predilection for embracing failure. We're afraid, in this country, of believing in our own ability to improve, to be positive and achieve. It's not what we're about at Rapton. Our pupils are encouraged to strive, to fulfil their dreams. And I'm not just referring to those who will go on to sixth form elsewhere, or to university. What's important to us is catering for the whole child, placing an emphasis upon our pastoral care. It engenders a nurturing family atmosphere in which every child really does matter."

Deborah McGillis nodded, unmoved by the passion of his rhetoric. "Which touches on our other issue tonight, that of schools being safe places to which we can trust the care of our children. Is Rapton immune, then, from the behavioural problems, from the bullying and knife culture which seem to infect so many of our secondary schools?"

"Of course not. I would say that the schools which are most at threat from such terrors as knife and gun culture tend to be located in inner-cities, and at Rapton we're lucky enough to be in the hills and valleys of semi-rural Lancashire, supported by a close-knit community. We don't tend to see the extremes you might get in London, for example, or even Manchester. However, it's important to remember that schools have never in fact been 'safe'. Bullying and wild behaviour have been a part of school life for centuries. Let's not attribute it solely to young people today. Let's just try to deal with it as firmly and as fairly as we have always done."

Deborah McGillis nodded. "So how might that be? If you have a difficult and disruptive child in your school who is exhibiting threatening behaviour, how do you handle that firmly and fairly?"

"In my experience," Stephen replied, "by the time pupils are old enough for their behaviour to be a serious problem, they are no longer children. I know it's politically correct these days to refer to students in Years 10 and 11 as children, but they're not. They are young people, and we do well to remember that and to treat them with respect. Of course they still need guidance, of course the laws of society applied as school rules need to be upheld, but these are young people with decisions to make about their own lives. The more we encourage them to take personal responsibility for those lives, the better. Anyone exhibiting difficult, disruptive, threatening behaviour is doing so for a reason, whether it's boredom or anger or low self-esteem. It's a very simplistic, knee-jerk reaction just to punish the behaviour. I would prefer to deal with the reason. It's the prevention rather than cure approach."

"And does it work?"

"In the majority of cases, yes. It's a long-term solution, sure, to take into consideration – for example – the class the pupil is in, the work they're being given, the classroom dynamics, their situation at home, and to act upon it. But it's far more effective than simply issuing detentions."

Deborah McGillis was looking at him with interest and he wondered what her impression had been of him before he had opened his mouth, whether she realised that his own job was as much about presenting an image as hers was. Smoke and mirrors, he thought. Sleight of hand. Nothing is what it seems. Not even me.

She said, "And what about those pupils for whom it's too late?"

He smiled. "I could not hold my head up and say I was doing my job if I believed for a minute, for even the most recalcitrant pupil, that it was ever too late."

Callum Bywater, looping his tie into the largest knot and shortest tail possible, glimpsed his reflection in the mirror above the fireplace and thought - *fucking hell, here we go.* September through July every fucking year. Same crap teachers. Same pissing-your-life-away lessons. No wonder half his mates were on weed. No wonder they went looking for excitement with their fists. You'd drill holes in your skull to relieve the boredom. This year, though. This year was different. Never been Year 11 before. You ruled the school when you were Year 11. Not that he hadn't been putting in an impressive bid for running it the last four years, but this year, this year it was his.

"Cal?"

He winced, grunted a response. His mother, coming in through the back door from her night-shift cleaning the local office block, he could hear her heaving the bags of shopping onto the kitchen worktop. She usually popped into the 24 hour supermarket on her way home from work, keeping the fridge stocked for him as she'd be gone again by the time he was back from school. He couldn't get his head round her running herself ragged doing two jobs when she could've played the benefits game and got money for nowt. But then she was too half-soaked and too knackered to be playing any sort of game.

She came into the doorway, looking so half-soaked and knackered he couldn't meet her eyes in the mirror. "D'you need money for school, love?"

"Nah. S'all right."

"How will you get your dinner?"

"Nip home. Make a sandwich." Rob it off a sprog. "You can go out at lunchtime when you're in year 11." So many kids vaulted the school gates come twelve o'clock she'd never know it wasn't true.

"All right then." She stood, watching him for a moment. "Your last year in that uniform, Cal."

"Yeah, I were thinkin' that."

She smiled. "Doesn't seem five minutes since it were your first."

"Seems like a fuckin' lifetime to me. Right. I'm off. See you later." Though he rarely did.

"See you, love." She half-raised her hand in goodbye.

There were maybe thirty, forty kids from the estate went to Rapton High. Some from the posh end where the fences weren't kicked in and they had gnomes in the garden (he and his mates used to nick them, but he couldn't be arsed doing that anymore), some from the Rottweiler'n'tattoo ghetto where the real psychos hung out, some – like himself - perched between the two. Down but not out. Back to the wall and still fighting. And then there were the other kids, from other council estates rougher than his own, from the terraces which snaked in endless rows into and through and out of town, from the boxy new houses up on the hills and some, a very few, from the other side of the tracks.

Like the boy walking in front of him now.

They were following the lane skirting the moors, school one way, farmhouses and barn conversions the other. The boy in front of him was carrying a bag slung heavily over his shoulder and Cal – who never carried so much as a biro – knew that his top button might be undone but his tie would be knotted to geeky perfection. He knew this because he'd known Todd Kershaw, top swot and minted with it, nearly all his life.

"Eh, Kershaw." A short stride and they were level.

Todd turned, button and tie as Cal had predicted. "Eh, Bywater. Good summer?"

He always said stuff like that, stuff grown-ups said. Like it wouldn't occur to him Cal had spent the summer hanging round the estate getting pissed and bored and forced to entertain himself with a bit of petty theft and vandalism. "Oh yeah," Cal mocked. "That five star Caribbean cruise were well sick."

Todd smiled faintly. "What did you do?"

"Nowt. What did you do?"

"Holiday." He shrugged, playing it down, Cal could tell. Probably had gone on a five star Caribbean cruise. "Weird to be back. Last year and all that."

"Yeah. Weird. Got them where we want them this year, though, haven't we?"

Todd frowned. "Who?"

"Them. Lord and that lot. Shitting themselves over our results."

"Why?"

Clearly Todd hadn't realised, as Cal had some time ago, that

Lord's precious reputation depended on his Year 11's GCSE grades. That this gave them all, as it were, leverage. "He's got to go easy on us, hasn't he? So he ends up looking good. Thought you were s'posed to be clever."

"I am," Todd said. "It's percentage A*-C results that count, not how many."

"Same thing." They had reached the school gates, stood on the periphery of concrete and parked cars, of wind-whipped voices and dark green blazers and the promise of anarchy. Cal liked that word. Anarchy. "See ya," he said to Todd. He'd spotted Josh and Connor and Liam kicking a bag around and strolled over to join them. Childhood mates or not, it wouldn't do his rep any good at all to be seen hanging out with Todd Kershaw.

Leigh surveyed her classroom. For this moment it lay before her a peaceful and welcoming refuge, supplied with stimulating resources, cheerful display boards, posters for *The Boy in the Striped Pyjamas* and Baz Luhrmann's *Romeo and Juliet*. The carpet had somehow remained remarkably free from scabs of chewing-gum and she had a brand new interactive whiteboard whose finer points she was going to master. She could feel her determination to succeed emanating from the walls. Yet shortly this room would ring with the clamour of adolescents, would be strewn with their coats and bags, hum with their odours. She knew well enough that for all her best intentions it could easily degenerate into a setting for dumb and sneering apathy, emotional outbursts, ritual humiliation. The trick, always but perhaps especially here at Rapton High, was not to let it.

The yard, deserted when she had climbed out of her car an hour ago, was now filled with pupils swarming, swaggering, skittering between the two storey concrete buildings. Rapton had been built in nineteen sixty-three, its architecture an homage to its time, and had spawned another building every decade since. There were now five, dropped at odd angles to each other and the main road, allowing plenty of scope for truanting and dark deeds in blind corners where the CCTV cameras couldn't reach. Closest to the main gate sat the Admin block, home to both the immaculately-suited office staff who steered well clear of the pupils at all times, and the school's senior management team, clearly sequestered as far as possible from anywhere they might conceivably be of any use. To the left of this, from Leigh's vantage point, were situated the Maths classes, the Science labs and the Tech rooms. Above them the IT suites and a Modern Foreign Languages department which had latterly dwindled to two ageing staff and a cassette player. To her right the Arts Block, Expressive and Performing Arts with its theatre below and Humanities above, plus the school's main staff room. Somewhere beyond these lay the canteen and the Sports Hall, complemented by boggy playing fields and shorn Astroturf, and finally, as distant from anywhere else as it was possible to be, was the English Department.

The Library spread across the entirety of the ground floor, above it six English classrooms plus the cupboard of an office which housed, somewhere behind the printer, books, resource material and stationery, Joss, the department's admin assistant. The English Block was the newest addition to Rapton, completed under Stephen Lord's auspices just two years ago, furnished and equipped as expensively as the school's budget would allow. It was, Stephen had explained to his flocklet of English interviewees as he had led their conducted tour of the school last summer, testament to how seriously he took the promotion of literacy skills. He had spoken at length and with plausible charm and enthusiasm about basic competency in English being essential to accessing the rest of the curriculum, about the mastery of English being the key to success. Leigh, initially wondering whether this was spin to ensnare them or a genuinely held belief, had caught herself being impressed.

Her gaze shifted to the yard below, where a cluster of children alert and anxious as meerkats, blazers hanging to their knees, huddled blinking at maps of the school. A saunter of teenage girls, their hair straw-bleached or tar-black, skin thick orange or beige, hung with self-conscious indifference around the walls of the buildings. In the centre a group of older lads, identified as Year 11 by the black stripe in the noose of their ties, were kicking a carrier bag around, the early autumn sunshine punctuated by their shouts and jeering laughter as the bag, weighted to give it ballast, sailed through the air and skittered across the tarmac between them.

At some point today, Leigh thought, I will be shut in this room with some of those children.

At the sound of her door opening she turned - Alan Jackson, her head of department, glancing round with approval. "Very nice."

"Thanks."

He smiled. He was a large and genial man, neither his size nor manner detracting from his air of authority. Leigh looked at him and thought of Bacchus, or Jupiter, incarnate. "All set?" he asked her.

"Yes, I think so."

"Any trouble, send someone down for me."

She grinned. "Bring it on."

Alan laughed. "Finn said he'd come and have a word with you, has he been in?"

"Finn ... ?"

"Finlay Macallister, Head of Year 11, English teacher extraordinaire. One of our strengths, up here in the ivory tower. You'll like him."

Will I? "Good," she said. She paused. "So what are they like then, my form?"

"Oh, they're not so bad. The usual mix. I don't think you've any of the wilder members of the Focus Group in there."

"The Focus Group would be ... ?"

"Lord Stephen's euphemistic name for the brighter of our prospective criminals."

"And they're wild?"

"Mm." For a fleeting moment his bonhomie was eclipsed. "Don't worry. It falls to me to teach them." He glanced out of the window at the boys kicking the plastic bag, almost but not quite spilling its contents, sending meerkats sprawling as they ran. "That's a few of them down there. Connor Taylor, Callum Bywater, Josh Ferris. Did you catch him on *News North West* last night?"

"I did, yes." She decided not to admit at this point that she had also read his articles in the Times Ed, that most of what he propounded there made absolute sense to her.

Alan shook his head, smiling ruefully. The bell rang.

Lord Stephen, she thought. So that's the way the land lies.

Sam Webster pressed his spine into the brick wall of the Arts Block, hoping that if he kept very still and didn't meet anyone's eyes, the shield of invisibility which he would need to survive five years at Rapton High would begin to grow around him. Having failed the grammar school entrance exam by one mark – a detail he had felt it unnecessarily cruel to have been given – he had wanted to go to West Park, the non-selective high school at the other end of the valley which boasted a new sixth form centre, a state of the art theatre and an Outstanding grade from Ofsted. But West Park was – unsurprisingly - over-subscribed and a mile out of his catchment area and the appeals his parents had launched had been unsuccessful. His mother was particularly upset that her little boy would be subject to the horrors of what was reputed to be the one of the roughest and lowest performing schools in Lancashire and so Sam was trying to be brave. It will be fine, he had told her. It can't possibly be as bad as everyone says. He had been resolutely cheerful when she had taken him to choose his new stationery and uniform, the right coloured pencil crayons and a set square he could see no use for; they had even laughed together over the monstrous size of the smallest blazer. When she had dropped him off in the deadlocked traffic outside school fifteen minutes ago he had seen in her eyes that her heart was breaking. And now here he stood, buttoned and tied into the bottle green uniform and trying to become at one with a wall.

The bell rang. At least, Sam gathered the bell had rung as suddenly the entire population of the yard began moving towards the entrances of the various buildings. He knew his form room was in Humanities, up on the first floor, but before the jostling, lurching queue he had joined reached the double doors something happened. It happened fast, in a blur of bodies and bags and green blazers, a bag thrust at him by an unseen hand. Confused, Sam instinctively clasped it to him, stepping backwards out of the mêlée into the relative emptiness of the yard, further confused to realise it contained something warm and moist.

As the queue continued to surge past him, he peered tentatively inside. At first he didn't understand what it was, this mass of fur and blood, the tiny paw. And then his stomach heaved.

A few years ago the school hall might not have accommodated a full assembly but now, with a falling roll due partly to a blip fifteen years ago in the birth rate but more to the growing success of its rivals, the populace of Rapton High could just squeeze inside its newly painted walls. Stephen insisted on the school being redecorated every summer, an expense he felt justified by the boost it must make to morale. His own, anyway, if no one else's. He was only too keenly aware of the critical scrutiny to which his every word and move were subject, and if there were times when he took this more seriously than he cared to let anyone know, there were also times when he didn't give a flying fuck. Was it such a crime to let the place look half-decent for at least the first few weeks of term? To behave as if they were living in Britain at the dawn of a new millennium and not some distant war-torn hell hole? Looking out across the field of pupils, his charges and hopes and challenges for another year, he didn't think so.

"Good morning."

He waited. The mass murmuring, aided by hissed threats and shushes from various members of staff, reduced, almost stopped.

"Welcome back." His gaze travelled across the hall, from the Year 7s pale and cross-legged on the floor at the front, to the Year 11s slouched in attitudes of cynicism and apathy on the seats at the back. From his new teachers, alert and weighing him up, to the old guard, weary and unimpressed from sun-up to sun-down. "I hope you've all had a good summer," Stephen began. "I hope you are all rested and refreshed and have come back to school ready to achieve even greater things this year than you did last. For some of you, last year was the year you really went for it. You had a fantastic year. You fulfilled your potential, and you have the medals and the certificates and the grades to prove it. For others of you, that wasn't the case. For some of you, today is the very first day of your time at Rapton. When I was a teenager, there was a poster – and it was everywhere, quite bizarrely, everyone had it – which said, 'Today is the first day of the rest of your life'. And whether we had a good year or a bad year, whether we're new to the school or for us the end is almost in sight, it's something that's true for each and every one of us. Today *is* the first day of the rest of your life. Today I want to talk to you about New Beginnings."

He can talk the talk, Stephen Lord, Leigh thought as she watched him. And he wasn't without a certain presence. Good-looking enough for looks not to be an issue, but not so much that he didn't need other charms in his arsenal. Early forties, she guessed, though his hair was prematurely silver, in his blue eyes a wit and intelligence which his detractors no doubt read as shallow cunning. Leigh knew only that the brief impressions she had gained of him at her interview and from his television spiel were at odds with Alan's wry comment and the pupils' derision this morning, that his writings in the educational press suggested a man of principle and integrity. She might have far from the full measure of him but she had no intention of wearing other people's opinions like second-hand clothes. Still listening, she let her glance flick across the acres of children, ignoring the murmuring and covert mobile phone fiddling to note the red velvet curtains either side of the stage on which Stephen Lord stood, the plaster walls hung with predictable prints – Van Gogh, Monet, Rossetti. A pity, she thought, they hadn't gone for Munch, Dali and Hieronymous Bosch but that might have been asking for trouble. Did they really need to freak the kids out even further with the pictures on the walls? She half-smiled, her wandering eyes catching movement at the double doors to the rear of the hall, a man sliding in unnoticed behind the rows of staff seated behind the rows of Year 11s. He was youngish, mid-thirties perhaps, wore his suit with no grace and his dark hair a shade too unkempt. He was also broad-shouldered, attractive and perceptibly furious. At her feet a boy was tucking an iPod earpiece into his ear, which would have escaped her attention had he not misjudged the volume of its tinny beat. Nudging his shoe very gently with her own, she held out her hand.

Later she sat with Joss in her room amid filing cabinets and broken computers, sipping the coffee Joss had made and exchanging essential information. Following assembly, Leigh had taught one lesson to a skittish bunch of Year 7s and after achieving nothing more than names on books and quelling pre-pubescent first-day-in-high-school hysteria she felt pathetically grateful for adult company. Joss, small and svelte with a shining cap of auburn hair and perception as sharp as her humour, was the perfect antidote.

"Photocopying," she was listing. "Stationery – ordering, unearthing and reclaiming. Texts in the cupboard at the top of the stairs. GCSE coursework, given to me, entered on the system and filed. Assessment data also given to me – senior management will be bugging me for it which means I have to bug you. Photo-copying. Exam papers in the red drawers. Emergency cover work in the blue ones and I do the cover. A confidential counselling service, ego-salving, coffee and biscuits at no extra cost. Oh, and did I mention photocopying?" She grinned.

Leigh laughed. "Where do you eat lunch?"

"Up here if you want some peace and quiet. The staff room if you can bear it."

"It's that bad?"

"Apart from the wailing, moaning and gnashing of teeth, it's quite pleasant. It's where Lady Penelope has her throne."

"Lady ... ?"

"Penny Arkwright. Don't tell me you haven't met Penny."

"I haven't met anyone, except Alan. He mentioned someone

called Finn... ?"

"Ah yes, the trouble-busting Mr Macallister. Any trouble with any kid, send for Finn."

Leigh tried to equate 'English teacher extraordinaire' with sergeant-major. "Because he's strict?"

"Because they respect him and they like him and he can bring them to heel with a look. When he has to he can also shout very, very loud." Joss grinned, glanced at the department timetable, one of many fluttering sheets pinned to the wall above her desk. "Penny's free now. Come on."

Joss paused halfway along the corridor between Leigh's classroom and her own dugout. "The décor," she whispered as she pressed down the handle of room EN3, "will tell you all you need to know."

Its display boards, Leigh saw immediately, had been papered in the frosty colours of sugared almonds and were bare except for titles in lavender italics, one of which contained a spelling mistake and a misplaced apostrophe. A wide shelf running the length of the rear wall of the room held neat piles of exercise books and *Harry Potter*; beneath it junk poked out between the gaps in the floral curtains. "Penny," Joss was saying. "This is Leigh Somers. Leigh, Penny Arkwright."

Penny Arkwright was a rotund fiftysomething with Alice in Wonderland hair and dressed from the frillier end of Marks and Spencer's Per Una range. Standing beside her Joss, in her black wrap-around, looked slighter and sharper still. "Leigh." Penny's voice was imperious, as though Leigh were at some sort of social disadvantage, her accent – Leigh noted – consciously refined local. "I was wondering when we were going to meet you. Has Alan been to see you? You've encountered Jocelyn, our assistant, of course. She can be quite useful if you need any photocopying doing."

Leigh glanced at Joss, miming Psycho knife-stabbing behind Penny's back. "Yes, Alan's dropped in for a chat. He tells me Joss more or less runs the department," Leigh smiled and held out her hand, as Penny had not. "Nice to meet you. Have you been at Rapton long?"

"Twenty-seven years," she said, with pride in her

achievement. "It's what the children here need, some sense of security."

"I'm sure." *Twenty-seven years? Blimey.* "People must come to you for advice all the time, with your experience."

"Oh they do, of course. I do have a certain kudos, you know, with the pupils."

"Well you will," Joss said," you'll have taught their grandparents. Oh look, it's nearly break. I'll put the kettle on. Chocolate biscuit, Penny?"

As Joss departed Alan arrived, sitting down heavily on one of Penny's desks. "Miss Somers has had to introduce herself to me," Penny remarked pointedly.

Alan paused, met Leigh's eyes. "Sorry Leigh, I've been meaning to take you round everyone but I haven't had chance. First day back and all that."

"It's fine," Leigh said.

"How were your Year 7s?"

"Excitable. Like trying to keep puppies in a basket."

He laughed. "Year 9 next. This is where the fun starts."

The door flung open and with it a brief blast of noise from the corridor. They all turned in surprise as the furious tousled man from assembly pushed it shut again. He stood with his hand against the safety glass to deter intrusion.

"What's up?" Alan was concerned.

"Did any of you notice a gang of Year 11 lads kicking a plastic bag around the yard this morning?"

"Yes, I did. Callum Bywater, Connor Taylor, Josh Ferris. A few others. Why?"

He sighed. "How old is this school year? Two hours? Two and a half? Fucking Focus Group are at it again. There was a kitten in that bag. I doubt it was dead when they put it in there, but it certainly was by the time they handed it to a Year 7 boy when the bell rang."

Alan drew in his breath. "Oh Christ."

"How's the boy?" Penny asked.

"As you would imagine. Tearful and scared and pleading to go home. Stephen's trying to prepare something to say to his mother. Alan, will you let Stephen know you saw who it was?"

"Sure. I'll do it now."

"My God," Leigh murmured.

The – now understandably – furious man looked at her for the first time. "Sorry, you must be Leigh. I was on my way to see you when all this blew up. I'm Finn Macallister." He held out his hand, added wryly, "Welcome to Rapton."

Stephen waited for Finn Macallister to round up the Focus Group and deliver them to his office. That this gang of fifteen year old boys had so carelessly committed such a cruel and vicious act shocked but did not surprise him. That they had done so within minutes of the new term was deeply depressing. He tried to tell himself it was not a sign of things to come. The ethos he had paraded on national television yesterday – the same ethos on which he had based his entire career - was one in which he believed with all his heart but it wasn't winning him any friends or going even halfway towards resolving the school's worsening behaviour problem. He suspected he should be torn between the short term solution of cutting his losses and resorting to permanent exclusions and the long term one of persisting with philanthropic principles which had yet to show results. He should be looking reluctantly at short-sharp-shock punishments, at sudden death reprisals. He should be promoting a zero tolerance discipline policy which would have the pupils wetting themselves if he so much as looked at them. He should be as fearful for his career and his sanity as his wife was.

"Mr Lord." Finn, three members of the Focus group gathered behind him in the open doorway, their faces ruddy with cocky bravado.

Stephen gestured towards the boys. "In here, please." Finn entered with them. Stephen raised his hand in dismissal. "It's all right, Mr Macallister. I'll take this from here."

Finn nodded. Paused before walking away.

Stephen looked from one boy to another. Connor Taylor: pug-faced and shaven-headed, the middle of five brothers, the youngest high on dope and drunk every Saturday night at the age of thirteen, the eldest on remand, Connor himself already a father, having impregnated last summer a slack-mouthed, crusty girl from Year 9. Josh Ferris: dark in a Mafia hood meets Neanderthal sort of way, incapable of anything above a G grade in any of his subjects and reputed to be handy with a knife. Callum Bywater: narrow face, spiky blond hair, an earring, aggressive, sullen and with an ounce or so of intelligence the gang's ring-leader for as long as Stephen had known them. All of them ranged before him, their eyes on his desk, the window, the framed photographs on the wall, darting to each other and away. He said after a moment, "There are no excuses or explanations any of you can give that I'm interested in hearing – "

"It weren't just us," Josh muttered.

"Perhaps not. The others will be dealt with later." His voice chilled the air. "Anyone else have anything to say?"

Apparently not.

He spoke, with unconcealed disgust and brooking no further interruption, humiliated -though they would not know this - because he had set himself the goal of putting his theories into practice by, before the end of this year, turning these boys around. He had wanted to transform violent thugs into young men capable of five decent GCSEs and a future which didn't include a criminal record. He didn't want, on the first day of term, to be admitting that it wasn't going to happen.

The silence stretched like a bubble blown through a hoop as Stephen could no longer trust himself to speak. Traditionally when interviewing pupils you left the door of your room open to protect both yourself and them. As five minutes ago he had left his ajar, Stephen had acknowledged that with it shut he might be tempted into meting out a form of justice he would regret for the rest of his life. If only a hand less culpable than his own might do it for him.

"Don't know why you're making such a big a deal out of it," Callum Bywater observed shortly. "It were only a dumb animal."

The boys rippled with barely repressed sniggers

Stephen looked at him, holding the gaze until Callum's faltered. "There are some, and just at the moment I find myself amongst them, who might describe you as dumb animals. It might be a fitting punishment for creatures twenty times your size to kick you around the yard. Sadly it's not within my power to arrange that. It is within my power to get you out of my sight, however, because I can't bear to look at you, and I think you'll find a large proportion of people in this school will feel the same way. Remember that in a few months time you'll be coming to me for references, for college courses and jobs. For the army, isn't it, Callum?"

Callum's throat was working. His eyes said *fuck you* but his mouth stayed shut. Which had to be, Stephen thought, something of a first. "In the meantime," he sentenced them, "isolation for the rest of the week and on report until I see fit. And I will be speaking to your parents before the day is out. Understood?"

Grunts, shrugs, a common refusal, or inability, to meet his gaze. Suddenly he could no longer bear to share the same air. "Go."

Three

Five minutes to the end of her first day. Leigh gazed across her rows of Year 10s, busy making notes on the difference between the opening scene of *Romeo and Juliet* as written on the page and as interpreted in the Baz Luhrmann film complete with guns, cars and petrol explosions. She knew that one girl on the register for this class was absent because she would be giving birth next week, that two of the boys had Asberger's Syndrome and that all of them were surgically attached to their Ipods and mobile phones. One of them, watching her watching them, said, "When do I get my phone back, Miss?" He had recently shaved off random areas of his eyebrows, presumably because he thought it lent him an avant-garde sort of cool, when in fact it made him look as though small animals had crept onto his pillow during the night and nibbled his facial hair while he slept.

She said, "When the bell goes."

On cue, it went. They looked at her, expectant. At least, she thought, they weren't trampling her in the rush. "Thank you, Year 10. Put your chairs up and your books on the front desk as you leave. I'll see you tomorrow." She handed back belongings as they passed and listened, as the door closed behind the last of them, to the emptiness of her room. Sinking down into her chair she closed her eyes for a moment.

"Miss?"

Opened them again. The boy who had entered was tall and dark-haired, dark-eyed, nice-looking beneath the obligatory sprinkling of acne, skinny with recent growth. And *smiling* at her. Leigh was almost taken aback.

"Are you our new form teacher, Miss?"

"I am."

He moved towards the coat pegs at the back of the room, his bag hooked over one shoulder. "What's your name?"

"Miss Somers." It had long since been erased from the whiteboard. "What's yours?"

"Todd Kershaw. I wasn't here at registration, I had to see to Year 7. I'm one of the prefects."

"I know. It's on the register."

He shrugged into his jacket, looked mildly surprised that this sort of fore-thought took place. "So what school were you at before?"

"St Mary's. South Manchester."

"What was it like?"

Leigh thought of her control freak Head of English, of her colleagues, prepared to do each other damage for the best grades, the best department, the best jobs. "Well. It wasn't like Rapton."

Todd grinned. "Nowhere's like Rapton, Miss. You'll see." Her expression must have given her away for he frowned. "You all right?"

"Fine. It's just a bit of a learning curve, first day."

He raised his eyebrows. "I heard about the kitten thing. How sick is that?"

"Well, very."

"Have they been excluded? Cal and the others?"

"I don't know." Something in his voice alerted her. "Is he a friend of yours, Cal?"

He hesitated. "We were friends at primary school. He was all right then. Naughty, but all right. Now – well, we get on but we've not exactly got a lot in common." He shook his head. "It's worse, somehow, when someone you know does something like this."

"Because it's a shock?"

"Because it's like you try to think well of them and they let you down. Again." He half-smiled, turned towards the door. "See you then, Miss."

She smiled back. "See you tomorrow Todd."

Staring at her laptop, at the little file icons whose acronyms she didn't yet understand, she wondered whether she should be trying to find her way round them or whether it would be simpler just to talk to Joss. There were a dozen questions she wanted to ask Alan but he had gone to a department heads' meeting and, to be honest, she was knackered. Sod it, she thought. I'm going home.

She shut down the laptop, stood up to switch off the projector, unlocked her filing cabinet for her handbag -

"Leigh."

Again, a voice from the doorway. Finn Macallister's, this time. Her skin prickled.

"Hey."

She watched him come to sit on the desk opposite hers, his suit and his dark hair messier still, but at least he had lost the furious look. He smiled. "Leaving already?"

"Is that all right? I mean, it's what everyone does?"

"Oh sure. Four o'clock, the place is deserted. Except for those kids with no homes to go to. Or homes they would rather not go to." He said it drily, though he wasn't joking. "How's it gone today?"

"Not bad." She admitted, "I'm not keen on Year 8."

"No one's keen on Year 8. Just don't give them an inch. Straight out, the minute they look at you the wrong way." He stopped. "Sorry. Why am I telling you this? How long have you been teaching?"

"Five years."

"There you go. But if you do need anything, I'm in the next classroom but one down the hall. Right opposite Lady Penelope." He smiled. "Oh, and Fridays? Some of us go to the pub for an hour, kind of ease into the weekend. You're very welcome to join us. Unless, you know, you have other stuff ..."

"No," she said. "I have no other stuff."

"Me either."

A pause. Not a lingering look, not even a fluctuation in tone, just a breath's pause.

She said, "Yeah, thanks, then. That would be nice."

"It's better than nice." Finn pushed up from the desk, ready to leave too. "It helps to prevent you from becoming a cynical, gibbering mess, so damaged by the horrors of teaching you're left drooling and incoherent and prone to fits of terrible violence. Or is that just me?"

She smiled. "Oh, I doubt it."

He grinned, went to the door. "See you tomorrow, Leigh. Sorry it's been such a crap start."

"Not your fault. It didn't really impinge on me. And there's a lot to be said for in at the deep end." She heard the words echo on the air as the door closed behind him, leaving her alone in her classroom knowing that the deep end was exactly where she was.

Stephen leaned across to top up their glasses. It was his favourite time of day, an hour's peace in the warmth of his kitchen, chatting with his wife over half a bottle of red, their children sprawled on the floor in the living room in front of *The Simpsons*. One day over, the next yet to begin, the sun stretching its last rays across the black granite worktop with false promises of a long evening ahead. By seven it would be dark and the children on their way to bed, dirty plates to stack in the dish-washer and the inevitable sense of gloom at the thought of another day on the other side of sleep. But just now, these precious minutes, relief at a summit conquered outshone the dread of the higher and more treacherous one looming ahead. I love my job, Stephen told himself as he took another sip of wine. Really I do.

"I didn't think," Claudia said, "there was anything you could tell me about that place that would shock me any more. But dear God. A *kitten*."

"Yes."

"Somebody's *pet*."

"Yes."

"You're raising sociopaths at that school."

"I would dispute that I'm the one raising them."

"So what happened? Did you exclude them?"

"No."

She looked at him.

"Four days' isolation. Don't," he said. "Don't make me explain myself to you."

"When have I ever – "

"Because God knows I'll have enough people demanding explanations tomorrow."

"Not least the Year 7 boy's mother."

"I didn't see her today. Apparently she didn't say very much."

"She was probably too busy ringing round other schools."

He sighed heavily. Claudia knew very well how little support he had from his staff and she knew why, she didn't need to hear him argue that extending these boys' summer holidays by excluding them would do no good, that it was better to isolate them for the duration of the school day, break and lunchtime included, and persist in attempting to educate them. She might not agree, it was true, but she understood because he told her often enough, that he still believed it his duty to do everything within his power to furnish them with some sort of qualifications and he wasn't going to shirk it in the name of vengeance. She also understood, as he did, that his staff would hang him for his idealism.

He said, "I don't know what the answer is. I only know that a knee-jerk reaction isn't it. If they're in isolation they can't upset anyone else in school, and they're not hanging round the streets or burgling people's houses or beating anyone up – "

"I know," she said softly.

He relented. She did know. She always knew, usually without him having to say a word. From the moment they had met fourteen years ago, it had been as though she had seen him with an empathy and a clarity no one else ever had. He would have said it was as though she could see into his soul, but he knew that not to be true, even in the most figurative sense. She looked after him, supported him, with the same good-humoured, rational calm with which she ran her catering business, and their household affairs, and brought up their children. Whatever storms he faced at school, home was always a sanctuary. He looked at her, this beautiful, wise, capable woman he had married and thought that she was now, as she had always been, so much more than he deserved. It had been a while before he'd stopped looking over his shoulder, fearful lest she should discover that he was so much less than she deserved.

"Da – ad."

The Simpsons must have finished. He looked towards the kitchen doorway, where his daughter Lucie stood with one sock hanging down, one golden plait untied. She climbed up onto his lap.

"Hi sweetheart." He kissed the top of her head. God forbid that in three or four years' time anyone would be thrusting an animal they had murdered into her arms, but then Lucie would not be going to Rapton. Both she and her brother would continue to attend the private school in whose preparatory years they were now. When Stephen compared the privileged education his own children were receiving with the bare knuckle fight which was Rapton High, he did not know whether to be ashamed of or grateful for his capacity for hypocrisy.

Todd fantasised about going missing.

Not on a regular basis or anything, just when the effort of staying resolutely cheerful and Rising Above It became too much, and the dark pit of reality which he spent his life pretending wasn't there threatened to engulf him. He longed then just to walk away, to disappear as if physical distance would solve everything. Sometimes it was only the suspicion it wouldn't that kept him here.

Tonight he'd returned as usual to an empty house. He liked this, sinking alone into its deep peace after having survived another day in the prison-asylum they called school. The house was a barn conversion which his stepfather, Vince, had snapped up the minute it had come onto the market ten years ago and it had, he never tired of reminding everyone, more than doubled in value since. Todd slightly despised Vince for his preoccupation with material wealth, but he loved the house, its origins still clear in the exposed stone and timber, the way you could vanish into a corner of it, never having to know who else was around, or have them certain exactly where you were. He swung through to the kitchen, all dried flowers and farmhouse pine without a glimmer of post-modern irony, to pluck a bottle of cream soda from the fridge and a bag of crisps from the cupboard. In his room beneath the eaves he peeled out of his disguise of Rapton Inmate and pulled into jeans and a black *Scouting For Girls* t-shirt, dropped his Ipod into its docking station and groped in his bag for the novel they'd started reading today in class. Holden Caulfield. His ticket out of here.

Surfacing a couple of hours later from the depths of someone else's angst, he trotted back downstairs to the kitchen. He preferred the evenings when he ate alone, rustling himself up beans on toast or a stir-fry from the bag in the freezer, crashing on the sofa with the lights low, pretending the house and its peace belonged to him. But tonight he could hear their voices before he was halfway across the hall, the growl and twitter audible even through the heavy oak doors.

"'Evening." Todd skated across the stone floor in his socks behaving, as he always did in their presence, several years younger than he was.

"All right, lad?" Vince sounded friendly enough. He was sitting at the island unit with a glass of lager – Sheryl, his loving wife, wouldn't let him drink it from the can - his square frame overflowing the bar stool on which he was perched, like a cube balanced improbably on a matchstick. His bulk and his weathered complexion, all those years on building sites before he'd become the boss, made him look like the sort of person you wouldn't want to mess with, though Sheryl insisted he was a teddy-bear. Yeah, Todd had thought, the kind of teddy-bear who'd knee-cap you if you looked at him the wrong way. But he knew this was unfair. Vince didn't much go in for knee-capping, and beneath the inarticulate bluster he did generally mean well. Todd just couldn't remember the last time he'd called him Dad.

"Todd, love. Are you having some tea with us?" Whatever her temper, Sheryl's voice was always excruciatingly shrill. Vince the teddy-bear had once mused that it reminded him of bird-song. Todd had said, *oh Jesus Christ* and been sent from the room. She stood now at the Aga she'd never been quite sure how to use, stirring something in a pan.

"Sure." He hitched up onto one of the other bar-stools. "What're we having?"

"Oh just something light. Have to keep a tight rein on what I eat at my age."

Todd wanted to say that forty-five and size zero was not a good combination, but he couldn't think how to phrase it without offending anyone. Vince told her she was in fine fettle for any age and she smiled. "It's easier, though, if you don't put on the weight in the first place. I don't want to be battling to get into my bikini for our holidays."

An instant tightening in the air between them. Todd looked from one to the other. "Where're we going?" This summer they'd hired a villa on the Amalfi coast. Todd, expecting to be bored out of his brain, had been granted his independence for the fortnight and free-fallen into an intense and euphoric relationship with Christie, an English girl his own age from the villa down the hill. One night on the terrace overlooking the ocean, beneath the tumbling bougainvillea, they had tenderly and fumblingly lost their virginity to each other. His head still swam with her. They texted and MSN'd and sometimes he could still taste her, still feel the silky warmth of her. It was a pleasurable kind of madness.

"Um ... St Lucia. It's in the Caribbean."

"I know. Have you booked? My GCSEs will have finished by the end of June." He stopped. Vince had shifted away from him. Sheryl's chirp had become that of a sparrow with a cat's paw at its throat. "What?"

"We've booked for the first two weeks in June," Vince said heavily.

"But ... "

"We know."

He stared at them, shocked into silence.

"You'll be able to get your revision done much better if we're not here," Vince reasoned, and Todd could see in his face that he had been talked into this. "Don't want us cluttering up the place while you're trying to work."

"And we hardly saw anything of you this time." Sheryl, her back to him, stirred busily at whatever odourless concoction she had in the saucepan. "It's not as if you enjoyed our company. Paying all that money to take you out there and you didn't spend five minutes with us."

"And it'll be much cheaper for you to go in June," Todd said bitterly. His throat felt tight. "Well thanks. Thanks a lot."

"It's not the money." Vince was unconvincing.

"Apparently it is. Didn't you hear what she just said?"

"You're a bit old now anyway, aren't you, to be trailing round after us? You'll be wanting to go away with your mates."

What mates? "That's not the point." Why did this matter so much? Why was he on the edge of tears? "Forget it, okay?"

It was the right thing to say. They wouldn't forget it, of course, but he had given them the excuse not to continue the discussion. That was what they did in this house, after all, not talk about things. Everything suppressed and sealed away so no one could at a later date be accused of saying something hurtful or blameworthy. He swallowed. "I'll get my own food later. Don't worry about me," he added acidly, before flinging back up to his room. He switched on his laptop, logged onto MSN, but for once Christie wasn't online. No one was there; no one he could talk to anyway. Sitting in the middle of his bed, he wondered how long it would take to pack a bag, walk down into town, get on a bus going anywhere. The eight hundred pounds in his bank account might last him ... how long?

And where would he go? There was no one to go to.

He'd known it since he was twelve years old. He was on his own.

Callum Bywater lived close enough to school to be able to leg it there and back in ten minutes, if necessary. He'd been glad of this often enough but today he would have liked to live a million miles from Rapton High and that arsehole Stephen fucking Lord. Isolation! What was the point of that? Coming on like he cared when everyone knew he was only out for himself. Even the teachers called him a wanker. Callum had heard them, when he'd been hiding behind the Arts block having a fag when he should have been in History, two of them, on their way to the staff room. He'd nearly laughed out loud except then he would have been discovered hiding behind the Arts block having a fag when he should have been in History. He'd loved it though, was saving it up to tell him at some appropriate moment. Assembly would be a good time. He'd cack himself, he thought they all loved him so much. It'd be pay-back time for thinking he could screw up Cal's chances of getting into the army. No one threatened Cal Bywater and lived.

Cackling like the villain in an am-dram panto he banged into the house. No one in. Never was, being as his mum was always at work and his dad had buggered off years ago. He grabbed a couple of cans of beer from the fridge and switched the telly on, flicking between CBeebies and assorted crap on the satellite channels while he drank. He'd wanted to hang round in town with the others, but Josh and Connor had parents who were pissed off when they were phoned up at work to be told their sons had narrowly escaped exclusion for kicking a kitten round the yard. They'd turned up at school at half past three to drag Josh and Connor into waiting cars. His own mother never received any messages from school, largely because Callum wiped the answer phone and intercepted the mail but also because she could barely read or write. This had embarrassed him when he was younger but lately it had become, like exclusions and Asbos and visits from the police, a badge of honour. My mum's illiterate, how hard am I? He did tell her the truth about some stuff, like the gas bill and family business, but she didn't need to know about school. He didn't see the point in worrying her. Didn't see the point in talking to her. Truth was, he couldn't see they had anything to talk about.

Because how was she his mum? How had someone so dopey and law-abiding, someone who had no spark or fight in her, produced him? He couldn't understand it. But then she'd always said he was more like his dad. He didn't like her telling him that, because as far as he was concerned his dad was a no-mark waster who sold crack to fund his own habit and never, on the rare occasions Cal encountered him, seemed sure what day it was. To be fair, his mum was well rid. But he wouldn't be living like this when he was her age, in a council house full of catalogue furniture and doing two crap jobs to pay for it. He'd have money and a bit of respect, the kind of car and house and bird other blokes'd kill for. He'd be well minted.

Later, much later, drunk on six cans of Stella and having eaten nothing but a Mars bar and a packet of crisps since lunchtime, he dialled for a pizza which he ate while watching some rubbish horror film Josh had lent him on DVD. Load of fucking bollocks. He'd have Josh tomorrow. Then he remembered about isolation and toyed with the idea of not turning up. He could … what? What else was there to do except go to school and see your mates, wind people up? In fact, whose fault was it he was in isolation in the first place? He'd seen them, watching from the window while they'd been kicking the bag around, Jackson and that fit new English bird. Couldn't have been her, she wouldn't have known who he was. It had to have been Jackson. Well he'd have to have eyes in the back of his head from now on, would Mr Jackson. The rest of the week in isolation then back in class. Cal grinned.

A second later he had stopped grinning.

Difficult to grin with someone's hand clamped round your face.

Four

Difficult to do much of anything with their other arm round your throat.

Callum, recovering fast and cursing into the palm held hard against his mouth, tried to buck but to his shame and fear he couldn't move. Not without having his neck broken. He could carry on squeaking and thrashing or he could wait. He chose to wait.

"I've got a knife. Now I can let you go and you can stay sitting nice and still, or I can use it."

It wasn't a voice you argued with. Cal nodded. The grip loosened and he gasped for air. The intruder moved slowly round from behind the sofa and lowered himself into the armchair opposite him. He was as tall as Cal probably, skinny but that tough, whipcord kind of skinny you didn't underestimate. Hair too short, face too pale, eyes like a door shut in your face. He had on manky jeans and battered trainers, some sort of biker jacket that'd seen better days. He took out a flick knife and began playing with it, turning it from point to end and back again on the arm of the chair. Cal swallowed. He didn't feel any freer for having been released. "What d'you want?" The surliness which usually came so naturally to him failed as his voice quavered. "There's nothin' here worth nicking."

"Don't want to nick anything."

Callum became aware of an urgent need to piss. He couldn't take his eyes off the knife. "So what d'you want? Why did you break into our house?"

"I didn't break in. Your back door's not locked. As for what I want … a few nights' kip'd be a start."

Callum couldn't get a grip on this. A straightforward burglary he could understand, beating him senseless par for the course. But this bloke had silenced him without really trying, hinted at violence and now expected to stay the night. What the fuck was going on? A cold realisation washed through him. Was this how these pervs worked now? Stalking you home from school, staking out the house, making their move long after dark, knowing you were alone … He stared at the knife and swallowed hard.

"What you gonna do to me?"

And the stranger laughed.

"Oh I don't know, Callum. Beat you at Scrabble?"

This just got worse. This down and out bloke who'd invaded their house and threatened to throttle him *knew his name*?

"Who the fuck are you?" he yelped.

"I'm Dean," he said.

Dean. He didn't know any Dean.

Hang on. Hang on. Wasn't his mum's brother called Dean?

Wasn't his mum's brother called Dean inside for armed robbery?

"Fuck," he whispered.

"Yeah," Dean agreed. "Fuck's about right."

Cal was sobering up fast. He croaked, "So what you doin' here?"

"Got out this morning. Thought I'd pay my big sister a visit." Dean was doing the knife thing again, point to end, point to end.

"My mum?"

"We've talked." Dean paused. "'Bout you, mostly. Thought I'd come and have a look at you. See if you're worth getting worried sick about."

Callum snorted. "She's not worried sick about me. She couldn't give a toss. She's never here."

Dean shot him a look which made Cal wish he'd kept his mouth shut. "She's never here because she's working to keep you in beer and pizza, you ungrateful shit. What d'you think she's doing while you're sat here slobbed out getting pissed?"

Cal stared. "How d'you know anythin' about us?"

"Because I can see for myself." He nodded towards the pizza box, the beer cans. "Because I rang her to tell her I was gettin' out and she told me all about you."

"Well you can't talk, where've you been the last seven years? What use have you been to her?"

"An' you're what, the model son?" He held Cal's challenging gaze. "No, thought not. She's not had a lot of help, has she? Yeah, I've been away. Well now I'm back."

Cal was uncertain. His menace was like waves, drawing quietly away then coming slapping back at you.

Dean sighed. "Fuckin' hell, Callum. Least you could do is get me a drink."

Bemused, he took another six pack of beer from the fridge, handed a can to Dean. They sat, ring-pulled, swigged. Cal said, "You could've just knocked on the front door like normal people."

"Always more interesting, getting into a place through the back door. Tells you a lot. Lets you surprise people."

"Gets you decked."

"By a fifteen year old kid?" The bleak humour was back. "Like to see you try."

"I'm not a kid." Sounded like one, saying that. Looked like one, surrounded by take-away pizza remains, drunk on cheap beer, dribbles of it down his shirt.

"Criminal record doesn't make you a grown-up, Callum."

"Made you one though, didn't it?"

Dean's voice when he replied was different. Serious. "No. It wasn't a bit of shop-lifting that made me grow up."

"Prison?"

Dean looked at him. "Any time you wanna take me on, feel free."

Cal shut up. Added, more cautiously, "So, what? You stickin' around?"

"For a bit. Mate's offered me a job up in Scotland end of next month."

"A job?"

"Not a bank job, dickhead. One with a wage. Like normal people."

Cal was disappointed. An uncle who'd done time for armed robbery might have been useful to have around.

Dean said, "So what d'you reckon, then? Gonna let me have a bed?"

Cal snorted. "Do I have a choice?"

"You always have a choice. Might not feel like it at the time, but you do. And that really is why I'm here."

Cal, watching him drain his can, understood that he was going to have his wits about him, having Uncle Dean around. Understood he'd never be sure which way he was going to jump.

Eight a.m. and sunshine filled the valley with a chill golden light. In a grassy corner near the school gates, Len the caretaker had propped his ladder against the sign at the entrance and was painting out the letter C someone had added to Rapton High. Leigh, lifting up the boot of her Fiat Punto to hoist out her plastic crate loaded with books and posters and examples of persuasive writing, heard someone call her name. Resting the crate on the inside rim of the boot, she looked around, saw Stephen crossing the empty car park towards her. "Morning," she greeted him.

He slowed as he drew nearer, smiled. "How did you get on yesterday?"

"Oh, fine."

"I had intended to pop in and see you, but events rather overtook me."

She remembered Finn Macallister saying almost exactly the same thing. "So I gather. Thanks, though. No, I was fine, really. Everyone seems very nice."

He raised an eyebrow. "Do they?" Indicated her crate. "Are you going upstairs? I'll give you a hand."

Rapton was only the third school at which Leigh had taught since becoming qualified, but she still didn't remember any headteacher carrying her bags for her before, or seeming at all likely to. "Lovely morning," she commented, trotting beside him as he strode, laden, while she had only her handbag to weigh her down.

"It is," he agreed. "Pity it wasn't like this last week."

"Or at any point at all during the summer." She glanced at him, decided to risk it. "What would you do today, then, if we didn't have to be here?"

But Stephen seemed unfazed by presumptuous smalltalk

from someone who had been a member of his staff barely twenty-four hours. "Oh, we'd probably take the children out for the day. York, Chester. The Lakes, maybe. One of our best days out," he added as they climbed the stairs to the English corridor, "was Bolton Abbey. Beautiful day, took a picnic, kids explored the ruins, paddled in the stream, clambered over the stepping stones, and we sat and watched. Funny, how little it can take to capture their imaginations. Make them happy. Right then." They entered her classroom. "Where do you want this?"

"Just plonk it down anywhere. And thank you."

"You're welcome. Leigh ... " He paused. "I know it looked bad yesterday. I won't pretend they're not a difficult year group, but there're some great kids in there."

"I know."

He nodded. "Well good. I'm glad you've seen that too. I don't want us to lose sight of them for the sake of the half-dozen who sometimes behave like mindless thugs. I'm sure Finn and Alan have said this to you too, but if you have any problems, anything I can help with, my door's always open."

"Thank you," she said again. "I'll remember that."

After he'd gone she unpacked her crate, plugged in her laptop, brought up her form register and checked her messages. It occurred to her then that messages of the snail mail variety would be delivered to her pigeon-hole in the staff room, and locking her door behind her, she descended the stairs and stepped back out into the sunshine.

It didn't take much in the way of perspicacity to spot that the main staff room was simultaneously a refuge from the storm and a slough of despond. A shelter from the abusive rampaging of the pupils, it provided somewhere reasonably comfortable to sit, a kettle, a microwave and a long, stained refectory-style table at which to work. One wall was lined entirely with pigeon-holes, another with notices and staff timetables. The windows of the third overlooked the yard, the brick walls of the opposite buildings and the encircling hills. Sitting in here alone during a free period, she could see, it would be a pleasant enough sanctuary.

But she was not alone now and the prevailing atmosphere was one of outrage.

"What message," someone was demanding as Leigh entered the room, "what message does that send out to the kids?"

"Ohh." Someone else sighed in despair. "He's lost it, so he has."

A woman in dress sense more nightclub barmaid than secondary school Maths teacher stood in the centre of the mêlée, her voice high with distress. "So I have to tell my Year 7s that there's no point reporting being bullied because the head's not going to do anything about it? Those psychos are going to be back in classes on Monday and nothing will have changed. They'll just be even more unteachable than they already are!"

"Nothing will have changed because he's more interested in his bloody Value Added than he is in the behaviour of the kids."

"West Park excludes and still has high Value Added."

"The head at West Park hasn't got her eye on Headteacher of the Year."

"He's not going to get to be Headteacher of the fucking Year if he doesn't do something about behaviour."

"He's not going to be Headteacher of anything. If Ofsted see any of this when they come in we'll be straight into Special Measures and then the whole HMI circus'll be in town. You know they're closing Mount View in Burnley? Kids' behaviour there wasn't much worse than it is here. Head was about as much use."

Leigh stood at her pigeon-hole, blindly collecting her post, trying to reconcile the image of Stephen as either a villain or a fool with the man who moments ago had been carrying her bags for her. Most staff were pitching in, but the loudest voices belonged to the woman with the inappropriate cleavage and a man of around retirement age, short and grey and watery-eyed. He shook his balding head. "He's out of his depth at Rapton, always has been. He's not tough enough for a school like this. All his liberal ideas about personal responsibility when what most of these kids need is a spot of corporal punishment. You've got to stand up to the Callum Bywaters of this world and he won't. He thinks if he can win the Focus Group round it's a feather in his cap. He won't accept you'll never win kids like that round and while he's trying the rest of the school's going to the wall."

"Only thing you can do with those scrotes is get them out." The Barmaid all but spat the words. "They don't want to be here, we don't want them here. They're going to end up dead or in prison in a couple of years anyway, let them get on with it. Let's concentrate on the good kids for once."

The sentiment was understandable enough, but Leigh felt disturbed by the vehemence with which it was being expressed, by the utter lack of sympathy with any of Stephen Lord's principles. Perhaps they had lived too long with the fall-out from his leniency. Perhaps they were even right. But there was almost a pack mentality to their bitterness, a *fight-fight-fight* chant behind the words. She left immediately, threading her way through to the door, the sour atmosphere still clinging to her as she hightailed it back to her classroom.

Barbara, Stephen's personal secretary, showed his visitor into his office then slipped discreetly away. "Mrs Webster." He rose to greet the mother of the child whose rite of passage into Rapton had been the receiving of a dead animal. "Please. Take a seat."

"No thank you." She remained standing, wrongfooting him as he had already sat down, and regarded him steadily. She looked like Sam, small and slender, same fine brown hair, same deep-set eyes. "I'm not here to have a conversation with you."

He should, he realised now, have been alerted by her silence yesterday. Instead, and possibly because at Rapton no one, neither staff nor students, ever did anything quietly or with circumspection, he had accepted her apparent calm at face value and with no small degree of relief. "I see," she had said, several times, when he had haltingly explained to her over the phone exactly why her eleven year old son was sitting weeping in his office. "I see. Yes I do. Of course I will." She had arrived within half an hour and swept Sam away with her, without seeing or speaking to Stephen himself. He had known at the time it had been a slip of integrity not to have had this interview with her then.

Now she placed Sam's Rapton High Diary and uniform on the desk between them. "He won't be needing these again."

Stephen took a breath. "Mrs Webster ... "

"There is nothing you can say."

"Not even 'I'm sorry'?"

"Well possibly you are. But it makes no difference. Neither does the promise I was made yesterday that the boys responsible would be dealt with, because if they'd known they'd be dealt with severely enough, they wouldn't have committed this atrocity in the first place. I'm only glad that if it had to happen, it happened now, before Sam was bullied to the point at which ... " She paused, as if unable to pursue that particular line of thought.

Stephen nodded. He had learned that listening and agreeing was the best method of defusing anyone's anger, that his attention and sympathy was sometimes all he could give and that – just sometimes - it was enough. He had learned it not from twenty years' experience of dealing on a daily basis with pupils, staff and parents, but from his wife.

"I would have kept Sam at home and taught him myself if necessary, but as it turns out we've been lucky. I spoke to the head at West Park this morning. She's offered him a place – apparently one of their Year 7s is off to the grammar school." She sounded wry, and Stephen understood that this would have been her first choice for her son, were choice not a fiction when it came to state school education. "So thank you for apologising, and for any action you might have taken, but it's too late."

"I understand."

"Do you." Her eyes narrowed, as though his understanding insulted her. "Do you have children, Mr Lord?"

"Yes – "

"And which school do they go to?"

"They're still at primary."

"But they won't be coming here." She waited for him to contradict her. He said nothing. "What sort of headteacher are you, that your school isn't good enough for your children, yet it's good enough for mine? That teenage boys can kill animals in the playground without fearing they'll be punished for it?"

"I think," Stephen said, "it's without caring they'll be punished for it. And that has as much to do with the backgrounds they come from as the school they attend."

"Is that what you have to tell yourself to get through the day? Rapton *is* the back-ground they come from." She paused. She was, he saw, trembling slightly. "My child shouldn't have had to go through what he did yesterday. It breaks my heart that he did. You're producing a generation of criminals and layabouts and you seem to think that if you keep your head down and public opinion up, it'll all be all right. Well it won't. You should know that if West Park were still full, and the education authority insisted Sam return here, I would be going to the press."

Stephen looked at her. She was, he thought, absolutely right. He leaned back in his chair. "I wouldn't blame you. If it had been my son, I'd feel as angry and outraged and protective as you do now. I can't defend what happened yesterday and I won't insult you by trying. But I am very sorry." He paused. "We do our best, you know, at this school. I'm only too painfully aware that sometimes it just isn't enough."

She hesitated, softened just a little by his honesty. "I'm still taking Sam out."

Stephen nodded, said again and with sincerity, "I understand." After she'd gone he closed his eyes. Part of the cause of Rapton's falling roll was the steady exodus of nice, well-brought up pupils to any preferable alternative their parents could find. This was effectively ratcheting up the proportion of the mad, the bad and the ugly to a majority level. At the current rate there would not be one decent, averagely intelligent child left in the school before the year was out. God help me, he thought.

If Leigh wasn't keen on her Year 8s, she suspected she

might quickly also become disenamoured of her Year 9s. Towards the back of the room a couple of girls had their phones out and their ear pieces in. Boys were surreptitiously – though less surreptitiously than they imagined – tearing strips of paper from the margins of their diaries to roll up, spit on and flick at each other. Several pupils had written nothing but the date. Several more had managed the title. A boy was kicking the back of the chair in front of him until the girl sitting in it turned round and screamed at him, "Will you fucking stop it!"

"Year Nine!" The hubbub lessened. Some of the pupils looked at her, some genuinely wanting to hear what she had to say, others with sullen contempt. "I gather from the amount of noise that the seating arrangement we have at present isn't working. I'm going to be reorganising where you sit during the course of this week, based upon how well you work next to the person you have chosen to sit beside today. Some of you are obviously doing fine. Others seem to be having difficulties where they are at the moment. Continue drawing them to my attention and I will do something about it. You have fifteen minutes left to finish the questions, or you will be finishing them at break. Does everyone understand?"

She remained standing at the front of the class watching them for the rest of the lesson.

A brew and biscuits in Joss's room at break was going to become one of the essential luxuries of the day. Especially as Joss made superlative tea and coffee and bought the department's biscuits at Marks and Spencer. Also as everyone popped in to exchange gossip, resources and advice, to vent fury or simply to whimper, piteously, for a few moments. Almost everyone.

"No Penny?" Leigh enquired innocently.

"Penny doesn't care to fritter her free time away with the likes of us," Joss grinned.

"Now, now." Alan, his considerable bulk blocking passage through the narrow room, sipped his tea. "She'll be in the staff room brown-nosing Senior Managemnet."

Joss choked on a biscuit. Finn, lounging against a filing

cabinet, smiled.

"I was in the staff room this morning," Leigh told them. "Doesn't anyone like Stephen Lord?"

"Not today," Finn said.

"But generally? It was unpleasant in there."

"Generally, people think Rapton's his Waterloo."

And are they right? she wanted to ask, but she was the new girl here. Despite the digs at Penny, she didn't think any of them would divulge their personal opinions just yet.

"How's Brian?" Finn asked. Alan shook his head. It had been announced earlier that morning that Brian Wilson, the Deputy Head responsible for Behaviour, had suffered a heart attack whilst walking his dog in Rapton Park. The news had been greeted with equal concern for Brian as for the school in his absence.

"Be surprised if we see him back this term," Alan predicted. "If ever, if he's got any sense." The bell rang. He sighed – "How many months have we been back now?" – and rolled through the doorway and off to his classroom, mowing a path through the children like a bowling ball through skittles. By the time the corridor had cleared it was a wasteground of empty crisp packets, polystyrene cups dribbling milk shake, pens crushed underfoot. Finn shook his head. "Not so much a school as a ghetto."

Leigh looked at him. They were standing together on the threshold of Joss's room but if she were invading his personal space he either hadn't noticed or didn't mind. She could see that his lower lip was slightly fuller than his upper, that there were gold flecks in the olive green of his eyes, that he wore no ring. Stop it, she told herself. Stop it now.

"For the record?" he offered. "Stephen's a decent bloke. Just a complete nightmare to work for." He saw her reaction. "I won't sit on the fence. Year 11s are my responsibility and I'm not looking forward to next week when Cal and Josh and the rest are out of isolation."

"Alan teaches them, doesn't he?"

"And Alan's the one who shopped them."

"They don't know that, surely?"

"Oh they will," Finn said grimly. "It's why Stephen should have gone for exclusion. God knows there's enough evidence in their files. Once they've got you in their sights there's no hiding from the Focus Group." She must have looked as alarmed as she felt because he smiled. "Don't worry. They've no axe to grind with you and they think I'm on their side. Christ knows why but it comes in useful."

A tidal wave of noise thumped against the wall of a classroom further down the corridor, the one outside which was strewn the lion's share of the litter. Following a scatter-gun attack of shouting a boy of about thirteen flung out, pausing to yell, "I'm not fucking going to Mr Nobhead Clarke!" before slamming the door behind him.

Finn said, loudly, "Oh yes you are."

The boy, seeing them for the first time, groaned. "Aw, shit."

"Yep. Off you go."

He went, dragging his bag, kicking walls and doors as he went.

"Jason Ryland," Finn explained. "Sadly misunderstood, as you can see."

"And Mr Nobhead Clarke?"

"Science teacher, Head of Year Eight."

"Any good?"

"Oh yes. And that," he added pointedly, "is Derek's class."

She didn't understand. "Should we see if he needs any help?"

"You can try."

Leigh walked to the slammed door, pushed it open. A paper ball sailed past her and hit the whiteboard. Children were lying on desks, texting, playing music. One girl was styling another's hair, her straighteners plugged in where the computer should be. A gang of boys were fighting in the corner. At the front of the class Derek sat on his desk wearing a frozen smile.

"Are you all right?" Leigh called.

"Oh yes," he replied. "It's going quite well now Jason's gone."

She looked at him. Derek Seaton had the long, thin face,

protruding ears and unfortunate overbite of Plug from The Bash Street Kids. He also apparently had the ability to become invisible. She said, tentatively, wary of undermining him, "Do you want me to … ?"

"Oh no," he said, as another boy emptied someone's bag out of the window. "You're new. They won't listen to you. I've been here two years and they don't listen to me."

She closed the door softly behind her. Finn was waiting. Her expression told him all he needed to know. He turned the handle, paused at the entrance as he surveyed the class. It was as if, Leigh thought, someone had suddenly turned down their volume control and Finn had yet to speak.

One of Stephen's more successful initiatives had been the introduction, a year ago, of a staff-student mentoring scheme. Each Year 10 and 11 pupil was assigned to a member of staff whose role it was to provide a confidential, largely pastoral advisory service. The quality of the support varied enormously according to the member of staff involved, and the support required according to the individual pupils, the minimum being a completed coursework agreement and a casual greeting every now and then in the corridor. Stephen liked to think he took his role more seriously than that. He had, he felt, come to know his four allotted students reasonably well over the last year, and took a particular and genuine interest in their progress. The boy sitting in front of him now, for instance, was set to be one of Rapton's shining stars. From a reasonably comfortable, reasonably stable background, he was in top sets for all his subjects, had achieved Level 7s in his Key Stage 3 SATs, had one of the highest CAT scores in his year and was predicted mostly A grade GCSEs this summer. He met every deadline for his coursework, was well-mannered, humorous and socially at ease. Stephen looked across his desk at the boy and wished fervently that he had the powers of replication by a thousand fold.

He said, "So. A little early in the day, I suppose, for one of our meetings, but I wanted to talk to you about your plans for this year."

"My plans for this year are to work like hell, get the grades, go on to sixth form and start my real life." Todd looked wry. "Is that what you wanted me to say?"

"Is it true?"

"Every word."

"Why do you say 'real life'?"

Todd hesitated. "I've never really fitted in here, have I? No offence. It's like, if your life is a performance, I showed up at the wrong theatre."

Stephen was intrigued. He knew well enough that Todd was among the handful of bright pupils whom four years ago the grammar school had chosen to reject. Its loss was very definitely Rapton's gain. "Do you think you'll fit in better at sixth form?"

Todd smiled. "I'd better. Otherwise there's no hope for me."

"I think," Stephen said, "that there is every hope for you. Certainly I have every hope for you."

"Thanks, sir." Todd blushed.

"I know I talk a lot about taking personal responsibility, but I don't think there's much that makes more difference, maybe especially at your age." He paused, decided to go for it and play the clueless adult card. "But perhaps you can help me out here, because I can't understand why so many pupils, Year 11s particularly, choose to abnegate that responsibility. Who do they think is going to lead their lives for them?"

"Um – I don't know." Todd looked taken aback by his headteacher asking not just for his opinion, but his advice. "I don't think they think like that. It's like another thing they're being told to do, and it doesn't really hit them till they leave why everyone was telling them they had to do it. Or maybe they're not used to having responsibility. Maybe they can't deal with it because it, like, scares them or something."

"So what would help?"

"God. I don't know. If you had people coming in, people who do the jobs they might do, tell them what grades they need and how much they'd earn and that they used to muck about at school as well, and look where they are now. I don't know."

Todd had told him three times that he didn't know, though clearly he did. Stephen nodded thoughtfully. "So perhaps a careers fair? Visits to local colleges? Talks by employers who take on apprentices, that sort of thing?"

"Well yeah. Except you kind of already do all that."

"Maybe nowhere near enough. Maybe we don't do it well enough. Maybe we need to stop complaining about pupils not taking their GCSEs seriously and give them more and better reasons to do so."

Todd half-smiled. "It's not rocket science, sir."

"No, it's the willingness to look for solutions. Which can be in short supply sometimes, Todd. Not for you, though. GCSEs, sixth form, then what? University?"

"Yeah, hopefully."

"Any thoughts where?"

Todd shrugged, his expression darkening. "Far away as I can get."

Stephen considered whether or not to pry and decided against it. Every teenager, even the Todd Kershaws of this world, had their problems, real or perceived. It went with the territory. But in his experience, boys like Todd had their support networks firmly in place. The last person he would choose to confide in would be his headteacher.

Callum Bywater slid his mobile from his pocket to check the time. Ten minutes to the end of this lesson. He glanced at Connor, Josh and Liam, who had their books open and their pens out in half-hearted mockery of work. Mr Macallister sat behind the desk at the front of the room, marking. It was so quiet Cal could hear footsteps from the floor above. A telephone ringing somewhere. His gaze wandered the room, from the broken ceiling tiles to unpicked blinds to stained and peeling walls. He groaned under his breath. "Thing with this isolation room, right, sir, it's well mingin'."

Macallister eyed him wearily. "It's a deterrent, Callum."

"A what, sir?"

"You're supposed to want to avoid being sent here."

"Oh right." He thought about it. "Doesn't really work then,

does it?"

Josh and Connor sniggered.

Liam said suddenly, "Is it right what they're sayin' about Mr Wilson? That he's had an 'art attack?"

Macallister looked like he was trying to decide whether or not it was all right to tell them. "Yes," he admitted. "Mr Wilson's in hospital."

"He's not dead, then?"

"No, Connor, he isn't dead."

The thought of the hole the deputy head's absence would create in the school's discipline procedures cheered Callum immensely. "Who's gonna be runnin' the isolation room and stuff?"

"Oh don't worry. It won't fall apart without him."

"Yeah, but who's gonna be runnin' it though? Won't be Lord, he won't want the bother."

"Be good if it's that new English bird," Josh smirked. "She's well fit. I'd give her one."

"*Josh.*" Macallister's voice was cold. "Show some respect for Christ's sake."

"Yeah Josh, you fuckin' stupid or what?" Liam was scornful. "They're not gonna put a woman in here, are they? We never get anyone nice who'll just talk to us. It's well not fair. I hate this school."

"I'm nice," Macallister said. "I talk to you."

"Yeah, you just give us a hard time though sir."

Macallister almost smiled. "Why would that be?" He stood up, collected together his belongings as the bell rang, waiting to hand over to the next member of staff to act as warder for an hour.

It was Derek Seaton.

Cal saw Macallister's face fall, heard him murmur, "Any trouble, ring me." Saw the mixture of disbelief and glee in Josh's and Liam's and Connor's eyes. He grinned.

"All right, sir?"

"Yes thank you Callum." Derek, watching the door close behind Macallister, took a pile of exercise books from a Mothercare carrier bag and glanced nervously at the boys.

"You've got work to do."

They grunted, shrugged, the tables in front of them entirely bare. Connor said, "Aah, does your mother care for you?"

He frowned, understood and folded the bag away. "Just bought something for my son."

They stared at him. "You've got a *kid*?"

"I have." He was so nervous, Callum observed, he couldn't look any of them in the eye. "Open your books and get on."

"Fuckin' hell," Josh breathed. "Someone's shagged him."

They spluttered with laughter. Liam ended up choking, his face red, tears streaming until Callum had to get up and thump him really hard on the back. Connor, quickly bored with cackling at someone who took no notice of them, took a piece of plain A4 from his bag and sailed an inept aeroplane across the room to Josh. Josh screwed it up and chucked it back. Connor tore a couple of sheets out of his planner and balled them to hurl at the wall behind Derek's head.

He looked up, twitching. "Stop that please, boys."

They ignored him. Cal looked at the three of them, launching paper missiles round the room, and decided he couldn't be arsed with any of it. Derek Seaton was too easy a target. Putting his feet up on the desk and lacing his hands behind his head, he sat back and watched.

Josh lumbered out of his seat, took the permanent marker he kept for graffiti purposes in his pocket, and drew an ejaculating penis on the whiteboard. Then he added his signature. Cal couldn't believe it. "Josh! How fuckin' stupid're you?"

"What?" Josh turned to him, frowning, looked back at his artwork. "Oh yeah." And tried to erase it with his sleeve.

Liam, meanwhile, had turned his attention to the room's only computer and was peacefully engaged in removing the letters from the keyboard. Having done so, he began to replace them in an order all his own. "How're you s'posed to spell 'twat' when there's only one 't'?"

"Boys." Derek's voice was thin with anxiety. "Sit down and get on now." He glanced towards the clock, checking his progress through this hour of hell.

"You wanna know what time it is, *sir*?" Connor, who had been looking for his own mischief to make, unhooked the clock from the wall, held it towards Derek, then let it slip to the floor and stepped on it. After grinding some of the shards of glass into the carpet with his heel, he threw it out of the window.

There ensued the briefest of silences. Derek grabbed for the panic button which linked to Stephen's and Brian's offices, but that morning Josh had snipped the flex and now it connected to nothing. Cal met Derek's pleading eyes and shrugged. They were acting like fuckin' lunatics, the lot of them, and he wanted no part of it. He'd led this gang for as long as it had existed, but he wasn't getting slammed back in here for another week.

Josh climbed up onto a desk.

"Get down." Derek's voice quavered.

"I'm not getting down. Have you seen the state of that floor? All that glass? Health and safety risk walkin' on that."

Connor followed his lead, the pair of them traversing the room from table to chair to Derek's desk while Derek flapped, gathering his papers away from their bootprints. Liam hauled himself up too, but hadn't foreseen that a computer work station was not going to bear his weight. It cracked and buckled, sending both the computer and Liam crashing.

And Callum still did nothing but watch.

"What's the matter with you Cal? Lost your bottle?"

"Just thinking what a bunch of wankers you are." Cal spotted Derek Seaton sneaking towards the door and gave him a wave. "You'll only get put in isolation again. Or excluded."

"You an' all."

"Nope. I ain't done nothin'. Uncle Derek'll tell them that. Won't you?" He glared at Derek, who swallowed and edged an inch closer to his escape. "Save it, we need to be around next week. I've got plans, me. More important shit to stir."

They stared at him, uncomprehending.

"Well who got us put in here in the first place?"

Still they stared. Shrugged. Did it matter?

"The Fat Man." Cal smirked. "Owes us big time."

Connor, frowning, dropped down to sit on the table bearing his footprints. "So what, we gonna get him?"

Liam and Josh joined him, their attention rapt. Cal nodded, glanced towards Derek. "Look at him, wetting himself. You can go," he called. "It was an accident, that clock. Go on. Fuck off. We're staying here. We've got business."

Derek, opening the door just wide enough to slide through, slunk gratefully away.

It's a bit of a learning curve, Leigh had told Todd at the end of her first day. She wasn't entirely sure how she would describe it now at the end of her first week. She only knew she was bone-weary, emotionally drained and wanted nothing more than to drive home and lie on the sofa with a cool flannel over her forehead.

Finn popped his head round the door. "That drink we talked about … ?"

She followed him to the pub, tailing his BMW Coupé in her Fiat Punto, past the buses and blazers of the grammar school, down the winding road of disused mills and narrow terraces, beyond which lay only the moors and the scarred hillside. As she climbed out of her car she could hear nothing but sheep acknowledging each other across the fields. It was a tougher, bleaker version of the village in which she lived. "Gosh," she said as Finn came towards her, his long dark coat flapping in the gathering wind. "*Wuthering Heights* country."

"There is a family called Earnshaw round here."

"There would be."

"Their kids go to the grammar."

She glanced up and down the empty street. "Is the pub even open?"

"It will be," Finn said. "Four o'clock on a Friday, just for us."

The pub was open as promised, but for now they were its only customers. The sunshine, so warm at the beginning of the week, had cooled. The scent of autumn was already in the air and she half-expected a fire to be burning in the open grate. Finn bought their drinks and they settled at a corner table.

"Who usually comes?" Leigh asked him.

"Oh, the PE crowd, couple of the IT teachers, Bob from Maths, Alan, Iona sometimes. It varies." He hung his coat on the back of his chair. "Have you met Iona properly yet?"

Leigh shook her head. Iona Lewis was the sixth member of the English department, a tall, dark-haired girl, ethereally beautiful and icily severe. "I've only really seen her wafting along the corridor."

He smiled. "The rest usually turn up in the next half hour or so. Tonight, I couldn't wait."

"Yes," she agreed. "It's been an interesting week."

He laughed. There was something of Wuthering Heights about Finn himself, she thought, his dark hair, green eyes, the brooding quality she'd noticed that first morning in the hall, but he was never so good-looking as when he laughed. She'd given up pretending she didn't find him attractive. The hell with it, she thought. Just enjoy it. "So," she said. "Finlay Macallister."

"Mm."

"Does everyone call you Finn?"

"Yeah. Or Mac. Or Tosser."

She smiled. "You don't have an accent."

"Born in Wilmslow. My parents are from Edinburgh. Moved here when I was eleven."

"So you grew up round here."

"Yeah. You're surprised. It doesn't show, you know, on the outside. And as I say, my family are Scots, so no webbed fingers or cross-eyes. I went to the grammar school. So did quite a few teachers at Rapton."

"Small world."

"Mm. But then it is, here. Too small sometimes. 'Local ways for local people'. You know the BBC actually thought about filming 'The League of Gentlemen' in Rapton, but decided it was just too weird for them."

She laughed. "So what's it like then, living here?"

"Oh, it has its up side. Perhaps it's the geography, being in a valley, I don't know, but there's a closeness between people above and beyond the whole interbred subculture thing. The schools don't segregate in the way they might do anywhere else. Kids from the grammar and Rapton and West Park know each other socially, romantically, form networks of friendships which might surprise you."

Leigh smiled. "That is a good thing."

"It is. But then again, one end of town has been entrenched in a running battle with the other end for decades. Families harbour grudges for generations. Feelings fester. It's unhealthy and insular and ridden with bigotry."

"And yet you didn't leave."

"Oh, I did," Finn said. "But I came back."

Leigh was intrigued. There was a story here which probably, five minutes into their acquaintanceship, he wasn't going to tell her but she still longed to know. "And was it the right thing to do, coming back?"

He hesitated. "Personally, I had no choice. I was a mess. Needed my mum." He smiled, self-mocking.

"I've been there," she sympathised.

He stopped, took a swallow of beer, glanced around at the abandoned pool table, the clusters of empty seats. It was almost visible, she thought, his decision to discuss something other than his personal life. "Professionally … I don't know. I think I've done some good at Rapton, but it can be bloody frustrating working for Stephen sometimes."

"How so?" She was intrigued; she had been wanting to hear more on why Stephen Lord was a nightmare as a Head since Finn had first said so and refused to apologise for it.

He hesitated. "I shouldn't be telling you. I should let you make up your own mind about him."

"But you already have told me, and I don't want to go the scenic route. If it affects what I do in the classroom, I need to know."

"True." He sighed. "Okay. The background is that Stephen used to be Deputy Head at St Thomas' in Halifax, and had great success with their behavioural issues. He was brought in at Rapton a couple of years ago on the strength of that. But St Thomas' had very specific problems which, luckily for Stephen, could be tackled and turned around within two years.

Rapton hasn't. At Rapton you're dealing with an aggression and apathy which is endemic. It has been for decades. You can't have that same impact because you can't change the culture the pupils are from. It's deeply rooted and self-perpetuating and all you can do is deal with it, and deal with the kids, as effectively and as firmly as possible."

"Maybe Stephen's just seeing the bigger picture."

"Ye-es, but he's seeing it through rose-tinted glasses. He sees it as crusading idealism but it's naïve and unrealistic and it doesn't work. Not here. It's what gets everyone's back up – we have to deal with that apathy and aggression on a daily basis and the support system that should be in place for us has been turned into a safety-net for the kids' self-esteem."

Leigh frowned. "But isn't it that he wants the school to provide for pupils a refuge from their backgrounds, to be a source of hope? Isn't that just what they need?"

Finn looked at her. "It's the beginning of term and already a kitten has been kicked to death and an isolation room destroyed. Tell me how focussing on hope and refuges addresses that."

"I think there are worse principles to be guided by, that's all."

His gaze didn't falter. "Right."

"If all someone knows is failure and deprivation and low expectations, what's wrong in offering them an alternative?"

"Nothing. But we also have a duty to protect and educate every child in the school and that means being tough with the Focus group and their ilk because being tough is what they need and understand. It's what they respect. They don't respect Stephen Lord."

She understood. "You don't respect Stephen Lord."

"I … have issues with him. He has issues with me."

"So it's personal."

"It's professional. I can't do my job as well as I'd like because he won't back me up."

"That's at the root of it, you don't have his support?"

"Exactly."

"Does he have yours?"

Finn let out his breath. "Don't tell me I need to give Stephen Lord my support. Jesus, you've been here a week and you think you have the answers?"

The edge to his voice sliced her skin like a paper cut. The pub door blew open with a blast of voices and the PE staff - looking as PE staff always did, even at Parents Nights and Awards Ceremonies, as though they were still on the field - whooped their hellos, their volume and ribaldry taking the small bar and Finn himself by storm. Leigh, stung into silence, slid away from him, letting him become engulfed by the crowd. When she rose, not much later, to leave, she glanced his way but his attention lay elsewhere.

Dean stopped in the centre of the motorway bridge and stared down into the endless stream of cars and lorries and vans, at the overtaking and lane-changing and cutting-in, at the remorseless speed and thunder, the hair's-breadth danger.

It was a long, long way to fall.

And if the fall didn't kill you, you hit the bottom and you didn't stand a chance. Maybe neither did the driver of the vehicle that got you.

He swallowed, wrapped his hands around the rail. Closed his eyes. The evening breeze blew chill against his skin, the traffic still rumbling steadily below him. He had never been afraid of heights, yet standing here like this made his skin crawl. He remembered again the car horns and smashing glass and screaming. Thought of his sister Julie who, when she had returned from her shift in the middle of the night to find him in her house, had begged him to stay for her sake, for Cal's. He thought of the job in Scotland and moving on and a new life.

Maybe it wouldn't hurt to hang around for a bit. He owed Julie that, after all. Had agreed to take a look at Cal and not much liked what he'd seen. He was busy overplaying things with the boy, from his entrance the other night through every time they encountered each other, on the stairs, in the kitchen. He wanted Callum nervous from the start, wasn't having him mouth off to him like he did to Julie and probably everyone else in his life. If he was going to make any sort of difference he had to have the boy taking serious notice.

But this, standing on the bridge, acknowledging his ghosts, had him shaking. He'd always been the only one who knew what had happened that night. The only one who cared.

Well not quite the only one.

Which was the whole point. Seven years inside, plenty of time to think about where it had all started to get out of control. Plenty of time to recall details, to work up a past grief into the sort of fury and determination that kept you alive. He didn't know how you traced a person when you'd never known their name, or what they looked like, or anything about them but the road they'd once lived on. It hadn't troubled him, this lack of one single concrete fact, when he'd been lying in his cell counting days and weeks. It had calcified his anger into something he could use. Now, free in the world, he was on the knife-edge of allowing the hopelessness of it to stagger him. But just being here helped. Already he'd had his suspicions confirmed; that the past is never behind you, it's bang up against the present and you can walk right back into it like it's a parallel dimension. Especially here, in the valley that time forgot.

He opened his eyes. Released his grasp. Rage and fear and the smell of death receded. The dying rays of September sunshine glowed along the crests of the hills and when he was done paying his debts, hundreds of miles further north, his future would beckon.

The afternoon sun through the the canopy of leaves dappled the path ahead of them, at its end the spreading lawns, daffodils and crocuses in the flowerbeds. Beyond this lay the playground. Even from here Spig could glimpse the bright, quick movement of small children, their shrill and distant voices. Sundays were rubbish, usually, nothing to do, nowhere to go, but walking in the park with Donna made things a bit better. Especially when she was happy. "How did it go, then?" he said. Like he needed to ask, but he knew she was dying to tell him.

"It were great." She had this really daft, soft look in her eyes. " We went to the pictures."

"What did you see?"

"That horror thing. It were well good. It had that bloke in it."

He started to laugh.

"Shut up," she said, laughing too. "You know, that bloke who was in that other thing."

"Oh him. *Was it an 18?"*

"I look older when I'm dressed up. Everyone says so. I can pass for eighteen easy."

Spig nodded. "Is he older than you, then? Your bloke?"

"Yeah." She added quickly, "It doesn't matter."

"No." He fantasised about older women, sometimes. Really old, like thirty or something. He was worried it might be a bit pervy.

"He's really kind. Dead sexy and that, but nice, you know? And ... " She paused. "He's ever so gentle."

Spig coloured. "Too much information, Donna."

"Oh I know, but just in case you thought ... He's not like that. He really cares."

"Yeah all right. We gonna feed the rabbits then?"

They always fed the animals when they came to the park, bought some bags of feed from the kiosk when they bought their own drinks and packets of crisps. Donna crouched, as she always did, right up against the wire, holding the feed in her hand so the rabbits nibbled her fingers, even though there were signs up telling you not to do that. "If you could do anything, in the whole world, what would you do?" She watched the tweedy coloured rabbit press its face to the gap, felt its pink snuffling nose against her palm. "As a job, I mean?"

Spig played through the glamorous, impossible alternatives in his head. Film star. Rock god. Striker for Man United. "Dunno," he said.

"I'd be a vet. It's hard, isn't it, to be a vet? You have to go to university and stuff. I could help out, though. I want to do my work experience at a vet's."

He said nothing. He envied Donna her conviction that if she only tried hard enough she could have a better life. She worked at school and talked about the future as though good things were possible. She didn't tell people she lived in a children's home because her mum was a druggie and she'd never had a dad. Not because she was ashamed but because she thought it didn't matter. She only looked forward.

She turned to smile at him and his chest felt tight and he half wanted to walk away. He wasn't supposed to have feelings for Donna. They were mates. Best mates, that was all.

Later, he would remember her like that, sitting in the gravel feeding the rabbits, happy and excited and full of ordinary hope. It would make his chest tighten in quite a different way.

Five

Stephen stood at the bottom of the stairs, gazing despairingly at the empty space where his children should be. "Luce! Hen! I'm going in five minutes. If you're not down here by then with your shoes on, I'm going without you!"

Claudia grinned at him from the kitchen doorway. "There will come a time," she said, "when they're away at university and it's just you and me and we'll remember these manic Saturday mornings with rose-tinted nostalgia."

"I'll be fifty-three by then. I don't even want to think about it. Lucie! Henry! Down here now!"

They came scrambling down the stairs, Henry with trainers unlaced, Lucie clutching a hairbrush and pink scrunchie. Claudia drily handed them their football kit and ballet shoes respectively, fixed Lucie's hair with three expert strokes. "Buy wine," she told Stephen over their heads. He smiled.

One Saturday a month he dropped Lucie at her dance class and Henry at his five-a-side training – to be collected later by Claudia – and drove another hour further north to visit his parents. They lived still in the small village west of Skipton, in the same house, in which Stephen and his brothers had grown up. He had always loved going back. Even now, when it took such a sizeable chunk out of his weekend and his parents could just as easily and would just as readily visit him, there was something about the sense of flight in the journey, something about sitting on their garden bench among the foxgloves and hollyhocks that assuaged his soul. And then there were his parents themselves, who had raised their sons with a kind, calm liberalism which prevailed in their house to this day. Stephen had not found it remarkable at the time, but he saw now that his growing up in an atmosphere of such gentle tolerance explained a lot about him, though he would never dream of explaining that to anyone else, especially not to the staff of Rapton High.

Today, however, was not for sitting amongst the foxgloves

and hollyhocks. His parents were in the midst of clearing out what they referred to as the garage, which had been in their home's former life as a farmhouse the stable block, and had found themselves unable to shift several monstrosities of furniture they had somehow hauled to the back decades ago and never looked at again. An hour later Stephen, panting and sweating through his favourite Gap t-shirt, was accepting a mug of tea from his mother and considering the merits of a life in the removals business. "What are you going to do with all this stuff?"

"We thought we'd give it to you." His mother grinned. He knew she could imagine as well as he could Claudia's horrified reaction. "I don't know. Auction? Antique dealer, do you think?"

"After twenty years in the garage? Your only serious option's the tip."

"Ah well." She didn't sound surprised. Most of her life had been a triumph of optimism over experience. Stephen, knowing this, felt a twinge of guilt at having dismissed her hopes so brusquely. He also knew that his status as favourite son conferred upon him certain kindnesses and responsibilities.

"I could look into it for you," he offered.

"Haven't you got enough on your plate?" his father said, adding, as it had been inevitable he would, "How's the new term shaping up?"

Stephen took a swallow of tea. How to answer? He selected carefully the details he served to his parents of Rapton, but they seemed to understand as much from what he withheld as from what he gave away. He said lightly, "Oh, you know, full of the usual challenges."

"You deserve a knighthood for what you do at that school."

He looked at his mother in surprise. His elder brother was a surgeon, his younger blazing some sort of trail in company law. When Stephen had been a classroom teacher he had felt the disparity sorely. But even his mother had never mentioned knighthoods before. The thought of the expressions on his staff's faces were he to receive any sort of recognition from anywhere made him smile. "It's just my job," he said and added, with rare honesty, "I'm not sure I'm doing it any better or any worse than anyone else. Truth is, Rapton desperately needs to be a better school and whatever I do, it's not going to happen overnight."

"But you can set things in motion," his father said.

"I know. It goes against the grain, because I've always believed in second chances and the measured response and letting people learn from the error of their ways. But you get to a point when it's not about that anymore, when it has to be about consequences."

His father nodded. "Try looking at it another way," he suggested. "If it makes it more acceptable for you to do, try looking at it not as consequences, but as justice."

"Justice?" Stephen was wry. "Don't you mean retribution?"

"What's wrong with that? Most of us, especially my generation, we read in the papers about the crimes committed by the sort of children you teach and we want them locking up. You can create a more tolerant society in your school if you think it's going to work, but there has to be some form of retribution or it isn't a society you've created, it's anarchy."

Stephen sighed. "Believe me, I know. But calling it justice will put the kids' backs up even more because it makes it more obvious I'm claiming the moral high ground. I've always wanted it to be about the results of their own actions and efforts, not about me meting out rewards and punishments from my throne in the clouds." He drained his cup. "If you think there's any way I can sell it to them without creating even more ill feeling, let me know. Because I used to believe that if you behaved with fairness and humanity, that's what you would get in return. I admit, I had a very sheltered life. I blame you." He smiled.

His mother took his empty mug from him and returned it to the tray. "You're too nice for that school."

"Don't. Being nice translates as having no backbone."

"Perhaps," his father suggested, "you have no choice but to wield your power with a bit more menace."

Stephen reflected that power and menace had never really

been in his armoury. Until now he had succeeded with a deadly combination of discussion, charm and high expectations. None of which stood a chance of working at Rapton. Maybe it really was time for the sword.

Finn loved Saturday mornings. When he woke alone, which he did more often than not these days, he loved the deep peace of his apartment, its complete absence of the noise and discord which characterised his working week. It felt a little like freedom.

There were always things to do, of course. The acres of empty time which lay deceptively before him when he opened his eyes were soon lost in a welter of friends to meet, films and plays to see, gigs to go to, of lose-yourself-for-hours shopping and boring essentials shopping and mind-numbingly tedious housework. Though he was as capable as anyone of loading and unloading dish washers, washing machines and tumble driers, he had not yet, in his thirty-four years, mastered the art of living tidily. His apartment in the converted Victorian mill should have been an ode to minimalist living; so white were the walls and unrelieved the wooden floors that a previous girlfriend had complained it was not so much a home as an art gallery stripped of the art. Finn thought his sliding piles of books, CDs and DVDs lent the place a more lived-in air but she had said no, that was just being untidy, and left him shortly afterwards for an IT consultant in whose home, Finn had since gathered, even the breakfast cereals were in alphabetical order.

This morning he switched on the coffee machine and snapped his gaze from the mess of newspapers and discarded clothing in what the estate agent's brochure had described as his open-plan living space to the uninterrupted view of the east Lancashire hillside beyond. He was thinking about new colleagues, and how what you expected was that they would be competent and easy to work with. You might hope they would be up for a laugh and a drink on a Friday afternoon, especially given the mad, the bad and the ugly with which the English department appeared to be staffed at the moment. But would you, in your right mind, and with ten years' teaching experience under your belt, anticipate them being so …

He let out his breath. Occupied himself with making the coffee. He'd spent so long entrenched in the daily slog, in feeling frustrated and pissed off at being Head of Year to a criminal year group in a failing school, mildly depressed at being alone (and lonely though it would have killed him to admit it), that the only response he had been daring seriously to entertain to Leigh Somers was denial.

So then he hadn't been breathtaken the moment he'd first clapped eyes on her, or acknowledged an urge when standing beside her to lift his hand to the conker silkiness of her hair. He hadn't noted the shape of her mouth or the curve of her breasts and spent hours trying not to think about them afterwards. He hadn't been keyed up with nerves when asking her to go for a drink, or been tempted to confess to her when she did his every triumph and torment. He wasn't so desperate for her to think him passionate about what he did that he'd chosen to launch a tirade against Stephen Lord (Christ!). And then, without meaning to, he'd insulted and offended her and she'd vanished before he could put it right.

Bloody hell, Finn.

He shook his head. Nothing like this, he reflected as he stirred his coffee and returned to his royal box view of the small town below, had happened to him for a long, long time and quite honestly, it scared him shitless. He'd become comfortable, in an atrophied sort of way, with a life that didn't look like it was going to deliver on any of its promises. Or, if he were going to be really hard on himself, as he frequently was, a life he'd succeeded in fucking up and couldn't find the energy to revive. He'd long since given up on the possibility of happiness.

He didn't find her achingly lovely. He didn't find himself at all lost in erotic thoughts.

He wondered how long you could be in denial without going completely mad.

The thing with Julie, Dean had always known, was that she

didn't ask questions. It was probably both her saving grace and her biggest downfall. One minute he'd been in prison and the next he was in her front room and all she talked about was the price of an Asda shop versus a Tesco one and the latest storyline in *Coronation Street*. He didn't know if he wanted her to ask about how the last seven years had been for him. Certainly didn't want to tell her. And there was something restful about her lack of curiosity combined with the kindness she showed him. He'd been jittery and aggressive all his life; why had he never realised before it was probably because he'd spent so much time with people who were jittery and aggressive back?

"Dean." She had been making a brew, picking her way through the crumbs and unwashed dishes to pour stale tea from its pot. "What's this?"

She held a piece of paper towards him. Dean took it from her. He'd never quite grasped why he, truant from more lessons at school than he'd attended, could read and Julie, listlessly present, could not.

He glanced at the letter. Read it properly. "Ah shit. Where was this?"

"Down the back of the breadbin. It's funny, quite a lot of our post seems to end up there." She frowned at him. "What's the matter?"

"I think you might want to ring the school."

He watched her make the call. Watched her face change as she listened to the explanation for Callum's sentence in the isolation room this week. Miserably she hung up, repeated to him the headmaster's words. "*Fuck*ing hell," Dean said. "What's the matter with him? You and me, we had a much harder time growing up than he has, we never did anything like this."

"It's not just him. There's lots of lads get into trouble like Cal."

"Oh well that's all right then. Does he do anything you tell him?"

She said hopefully, "He does if he wants to."

Dean tried to hang onto his patience. "He's out of control,

Jules. I don't know what you think I can do with him. It's gonna take a lot to undo fifteen years of you letting him do what he likes and making excuses for him." *And I've got my own shit to deal with.* He looked at her steadily. She glanced away.

The back door banged. Cal, looking wrecked and stinking of weed, slung into the living room and, recognising trouble in the air, looked from one to the other. "What's the matter with you?"

Dean told him.

"I didn't *know* there was a kitten in the bag, all right?" His tone was defensive-aggressive. "I didn't put it there, did I?"

"Are you sure about that?" Dean demanded.

"What's it got to do with you?"

"Of course he's sure." Julie couldn't help herself. "He's got in with a bad lot at that school. They won't leave him alone."

"That's right," Cal smirked. "Victim of circumstance, me."

"That's not how your headmaster describes you."

"No well it wouldn't be, would it? He's a fucking wanker. Ask anyone."

Dean folded his arms.

Callum cursed. "All right, so it was sick, it was a mistake. What do you want me to do about it? I joined in kicking a bag round the yard. Fucking hang me for it."

"Don't tempt me. Get upstairs," Dean said wearily. "Get a wash. You stink. Then get back down here and we'll try having this conversation again."

"I don't want to have this conversation again."

"Tough. You owe it to your mother."

Callum shrugged. "Why should I do what you say?"

"Because," Dean replied evenly, "if you don't I'll put you through the middle of next week."

Callum slung sullenly out of the room and thumped up the stairs, slamming the bathroom door behind him.

Julie said, "Don't be too hard on him."

Dean looked at her in disbelief. "You want me to knock some sense into him or not?"

"It's just, he hasn't had a man around the house for years."

"Yeah. It shows."

Her tears brimmed and fell. Dean recalled her as a teenager, quietly practical, full of foolish hope. She'd been pretty in a pale and wispy sort of way. She stood before him now, overweight and doughy-faced, her blonde hair thin and limp, hands roughened, hope gone. "Sorry," he muttered.

The house was suspiciously silent. Todd frowned as he descended the stairs, two at a time as usual. Saturday and no drone of the Dyson, no whirr and swish of the dishwasher, no trilling laughter to Jonathan Ross on Radio 2. He padded into the kitchen, where Vince sat in his customary place at the island unit, the Daily Mirror spread in front of him, a mug of coffee in his hand. "Morning," he greeted Todd without looking up.

"Morning." Todd opened the fridge and poured himself some milk. Started to ask. Decided he didn't care. Vince, however, drained his coffee mug and closed the newspaper's weekend supplement.

"Sheryl's at her health club."

Todd, unable to come up with a suitable riposte, grunted.

"So it's just you and me."

He groaned inwardly.

"I thought," Vince suggested, "we could have a bit of a lads' day. Bit of bowling, catch a film, Pizza Hut after."

"I'm not twelve."

Vince looked at him. "Well, I know you're not. I know that."

Todd gritted his teeth. He felt furious and upset again, as of course you would if someone offered you a fun day out, all expenses paid. What was the matter with him? "I've got stuff to do, that's all."

"Can't it wait?"

"No."

Vince sighed heavily. "Todd. What's this about?"

"You don't give a shit what it's about."

Silence. Todd swallowed. He didn't swear much, and certainly not in the presence of Vince and Sheryl. "Sorry," he muttered.

Vince said, "Well I do, as it turns out. Give a shit. I have done all these years, as you well know. If it's about this holiday … "

Todd shook his head. "It's not just that."

"What, then?"

He couldn't speak.

Vince said, "I know, I'm not much good at talking, listening, all that. But if you want, you know, I'll give it a shot."

He nodded. Grappled for some sort of composure. "Thanks." He couldn't talk to Vince any more. He could sit in the same room facing the television with him, but that was about it. Even when he had been able to talk to him it had been about stuff you did, not stuff you felt. Sheryl's arrival had changed everything but maybe it would have changed anyway. Maybe even if she weren't here, even if his mum were still around, he'd still feel like this. Like what he really wanted to do was cry, *I don't know who I am*. And how soft was that?

He said, after a moment and with some small degree of calm, "I'm gonna go out for a bit."

"All right." Vince returned to his newspaper, saving face for them both. "Take your phone."

Years ago, before gangs of hooded youths ruled the streets, before tagging and Asbos, before the discipline at Rapton High had become a joke, the park had been a pleasant place to be. Now the violent, criminal and amoral activities which took place there under the cover of darkness contaminated it throughout the days. Though the rusting slide and swings remained, no parent would allow their child to toddle through the undergrowth of used condoms and syringes. No elderly visitors took afternoon strolls along the leafy paths, for those paths were shrouded by trees and bushes and who knew what might lurk within even during the hours of daylight, to mug or maim. No one felt safe.

Todd didn't much care about feeling safe. When the centre of him felt as though it were cracking apart, a few Asbo kids were the least of his worries. He sat on the cold grass, yards from the deserted playground, within sight of the boarded up kiosk and the empty cages which had contained rabbits and chickens before someone had set fire to them. He couldn't bear being in the house he'd always loved, but being alone was hardly a comfort. He'd always told himself that when he went to university he'd be free, be himself, be presented through his own independence with some sort of truth. What would it matter then who he'd been? But that was three years away yet and it looked like he'd have gone mad long before then.

"Bloody hell Todd. What you doing here?"

Todd looked up at the boy standing in front of him. He smiled wryly. Great. Alone in Rapton Park with Callum Bywater. "All right?"

"Yeah." Cal dropped down onto the grass too. "Don't see you round here much."

"No." Cal was, he knew, one of this place's resident ghosts. A tormenting spirit. "Just escaping for a bit."

"Yeah?" Cal took a packet of fags from the pocket of his hoodie, lit one, offered the packet to Todd.

Todd shook his head. "No, thanks."

Cal shrugged – *please yourself*. Todd watched him smoke, listened to him bang on about how crap school was because the teachers all hated him and nobody gave a toss. "It's all bollocks anyway cos when're we ever gonna use any of that shit? We get Stephen fuckin' Lord who hasn't got a fuckin' clue about anything isolating us cos we're bored out of our heads with all the mindless crap they're trying to fill us with. Nobody listens, there's no point to any of the lessons and the teachers are so far up themselves they can't see out or they're fuckin' useless ... "

Todd said nothing. It was so far from his experience of education at the same school that he didn't feel there was anything he could usefully add. He remembered a winter's afternoon in a primary school Art lesson, the windows running with condensation, the tables a chaos of empty egg boxes and toilet roll tubes, of tissue paper and PVA glue, everyone's hands covered in paint and sticky bits of newspaper. Cal had made a model of a tyrannosaurus rex and their teacher had stopped the lesson to show everyone, to praise him. Cal had turned pink with pleasure and embarrassment and for the rest of the afternoon in the warm, damp classroom he had been kind to everyone. Later, when the teacher and her assistant had been clearing up the mess, Todd had slipped back in to collect his pumps and heard the teacher saying that no one should ever give up on Callum Bywater. The words and the sentiment had struck him even then, half his lifetime ago. Ever since, when Cal was getting into trouble or rambling on like he was now, Todd remembered him with his model of a T-Rex, remembered him being proud and pleased, and he tried to say something nice to him. He'd never had any bother with Cal, and he didn't know whether it was because of their shared history or a grudging respect or what. It meant he didn't fear Cal, as a lot of others did. He didn't much like him, but then he thought of that little kid, who must still be inside Cal, and liking him somehow became irrelevant.

Cal, mistaking as people often did Todd's silence for complete agreement with their point of view, threw his cigarette butt into the grass. "Bet you can't wait to get out of that shit-hole either. What're you gonna do, then? When you leave?"

"Sixth form, probably." Todd spoke lightly, as though it were not his life-line, held his breath waiting for the inevitable searing mockery. It didn't come. Cal just made a face. A yeah-well-you-would kind of face.

"Joining the army, me. Bring it on."

Todd wanted to know what it was about joining the army that Cal thought would solve all his problems. Didn't know how to phrase it without causing offence. "Do you need GCSEs or anything?"

"Cs in Maths and English if you want to be an officer. Nowt if you wanna be a regular soldier, though. You go for a couple of days, like sort of work experience or training or something – assault courses and that - and they interview you and stuff. See if you like it and if they like you."

It was the most enthusiastic Todd had ever known him. "So you don't fancy being an officer then?"

"Nah. Can't be arsed. What's the point?"

"More money?" Less chance of being cannon fodder?

Cal looked at him. "Yeah. Maybe. That what you'd do, then?"

Todd shrugged. He couldn't imagine anything worse than joining the army.

"Not that you have to worry about money."

Todd frowned at him. "What d'you mean?"

"Well your dad's minted, isn't he?"

And Todd heard himself say – "He might be, but he's not my dad." *Fuck.* Why? Why had he had to mention that? Last thing he wanted, to talk about Vince and Sheryl. He took a breath, aware that Cal was watching him. "He's my step-dad."

"Oh yeah. He brought you up though." Cal sounded bizarrely impressed. "Who's she, then? The skinny bitch?"

Todd wished she could hear him. "She's his second wife. They got married last year."

Cal looked at him. "You're as screwed up as the rest of us, aren't you, 'cept you live in a fucking mansion."

"It's not … " But then it probably was, compared with where Cal lived.

"Don't know where my dad is, don't even know if he is my dad. Shacked up with some slapper somewhere. It's just me and me mum and Uncle Dean." He curled his lip as he said the name.

Todd, relieved to be out of the confessional spotlight, probed, "Uncle Dean?"

"Me mum's brother. Just done seven years for armed robbery. Turned up at the house acting hard and now he thinks he's my fucking dad. He's been in jail, and he's lecturing me about being in isolation? It's a bit – what's the word?"

"Hypocritical?"

"That's the one."

"Does he know you want to join the army?"

"Hasn't bothered asking. Just assumes I'm going to go the same way as him. Pisses me off, I tell you." Cal paused. Grinned. "Mind you, if he hadn't got caught, he'd be minted an' all. Five hundred grand, he stood to clear."

Todd whistled. "Change your whole life, that sort of

money."

Cal said, with feeling, "Any sort of money'd change my life."

"I suppose," Todd added after a moment, his gaze fixed on the black depths of the trees beyond the playground, "it's all about risk. What are the chances of getting caught compared with what you stand to gain? And how much does what you stand to gain matter?"

"How'd you say no to the chance of that sort of dosh? You'd have to be sure of the odds," Cal said thoughtfully. "You'd have to be fucking sure you knew what you were doing."

Ambushed by the demands of Monday morning, it was break before Finn was free – and even then, he was supposed to be on yard duty – to seek out Leigh. But she had been swifter than he and was already in the office with Joss and Iona, making coffee and opening a new chocolate biscuit selection. Finn paused in the doorway, waiting for her to glance his way. She had her hair tied into a knot at the nape of her neck like a dancer.

"Aren't you on duty?" Joss reminded him.

"Yeah, just … "

"Just?"

"Avoiding going," Iona said.

Having obviously become both invisible and inaudible to her, he gave up.

Returning to the English block after his stint on break duty, he encountered Alan coming in the opposite direction. "Had enough already?" Finn greeted him.

Alan smiled, rolled his eyes. "Left the *Of Mice and Men DVD* in the car."

"I'll walk with you." He wanted to be upstairs grabbing a drink, filling in Risk Assessment forms for a pending theatre trip and grovelling to Leigh, but this morning had been Alan's first lesson with the Focus Group since their release from isolation. "How were they?"

"Strangely subdued. I didn't know whether to be suspicious or grateful."

"Monday morning," Finn reminded him. "They're still asleep. I wouldn't be lulled into a false sense of security."

"No, no."

"What did you do with them?"

"I did what you have to do with the Focus Group following an Incident. Pretended it hadn't happened."

"Ah. The blessed Clean Slate Strategy." The Clean Slate Strategy favoured by Stephen Lord was pretty much implicit in the school's behaviour policy, though it hardly squared with the weighty discipline files maintained by Brian Wilson and seized upon by him as evidence in the face of an impending permanent exclusion. Both Finn and Alan understood perfectly that each child should be allowed to start afresh every lesson, that everyone deserved second chances and that from their own point of view, minimising the after-effects of a behavioural catastrophe was often the only way forward for their own sanity. Where it fell down, as everyone except Stephen seemed to be painfully aware, was that second chances rapidly became hundredth chances and the worst pupils, who never turned up to their detentions and whose parents when contacted were of the view that the school was solely responsible for their offspring's misbehaviour, delighted in the knowledge that they would never receive serious or long-term punishment for anything.

"Exactly. I gave them a power point presentation on the historical and social context of *Of Mice and Men* and I wouldn't use the word attentive, but for the full fifty minutes nothing was hurled across the room, no one was hurt and nobody mouthed off."

"Do we call that progress?" Finn wondered.

"We call it peace." The words were barely in the air before he stopped dead. Ten yards across the car park, Alan's beloved Rover now sat with a jagged hole in its windscreen and a brick sitting neatly in the driver's seat.

By the beginning of her second week, Leigh had learned to identify the categories into which the pupils fell: the hard-faced girls who refused to meet her eyes, or did so only with contempt; the loud boys who flirted with and tried to charm her; the children of both sexes who kept silent, kept their heads down, desperately minding their own business; the friendly, well-balanced ones who held doors open for her and apologised if they got out of hand. She noted the voluntary segregation, more pronounced here than anywhere else she had taught, that the boys and girls generally found each other irritating, their conversation superficial and sexually oriented, the attack/defence nature of their interaction. Humour was almost always used to mask feelings, everything hanging on maintaining a façade of credibility or cool. It was a question, she quickly realised, of survival.

She shared these observations with Iona and Joss as they ate lunch in Iona's class-room. "Where're the others?" she'd asked, meaning – *where's Finn?* Her annoyance at his rudeness on Friday had quietly and ruthlessly worked itself out of all proportion over the weekend, so that when he'd popped into Joss's office at the beginning of break she hadn't been able to look at him. She didn't know what was the matter with her.

Except, of course she did.

"Alan's on duty," Joss listed, "Lady P takes her luncheon in the staff room, and Derek drives as far away as he can and eats in his car quivering to Classic FM. Finn'll be here in a minute."

Which he was, pulling out the chair beside Leigh's, peeling open his sandwich carton. Her skin burned at his proximity. "So," he said. "What are we talking about?"

"Leigh's initiation into Rapton." Iona supplied the details.

Finn listened. "That's what being a teenager is about, isn't it, survival? Surviving the pitiless judgement of your peers. Surviving being incarcerated in a place like this for five years having teachers drone on about Macbeth and quadratic equations when you know you're going to be a brickie."

"It wasn't like that for you, though," Joss pointed out, "at the grammar school."

"No, but it's what it's like for them." He brandished his sandwich in the general direction of the yard. "That's why schools like Rapton are the way they are. We try to make confused, disenfranchised kids conform to standards and expectations which are meaningless to them. Why can't we just try to teach them basic literacy and numeracy skills then train them for the trades and professions they might stand a chance of being good at and interested in? Sorry." He grinned, met Leigh's eyes. She managed to hold his gaze for a moment before flicking away. "Holding forth again. Not that I feel strongly about this or anything."

"No, you're right." Iona tucked a strand of her glossy black hair behind her ear, peeled back the lid of her yoghurt. "But we're as trapped as they are."

Joss snorted. "Only we don't stand on tables swearing at them."

"Don't you?" Iona smiled. "I do."

"No you don't. You just stare at them and raise your eyebrow. I've never seen such a terrifying eyebrow. I don't understand," Joss said helplessly, "why we can't just expect cooperation and good manners as an absolute given. No exceptions, no excuses, nothing."

"Well we should," Finn agreed. "Some of us try to. But the kids bring to school what they learn at home. It's all they know. We just have to try to show them an alternative."

Leigh frowned. How was it that everything he was saying now made sense? Was it just his reasonable tone of voice compared with his pissed-off one the other night? Maybe he was a nice guy driven to the edge, not an arrogant one intent on patronising her. She said, "But on Friday you said Stephen thinks the home environ-ment can be overcome when it can't."

He nodded. "In some cases."

"*Why?*" Joss bemoaned. "One rule for home: use foul language, tantrums, and bad manners to get your own way. Another rule for school: don't. It's not difficult."

Iona said, "What was it like at St Mary's, then, Leigh? Paradise?"

"Far from it. But not as extreme as Rapton. Not as ... savage."

"Catholic schools, you see," Iona declared. "Can't beat them for discipline. Must be the nuns."

Leigh smiled. "It isn't a convent. It just had a very different catchment area. All pushy middle-class parents with - "

"Snotty, arrogant brats?"

"Pretty much," she admitted. "But I was never told to fuck off. No one slaughtered an animal in the playground or vandalised teachers' cars."

Finn sighed. "It's getting worse. 'Things fall apart; the centre cannot hold; Mere anarchy is loosed upon the world'."

"Yeats," Leigh recognised in spite of herself. "*The Second Coming.*"

Finn laughed. "See, mark of a good English teacher, quoting poetry even while he eats his sandwiches."

"Mark of a pretentious git," Iona said.

He grinned. "Tea, anyone? Leigh?"

He had risen to fetch the kettle and was looking down at her, still smiling. They were perhaps four feet apart yet warmth suffused her as swiftly and thoroughly as if they were touching. "Thanks, but I need to go and set up for my next lesson." *God*, she thought, this is going to be distracting.

Back in her classroom, she clicked onto the first slide of her power point for her lesson on autobiographies, then went to the cupboards along the rear wall to collect exercise books from the Year 7 basket. From the corridor she could hear the heavy fall of running footsteps, shouting and belches of laughter. Focus Group, she thought, causing havoc. At the same moment her door burst open and the Focus Group causing havoc were in the room with her.

"All right, miss?" Five of them clustered around her door, which they had slammed on another of their pack outside, jeering and gesturing at him through the glass. Leigh sighed inwardly. Whilst she recognised them en masse she could not have assigned to them their individual identities; she knew they were called Josh and Ryan and Connor and Callum and Liam, as were most of the boys in the school, but she could not have said which was which. She continued to sort through the books, waiting for them to leave as volcanically as they had arrived.

EXCLUDED

After a few minutes they grew bored with mocking someone through a door and turned, one by one, towards her. Aware of their sudden quieting, she glanced up, saw that they were swinging over the desks, crouching with their thick boots on the clear pale grey surfaces, their jaws working as they chewed. One came to sit on the low cupboard beside her, and she tried not to recoil from the stench of bad breath and cigarette smoke. "Something I can do for you?" she enquired.

They cackled and she understood that the nature of their intrusion had changed. She looked from one to the other, trying to think of something to say which would not be wilfully misconstrued. She decided to go for friendly and unfazed. "We haven't met, have we? I'm Miss Somers."

"Yeah, we know who you are." Skinny, spiky blond hair, ring-leader material. "We seen you around."

"You was the one watchin' us when we was kickin' that bag about."

"Were it you grassed us up?"

Leigh frowned. "How could it be? I've no idea who you are. But if I had known, you can be certain I would have done."

One of them snorted, lay flat out on his desk and scratched his balls. Someone else sniggered.

She said, "I've got a lesson in here in a minute. Year 7."

"So what? You want us to piss off?"

"Yes please."

The boy sitting on the cupboard edged closer. She could feel his leg against the back of her skirt, his foot enter the space between her feet. They had all crept forward a few significant inches. "'S not very nice of you, miss."

"You wanna be nice to us. Keep us on side."

"Do I?" she said blandly, stepping forward, away from the boy lurking behind her. Another pushed up from his desk to crowd her from the side. The boy lying on his back rubbed his hand up and down his groin. They were laughing. Leigh prayed her hammering heart could not be heard, that her face displayed nothing but composure. She said, "Please leave. Now."

A third stood to block her from the right, not one of them

touching her yet besieging her all the same; she was only average height with her shoes on and they eclipsed her view of anything but themselves and the ceiling. She could see with too much clarity the sweat stains on their uniforms, the rage of their acne, their bubbles of saliva as they leered down at her. The supine boy rolled onto his side, facing her, and lifted his hand to his zip.

"What the hell," Finn's voice, loud and severe, "is going on?"

Leigh knew that if her expression had not betrayed her to the boys, it did to Finn. They melted back from her as though she were suddenly aflame.

"Ain't even done nuffin'."

"My office," he thundered. "*Now*."

They slouched away. He closed the door behind them. "Are you all right?"

"Yes."

He frowned at her. "Are you sure?"

That he asked again, because he had the perception to see she was not all right, almost undid her. She felt shakier than she had when the boys had been upon her. "I'm fine." She made an effort to control her voice, her tear ducts. "Really."

"Tell me what happened."

She sketched in the details, seeing as she did so the clench of his jaw, the darkening of his eyes.

"Right," he said grimly. He paused. "Give me a minute. If I go out there now I might just kill them."

Joss entered Leigh's room as her cherubic little meerkats were embarking upon spider-diagramming their life stories. "Finn says can you pop into see him for a minute. I'll mind the babes."

He was in his office, shirt sleeves rolled up, jacket over the back of his chair. His voice, as he had been castigating the Focus Group, had thundered through every classroom in the department. "Leigh. God. I'm so sorry about that."

"It was hardly your fault." She perched against the edge of his desk.

"Are you all right?"

"I was just a bit shaken, that's all. I'm made of sterner stuff than that."

He looked at her appraisingly. Even to an objective eye she would be young and pretty and vulnerably slender. Hardly anyone's idea of a physical manifestation of stern stuff. He didn't doubt her spirit for a moment, but he could see how the Focus Group had seized on her as prey. He said, "I want to take it further."

She shook her head. "They were just behaving like prats. Stupid little boys, showing off. Don't give them the satisfaction of thinking they got to me."

"It's sexual harassment."

"It's par for the course." She shrugged. "But they step out of line with me once more and you can throw the book at them."

His eyes searched hers. "You're sure?"

"I'm sure." She smiled. "Thank you, for being there."

Finn, still looking at her, tried without success to find something to say which might sound more like professional courtesy than personal concern. Instead he seized the moment. "And I'm sorry too, about Friday night. I invite you for a drink and then I go off on one and insult you. It was unfair of me and I am sorry and you probably think I'm a complete arse."

"No." She looked touched, surprised. "I mean yes, it was a bit unfair, but I wasn't listening to you properly and I just think you care about what you do."

"I do. And I am a complete arse."

She smiled.

"Friends?" he said.

"'Course." She stood up. "Better relieve Joss. Thanks. I'll see you later."

He watched her go, recalling how the intensity of his anger had bewildered the Focus Group; though not nearly as much as it had bewildered him. Though he detested intimidation of any kind, he did wonder guiltily whether he would have raged quite as effectively on behalf of any other female teacher in the school.

His telephone rang. It was Stephen.

The CCTV footage left no doubt. Though all the members of the Focus Group were present, the boy who had launched the brick at the windscreen of Alan's car was Liam Clough. Finn, Alan and Stephen watched the tape through twice, the boys swinging across the yard like baboons in a wildlife park, the absence of sound rendering their open mouths and contorted expressions more lunatic yet. They had circled the car, kicking the tyres, bouncing on the boot. And then Liam had picked something up from the ground, drawn back his arm. "I think," Stephen said as their second viewing drew to a close, "that that would stand up in court."

Finn and Alan looked at him, taken aback.

"I'm assuming you want to go to the police?"

"Oh yes." Alan recovered sufficiently to state his intent. Prevaricating with Stephen Lord got you nowhere. "But I also want him excluding. Permanently."

"Of course," Stephen replied. "I was taking that as read."

Finn frowned. "Have I missed something here?"

Stephen gestured. "Enough is enough. Things are already far worse than they were last year and we're only a couple of weeks in. I don't think we stand a chance of taming the Focus Group and I know it was my hope to perform miracles with them but I honestly can't see it happening. If I have to sacrifice them for the sake of the rest of the school, so be it."

Finn blinked. "Run that by me again."

"No." Stephen was rueful. "You heard me right."

Stephen put down the novel he was trying to read in favour of watching his wife undress for bed. He was constantly trying to read novels, partly because he feared the literary world was in danger of becoming closed to him forever, and partly because he had once, dammit, enjoyed reading them. But these days a page or two as he was falling asleep was the most he could manage, and the list of books into which he had delved no further than the opening chapter grew longer year by year. He tended, when they were available, to watch the films instead, a practice he would have deplored in his pupils and which he had no intention of admitting to the English

Department. Though he had this week overheard Leigh Somers and Finn Macallister debating the merits of James McAvoy's and Keira Knightley's performances in *Atonement*. Had wanted to join in the discussion himself but suspected it might be an intrusion. So here he lay, another novel face down on the bedside table, Claudia's shell coloured silk camisole whispering to the floor.

He liked that she carried a little more weight now than she had when he had married her, appreciated the rounding of her body which she complained about on a regular basis. Her blonde hair and even features lent her a Grace Kelly style serenity whilst also belying – as possibly Grace Kelly's had too – a rigorous commonsense and steeliness of intent. He smiled, thinking this, and she caught his eye in the mirror.

"What?"

"Just thinking how beautiful you are."

She threw her hairbrush at him.

"What? *Ow*. That is what I was thinking."

Claudia laughed. "I'd love to have seen their faces," she said.

"It was worth it," he admitted, recalling Alan and Finn in his office this afternoon, their patent astonishment at his readiness to exclude a member of his beloved Focus Group.

"So what did it?" Claudia asked. "Did you finally reach the end of your tether with them?"

"That, yes. Also we have Ofsted due before the end of the year and I need to show that steps have been taken to address pupil behaviour." He paused. "It's not been enough to promote the image of the school, to build new sports halls and IT suites, to try my damnedest to drag the place up there with West Park and the grammar in terms of facilities and meeting the needs of our kids. If Ofsted come in and nothing's improved, we will go into Special Measures this year. And so will my career. Left to my own devices, I'd be perfectly happy to slog on trying to make things better according to my own beliefs, but I do know that's not how the real world works. I'm not going to have everything I've worked for destroyed by a small group of jeering thugs."

Claudia looked impressed. "Bravo. About time."

"And something my father said at the weekend, about not thinking of it as the consequences of a punitive society, but as the justice of a fair one."

"Which is what you've always been about."

"Mm. It's going to be a battle, though. I feel less like a force for justice than like King Canute."

She laughed, knelt on the bed and leaned over to kiss him. "Oh Stephen. The jeering thugs at that school need someone more jeering and thuggish to sort them out, not you. What dark deed is it you think you committed in some past life that you still have to atone for it with tolerance and forgiveness?"

He reached for her. "You know all my dark deeds," he said seriously.

"In that case," she said, kissing him again, "I can't see you have anything to fear."

Six

Late September rain slashed against the windows of the corner shop, a blustering wind rattling the glass in its frames. Dean stood in the queue at the till, listening to the elderly customers complaining as if somebody had promised them a lifetime of blue skies and sunshine and reneged on the deal. A few weeks ago he hadn't been able to stroll down to the local shop to buy a newspaper and feel the rain on his face, though years ago no doubt he'd complained about it too. Be careful, he thought, what you whinge about because it might turn into a fucking luxury.

The queue moved teeth-grindingly slowly but it wasn't as if he had anything to rush home for. Day-time television and the sports pages about summed it up. Nothing to do and nowhere to go and he could be sixteen again, desperate for something, anything, to look forward to, a bit of excitement. Sod all round here to give anyone hope or ideas or motivation. No wonder the kids turned out the way they did. Nothing changed, it just got worse.

No one had looked at him twice in the shop, though there was a bit of an atmosphere. They knew who he was. He was staying away from the pubs and the other estates, from the people who maybe thought he owed them. No one here was likely to be scared of him because he was hard or bent on revenge because fifteen years ago he'd broken into their house and nicked their telly. Most likely they thought he was a dickhead for having got involved in a robbery with a gang of greedy, stupid lads, a robbery where there'd been so much money at stake it'd had the police crawling all over it from the outset. Most likely they thought he'd deserved to be banged up for a sight longer than he had. Most likely they were right.

Trying to tell Cal (who wanted to join the army for Christ's sake! What the fuck was that about?) that there was nothing cool about being a convicted criminal, certainly nothing cool about a stretch inside, he had realised that this prison system, which was meant to be a joke and only churn out criminals better trained for the job, had actually worked. He wasn't going back. He wasn't staying here either and this was kind of the point. He and Cal were rubbing along and pissing each other off in equal measure. The boy listened to him now and again, though he made a great show of pretending not to, but Dean knew he was kidding himself – kidding them all – if he thought a few weeks of him acting tough were going to change anything. Cal needed rewinding half a dozen years and starting again. And it wasn't just that given the time and energy he didn't think he could do it. It wasn't anything to do with Cal. He couldn't stick around because here there was no escape. In every park, on every street corner the memories were so vivid it was like watching a film of his past and it wasn't getting any easier as the days went by. It wasn't about laying the ghosts by seeking out the truth either because he knew exactly what had happened. He had been there. Seen it all.

He paid for his paper. The man behind the till didn't even look at him.

Taking a right turn instead of heading back to Julie's, away from the streets of litter and terraces surrounding the estate, he pressed on through the centre of town, past the health centre and the cricket ground, beyond the mill apartments and the twenty-four hour supermarket. Up the cobbled street with its banks and cafés and estate agents, independent businesses smarter than the grubby chainstores, past the market and the traffic lights at the box junction. He could have done it all with his eyes closed.

And here he was. On the Old Road.

Where to start.

There was no answer, at the first few houses he tried. He should come at night, he thought, when they'd be home, instead of in the middle of the day when they were out working to pay the mortgages on their big Victorian bay-windowed semis and mill-owners' mansions. He tried a fourth house, taking the tarmac path to the heavy door with its engraved glass panes, rain dripping down his face as the wind gusted around him. And the door opened.

The curiosity on the face of the elderly man who'd opened it creased almost instantly into suspicion.

Dean understood. He knew the sight he made, soaking wet, shorn head, cheap clothes. He knew he was going to sound dodgy at best. Wasn't a lot he could do about that. He plunged in. "I'm trying to track someone down. Need to find out who lived in these houses twenty years ago."

"Who is it you're after?" Half a foot shorter than Dean, with sparse white hair and a cardigan the colour of cat-sick, his tone of voice said he wasn't going to be intimidated. That's me, Dean thought. Sort of bloke who intimidates the old folk.

"That's the problem," he admitted. "I haven't got a name."

"Well I lived in this one. Have done half my life."

Not here, then. His guts had been twisted up at the thought that the end of his quest lay behind one of the doors on this road. Within touching distance. A sudden squall of wind against his back had him hunching his shoulders, water seeping into his collar. He winced.

"I'm not asking you in," the old man said.

Well no. That would obviously be stupid, wouldn't it. I could rob you blind and leave you for dead. Might have done once. The first bit, anyway. He said, "No. S'all right."

"Is it a family you're looking for?"

"A bloke. Friend of a friend, sort of."

"And this was twenty years ago?"

"Give or take." He shivered but the old bloke was getting into it now.

"What did he look like? Ah, now, what sort of car did he drive? I might remember that."

"I don't know."

"Hmm. Will he have moved on now?"

"Probably."

The man with the cat-sick cardigan looked at him. Said, with sympathy, "You wouldn't know him if you found him, would you." Dean was silent. "I don't want to put you off, but it sounds a bit of a wild goose chase to me."

"Yeah. Well. It might be."

"I'd ask around for you, but there's not a lot to go on."

"There isn't," Dean agreed tightly. He'd asked around himself, the last couple of weeks, pubs, bookies, corner shops. No one'd known anything. He hadn't reckoned on this, old people trying to be helpful and feeling sorry for him. He felt absurdly ashamed. "Thanks anyway."

He turned and walked away through the rain.

Itchy with curiosity he could no longer ignore, he followed the road higher up into a different kind of rich man's land. Here the roads were quieter and broad, tree-lined, their houses set behind gates and at the ends of drives, gardens flourishing, lawns tended. His heartbeat had begun to quicken already. Higher still, past farmhouses and barn conversions, the moor beginning the other side of this drystone wall and stretching beyond the clump of trees ahead to the horizon. He stopped and swallowed and could hardly bear to look.

It had changed, of course it had. Tarmacked drive leading across the field to it now. Five-bar gates you'd have to get out the car to open and shut. Extension, new kitchen, proper bathroom, on the market for a quarter of a million. Twenty-first century property boom gone mad. He'd rung the estate agents when he'd seen it was up for sale, learned it was empty, the owners moved out a couple of weeks back to secure their new home in Cheshire. It was, apparently, proving a difficult house to sell, despite its extensive renovation work. He had lacked the courage to come and take a look until now.

And even now, he couldn't get further than the bottom five-bar gate. His memory skittered away from images of the house as it had once been. Instead he thought of Julie and Callum, of promises and debts. Of that other promise, made a lifetime ago. He'd done his best, was as sure as he could be without knowing the upshot that it'd been the right thing. Yet like a ghoul at the window it clawed at him still.

Emily Jordan skipped through the school gates halfway through first period. Her asthma review had been due at the local health clinic last week, but her mother had been unwilling to disrupt Emily's routine at her new school until she was reasonably sure her daughter knew what that routine was, and consequently the review had been postponed until this morning. Emily had blown into a tube and answered some questions and been given two new inhalers, and her mother had bought her a magazine and some chocolate from Asda before dropping her back on the road outside school.

Arriving late into an empty yard felt weird; it was usually so full of other pupils she couldn't see from one building to the other, had to have her wits about her crossing the tarmac to avoid footballs, elbows, insults. The quiet and sense of space now was dizzying. But it was the third week of term and as Emily was able to navigate the school grounds without a map, she felt confident of reaching Mr Macallister's classroom without becoming hopelessly lost en route. After first visiting reception to let them know she was back in school, she set off through the main doors on the labyrinthine trail towards the English Block.

In ground-floor classrooms pupils sat, working, hands raised, others sauntering about. Teachers either sat working too or stood, hands on hips, writing on the board, speaking to the class. She could hear the heavy thump of footfall from inside the gym, the shriek of a whistle. A grown-up she didn't know was carrying a box of papers, holding down the top sheets to prevent them being whipped away by the wind. Emily ducked out of the wide area of yard into the short-cut she and the other Year 7s had discovered last week, a narrow strip between the Arts Theatre and the Chemistry labs, no windows to the latter and black-out curtains to the former. It was called, though she did not know this yet, The Tunnel, and offered such an easy and already familiar route from one area of the school to the other that it hadn't occurred to her it might not be a safe place to be alone.

She was halfway along, listening to the echo of her footsteps and thinking about her English lesson and the biographies of each other they had begun writing last week, and the funny autobiography Mr Macallister had written and shown them on the whiteboard – everyone in her class wanted Mr Macallister to be their English teacher *forever* – when suddenly she was pinned to the wall of the Science block, the boy's wet red lips and narrowed eyes inches from her own. He stank of smoke, his hand on her throat hurt and between them she saw glimmering the long silver blade of a flick knife.

She whimpered.

"Not gonna hurt you. Just want your money."

She thought of the coins in her pocket, her dinner money and bus fare, her mother sitting beside her in the car counting it out only a few minutes ago. She wanted to cry. It wasn't going to be enough. "I've only got two pounds fifty."

He looked annoyed. "It'll have to do."

She could feel her legs trembling. She hardly dared breathe, let alone move. He grabbed her shoulder, twisting her round to gain access to her bag. "Well fuckin' hand it over then."

She dropped her bag to the floor, knelt to unzip it. Her hands wouldn't work properly and he was holding the knife really close to her face, she could feel his impatience quivering along the blade. Her searching fingers found the edges of the fifty pence and she scrabbled for the rest, pushed it at him, feeling sick as the heat of his hand snatched at hers. Then either she moved too fast or he'd lied, because she felt the faintest scratch across her cheek and she knew that he'd cut her.

"Ah, Emily." Finn glanced across as she slipped into his room, dropped down into her place. "I'll be with you in a minute, I'm just explaining something to Luke." He turned back to Luke, a delightful boy with no grasp whatsoever of written English, and only a passing acquaintance with reading it. "Now then. The reason we use sentences when we write ... "

"Sir ... " A child from Emily's table.

"Yes, just one moment."

"Sir."

"Okay. Hang on."

"*Sir.*" More urgent this time, more than urgent. Distressed. Finn turned. Saw Emily's paper-white face, tears streaming and dripping from her chin, the nick of blood on her cheek. He had crossed the room to crouch beside her in a second.

"What happened?"

She shook her head, unable to speak.

"Come and talk to me outside."

She stood, trembling, the rest of the class shocked into silence. Finn led her gently out into the empty corridor. "What is it, Em?"

"He took all my money off me. I haven't got any bus fare, I won't be able to get home."

"Don't worry about that, I'll give you your bus fare. Who took your money?"

"The boy with the knife."

Finn's insides went cold. She began to sob. "I was so frightened."

"Josh Ferris." Finn was so angry he could barely speak. "She described him perfectly and I've checked the register, he wasn't in class but he is in school."

"All right." Stephen rubbed his forehead. "Where is Josh?"

"In his Maths lesson."

"Let's make sure he stays there. I want to talk to Emily first."

"He needs excluding, Stephen."

Stephen hesitated, which enraged Finn further.

"Excluding Liam obviously wasn't deterrent enough, was it? We can't have the Focus Group getting away with threatening children with knives because two exclusions in one week will look bad for the school. We were lucky, with the kitten incident, that Sam's gone to another school and his mother let it go. I can't see Emily's parents letting this go, can you?"

Stephen nodded slowly. "I know. And I know you're upset. So am I. I know we have to be seen to be dealing with this."

So fucking deal with it, Finn thought.

Leigh pinched some coffee and biscuits from Joss and sat him down in his Head of Year office. "If you had seen that little girl's face … " Finn shook his head. "I could have cried for her. My kids, Leigh. My bloody year group. But if Stephen won't back me up, what can I do?"

"Maybe he will back you up. He excluded Liam."

"I know. But because he's been so soft in the past we have this culture where the worst kids think they're running the school. Whatever sanctions Stephen puts in place now – and I have known him to be all talk and no follow-through, by the way - that's not going to change overnight. I'd hoped excluding Liam'd keep a lid on things for a bit." He sighed. "I can just sense things spiralling out of control and I don't understand why. What's the matter with them? I know they don't want to be in school and they don't care about coursework or exams or any of that, but holding an eleven year old girl at knife point for two pounds fifty? He laughed, you know, after he'd robbed her. Chased her across the yard with the knife and laughed. Whose good is it going to serve keeping him here?"

"What're his parents like?"

"Ineffectual, clearly. And what also worries me is even if we do get rid of the Focus Group one by one, the level of behaviour is already having a ripple effect through the rest of the school. Year 10'll be next."

"Year 9 have already started."

"Oh God." He sipped his coffee. "Thanks, for this. For listening to me rant. Again."

"Don't thank me. You might be listening to me one day."

He smiled. "With pleasure. I owe you." Looking at her, seeing the sympathy and humour in her eyes, realising she had given up a free lesson to listen to him, his misgivings receded further still. Surely the point of a gut feeling was you went with it despite yourself, despite your past and your defensive cynicism and your stubborn refusal to recognise something wonderful when you saw it? He wanted to say – no, let me thank you, let me take you out to dinner. Let me take you home.

His telephone rang.

"I have Josh in my office," Stephen said. "I thought you might like to be party to the conversation we're about to have."

Cal slung his bag on the sofa. "It's like living in a fucking war zone, being at that school."

Dean didn't look up from his newspaper. "How's that, then?"

"You're advancing, right, with your troops, middle of the battlefield, look up - and half your mates have been blown away."

Dean frowned at him. "You've lost me."

"Fucking exclusions."

"Maybe you wanna be a bit more careful who your mates are."

"Yeah right, I'll start hanging round with the prefects, shall I?" Cal went into the kitchen, opened the fridge. "Fancy a beer?"

"So - " Dean took a swig from his can. "Why're your mates being excluded?"

"Ah, any crappy little thing they can hang on them. It's like the Lord's on a purge."

"A purge?"

"It's the right word. It means like getting rid of all the shit. I looked it up once. I'm not stupid."

"Right. Touchy but not stupid." He paused. "The Lord?"

"It's what they call him. Not descriptive enough if you ask me. Stephen Lord, the head of Crapton. Big Mac's no better. I used to think he was sound."

"Big Mac? You don't half talk some shit, you."

"Mr Macallister, Head of Year 11. He's not that big. Six foot or something but not exactly a brick shithouse." He ambled back into the kitchen. "Talking of Big Macs, there's no food."

"There's loads of food."

"Nah, but stuff you cook, not stuff you eat. D'you wanna get a take-away?"

"I've just got out of prison, haven't I? What money do I have for take-aways?"

Cal grinned. "Who said anything about paying?"

"Don't even think about it." He hauled out of his chair and came to stand with Cal in front of the open refrigerator. "I'll cook us something."

Cal started to laugh.

"Fuck off," Dean told him sternly. "I will and you'll eat it."

One of the really unfair and annoying things about the current antics of the Focus Group, Todd thought, was that as far as most of the Year 7s were concerned, it tarred them all with the same brush. Wandering that afternoon in the general direction of home – which he had dwindling interest in reaching at all these days – he came upon a Year 7 boy lingering alone at one of the entrances to the estate which lay behind the school. Todd slowed his pace and the boy looked more anxious still. Todd, who would have described himself as fairly tall but pretty weedy and about as menacing as Bambi, understood that the black stripe in his tie might have been a treble six tattooed on his forehead. "You okay?" he asked.

The boy – whose name, Todd remembered from a previous vague encounter, was Zak - looked nervously up at him.

"It's all right." Todd raised his hands in a gesture of surrender. "Honest. I'm one of the good guys." Whatever that meant. "What's up?"

Zak was uncertain. "One of those boys lives near me."

"What boys? Oh. *Those* boys." It was not only inside the school gates that the reputation of the Focus Group struck fear into hearts. Most of the residents of Rapton had endured some appalling encounter with them. Todd quite saw that if you came from the same estate you'd feel there was no escape. "Where d'you live?"

"Down there." He pointed. It was the street on which, Todd felt sure, Cal Bywater lived. Cal was guilty of a lot of things but Todd couldn't imagine him beating up a little boy just because he lived on the same street. Then again, he couldn't get his head around the reason for Josh Ferris' exclusion. Why would you do something like that? The impulse to hurt anyone was so alien to him he couldn't get any sort of purchase on it.

"D'you want me to walk you home?" he offered.

Zak smiled gratefully.

It was a long time since Todd had had reason to enter the Rapton estate. At the far end it was, just as he'd remembered, a wasteground of boarded windows and cars with bricks where their wheels should be, front gardens the final resting place for old washing-machines and rusting bicycle, litter ankle deep, feral dogs sniffing and peeing along the low brick walls. But on the way to this domestic armageddon lay streets of houses with new front doors and frilly blinds at the windows, their gardens filled with autumn flowers and neat little lawns. It was beside one of these, and midway through a slightly baffling discourse on the merits of the latest series of *Dr Who*, that Zak stopped. "Thank you."

Todd looked at the house, at the large toy rabbit in the window of a bedroom, at a row of cards on the living-room sill. "Someone's birthday?"

"My sister's." Zak wore the expression of a weary elder brother.

"Sisters, eh? What can you do?" said Todd, who for years had longed for brothers or sisters of his own.

Zak grinned. "Seeya!"

Todd watched him go, running up the path to the front door, announcing his arrival through the letter-box. He was four years older than Zak. He might have been twenty. Turning away, he walked another hundred yards or so down the hill towards the bleak navel of the estate, where teenage mothers pushed their buggies past the graffitied walls of burned-out houses and tattooed men loaded packages into and out of wrecks of cars. He felt uneasily that he was somewhere he shouldn't be, gazing upon a site of past atrocities which at any moment might waken to ensnare him.

And so they did.

"Oi! Todd! What you doin' round 'ere?"

Cal. Halfway down the other side of the street, a four-pint plastic container of milk in one hand, a six-pack of Stella in the other.

"Umm ... " Todd scraped his shoe on the side of the kerb. "Well – just ... nothing." As an explanation it didn't exactly hang together, but Callum didn't seem to mind. He sauntered across the road.

"Did you hear about Josh?"

"Yeah." He said it non-committally, uncertain whether Josh was being cast as ruthless hero or wronged victim.

But Cal rolled his eyes. "Twat. A little kid, what's that about? He's fuckin' mental, Josh. I mean, there's stuff you don't do, right?"

"Right," Todd agreed, masking his surprise that Callum was admitting to scruples.

Cal frowned at him. "You're one of them prefects, aren't you?"

"Yes," Todd said warily.

Inexplicably, Cal grinned. "D'you want to come and have a beer?"

"Erm ... "

"Go on. Uncle Dean's cooking me tea. Should be good for a laugh."

Why not? Todd thought. He smiled. "Yeah, all right. Thanks."

Cal's house, perched on the uppermost rim of the estate, was neither vandalised nor derelict. It just looked, Todd thought, with its peeling paintwork and smeared windows, as though it needed someone to care for it. He followed Cal round the back to the kitchen door, stepping over empty crates and bags of rubbish en route. Inside a wiry bloke in baggy jeans and a stained t-shirt was pushing sausages and bacon round a frying-pan with a fork. "Got the milk," Cal told him, opening the fridge and dropping the plastic container inside. Added, for Todd's benefit and not without a degree of mockery, "This is me Uncle Dean."

"Ta." Uncle Dean glanced at Todd and frowned, but more in enquiry than objection. "Who's this?"

"Todd," Cal replied laconically. "He's a prefect."

"Is he now?" Dean, smiling – sardonically, Todd thought, like at some private joke – gave him a longer look, his expression changing as though everything Todd was, was not only visible on his skin but took only the most fleeting of moments to comprehend. He nodded. "All right, Todd?"

"Yeah. Thanks." Todd took a slurp of the beer Cal had given him, wiped his mouth with the back of his hand.

"Is this it, then?" Cal said. "Is this you cooking my tea? Sausage and bacon?"

"Fuck off," Dean replied amiably. "There's eggs as well. What more d'you want?"

"A nutritionally balanced meal containing each of the major food groups," Cal replied.

Todd laughed, spluttering his beer.

"What are you complaining about? There's protein, stick some fried bread in you've got your carbohydrate. Bit of tomato?"

"We don't have tomato. We don't buy fruit and fucking veg, had you not noticed?"

Dean came close to laughing. "Todd? Sticking around to have your arteries clogged?"

"Sure," Todd grinned.

They ate around the kitchen table, a three foot square of red drop-leaf formica, the remains of previous meals crusting its surface. But then the remains of previous meals crusted every surface; the floor crunched underfoot; the fridge and the sink reeked of decay. At least, Todd thought, the sausages were good.

Cal stabbed a piece of fried bread into the runny yolk on his plate, resuming a conversation which Todd presumed had begun long before he'd turned up. "See, me, I won't be hanging round here after next year. Fuck all to do in Rapton. That's why I want to join the army, get out of here. Travel a bit."

"Oh right," Dean said. "Iraq. Afghanistan. All the hot tourist spots."

"Beats seven years staring at the inside of a cell, doesn't it? Don't get to see much of the world doing that."

Dean's rein on his anger was impressive, Todd thought. Scary but impressive. Obviously the pulse in his temple and the set of his jaw were imperceptible to Cal. That or he just didn't care.

Todd cleared his throat. "Food's good, Dean."

"Thanks." Dean turned to him. "Have we met before?"

Cal snorted. "How're you gonna have met him before? He

was like, eight when you went inside. Same as me."

"Yeah all right, shut the fuck up, I'm just being polite. Is your family local, Todd?"

He nodded. "My step-dad's Vince Kershaw, he's got a building firm in the valley."

"I know Kershaws."

"He's always lived round here so yeah, I suppose we're local."

Dean squirted a fart of ketchup onto his plate. "And your mum?"

Todd hesitated. "She died when I was twelve."

Something unexpectedly approaching sympathy in Dean's eyes. "Must've been hard for you."

"It was."

"Was she a local lass too?"

Cal looked at Dean in disbelief. "Fucking hell, doesn't do much for your social skills, does it, prison? Leave him alone, will ya, he's tryin' to eat."

Bizarre, Todd thought later, lying in bed, Mika playing inside his head courtesy of his iPod's ear-piece. He'd arrived home to darkness, Vince and Sheryl out at someone's fiftieth birthday bash, the house cavernous around him after the Bywaters' council semi. From seeing Cal doing something as normal as buying milk, through his edge-of-aggression banter with Dean, to having his tea cooked for him by an armed robber. The whole encounter had been seriously bizarre.

And Dean asking about his mum. Todd stared up into the airy darkness, his chest aching. It had taken months to stop aching so much he cried when he thought about her. Years before he no longer thought about her every day. He remembered realising, when he was about fourteen, that he had it cracked. He could deal with being an orphan. He wasn't cool with it exactly, but he could handle it. And he'd had Vince.

And then Vince had Sheryl.

He rolled over and reached for his laptop, logged on. Christie was there – he could swear she spent most of her life on MSN – and he typed *Hey*.

- *Hey you,* she wrote immediately. *What you up to?*

He told her, describing the evening in brief but amusing detail. Christie was fascinated, but then her father was a university lecturer, her mother a GP and they lived in a leafy suburb of York. She probably didn't have much to do with armed robbers or lads like Cal.

- *And how's the wicked stepmother?*
- *Wicked's too cool a word for her. Evil stepmother.*
- *It's that bad? Are you really fed up?*
- *Yeah, fed up and lonely ... and missing you.*

He rubbed his eyes, the glow from the screen was making his head ache a bit. *I'm unravelling*, he wanted to add, but there was some stuff you just couldn't tell anyone.

Dean sat on an upturned crate in the scrub of land Julie called the garden, trying to sink enough Stella to put him to sleep. It'd help if he were warm, instead of out here shivering in his t-shirt, but he felt tethered in the house, his intent drained out of him by too many distractions, too much emotional baggage. He had enough emotional baggage of his own, for Chrissake. Tonight, for instance. Was he mad, jumping to conclusions? Had he been focussed on the same thing for so long he was seeing connections where there weren't any?

Or was he right.

"Eh, Dean." Cal, backlit by the light from the kitchen, closing the door and coming across the mud and the grass toward him. "What you doin' out here?"

"Getting pissed."

"Might join you."

Dean tossed him a can. Cal caught it, snapped it open, slugged it back. Dean watched him. "Who were that lad, then? Not the sort of mate I'd have thought you'd have."

"Todd's all right. Can't help being a geek." Cal wiped his mouth on his sleeve.

"Is he the same age as you?"

"Yeah. Known him since primary school. Lives in one of them barn conversions up top. Step-dad's minted."

Dean looked at him through the darkness. "It's not everything, having money."

"Yeah, like you'd know." Cal perched on a broken down bit of fence. "Have you ever had stuff? Like major stuff?"

"Nah." He was pissed. He slid off the crate to lie on his back on the cold and rutted ground. The stars were spinning.

"Is that why you wanna start over? Have a proper job an' that?"

"Sort of." He pressed the heels of his hands over his eyes. "Have something that's not about being scared and using me fists. Having a life that's nothing to do with coppers and getting hurt and being banged up. Having something to look *forward* to, for fuck's sake."

"You could have that here, couldn't you?"

"Nah."

"Dean." Cal's voice seemed to come from a distance. "Why've you really come back?"

And Dean said, "I'm looking for someone."

"Who?" Instant interest. "Who you lookin' for?"

"Some bloke. You wouldn't know him. He might not live round here now."

"Everyone knows everyone in Rapton. You could ask, like down the pub or summat."

"Yeah. I have. It's like a brick wall. Trouble is, I don't even know his name."

"What do you know?"

"He used to live on the Old Road."

"Is that it?"

"Yeah."

"Fuck."

Dean laughed. Miserable-drunk, desperate and laughing. What was that about? Madness. All the years in jail, driven him over the edge. Only thing that kept him going a – what had that old fella said? A wild goose chase. He felt the steel harden around his heart.

There were days, Stephen thought – no, in fact there were *weeks* – when the walls of Rapton High closed steadily in on him, inch by inch, and a giant ball began rolling slowly but ineluctably towards him, and he might be a lot of things, but none of them was Indiana Jones. Only a few short weeks ago he'd been describing to Deborah McGillis on national – well, regional – television the 'nurturing family atmosphere' he tried to foster at his school, impressing upon her that knife and gun culture were pretty much unknown, implying he received a high level of support from the 'local close-knit community'. Had he even believed it at the time? What would Deborah McGillis's reaction have been had he told her that the atmosphere was actually that of a dysfunctional family, that the knife culture was alive and well and no doubt guns not far behind it, that close-knit community translated as inbred, parochial paranoia?

"I'm trapped," he told Claudia.

She looked at him over the top of the novel she was reading. "Now who's paranoid?"

"I know, I know. I'm dealing with it." But Finn Macallister had looked at him with scorn this week, and he had felt something inside him recoil. Finn was, he knew, one of the best members of his staff: rational, down-to-earth, good with the kids. They'd had their differences but Stephen recognised that he could also be one of the most supportive. To have someone you liked and respected look at you as if they didn't think you were up to the job was humiliating and unpleasant. It had been Finn's response as much as Josh Ferris' actions which had led to the boy's exclusion.

"Well why don't you get Finn on side?" Claudia suggested. "Have a meeting with him, decide on the best way to handle Year 11 together? It doesn't have to be lonely at the top."

He looked at her. "You know, you should be doing my job."

"Yes. It sounds so appealing."

He smiled ruefully. "The trouble is, I can't move on until Rapton's a better school. I need a decent Ofsted and a list of glowing achievements behind me."

"And you need to start by taking control and then keeping it. They're children, Stephen. Nasty kids. Don't let them grind you down. You've worked so hard to be a good Head. It's not your fault Rapton's what it is. You'll never change those children because you'll never change the families they come from. It's a losing battle."

"Thanks."

"I don't mean it like that. You know I don't. But it's a situation you can only deal with, you can't overturn entrenched values and low expectations when they're rooted in the community. But you can deal with it to the best of your ability, and surely that's what Ofsted and anyone else will be looking for? Your next school could be the one you never want to leave. Rapton's just another stepping-stone. An unsteady, slippery one which might tip you into the rapids, but a stepping-stone nonetheless."

He nodded. "You're right."

"I always am. It's taking you such a long time to accept that." She smiled. "Stop fretting. It'll be fine."

Leigh, turning to lock her classroom door, found Todd beside her. "Sorry Miss. Forgot my PE kit."

She stood aside for him to pass. "No problem." There was something up with Todd, she thought. He'd been increasingly withdrawn this week, sitting alone at registration and form time, reluctant to engage in conversation. "Are you okay?" she asked him now.

He retrieved his PE bag from the floor beneath his desk. "Yeah, just, you know. Stuff."

"Stuff's a bugger, isn't it?"

He looked at her and half-smiled. His eyes were shadowed. "It really is. Thanks, Miss."

She gestured – *any time*.

The corridors, at break and lunchtimes, were intended to be tranquil, child-free environments. Removing the children from the environment, however, often took the whole of break to achieve. Leigh sat with Joss in her office, waiting for the tea to brew and listening to Finn's voice growing steadily louder as he strode the length of the building, from his own office to Joss's, turfing out pupils on the way.

"Right, off you go, ladies and gentlemen, downstairs please.

Could you clear the corridor? Outside, the sun's shining and it's so good for your skin, all that Vitamin D. Can you not hear me down there? Shaun, will you stop swinging off that door frame? Shall I say it a bit louder? *Off the corridor*. Was that better? Yes, that means you too, Leanne. Take your food outside. No, Miss Somers is having her break too. Downstairs. Now. CAN WE MOVE OFF THE CORRIDOR? THANK YOU!!" He burst into Joss's office. "*Fuck*ing hell."

"Cup of tea?" Joss said.

Leigh was grinning. "Tough morning, Finn?"

He let out his breath, gratefully took the mug Joss held out to him. "Thanks. Jeez. I hate to be the harbinger of doom or anything, but it's getting worse, isn't it? The atmosphere around school?"

"It is," Leigh agreed. "And we haven't even got to half-term."

"It reminds me of that song," he mused. "By the Kaiser Chiefs."

Joss said, predictably, "What song by the Kaiser Chiefs?"

"*I Predict A Riot*."

Leigh winced. "God, I hope not."

"I do, though." He shook his head. "Maybe I'm wrong. I hope I'm wrong. Anyway. What did we watch on TV last night?"

But Leigh had something on her mind. "Do you know Todd Kershaw?"

"Sure. Nice lad."

"Very nice. He's in my form."

"I know. Iona's got him in her top set. Straight As and A*s, apparently."

"Yes. Really enjoying *The Catcher In The Rye*."

She paused. Finn waited.

Leigh said, "It's just … he seems a bit … down."

"He's a teenage boy."

"Yeah," she nodded, admitting the implication. "Just my antennae twitching."

"Do you think I should have a word with him? Casually?"

"I don't know. I'll keep you posted."

"Okay." The bell rang. "Oh bloody *hell*," Finn said.

After he'd gone, and with a free period ahead of her, Leigh put away the biscuits, collected together their empty mugs. Joss sat, watching her, an amused and knowing expression on her face.

"What?" Leigh said.

Joss gestured innocence. "Nothing."

"Joss."

She grinned. "*Nothing*. Enjoy your free. See you later."

Leigh sat at her desk, gazing blankly at a pile of Year 11 coursework. She understood that in the presence of Finn Macallister the extra layers of protective skin she wore in school peeled away, leaving her vulnerable and a little bit shaky and distracted with desire. And Joss could see this? Could Finn see it too? If he could, it clearly didn't repel him, for still he sought her out to talk to, to share lunch with, to accompany him to the pub. He had been, since that initial snarl, unfailingly friendly and attentive and helpful. Did that also mean he might want to take her into his office with him and lock the door? She tried to measure his response to her by his response to the other members of the department, but when some of these were Alan, Derek and Lady Penelope, it really didn't help. And she did enjoy it, the frisson of attraction whenever he was near. It was just that sometimes – all right, much more often than sometimes - when he was distressed, when he laughed, when he met her gaze, it went a little bit deeper than that. All right, alone in his presence all she could think was *touch me now*.

In at the deep end, she thought. Ain't that the truth.

Alan had suspected from the moment he had given their names to Stephen following the kitten incident that there would be a marked and irreparable shift in his relationship with the Focus Group. The brick through his windscreen had rather cemented that suspicion but he didn't feel any real sense of foreboding until the day they began ignoring him.

He had, as usual, laid a copy of *Of Mice and Men* in each of the boys' places along with their ripped and graffitied excuses for exercise books, projected the lesson's aims and objectives onto his Smartboard and sat marking Year 9 descriptive writing pieces whilst waiting for the bell to ring. Also as usual by the time his charges had hauled themselves up to English from break, stopping on the way for a sneaky fag and a spot of light bullying, almost fifteen minutes of the lesson had been wasted.

"Right," Alan said sharply, as they began slouching into his classroom. "Let's make a start."

None of them so much as glanced in his direction. A couple sat on the tables, one or two others heading to the back to kick against the cupboards and peer out of the windows. Someone else launched his bag across the room at knee-height so that it collided with a bookcase and sent a dozen copies of *A View From A Bridge* flapping to the floor.

Alan said, "Sit down please."

Cal Bywater strolled in, pulled out a chair and put his thick, black booted feet up on the desk. In Alan's experience, any instruction given by a teacher was complied with after a minute or two, to create the impression that the pupils were not obeying an order but acting as they chose. He wryly understood the adolescent need to appear autonomous. So he gave them a couple of minutes. Nothing changed.

Following the kitten, and the windscreen, and the knife incident, Alan was losing not only his tolerance but also any residual respect or goodwill he might ever have had for these boys. "Sit down," he repeated. "Open your books. We're carrying on from Chaper Three."

"Fuck off," someone muttered.

"Fair enough," Alan replied, "if that's the way you want it." And he sent for reinforcements.

As Finn entered the room, several of the boys magically discovered they were now quite able to take their seats. Finn addressed the others. "Sit down. Open your books. Read. I'm prepared to go through this with you every single lesson until you can manage to do it all by yourselves. It's what I get paid for. But a blanket refusal to work results, as you well know, in a trip to the Head and pretty quickly after that, a trip off the premises. You might not want to be here. Fine. If that's your attitude, we don't want you here either. You might remember that this time next year when no one'll employ you and no college will accept you because you failed to get a D or a C in English."

Cal Bywater said, "I'm joining the army, me."

"Good," Finn replied. "Best place for you. Any more trouble, Mr Jackson, let me know."

Alan nodded. He glanced at the boys, who either refused to look in his direction or stared at him, remorseless and stony-eyed. For the first time in more than thirty years of teaching he was uneasy.

Immediately he changed his plans for the lesson. No hope of a class discussion of the characters of Lenny and George with close reference to the text now. Instead he brought up the notes on screen, said, "Copy those down in your books. In silence." And retreated to his desk.

For as long as thirty minutes there was relative calm. True, not all the boys were writing, but they were fairly quiet and he was happy to ignore the glances and sniggers and notes passed between them.

Then Callum Bywater announced, "Finished."

"Read on," Alan instructed.

"Nah." Callum pushed back from his desk, tilting his chair to rest on its back legs. "Can't be arsed."

"Out." Alan stood up. "Go on, out."

Callum rose too. "Don't feel like it."

One by one the other boys pushed to their feet, the legs of tables and chairs scraping on the parquet floor. Together and ignoring his commands which had become pleas, they moved closer to encircle him. Alan understood that the notes and looks exchanged through the lesson had been the planning of a military operation. Looking up into their sneering faces, he wondered was this what drowning felt like. Being wide but not especially tall, their height and number pressed in on him in the confined space between his desk and the wall, their combined torsos and limbs a great deal harder and stronger than his, their will compacting him as effectively as their bodies. All he had in his favour was the knowledge that in a minute or two the bell was going to ring.

"Boys, come on, sit down." He was beginning to sweat. They could probably feel it. Certainly smell it.

"You grassed us up." The delightful Callum Bywater. "We got put in isolation because of you."

"You were put in isolation because you killed an animal." He couldn't help it, even now. "The yard was full of people who saw you."

"It was you went to Lord. Liam and Josh'd still be here now if you hadn't done that."

"Liam and Josh are masters of their own fate. Move away, sit down and we can finish the lesson." Not that, even if they did the unthinkable and obeyed him, he had any intention of continuing to teach them, but it helped to sound confident. Trouble was, he didn't sound confident. His voice had come out reedy and uncertain.

Cal laughed. "Masters of their own fucking fate? What're you on?"

The boys crushed closer. Alan swallowed. Apart from the heat, and the stench of their sweat as well as his own, the stale smoke on their breath, he realised that his balls were less than inches from their grasp.

The bell rang.

No one moved.

A moment. An exhalation. He felt their muscles relax. "Come on," one of them said. "Get the fuck out of here."

The instant release of their pressure dizzied, almost felled him. He steadied himself against the desk for a moment, fearing for his heart, his blood pressure. Only Callum remained in the room.

"Get you next time," he jeered.

Alan moved towards him with as much speed as he could muster. Callum stepped out into the bustling corridor where he waited, still smirking. "You wanna lose a bit of that weight, Fat Man."

Alan lurched into the doorway. Right and left pupils were exiting through the fire doors, down the stairs, trailing bags and laughter and shouted abuse behind them. At the far end Finn was reminding them to move off the corridor.

"Think you can catch me?" Callum taunted. "Like to see you try."

Alan, when not recovering from coming close to being crushed to death, was nimbler on his feet than his size might suggest. He had been a good dancer in his youth. Making one last ditch effort before he crumpled into a nervous heap, he launched himself into the corridor, past a bemused Todd Kershaw, the edge of Callum's bag just within his reach. His finger-ends grazed the stitched canvas, gained purchase on the flapping tie of a pocket. But Cal, jerking out of his grasp, swerved, banging the fire door open, Alan fast at his heels. At the top of the staircase he stopped, too abruptly for Alan to slow his pace, and turned into the Fat Man's path.

And Alan, bouncing off him, off-balance on the top step, fell flailing through the air.

Seven

"I didn't push him."

Finn exchanged glances with Stephen. Having separately and at some length interviewed each member of the Focus Group, they had a fair idea of exactly what had taken place in Alan Jackson's classroom that afternoon. Stories varied in their details: the degree of malice in their crowding of Mr Jackson; the identities of the boys closest to him; the extent to which Sir had provoked them and should therefore take some of the blame. On one point, however, they were unanimous - the only one of them not to have legged it as soon as the bell went was Cal Bywater.

Finn stood against the window, the heat from the radiator burning the backs of his thighs, wishing he could look at Cal and see a child instead of a convict in training. He said calmly, "What did you do?"

Cal shrugged. "Same as the others."

Stephen sighed. "So you refused to participate in the lesson Mr Jackson was attempting to teach and were then involved both in verbally abusing him and in the resulting assault which consisted of physical intimidation and actual bodily harm?" The more furious he was with a pupil, the cooler and more formal Stephen became, Finn had noticed. Perhaps it was about putting some essential distance between himself and them. Frightening them with the use of vocabulary they might not fully understand.

But Cal was brighter than that. "We were just winding him up. We weren't gonna do nuffin'."

"Yet you did do something."

"Yeah, I went out the room. I went onto the corridor. He were chasing me. I got to the top of the stairs, turned round and he went flying past me. It weren't my fault."

"So you say."

"Right, there was loads of other people on that corridor. They're my witnesses."

"Most of the other people in that corridor, Callum, are so used to you creating mayhem wherever you go that they weren't really paying attention. The only person who could corroborate your story is Mr Jackson, and since he has not yet recovered consciousness he can't, even if he would. The police are waiting to interview him, just as they will be waiting to interview you."

Finn watched Callum swallow hard, saw panic skitter across his eyes. "I didn't do nuffin'."

Stephen sighed. "You didn't do *any*thing. Let's look at what happened, shall we? You and the rest of the Focus Group have been causing serious trouble ever since we came back to school. This afternoon your target was Mr Jackson and after being rude and disruptive you assaulted him in his classroom. A few minutes later he's being taken away in an ambulance. How does it look, Callum? If he wants to press charges, who is anyone going to believe?"

Cal's face constricted. "That's well not fair."

"Yes, you're quick enough to say something's unfair when it applies to you but you're incapable of applying it to anyone else. What's fair about the way you treat people? Why is it fair that other pupils should be frightened and have their learning compromised because of you, or that staff should have their lives made more difficult because you don't know how to behave?"

Cal struggled to mask his tears. "I fucking hate you."

"The truth is unappealing, isn't it?" Stephen was colder still. "And to be honest I'm not too enamoured of you either at the moment. But this situation is not of my making."

Outside Finn gave Callum a moment or two to compose himself before returning him to the fray. For all his cocky mouthing-off, Cal had clearly been shaken by Alan Jackson's fall, by the sight of him out cold at the foot of the stairs, one leg at an angle which had made Finn's stomach twist. Cal, failing at sounding belligerent, said, "What if Jackson says it's me for revenge, you know, for us winding him up? Will I be arrested?"

"I don't know." Just less than half his age and already Cal's experience of the law was far greater than his own. The boy had a string of convictions long enough to hang your weekly washing off, all of them petty crimes of which he had been irrefutably guilty. So Finn didn't understand why, in spite of everything, he instinctively believed him now. "You need to find a reliable witness from the other people there, Cal. Not one of your mates, or someone you can bully into saying anything you want. Someone who actually knows you're telling the truth."

Cal nodded slowly.

"All right?"

"Yeah." He shifted his shell of aggression back into place. Once he stepped back out onto the battleground he was going to need it. His gaze rose to Finn's, crashed away again. "I didn't do it, you know, sir. I didn't push him."

Finn watched him go. He wanted a drink. Wanted to drive at speed through the school gates and not stop until he was on a wide and empty road somewhere far away from Rapton. Alternatively, to sit in a tranquil place with someone he could trust to soothe his soul.

He wanted Leigh.

"How fucking stupid are you?" The disgust in Dean's eyes was as abrasive as his words. "And don't tell me again it wasn't your fault because he was coming after you, wasn't he, which he wouldn't have been doing if you hadn't acted like a twat in the first place. Has he come round yet? Is he talking?"

"I don't know," Cal said furiously.

"Why don't you know? Ask someone. Make it look like you care. A little bit of fake remorse goes a long way. How is it you think you're so fucking clever and you haven't managed to work that out yet?"

"Get off my case!" Cal shouted. "Do you want the cops round here asking questions?"

Dean held up his hands. "Hey, I'm clean. They've nothin' on me. Doesn't sound like I could say the same about you though, Cal. What're you scared of?"

Cal was silent. Dean pretended to carry on reading his

newspaper. After a minute Cal said, "If Jackson stitches me up, I could get what, six months? Fucks up my chances of the Army taking me next year. If he doesn't, Lord'll exclude me anyway and how will that look?"

Dean glanced at him. "What was wrong with keeping yourself out of trouble to begin with?"

"Aw, fuck off, you sound like them."

"I'm not 'them' and I never will be. But I've had a bit of sense knocked into me the hard way. I've said it to you once and I'll say it again: there's nothing cool or clever about being banged up. There's nothing heroic about being a trouble-maker because once you're stuck with that reputation it can ruin your life. You're at the thin end of it now. Don't let it go any further."

Cal was quiet for a minute. "I never touched him, all right? I just wanted to scare him, let him know he couldn't mess with Cal Bywater."

Dean looked at him. "And now you're the one who's scared. What's it gonna take for you to stop acting like a dick-head? Or are you gonna wait till it's too late?"

Cal shrugged. Added, less aggressively, "So help me out here."

"I thought you didn't want me on your case." He sighed. "What do you want me to do?"

"Come up the school. Talk to Lord and Macallister for me."

"Me? Talk to teachers?" He hesitated. "I'm not much good with authority, Cal. I'll say the wrong thing, piss them off. They'll take one look at me and decide you're guilty."

"You won't even try?"

His temper slipped. "I'm not your dad."

"No," Cal agreed bitterly. "I haven't seen my dad for years. Last I heard he was on Moss Side selling crack."

Dean was silent for a moment. If nothing changed, in another couple of years Cal himself'd be on Moss Side selling crack. He knew how this worked. He hadn't exactly escaped the whole fucking depressing cycle himself, had he? He said, "Army's your best chance of any sort of life, isn't it Callum?"

"Well yeah."

"And I promised your mum." He took a breath. "All right. When do we go?"

Finn dangled their basket as he studied row upon row of bottles. "Red or white?"

"Red." She watched him narrowing their options from red to New World to South African, plucking two from the shelf. His neck bare of the noose of his tie, a hip and battered leather jacket over his shirt, dark hair even more dishevelled than usual, he looked too much of a free spirit to be a teacher. She had been packing away her laptop at the end of the day when he had stridden into her classroom telling her he had to leave, right this minute, and it would save his sanity if she would come too.

"How's Alan?" she had asked. His fall and Callum's probable responsibility for it had shaken everyone, including Derek, usually too deeply mired in his own shortcomings to afford concern for anyone else, and Penny, too self-absorbed to care.

"Concussed and can't remember what happened, badly broken leg, otherwise as okay as he can be. But we're not telling Callum Bywater that." He gestured, uncertain whether this was the right line to take or not. "Come on," he pleaded. "Let's get out of here."

She'd smiled. "Where are we going?"

"*Any*where."

"We could go to my house. It's a really healthy distance away. We could crack open a bottle and I could cook us some dinner." Even as she was saying the words she had been appalled. Why was she taking this risk? Was she mad? Maybe his only feelings towards her really were those of a friendly colleague. Maybe the idea of being alone in her house with her was filling him with horror.

Finn, however, looked surprised and pleased. "I'd love to. But we could both cook."

She'd felt herself weaken with relief. "Great." Thought of the scant contents of her fridge. "Though first, we both have to shop."

So here she was, standing beside him in the wine aisle of Tesco, full of nervous excitement at the prospect of their evening together, while a mile or so away Stephen was despairing over his school and Alan lay drifting in and out of consciousness in a hospital bed.

"I'm not going to feel guilty," Finn said without much conviction, dropping their carrier bags into the boot of her car. "If Stephen doesn't take some time out tonight more fool him. Sometimes you just need to step away for a while."

"Then step away. From now on, until tomorrow morning, school is a forbidden subject."

He smiled. "Sounds good to me."

He followed her the half dozen miles north-west, where small towns and suburbs gave way temporarily to open moors and farmland, to a village you might drive through on the way to somewhere else, its pub and church and single street of shops not much of an enticement to hang around. But it was peaceful and the air was clean and the hillside views, as she had promised him, were spectacular. "It's a retreat," he said, gazing round.

"It is." She tried to remember the state in which she had left her house this morning. Last night's washing-up in the sink? Clothes on the floor? Dust lining the shelves? And if all this were the case, would he care? Fingers crossed, she turned the key in the lock.

Let out her breath. A used mug on the floor by the sofa, piles of papers on the coffee table, a vase of dying flowers and crumbs on the kitchen worktop. It could have been a lot worse. "Ignore the mess," she said.

"There is none. You should see my place." He looked around at the bookshelves lining one wall, the racks of CDs, a tapestry throw over the sofa by the fire. In the little kitchen beyond a small rectangular pine table and two chairs sat beneath a blue and yellow seascape. "It's really nice."

"It was already done up when I bought it."

"It's not that, it's the atmosphere, it's so warm and calm. You just want to sink right into it."

She laughed, self-mocking. "That'll be me, then."

"That is you." He smiled and her skin prickled. He peered though the window. "Sun over the yard-arm yet?"

He opened one of the bottles, poured them both some wine. Leigh unpacked their shopping, tumbled new potatoes into a pan and switched on the heat, stretched to reach olive oil from a shelf, acutely aware of him watching her. "What would you have done," he asked her, taking a mouthful of wine, "if you hadn't gone into teaching?"

She opened her mouth to object.

"Doesn't count. That's not talking about school, it's talking about us."

She liked the 'us'. "I don't know. I always hoped something more glamorous and exciting would occur to me, but it didn't, and the money and the security of teaching were a big attraction." She picked up her glass of wine, sipped from it, put it down again. "It's not as if I ever had a burning vocation to do anything else. And as it turns out, I enjoy it, most of the time, and I think I'm quite good at it, most of the time. How about you?"

He twirled the CD rack which stood on the worktop, glancing through the albums while he talked. "I had ideas of becoming a travel writer. After uni I back-packed with a couple of friends while we were putting off deciding what to do with our lives. We rode and flew and hiked across Southern Africa, Australia, North and South America, most of Europe. I don't think I was in the same place for more than a week in nearly two years. I kept a journal, fancied myself as a kind of Bill Bryson, writing these supposedly witty, opinionated accounts of every place we went. I wanted to create something personal and a bit wayward, an antidote to all those bland, factual travel guides that tell you everything and nothing. Anyway," he shrugged, "stuff happened. I never finished the book. I did get a job working with teenagers at a summer school, realised I liked it a lot, liked *them* a lot … " He stopped. "I have never met," he said, waving an Aerosmith album at her, "anyone else with such a comprehensive and catholic collection of music. It almost beats mine."

"Put some on, if you like." She watched, imagining him in

shorts and hiking boots, sweaty and suntanned at Ayers Rock, the Grand Canyon, the Acropolis, as he selected Jack Johnson's *In Between Dreams* and slid it into the slot. "It's all the music I've ever listened to," she admitted. "I've never thrown anything away. How could you? Music represents your life. I hoard it like other people hoard old photographs."

"I can tell." He grinned, teasing her, stopped at another album. "The Bangles," he said reverently. "I had such a huge crush on Susannah Hoffs when I was about thirteen. She always looked like the girl who might." He smiled. Paused. "I swear she kick-started my attraction to women who were trouble."

Leigh, distracting herself with unwrapping their steaks, emptying salad onto the chopping board, looked back at him. "You're attracted to women who're trouble?"

"I was. I grew out of it eventually. Not until I'd married one of them. Can I do that?"

"Sure. Steak or salad?"

"Both. I'll multi-task." He smiled, handed her back her wine glass and poured a drop of oil into the pan. "I met Carla when I was twenty-three, half-way through that tour of Australia I was telling you about. We had this ... interlude, which looking back, four nights in a Brisbane hotel, it's nothing. But at the time it was wild and mind-blowing and I'd never met anyone like her." He shook his head, despairing of his own naivety. "Anyway. We stayed in touch. Back home that Christmas we met up again, picked up from where we'd left off. I was dazzled by her. I thought she was exotic and exciting and it turned out what she really was, was barking mad. My friends warned me off. My family was horrified. But we married, stayed married four years, during which time she became madder and everything got scarier until I couldn't take it any more. It wasn't the most amicable of separations." He looked wry. "She torched my car. Poured urine through my letter-box. I wouldn't have minded so much if I'd deserved it, but she was the one who'd been sleeping around."

"My God," Leigh said. "Weren't you ... traumatised?"

"Yep. Scarred for life. I hide it well. Do you want any

dressing with this?"

"It's in the fridge."

He opened the door, surveyed the refrigerator's contents, found the vinaigrette. "Seriously? She scared the hell out of me. She's why I'm standing here talking to you now, in a way. We were living down in Bristol. After we split up and things got really nasty I came home to my parents to lick my wounds and never went back. Susannah Hoffs has a lot to answer for."

"Martin used to like Kylie Minogue. The Jason Donovan years."

"Bloody hell." He took a mouthful of his wine. "How long were you with him?"

"Too long. We met at uni, moved down to London together, he went into banking, I did my PGCE, we split up. Made a killing on our flat though so not entirely an everyday tragedy."

He smiled. "I used to wonder, is it so easy to fuck up and make the worst mistake about the person you think you want to spend the rest of your life with, or is it just me?"

She shook her head. "If it's you, it's me as well. I know as many people who're single and searching as those who're happy and settled. You can't really arrange to meet the right person, can you? It's the luck of the draw."

"Oh good, so nothing to do with lousy judgement or thinking with my dick, then?"

She laughed. "Well there is that."

He grinned, holding her gaze. Their steaks sizzled in the pan and Jack Johnson was singing about Good People. "See," he said, "it's the perfect evening. Great food, good music and I've unloaded all my baggage onto you and you'll never want to do this again." He caught his breath, looked uncertain.

"Won't I?" She said it lightly and smiled, though her heart was racing. It never changes, she thought. Someone you like likes you back and you're sixteen all over again.

"So … my place next time?"

"Go on then. It'd be only fair."

"Can I have a word?"

Stephen looked up. The man marching belligerently across

the empty car park towards him was overweight and shaven-headed, wearing work boots and jeans and a thick wool shirt. He was also, Stephen remembered with a sinking heart, Liam Clough's father.

"Certainly." He glanced towards the windows of the buildings around him, hoping that from one of them someone was watching.

Roy Clough advanced until he was within a flying fist's distance of Stephen's face. "I want to know why you've not excluded Callum Bywater."

Stephen took a breath. "Well ... "

"Because he's assaulted Mr Jackson, I've heard. Thrown him down the stairs. All our Liam did was break his bloody windscreen."

"Yes, but we have Liam on camera breaking Mr Jackson's windscreen. The extent of Callum's involvement in what happened yesterday is yet to be clarified – "

"Don't give me that. He's the worst of the lot, Cal Bywater. Any trouble, he's at the bottom of it. Always has been."

"I don't doubt it. And when Mr Jackson has made his statement to the police, if it incriminates Callum, I will be dealing with him. If he's guilty, he'll pay the price. Just as Liam did."

Liam's father looked, just slightly, appeased. "It's in the hands of the police, then?"

"Of course it is. It's a possible assault, as you said, and I won't have anyone, neither pupils nor staff, assaulted in my school without redress." He waited, took half a step away, signalling a conclusion to their exchange.

"Only I'm not happy Liam being excluded when Callum Bywater gets away scot-free."

"I understand. That isn't going to happen."

"I just want what's fair, you know?"

"Oh I do," Stephen promised him. "Justice is uppermost in my mind, Mr Clough, I can assure you of that."

In the safety of his office he closed his eyes. Heard the familiar rattle of cup on saucer as Barbara – who didn't believe in mugs – brought him his tea. "Are you all right?" she asked.

"I've just been accosted in the car park by Liam Clough's father."

"Oh, you don't want to get on the wrong side of them. Local mafia, the Cloughs. And that other boy you excluded with the knife, Josh Ferris. They're related, you know, the Cloughs and the Ferrises."

"They would be. So what should I expect then? A horse's head on my desk?"

She didn't look as though she thought this remotely amusing. "I wouldn't be hanging round on my own after school, especially now it's getting dark earlier. And I'd watch my rear-view mirror too."

He looked at her in disbelief. "It's the twenty-first century, Barbara."

"It's Rapton, Mr Lord."

After her first lesson reading Harry Potter with Year 7, the supply teacher drafted in to cover Alan's classes trilled to Joss and anyone else who would listen that the children were delightful and diligent and she couldn't understand why the school had such a terrible reputation. By break, following the hard-eyed girls and loud-mouthed boys in Year 9, she was looking pale and her hand trembled holding her mug of tea. "The invention of the mobile phone," she shuddered, "was a terrible thing."

"Oh I don't know," Joss said reasonably. "I have teenage children and I wouldn't want them to be without theirs. But I agree they shouldn't be used in school."

"Those boys were *spitting paper*."

"Yes, they do that. If they think they can get away with it. Go through the behaviour code," Joss advised her. "Don't take any nonsense."

After she'd returned fearfully to her classroom, Joss turned to Penny. "She's got what's left of the Focus Group next. Do you think I should go in with her?"

Penny tossed her Miss Piggy mane. "Oh for heaven's sake. She's a teacher, isn't she? She'll be getting paid three times what you are."

"True, but what happened to Alan hasn't subdued anyone. If anything it's whipped the kids into even more of a frenzy." *Or hadn't you noticed?*

"Which as a qualified teacher she should be able to deal with." Penny would not be swayed into any misguided notion of sympathy. "They're children, Jocelyn, that's all."

Joss went to find Finn, who was standing in the doorway of Leigh's classroom, looking at her in that amorously enchanted way Joss was surprised the whole department hadn't noticed yet. Ignoring that – for now – she explained.

"Let me know," he said. "I'll pop in at the beginning, but keep an eye on her and let me know."

Joss turned off her radio and wedged the door of her office open. Watched Finn shepherd the boys into Alan's classroom, exit again a few minutes later to return to his own class. Listening, waiting, she filed a set of coursework, unpacked a delivery of stationery. Became entirely immersed in compiling a new set of class lists with all relevant data and forgot, completely, about the supply teacher and the Focus Group.

Until, twenty minutes into the lesson, the supply teacher came scurrying down the corridor with her coat over one arm and her bag on the other.

Joss flew to the doorway. "Wait. What's happened? Do you need me to ring Senior Management?"

"I have never … " The poor woman was in tears - " … in all my years of teaching, never encountered such rude, disgusting behaviour … "

"What have they done?" Joss looked down the corridor towards the classroom. All she could hear was a bark of laughter, the scrape of chair legs.

"I'm not staying. You can do what you like with them." She headed towards the fire doors at the top of the stairs, Joss at her heels.

"Wait, let me … what did they do?"

She stared for a moment at the supply teacher's departing back, then whisked down the corridor to Alan's room. Two of the boys stood on tables beneath the open windows, their school trousers around their ankles, calling to passers-by below and waving their penises in the morning breeze.

Joss, unnoticed, backed silently away towards Finn's room.

The arrival of Tracey Ferris in Reception would have caused consternation and then panic had any of the Reception staff been present to witness it. As it was, when Josh's mother turned up the desk was unmanned, the foyer empty even of children exhausted from their beck-and-call reception duties. Having the apparent freedom of the school, she lumbered along the path she had trodden so often during Josh's school career, from the front door to Stephen Lord's office.

Stephen, sitting at his desk drafting a letter, subliminally aware of unfamiliar footsteps in the corridor outside his room, might have been taken by surprise had Tracey Ferris' body odour not reached him first. He looked up, his heart dipping for the second time that day, to find her heaving herself across the threshold of his office and as he rose in pretended greeting to defend his territory, it crossed his mind to open a window on the way.

"Mrs Ferris. How can I help?" And how the hell had she got this far without anyone stopping her?

"It's not right what you did to our Josh."

"This would be your Josh who held an eleven year old girl at knife-point, would it?"

"Not if you're letting Callum Bywater get off with GBH on a teacher."

Stephen felt his limbs grow weary. He restrained himself from sighing. "Whatever Callum Bywater is or isn't responsible for, and no one is talking about GBH, it has nothing whatsoever to do with Josh." Or you, for that matter. He could see she was trying to manoeuvre herself into a seat and, taking a step forward to prevent her from doing so, almost gagged. Didn't she know? Had no one told her? Stephen guessed she weighed twice as much as he did but even so, was it really impossible to wash that amount of flesh on a regular basis? He reiterated: "Josh's exclusion has no bearing on anything else that has happened in school this term. I can't discuss the disciplining of another pupil with you, any more than I would discuss your son's with anyone else."

"Yeah, but, it's not fair though, is it?"

"I don't imagine the child he assaulted and frightened out of her wits thought it was fair either." *And we have had this conversation.*

"He were only messing."

Stephen took a breath. "Ms Ferris, there are misdemeanours which in the outside world constitute 'only messing' and those which don't. I don't think it would be fair of me to mislead your son as to which is which. Had he threatened a child in the street with a knife, he would have been arrested and charged with assault with a dangerous weapon. If I let that go because it happened on school premises, it would be tantamount to condoning a crime. Do you understand?"

"Don't talk to me like I'm one of the kids!" A disturbing aggression flared in her eyes, reinforcing Stephen's conviction that most deranged pupils learned their psychosis at their mothers' knees. "I'm sick of coming in here and you lecturing me like you think you're better than me! Just because we don't talk like you don't mean we 'aven't got rights!"

"No, of course not, I wouldn't for a minute ... " He had to back rapidly away as she bore down on him, his calves hitting the seat of one of his visitors' chairs.

"I'm gonna be tellin' Josh's dad what you've accused him of when Callum Bywater's smacked a teacher. You'll not be all smarmy once he's got you in here. He won't listen to reason, like me."

Over her shoulder in the open doorway he saw, to his enormous relief, Joss Monroe. "Is it urgent, Joss?" he asked hopefully, his voice a note higher than usual.

"It is actually. You're needed up in English. Could I get ... your visitor a cup of tea?" Her eyes said everything to Stephen. Tracey Ferris saw only a polite mask.

"I'm not hangin' about. I've said what I come to say. You just remember," she spat in Stephen's direction, "when you deal with Callum Bywater. Our Josh has his rights."

She lumbered away, the corridor seeming to rock under her

tread. Joss met Stephen's eyes. "Dear God," he murmured. "Now. What is it?"

Joss smiled ruefully. "You're going to love this."

Cal and Dean sat in Dean's car, staring through the windscreen at the sports hall, at a line of Year 10s in their PE kit jogging out towards the Astroturf. For a long moment neither of them had spoken.

"I can't believe," Cal muttered finally, "you're such a fucking wuss."

"Say that again and you'll get my fist where it hurts. And don't swear. In there, I mean. It won't do you any good. Teachers don't tend to be won over by fifteen year old kids swearing at them."

"I'm nearly sixteen."

"Whatever."

Another silence.

Cal said, "We are going in, then?"

"I said I would, didn't I?" But his guts were twisted and he couldn't get rid of the sour taste in his mouth. He'd never been one of those boys jogging cheerfully out to the football pitch. Never carried a bag, owned a pencil case, worn all the items of uniform at the same time. He'd spent most of his five years at Rapton bunking off, in detention, internally excluded, suspended. Sometimes he'd fallen asleep at the back of classrooms because it was quieter and warmer than where he'd spent the night. Sometimes he'd got on all right with one of his teachers but something had always happened to wreck it. He should have looked forward to leaving but he'd known there was nowhere to go. And sitting here now in the car park which had once been the yard, facing a hostile reception from whoever this Stephen Lord might be and a hostile silence from the boy sitting beside him, he felt sick and uneasy and – "Oh for fuck's sake," he muttered. "Let's get it over with."

Stephen sent the offending members of the Focus Group home, telephoned their parents, rearranged staff to cover the rest of Alan's lessons for the day and called Finn into his office. "Will you work with me on this?"

"Of course." Finn had the grace not to look surprised. Stephen knew well enough that his staff considered him reluctant to listen to them or rate their opinions and lacking in any talent whatsoever for engendering any sense of team spirit. He knew from past disbutes that Finn Macallister was among them. He said, with suitable humility,

"Where do you suggest we start?"

Finn cleared his throat. "Well – a Year 11 assembly telling them that due to recent events we now have a zero tolerance approach to discipline. Explain that that will mean swifter movement through the behaviour code, mobile phones confiscated on sight and only returned to parents, point blank refusals resulting in a week's isolation. And so on. Stiffer sentences, basically. And then an assembly for the rest of the school telling them the same thing. For starters."

Stephen nodded. His telephone rang. "There's a … " Barbara discreetly lowered her voice " … Dean Bywater to see you."

"Who's Dean Bywater?" He looked the question at Finn.

Finn sat up a bit straighter. "He's Callum's uncle. I remember him."

Stephen wanted to crawl underneath his desk and stay there for the foreseeable future. "Is he alone?" he asked Barbara.

"He has Callum with him."

"Wonderful. All right. Send them down." He hung up, looked at Finn. "What's he like, Dean Bywater?"

"Just done seven years for armed robbery."

Stephen closed his eyes. Opened them again.

"I'll stay, shall I?" Finn offered.

Stephen nodded.

"Mr Bywater. I'm Stephen Lord." The headmaster offered his hand which Dean, immediately wrong-footed, shook. "This is Finlay Macallister, head of Year 11. Please, take a seat. You too, Callum."

Callum looked uncertain, like he'd never been invited to sit down in Lord's office before.

"Now." Stephen Lord, clearly determined not to be intimidated by anyone, smiled. "I'm glad you've both come in. We've had further developments. Mr Jackson regained consciousness last night. He has a complicated fracture of his right leg and won't be back in school for some time. But he has no memory yet of what actually happened, which leaves us in a slightly difficult position regarding you, Callum."

Dean cleared his throat. Neither of these men was any taller or broader than he was himself. They seemed civilised, reasonable. He knew, looking like he did, being who he was, that his presence in the room could be a palpable force. And it might have been, had he not been seated on a low-slung foam chair feeling like hell. He said, "What's difficult? If he doesn't remember what happened, you've got to assume Cal's innocent."

"We don't have," Stephen Lord said mildly, "to assume anything. This isn't a one-off, Mr Bywater. Callum has been causing us some considerable problems for … " He obviously wanted to say 'years' " … weeks now."

"Yeah. He knows he's been f… stupid. We're not saying he's a saint. We're saying he didn't do this." Dean's voice was tight, emphatic. "You can't exclude him for something you don't know he's done."

"There is also the fact that Callum and several other boys assaulted Mr Jackson before the incident on the stairs."

"Yeah, that was … really stupid. And he's sorry about that. Aren't you Callum?"

Callum grunted.

Dean glared at him.

"Yeah," Cal mumbled. "Sorry. Stupid."

Dean took a breath. "Look. I'm living with Cal and his mum at the moment. I've promised her I'll look out for him. I know he's been trouble. What he really wants is to get out of school and join the army. If I can't persuade him that doing that means keeping on the straight and narrow for the next year, he's all yours. But for now, let him stay in school. He gives you any grief, he'll have me to answer to."

Mr Lord said, "Callum … ?"

Cal grunted.

Dean said, "Really not making this any easier for yourself, Cal."

"Yeah." Cal tried again. "Yeah, I didn't push Mr Jackson down the stairs. I've told you that. Yeah, I'll behave. All right?"

Dean held the glare for a moment, looked back at Lord and Macallister. "He's a bit behind when it comes to manners but -"

The world tilted.

For a moment he didn't understand why, what it was he'd seen. He just stopped, as abruptly as though someone had cut off his power supply, and stared.

And sixteen years fell away.

Fuck. Nausea in his throat. His hands were shaking.

Sweating, he jerked unsteadily to his feet. "Right, well if we've got that sorted. Thanks, for … " He couldn't go on.

"Thank you for coming in," Stephen Lord replied swiftly, following him to the door. "What we'll do is put Callum on Head of Year Report, so Mr Macallister's aware of what he's getting up to, and take it from there. The situation regarding Mr Jackson is on hold for now."

Dean nodded. "Come on Cal. Don't want to take up any more of these gentlemen's time."

Cal, looking bemused, followed him out of the door, through reception, out into the yard. Drew level with him as they reached the car. "What the fuck was that?"

"Shut up." Dean's voice was rough. "I got you what you wanted, didn't I?"

"So why're we running? You're not scared of them in there? Didn't have you down as a fucking coward, Dean."

Dean hit him, his fist connecting with Cal's nose with enough force to send him stumbling back across the tarmac. Cal yelped, his chest heaving, stared at Dean in shock and pain. "You had it coming," Dean yanked open the car door, got in, started the engine. His tyres squealed as he sped out of the gates onto the road, leaving Cal, bleeding and tearful, behind him.

Todd, on an errand from his Science lesson, stopped off at the boys' toilets en route. If he waited till lunchtime they'd be packed and stink of smoke, and his Science teacher wasn't going to notice another minute or two. But as he crossed the threshold he heard a sound, a soft gasping, which sounded like somone either crying or jerking off. He didn't want to witness either but he did need to pee. Shutting the door loudly behind him to announce his arrival, he rounded the corner and saw to his surprise Cal, ineffectively wiping blood from below his nose and – even more shockingly – tears from his eyes.

"You all right?" Todd ventured.

"Do I look all right?"

Todd hung around uncertainly. "What happened?"

"Dean happened."

"*Dean*?"

"Yep." Cal dabbed again at his nose. "Why are there no fucking mirrors in this place?"

Because people like you would smash them up. "Why did he hit you?"

"'Cos I called him a coward."

"Smart move."

Cal glanced at him. "Yeah all right. I dunno. He's been, like, wired all day. Like coming into school freaked him out or summat."

Todd considered. There were a lot of questions he'd like to ask, but you had to be careful what you said to Cal Bywater, even if you had eaten egg and sausage at his house. He said, "You want to get that looked at, he could've broken it."

"It's not broken. How do you know if it's broken?"

"It looks a bit wonky, I suppose. And hurts a lot."

Cal winced. "Jackson doesn't remember what happened, you know. Everyone thinks I pushed him, but I never. Lord won't believe me. I fuckin' hate him, he's gonna wreck everything for me. Macallister," he added with disgust, "says I've got to find a witness."

"Well, I was there."

Their eyes met in realisation.

"You saw what happened?" Cal stared, his face bright with unexpected hope.

"Yeah," Todd said. "Yeah. I did. I'll go and tell them, shall I?"

He paused outside Mr Lord's door. Knocked. Entered. "Sorry." Mr Lord was sitting at his desk, Mr Macallister standing at the window. "Sorry. It's just, there's something I need to tell you."

Mr Lord said, "Is this anything to do with Callum Bywater?"

"Yes."

They looked at each other. Mr Macallister gestured towards a chair. "Come in, Todd."

He sat. Saw them waiting, expectant. "He didn't push Mr Jackson down the stairs. I saw what happened."

Mr Lord sighed. "Go on then. From the top."

"I'd just come out of the classroom after the lesson. The corridor was really loud and busy, you know what it's like, everyone making for the stairs, sometimes I think it must be a bit scary for the little kids, they just get swept up and carried along. Anyway, I could hear you," he looked at Mr Macallister, "telling everyone to move along and then Cal came out of Mr Jackson's room, saying something snidey, like he does. Then he waited and said something else, something about Mr Jackson not being able to catch him. Mr Jackson was in the doorway by then, and he came really quick out into the corridor and he tried to make a grab at Cal. I think he might have caught hold of his bag. Cal pulled away and went through the fire doors and Mr Jackson went after him. Cal stopped at the top of the stairs and Mr Jackson – well, no disrespect, but he couldn't stop as quick as Cal, he'd built up a bit of momentum by then and it was like he had to keep going. He kind of ricocheted off Cal, and lost his balance. He just fell. It was a bit frightening, to be honest. Nobody pushed him, or tripped him or anything. It was an accident. And I'm not saying this because I'm Cal's best mate, which I'm not. Or because he's threatened me, which he hasn't. It's just the truth, that's all. It was an accident." He stopped talking. For a second no one else started. Then Mr Lord said,

"Thank you, Todd."

"Does it help?"

Mr Macallister smiled. "Depends whose side you're on."

Dean, knowing he wasn't going to have patience with a series of five-bar gates, abandoned his car on the road and hiked up the tarmac drive thinking that seventeen years ago it hadn't seemed this steep. It wasn't much after four o'clock but already dark with threatening rain, and up here with no streetlamps to guide you, the cottage seemed a lonely place. He cupped his hands to the windows and peered in at pale walls and a cheap charcoal grey sofa at the front, at a glossily empty kitchen in the extension round the back. It'd be a piece of piss to break in, hole up for a bit. Get his head together after the shock this afternoon which still had him reeling. But breaking into the house would be like breaking into the past, and once in there'd be no getting out.

He sank to the ground, crouched beside the kitchen door looking at a fenced-off square of land with a bit of grass the moor was reclaiming as its own, and a few shrubs someone had planted then never much bothered with. He'd hit Cal. Not that the boy didn't ask to be hit on a daily basis, but he still felt bad about it. You didn't hit kids, no matter how tough they thought they were. You especially didn't hit your own nephew when you were supposed to be building bridges.

He was trying to avoid it, the elephant in his brain. And it wasn't working, because he was squatting here in the lowering dusk with his head pounding and his eyes smarting and everything he'd spent the last few weeks trying not to think about was shouting inside him. No pretending any more. No talking airily to himself about the past like it was some sort of philosophical concept that had nothing to do with him. Because it was his past, their past, and he was mired in it like treacle. Quicksand. He didn't know what he was mired in it like, but he did know there was no escape. And he did know there was no happy ending.

It'd taken him half an hour to stop shaking, after he'd left the school, after he'd left Cal bleeding in the car park. Another half an hour to talk himself out of walking back in there and doing the kind of damage that'd end up in them throwing away the key. All these years the thought of revenge had kept him going like it was his life source or something and here he was, thinking twice. Thinking what it really meant to connect your fist with another man's face, to have his blood on your hands. But he couldn't trust himself. Not after that gut reaction this afternoon. Couldn't live here feeling like this every day, nerves jangling, fists bunching, knife in his right-hand pocket. Supposed to be a new start, for fuck's sake.

Slowly he pushed to his feet, tramped back down to the car, drove to the offices where his sister worked. To tell her he was leaving.

Todd rang the front doorbell of the Bywaters' house, heard Cal yell, "S'open!" and edged inside. Cal was sitting in front of the television with a six pack, watching some posh woman showing a badly dressed middle-aged couple round an over-decorated house. Todd, momentarily distracted by the posh woman's tits, also gazed at the screen. Cal nudged him with his foot. "Well?"

"Well … yeah. It was okay. I told them and they listened and Mr Macallister said I'd done the right thing coming to talk to them."

"Macallister's full of shit."

"He's all right. He believed me. I think he believed you."

Cal was unconvinced. "What about Lord?"

"Who knows. Hard to tell what's going on behind that smile."

"So, what? Am I back in tomorrow?"

"I don't know. You could just turn up. Maybe he'll ring you."

They both looked at the phone. It sat, unforthcoming, on the sideboard. Cal said, embarrassed, "Listen. Thanks, you know."

"S'all right."

"Nobody ever stuck up for me before."

Todd couldn't think of an answer he wanted to give to that one. "Dean not back, then?"

"Nah." Cal passed him a can. "He's well weird, you know. I don't know if it's being banged up all that time or if he was always weird."

Todd took a swig. "Weird how?"

"Like jumpy. Moody. Like, a bit mental."

"Jesus."

"He's got this tattoo. Right at the top of his arm. It's little wings, like peace or that. And a D. Why'd you have your own initial tattooed on your arm?"

Todd shrugged. "What do you actually know about him?"

" 'Actually'," Cal mocked, "nowt. He's me mum's little brother, he went to Rapton, did loads of burglaries and stuff, ended up inside. End of. Oh and – found this out the other day – me mum says she fell out with him because he went missing when she were pregnant with me, and she needed him around."

"Why did he go missing?"

"Fuck knows. And he says he's lookin' for someone."

"Who?" Todd said stupidly.

"Dunno. *He* doesn't know. Someone from before he got banged up, I s'pose. All he's got is where he used to live, on the Old Road." Cal, emboldened by alcohol, pushed to his feet. "His room's open, there's all his stuff out on the side. Let's have a look."

Todd frowned. "What if he comes back?"

"We'll hear the car. Come on. Two minutes."

The room smelled stale, the window sill and the furniture powdered with dust and dirt. Todd thought that if you cleaned it up, put in a new window, filled the cracks in the plaster, it wouldn't be half bad, then despaired because that was the sort of thinking ten years with Vince taught you. Dean's possessions, such as they were, lay heaped on the top of a broken chest of drawers, as though thrown there after unpacking. Or waiting to be packed. How old was Dean? Thirty-five, at a push? What must it be like, Todd wondered, to get to that age and for this to be your whole world? He thought of Dean, frying egg and bacon in the kitchen downstairs, trying to make conversation with him. It was sort of sad.

Cal sat on the edge of the bed, picking stuff up and putting it down again, but carefully, for even he was aware of the consequences should Dean discover their snooping. Todd watched, straining to listen for the sound of a car outside, interested against his better judgement in these fragments of a man's life. A pile of coins, an old comb, a pack of cards. Photographs – Cal's mother holding a baby Cal, a photo booth shot from around the same time of a teenage girl with dark curly hair, smiling prettily, nervousness around her eyes. "Who's this?" he asked. Cal shrugged. He turned the photo over, but there was nothing written on the reverse. There were a few rock or heavy metal CDs, bands with names like *Slayer* and *Megadeth* and *Anthrax*. A three-quarters full bottle of vodka. A thin silver chain. "It's not much," Todd said, "to show for a life."

Cal looked at him, misunderstanding. "It's nothin', is it? It tells you nothin'."

Stephen entered the kitchen still wearing his coat and shoes which he usually discarded in the hall, still carrying his briefcase. In the next room his children lay sprawled on the floor in front of *The Simpsons*. Thank God, he thought, there were some traditional features of family life on which he could still rely. Claudia looked up from the bottle of olive oil she was opening. "Hi ... *Stephen*. What's happened?"

"You would not believe," he said wearily, "the day I have had."

She went to him, wiping her hands on a tea-towel, hugged him hard. "Come here." She took his briefcase out of his hand, lifted his coat from him. "Sit down." She poured him an inch of scotch. "Spill."

He did so. Liam's combative father. Josh's mountainous mother. The penis-waving boys. The fleeing supply teacher. The armed robber who'd talked more sense than anyone else and then fled. His A* student becoming witness for the defence.

She listened with sympathy. "What about Finn Macallister?"

"He was," Stephen conceded, "calm, supportive and a pillar of strength."

"There you are then. If you're going to snatch triumph from the jaws of disaster, that's where it'll lie. Better staff relationships. People listen to Finn."

He nodded. People did listen to Finn. For all the run-ins they'd had in the past, he listened to Finn. But. "I don't know if I can go through another day like that in the name of better staff relationships."

"Of course you can. It's what they pay you for. You'll come through in a blaze of glory, get a decent Ofsted and move on to a nice middle-class school full of happy, well-balanced children and fulfilled, supportive staff."

"I'm going to die and go to heaven?"

She laughed. "You'd still be a teacher in heaven? I know. You've had a really crap day. Tomorrow will be less crap."

He looked at her. "How are you so annoyingly, virtuously positive?"

"Because what's the alternative? Seriously." She kissed him, stroked back his hair. "What would make you feel better?"

Their children padded in, leaving the theme music and closing titles of *The Simpsons* playing to an empty room. Lucie hopped up onto a barstool beside him. Henry fetched his reading book. "This one's ace, dad. It's all about traction engines."

Stephen and Claudia exchanged a mystified glance. "Half-term," he told her. "I know we've left it really late, probably too late, but half-term, a villa in Tuscany. Just the four of us. Anywhere, actually, just the four of us. Marooned, preferably."

She smiled. "Expedia here I come."

Cal, lying awake in the dark, heard the creak of the stairs, the click of Dean's bedroom door. After a moment he got up, padded out onto the landing, pushing Dean's door open further with one finger. In the orange glow from the streetlight through the uncurtained window, he could make out a holdall on the bed, Dean sweeping the pile of junk he and Todd had sifted through earlier into it.

Cal felt his throat tighten. "Where you goin'?"

Dean didn't glance at him; clearly his presence was no surprise. "Scotland. That job I told you about."

"End of October, you said."

"Yeah well, he wants me up there now."

Cal said nothing. He didn't believe him, and he didn't want to give Dean the satisfaction of knowing he was bothered, but somehow he couldn't help himself. "So what were you goin' to do, just sneak out in the middle of the night?"

"Yep."

"Does me mum know?"

"Where d'you think I've been?"

"What did she say?"

"Well she weren't happy." He paused. "I can't stick around, Cal."

"Not because of some crappy job though."

Dean picked up his bag from the bed. "You gonna behave yourself while I'm gone?"

"What's it to you?"

"It's nothing to me, is it? It's your life you'll be fucking up if you don't." He swung past Cal, out onto the landing, was halfway down the stairs when Cal said,

"I'll come with you."

Dean halted. Looked up at him in the borrowed light from outside. Cal knew he could see the swelling round his nose, the dried blood still crusting one nostril. "I shouldn't have hit you."

"I've been hit harder than that."

"Doesn't surprise me." He went down the rest of the stairs, Cal at his heels.

"Let me come with you."

"You're not coming with me, Cal. You've got stuff here." They were out the front door, on the pavement.

"You've got stuff here too. That's why you're goin'. Nowt to do with some stupid job. You've got stuff here you can't face up to and you're running' away.

Dean said nothing.

He blundered on. "What's the matter with you, anyway? You tell me I can't be trusted? You're supposed to be lookin' out for me. You promised them at school. You promised me mum."

"I know. I'm sorry."

Cal didn't know what made him feel worse, Dean abandoning him or regretting it. "What's happened, Dean? Why have you gone like this? Is it summat to do with that bloke you're after?"

Dean paused with his hand on the door of his car. "Yeah. That's about the size of it."

"You're leavin' cos of him? Some stupid bastard whose name you don't even know? You're puttin' him first?" Cal's face was creased, his voice cracking with emotion he didn't want to feel. "You laid into me because of him?"

Dean took a breath. "I hit you because you were right. I am a coward. Something happened, years ago, and I did nothing. Being here, it's like being up to my neck in it all over again and if I hang around, I am gonna do something about it and there'll be trouble like you wouldn't believe. And I don't want trouble, Cal. I want a fresh start."

Cal was fascinated. This sounded like something he wanted to hear. "Why would there be trouble? What did you do?"

Dean hesitated. "It's not what I did. It's what I know."

Finn sat at his desk in his office writing notes for the speech he was to make at his Year 11 assembly. He couldn't decide whether to go for more-in-sorrow-than-in-anger or just plain anger. Truth was, he was too distracted to decide much at the moment. In a few days' time it would be half-term and while in normal circumstances a week's holiday would be cause for celebration, it also meant a week without seeing Leigh. Unless he did something about it. Unless he was misreading signals and she couldn't imagine anything worse than spending all or part of her precious half-term with him. One of the long-term consequences of having been married to a madwoman was that you lost all faith in your ability to read people.

"Sir." Callum Bywater, three feet into the room and looking

edgy.

"All right, Cal?" Finn put down his pen and swivelled to face him.

"Yeah. Just thought I'd come and see you."

"Fine." He wasn't going to ask him why he wasn't in Form Tutorial. He really didn't want to know. He did want to know what had happened to Callum's nose, but he was choosing his moment with that one. "Have a seat." But evidently Cal had too much going on in his head to be able to sit down. He ambled towards the window, stood looking out at the school buildings, the playing fields which lay between them and the road. "Anything I can do for you?" Finn asked.

"No, it's just like ... " He didn't know what it was like.

"A social call?"

"That's the one."

Bloody hell, Finn thought. Social calls from Callum Bywater. He didn't know whether he shouldn't feel more uneasy. "How's your uncle looking after you?" he asked casually.

Cal's jaw clenched. "He's gone. Fucked off last night."

"For good?"

Cal shrugged. Finn, watching him, was going to ask how he felt about that, realised he didn't need to. Cal, all surface indifference, was tense as hell. There was more than a fighting chance of that tension erupting at some point today. He sighed inwardly. "Cal, you know, just try keeping your head down."

"Sir." Another one. Todd Kershaw, this time. "Miss Somers says have you got any Temporary Diaries?"

"Yeah, hang on while I find them." Finn began rooting through his overflowing in-trays. Todd waited obediently.

Cal smirked. "She's well fit, Miss Somers. You fancy her, don't you, sir?"

Bugger, Finn thought. Why do they only notice the things you don't want them to notice? He laughed, as though fancying Leigh were an amusing conceit. "Nope, can't find any, Todd."

"They're in your filing cabinet, sir. That's where you got them from last time."

"Oh right. Thanks."

"Where's this, sir?" Cal was examining the photographs Finn had pinned to a cork-board on his wall to remind himself that he'd once had a different life.

"I went travelling when I finished university. All over the world. That's Los Angeles, Venice Beach. That's the Okavango swamps in Botswana. That one just below is Hong Kong."

Cal whistled. "I wanna do that. Go to all them places."

"Then go. Make it happen. The world is your oyster."

"Bet you had loads of money though."

"I didn't, as a matter of fact. I had to work myself into the ground to pay for it."

Cal looked at him. "You live in them mill apartments, don't you?"

"I do." The kids saw him driving in and out, shopping in town. There was no hiding. He found the Temporary Diaries and handed them to Todd. "There you go."

"Thanks."

"Right, I just need to remind Miss Somers about assembly," Finn improvised. "I'll take these to her." Todd passed them back, dead-pan. The boys watched him go.

"What did I tell you?" Cal said. "Shagging." He paused. "Dean's gone."

Todd's eyebrows went up. "Where?"

"Dunno. Scotland or something."

Mr Macallister was probably about the same age as Dean Bywater, Todd thought. Mr Macallister with his university degree and his flash apartment, his years of travelling the world, his half-decent job. He wondered was Cal remembering Dean's meagre possessions and drawing the same comparison. "Was it because of us? Did he find out we went through his stuff?"

"No. It weren't nowt to do with us. It was 'cos of something what happened years ago. Pisses me off, I tell you. He comes back, acts like he's fuckin' *cares* and then … " He stopped. Todd saw that his face had reddened, that his throat was working. Cal swallowed hard. "I've been thinkin' about what we said, in the park. About risk. Chances of getting caught against what you stand to gain."

Todd remembered. "And you said you'd have to be sure of the odds."

"Oh, I'm sure all right."

Was this typical Cal Bywater bravado, Todd wondered, or was there something going on here? He didn't like Cal's jitteriness, the gleam of trouble in his eyes. "What's going on?"

Cal looked at him, his expression an uneasy mix of bitter anger and triumph. "Pay-back time."

Mr Macallister was back. "Have to turf you out I'm afraid," he said. "Meeting with the Head." He looked at Cal. "If you want to talk to me, if you need anything, any time, come and find me."

"Sure," Cal said.

"The pair of you."

"Yeah all right sir." Cal assured him. "We know where you live."

In the week before half-term Joss watched helplessly as chaos ran through the school like a plague of rats let loose into the corridors. Across every year group pupils grew increasingly rude and disruptive, apathetic and careless. Truant clusters of them skittered down the corridors during lessons, hung out in the Tunnel and on blind corners. Teachers issued sanction after sanction. Two more isolation rooms were set up, requiring resentful staff to man them. A record number of pupils were sent home, sent to the Head, placed in detention. Teachers queued to phone parents. Fights between gangs of both sexes broke out in the yard at lunchtimes and break, in the road after school. In the English Department Iona, who never shouted at her classes, was shouting. Derek sat helplessly as class after class abused him, ran riot destroying displays, slashing the whiteboard. The new supply teacher for Alan's classes spent non-contact time shaking in the staff-room. Joss, finding her terrorised by a group of Year 9 boys who refused not just to do anything she asked but to acknowledge her presence at all, went next door to Penny's room.

Penny, Acting Head of Department in Alan's absence, was marking books. Her class of twenty-four top set Year 9 pupils sat peacefully writing. Joss, approaching Penny's desk, took note.

"I think the new supply might appreciate some support," she said quietly.

Lady Penelope glanced up at her. "You go in there with them, then."

"I've been in. It didn't make any difference. It's chaos, it's horrible and I'm not," Joss added, "a senior member of staff."

"Well I can't go in." At her most self-important. "I'm teaching."

Joss let her eyes travel over the molehill of marking, over the quiet, occupied children. Over the screen of Penny's laptop unaccountably frozen on package holidays in Cyprus. "I could sit with your class while you have a word," she offered.

Penny snorted. "Don't be ridiculous. I'm far too busy. And how could I leave them with you? They're a top set."

Joss, too furious to speak, returned to her office to ring for one of the Senior Management Team. Not one of them was answering the phone.

"Are you on your way home?" Claudia, the cordless phone in one hand, dragging the last suitcase out into the hallway with the other. "I'll ring back later if you're driving."

"I'm not driving," Stephen said.

She heard the misery in his voice and stopped to give him her attention. "Another tough day?"

"Mm." He sounded as though he could barely speak.

"You're still at school?"

"Just about to leave."

"Good. I've packed for us all. Mum and Dad are picking the children up from school. Plenty of time before we need to leave for the airport and you don't need to do anything other than change. Listen," she said. "It's half-term, we're going to Italy, and everything will be seem so much better, I promise."

"I don't know this time."

"Stephen." She heard the despair in his voice as she had heard it so often these last few weeks. "It's just been a really bad start to the year, that's all. It'll get better. Trust me. You know I'm always right."

Finn waited while Leigh parked alongside him in the covered entrance to the mill, all tall brick archways and tubs of plants, the river running alongside silver in the fading evening light. They had spent the usual Friday hour or so at the pub with Joss and Iona, some of the PE staff, the dour woman from InHumanities, the overgrown Labrador of a trainee from Maths. But so stressful and soul-destroying had been the preceding week that everyone except the Labrador had been too exhausted to celebrate. Most of them, Finn thought, would spend half-term asleep or weeping or searching the jobs pages of the Times Ed. Eventually the shared weight of depression had become too much and across the table he and Leigh had wordlessly arranged to leave. "It has been," she told him on their way out of the pub, "a baptism of fire."

"I know. Do you still want to do tonight, or are you too fed up?"

"No, no. I'd be even more fed up if I had to go home." She'd smiled.

"Good. I'd be even more fed up if you had to go home." He'd smiled too.

She'd laughed. "All right then. Race you back."

He led her now up the steps and through the security door into the mill's stone and chrome foyer, into the lift to his apartment. The relief he'd felt giving in to wanting her seemed to have sent the wanting of her off the scale. Several times this week he had woken from dreams of her so erotic he couldn't look at her the next day without feeling the heat of them on his skin. Being enclosed with her in the confined space of the lift was tempting to the point of being unbearable. He tilted his head a little to study her profile, the shape of her mouth which he was longing to kiss, the triangle of nakedness between her collar bones and her cleavage.

"What are you doing?" She was smiling and blushing at the same time.

He smiled too. "Raising the temperature."

The lift pinged open and they were at his door, through it and into the wide open space of his apartment. He watched as she gazed round at the high white walls and wooden floors, the panoramic view of the hillside. He looked at the hopeless mess of music and books and clothes, the old leather sofas, the spiral staircase in one corner leading to the mezzanine platform which was his bedroom, trying to see it all through her eyes, to read what it told her about him.

"Wow," she said. "This is *so* cool."

He laughed. "Drink?" He opened a bottle of wine, switched on the CD player. Jack Johnson's *In Between Dreams*. She turned in surprise, away from the view, towards him.

"We have the same album."

"We do."

She sat down on one of the sofas, sliding out of her shoes to curl up on the cushions. He handed her a glass of wine, sat not on the sofa opposite, but on the empty seat beside her. So much scope for accidental touching. "Thank you."

"You're welcome." He raised his glass. "To half term."

"Amen."

He took a mouthful, put down his glass, ran his hands through his hair. "Aaah. Leigh. I'm so sorry we got off to such a crap start."

"We didn't. It was just … a misunderstanding, which … "

"Was my fault."

"You were stressed, being proactive and supportive, dealing with everyone else's chaos as usual. And you snapped. At me." Humour in her eyes, for which he was grateful.

"I love teaching," he said. "I do. It'd drive me mad to progress so far I spent all my days in an office tussling with budgets and targets but this year, this last year … " He shook his head. "Sometimes, you know, I get so fucking disenchanted."

She nodded, sympathetic. "Why wouldn't you?"

"I thought after ten years, I'd have something to show for it.

A half decent CV. A sense of achievement, satisfaction, even."

"But isn't that just your perception because this term's been so awful?"

"It's how I feel. Sometimes I get so annoyed that the wrong people get promoted, those who can't hack it in the classroom, those who're full of fine words and can't carry through an action plan, because of which the whole school starts to fall apart."

"Have you applied for promotion?"

"At Rapton? Are you kidding? Oh, Leigh." He leaned back, so he was staring up into the shadowy heights of the ceiling. She rested her arm on the back of the sofa, her cheek in her hand, watching him. He turned his head to look at her. "Am I bitter and twisted?"

"Yeah."

He smiled. "Thought so. And it's not just school, you know. It's … " His smile faded. "I've been on my own a while. Haven't had a relationship that worked since Carla. I always thought I'd be happily married one day, always wanted kids, and I've kind of given up on it ever happening."

"What, with you being over the hill, you mean?"

He laughed, in spite of himself. "Oh, it's fine with you here, mocking me, but when you're on your own and all you can see are your failures … It's easy to lose your sense of perspective sometimes."

"You weren't talking like this the other night, at my house."

"I was making light of things. Wanting you to think well of me."

"And now you don't want me to think well of you?"

He touched her hair, as he had been yearning to for weeks, stroked a long dark lock of it while he tried to conjure up the right words.

She said, "Shall I tell you what I think of you?"

He narrowed his eyes. "Do I want to hear this?"

"You might." Her lips twitched. She caressed his arm with the back of her finger, the lightest touch through the cotton of his shirt. It felt to him like branding iron. "When you growled at me, I overreacted, felt hurt. Shush, don't you dare apologise again. I overreacted because when we're having lunch with everyone I watch your hands and your mouth and I want you to touch me. I see you sometimes in the corridor, in your classroom, and I imagine how you look when you come. In meetings when you sit opposite me I want to slide my foot out of my shoe and massage your crotch under the table. So on balance, yes, I do think well of you." She was smiling but also watching his eyes for his reaction. Which was, he thought, the wrong part of his anatomy to be watching.

"God. I want to say all that. I feel all that. But first I'm afraid I'm going to have to jump on you."

"No, please. Just take me, any time now."

He started to laugh, cupped her face in his hand, and kissed her.

She woke to grey dawn sifting in through the blind, to the warm tangle of the duvet, Finn's knee against her calf, his curled hand brushing her shoulder. She watched his face for a little while as he slept, tracing with her eyes the curve of his lips, the line of his jaw. Last night they had made love fast and hungrily, each brief and burning caress tipping them closer, then closer still. The second time he'd slowed it right down, made it tantalisingly, lingeringly sensual. Made her come, explosively. Afterwards, stumbling into his kitchen, they'd cooked dinner half-dressed, eaten barely any of it, drunk with wine and sexual excess, and fallen back into bed again. She didn't want to go anywhere else, be anywhere else, ever.

Except she had to.

On her way back from the bathroom she paused beside the window, fascinated by how vast the surrounding hills seemed from up here, how small the streets below. It was very early still, the town barely stirring. One car on the road. No passers-by. Leaning in to the glass she could glimpse the river, the edges of the flower tubs.

Someone slumped against a parked car. A boy. A boy she thought, even from this distance, she recognised.

She frowned. It would be chilly out there, and he wasn't moving. "Finn." She padded quickly back into the bedroom, knelt on the bed, touched his shoulder. "Finn."

He pulled on jeans and a t-shirt, took the stairs instead of the lift, the stone floor of the foyer hard beneath his bare feet. He could see before he reached the car and the flower tub between which the boy's cold and lifeless body lay, that he was Cal Bywater.

Eight

Leigh halted a yard away from where Finn squatted beside Cal's body. "Is he - ?"

"There's no pulse." He looked back at her, stricken. "Will you ring? I'll stay with him."

She nodded, ran back upstairs, made the call from her mobile. Gathering up his jumper and shoes she returned. "They're on their way. Here, it's cold."

He pulled the jumper absently over his head. "Thanks."

"Is he ... " she began again. "Can you tell ... ?"

He shook his head. "He reeks of alcohol. But there's nothing ... no sign of ... I don't want to move him."

She could scarcely stand to look at the scuffed and muddy black boots, the torn jeans, was thankful Finn was blocking her view of the boy's face. "Why is he *here*?" she breathed.

Finn swallowed. "I think he might be here because of me. It was the last thing I said to him. 'If you need anything, come and find me.' The last thing he said to me was 'I know where you live.'"

"Oh God." There were tears of shock in her eyes and she felt a fraud. "I didn't really know him."

"I've known him since he was eleven years old." His voice was hollow. She reached down to him, glimpsed the boy's profile as she did so. No obvious injury, yet he did not look as though he were sleeping. It was, rather, an absence. She understood why it was said of people who had died that they were gone.

The emergency services were not long in arriving. Finn pushed to his feet as the first police officer approached.

"Did you find him?"

"Yes," Finn said. "I'm a teacher. He's one of my pupils. Callum Bywater."

The policeman knelt beside the body. "Oh yes. We know Callum." He looked back at Finn. "D'you live up here?"

"Yeah." Finn gestured. "Number twelve."

"We'll need to come up and ask you a few questions, take a statement. Be ... half an hour or so?"

"Sure." Their cue to leave. Back in his apartment he turned to her. "Jesus Christ."

She held him. For a long moment neither of them spoke.

"I need a drink," he said finally. Wiped his eyes with the back of his hand. "Fucking hell, Leigh."

"I know." Her hands were shaking as she picked up the glasses, scotch splashing as she poured it. "Do you think he passed out down there? Alcoholic poisoning or something?"

He lifted his hands helplessly.

"After the police have been, should I ... do you want to be on your own?"

"*No*. God, no. Come here." He hugged her again. "Everyone says it, all the time, when someone his age dies, it's become a cliché, but God. What a *stupid* waste."

The same police officer who had spoken to them outside was with them, as he had predicted, half an hour later. "DS Mike Whelan." He shook their hands. "You two all right? It's a shock, isn't it?"

"It is. Come in, have a seat." They sat, Leigh and Finn on one of the leather sofas, DS Whelan on the other. "Have you any idea yet," Finn asked, "what happened?"

"Too early to say. There's a head wound, but it's hard to tell. He'd been drinking, and it was cold out there last night ... " He shook his head. "Did you know him well, Mr ... ?"

"Macallister. Finlay Macallister. This is Leigh Somers. We're both teachers at Rapton. Yes, I did know Callum. I was his Head of Year, and I taught him English when he was lower down the school." He paused. "Callum had been in a lot of trouble at school lately. Yesterday I told him that if he needed anything, he should come and find me. It could be coincidence, but that might be why he was here."

"Looking for you?"

"Possibly."

Whelan was making notes. "Is there any specific reason he was in trouble?"

"You knew Callum. He never needed a reason. His uncle

had been staying with him, though. Dean Bywater. You might know him too."

"Aye. We'd heard he was back."

"He's gone again, apparently. Cal seemed a bit – uptight about that yesterday."

"You don't know whether anything happened between them?"

"I don't, no."

"There was an incident at the school the other day, I understand, in which Callum may or may not have been involved."

"Alan Jackson, yes. He fell down some stairs, can't remember whether or not Cal helped him fall. Cal denied it and another boy, who was a witness, also says Callum didn't push him. In fact, that is something that happened between Cal and his uncle. Dean came in to discuss the situation with us on Thursday."

"Is that what the trouble with Callum has been about?"

"That," Finn said, "was pretty much the last straw." He explained the details, sighed. "I can't take this in. What's your best guess, about what happened to Cal?"

Mike Whelan considered. "Don't quote me, because there's a long way to go yet, but my best guess, unless anything else comes to light? It'll go down as misadventure."

The relentless drone of the vacuum and the even more relentlessly crap music Jonathan Ross played on a Saturday morning were audible from the top of the stairs. Todd jumped down three or four steps at a time, bumping down into the hall, to collect the bag and trainers he'd dumped there last night. Before he could safely abscond with them to his room, however, Sheryl had pulled open the door to the kitchen, the noise of the Dyson thankfully drowning out the more piercing notes of her voice. "Yes, you can move all that, put it away in that black hole you call a bedroom."

"I am moving it," Todd said mildly.

"I'm sick of you, leaving your junk round the place for me to tidy up, thinking I'm going to spend my time fetching and carrying for you – "

"I'm *moving* it, all right?" Already he was exasperated. 'The change', Vince mouthed at him whenever Sheryl embarked upon one of her rants. Todd wasn't sure whether he was supposed to be capable of understanding and patience beyond his almost sixteen years, or whether Vince just expected him to be as long-suffering as he was. Vince didn't know that in his absence, Sheryl's rants took a more vicious and spiteful turn. He had never witnessed her driving Todd to the edge of fury and tears.

She said now, "I don't know why you have to hang round the house at the weekend anyway. Why can't you go and get a job, like other lads your age? Or are you too soft for a bit of hard work?"

Todd looked at her in disbelief. He had come to realise she deeply resented his presence in the house because he was a continual reminder of his mother, Vince's beloved first wife. Realising it had never made her any more bearable, though. "I'm trying to get good grades in my coursework, so I can go to sixth form, get my A levels and leave. Which I'd have thought you'd be glad of. Why would I jeopardise that for a few quid earned working in some manky job?"

"No, you'd rather sponge off Vince."

What, like you, you mean? The countless retorts he didn't make. "I don't sponge off him. I don't ask him for money. I've got my own money."

"And we know where that came from."

"Yes we do. It came from my mum." There were things she wanted to say to him about his mum, he was aware of that. Nothing he didn't already know, just bile bred of her own insecurity, her own avarice. It didn't stop him hating her so much he sometimes wished her dead.

"Anyone here?" Vince, having entered through the yard door, was making his way through the utility room and the kitchen. "Todd! Sheryl!"

Sheryl's expression changed as effectively as if a child had erased her nasty face and drawn a nice one in its place. "Hello sweetheart," she trilled. "Lovely to have you home for your lunch. I've some nice sausage rolls in the fridge."

She teetered away. Todd sank down onto the stairs and watched her sourly.

Vince moved into his line of vision. "Todd."

"Yeah."

He hesitated. "You don't know a Callum Bywater, do you?"

"Yeah, 'course I know him. He's in my year at school." He watched Vince's face. "Why? What's he done now?"

"I heard something, in town this morning." Vince looked worried. "It isn't a rumour, everyone seems to know something about it. Callum's dead."

Todd couldn't react. The words made no sense.

"They found his body down by the old mill early this morning. Bit of a mystery what happened to him, apparently."

Todd almost laughed. "Cal? He can't be *dead*."

"I'm sorry, Todd. I didn't know you were mates."

"We're not … " He stopped. "Are they sure? That it's him, I mean?"

"It seems so."

Cal's dead. Cal's dead. "Fuck," he whispered.

Vince nodded. "I know."

Todd sat for a minute, numb with disbelief. Then suddenly he needed to move. "I'm gonna go down into town."

Vince frowned. "I'll come with you."

"No. I mean, thanks, but I want to be by myself."

"Sure that's a good idea?"

"I need some stuff for school. Stationery and some … might call in at the library for … there's a book I could … reserve, or something. " His mouth was operating independently of his brain, as if Vince's news hitting home was causing interference on the line. "Shit. I just want to go for a walk."

"'Course you do." He squeezed Todd's shoulder. "See you later. Take your phone."

Late October, dusk at four, dark by five. Todd had spent the afternoon trudging through town with only the vaguest notion of where he was going, and no clear idea what to do once he got there. He'd stared unseeing at library shelves, a café's menu, racks of cheap stationery. In the end he headed for the park, sat down on the same cold, damp piece of grass on which he'd had his first real conversation with Cal for years. They'd talked about how crap school was, he remembered. About Dean, and Vince and Sheryl. About Cal joining the army. It was this last memory which upset him the most, Cal talking about his future. He didn't want to cry, exactly. He wanted to yell with rage. Because Cal had never had the chance to redeem himself and now he never would. Six months ago, six weeks ago, Todd would hardly have registered it, would have made some passing, shocked comment and moved on. Today he couldn't get it out of his head.

Cal's dead.

The park at night was not somewhere you wanted to be. In broadest daylight there was something eerie about the place. Already, barely five and the shadows were dark and deep in its furthest corners, the gangs of youths who would ride the creaking swings and roundabout through the night, drinking and smoking and beating each other up, had begun to form. They were Todd's contemporaries at school. Had Cal been one of them? Had he sat here getting pissed and stoned in the cold? He thought of his own life, his incipient row this morning with Sheryl, the thoughts passing through his mind last time he'd sat in this park. Todd glanced towards the hoodied kids in the playground, seeing the attraction of getting drunk out of his skull. He could never join them. He was too well-spoken, too bright and soft and middle-class. They would kick him to the ground for being different.

Instead, he slipped away.

He'd never been in Rapton police station before. It had a tiny little entrance with two orange plastic chairs and a grille through which to speak to someone. He glanced at the posters on the boards about Neighbourhood Watch and Cracking Crime. A face appeared behind the grille. It didn't look particularly friendly. "Hello." He sounded, even to his own ears, about twelve. "I wanted to talk to someone about Callum Bywater."

The face was unimpressed. "And who're you?"

"Todd Kershaw." He hesitated. He didn't know whether this

was hypocrisy, or a lie, or maybe, in some strange and twisted way, after all the truth. "I was Cal's friend."

Ten, fifteen minutes of sitting on one of the orange chairs and a middle-aged man in a rank brown suit entered from a side door. "Todd Kershaw?"

"Yes." Todd stood up quickly.

"DS Mike Whelan." The man - shorter than he was, more heftily built - shook Todd's hand, which Todd appreciated. "Come with me."

It was, Todd supposed, what they called in police series on television, an interview room. It was also, frankly, a bit of a disappointment. Second-hand furniture and peeling grey walls. Nothing remotely intimidating or official about it.

"Have a seat. What can we do for you, Todd?"

"I wanted to ask someone about Cal. How he died, I mean."

"Head injury. That's all I can tell you, I'm afraid."

He nodded. "Because it's confidential?"

"Yes. Also because it's all we know. For now. Were you good friends with Callum?"

"Not good friends, exactly. But … you know. I had dinner at his house the other week."

"With the family?"

"His mum wasn't there. With Cal and Dean, his uncle."

"You wouldn't know where Dean is, would you?"

Todd shook his head. "Cal didn't say. I don't think he knew really. I think he might have said Scotland."

Mike nodded. "Big place, Scotland. Any idea how Callum might have felt, about Dean leaving?"

"Yeah, he was upset. He tried to hide it, like he tried to hide everything else. But when he told me about it, he was nearly crying."

"So he had a good relationship with Dean?"

"I think he respected him, but he pretended not to. He pretended he didn't want him around, but he did." Todd paused, remembering Cal's bravado the night they'd been snooping through Dean's things. "Did you know Callum?"

"Oh yes." He half-smiled. "I know you too. Vince Kershaw's lad."

Todd wasn't surprised. Vince was pretty well-known, in a good way. "That's Rapton, though isn't it? Everyone knows everyone. Everyone knows everyone's families and pasts, everyone's related. You know that thing, six degrees of separation? It's like one degree of separation in Rapton."

Mike smiled. "Kind of useful, in my line of work though."

"Yeah. It would be."

"Is there anything you can tell us, Todd, about Callum over the last few weeks? Anything he was up to, anything he said, that you think might be important? Or just unusual?"

Todd took a breath. "That's why I'm here. I don't know if it's important. It probably isn't. It's just something that when I think about it, it makes me stop. Do you know what I mean?"

"Yes," Mike said. "I know what you mean."

"It's about taking risks. We were talking about it, weeks ago, me and Cal, about Dean and his armed robbery and all that – you know about that?" The policeman nodded. "I said, you had to weigh how likely you were to get caught against what you were likely to come out with. And Cal said, you had to be sure what the odds were. He said that again to me, yesterday in Mr Macallister's office, he said he was really sure of the odds. He said it was 'pay-back time'. There was something in the way he said it, it made me think he knew something, or he was going to do something. I don't know. I might be wrong."

"But he definitely gave you the impression he was up to something – what? Stupid? Illegal?"

"Yeah. Either of those." He said again, "I might've been wrong."

"Well you might. But we have to take it seriously."

"Why?"

"Because, Todd, he said it the day before he died."

The words struck him hard. It was as if every so often reality dealt him another hammer blow. He nodded. Whelan was looking at him with what he suspected might be sympathy. "Come on, Todd. I'm at the end of my shift and it's been a very long day. D'you want a lift home?"

The woman who answered the door was not Cal's mother.

Finn was sure of this, even though Julie Bywater had never attended a parents' evening, never turned up at the school to discuss her son's behaviour when requested. Finn had always suspected she never received the letters, or the phone messages. He suspected, moreover, she was functionally illiterate, though he couldn't remember now what had initially sparked that thought. But the woman who answered the door was far too young to be Cal's mother. "I'm Finn Macallister," he explained himself. "From school."

She stood aside, as no doubt she had stood aside so many times since the news had burned its trail through Rapton yesterday, for visitors paying their respects. Friends and neighbours whose own children were no worse nor better than Cal; on the Rapton estate, their numbers were many. Finn stepped into a hall so tiny one more step took him into the sitting room and there she was, alone on the sagging sofa, her face melted with grief.

"I'm so sorry," he said.

The guardian of the door went to switch on the kettle. He could see this was her role, admitting visitors, making tea, getting them through the hours. Julie Bywater raised her eyes – Cal's eyes, he thought, stricken – to his. "Are you our Callum's teacher?"

"His Head of Year." He didn't think she knew what that meant. He wasn't sure he did. "I've taught him, yes. I came to say how sorry I am. I can't begin to imagine what you must be going through."

"I can't take it in." She didn't seem to mind, or care, that she had no real idea who he was. "I'm crying and crying and I can't take it in. I keep thinking, it'll be over tomorrow. If I can just do today, it'll all be back to normal tomorrow." She shook her head. "I can't find anyone. I can't find his dad, I can't even find Dean and he was here … " She tried to remember when it was Dean had been there - " … was it yesterday?"

"Thursday." The woman who was making tea handed Finn a cup. "It was Thursday Dean went, love."

"If there's anything at all I can do," Finn said helplessly.

Julie looked at him earnestly. "His things from school. All

his books. I'd like to have those, if that's all right."

"Of course." Finn's heart sank further still. He knew what Callum's books looked like – torn covers, graffitied pages, obscene scribblings. A date, here and there. A title, perhaps. What comfort, what reassuring memory of her son, was she going to draw from those? "I'll get on to it."

"Wasn't it you that found him?" she said suddenly, this detail rising through her misery to the surface.

"It was. I live in one of the mill apartments."

She nodded slowly, as though the digestion of any information took time and emotional effort. "How did he look? Was he … ?"

Finn knew that he would have told her this even had it not been true. "He didn't look as though he'd been in pain or afraid. He looked as though he'd fallen asleep."

Her tears spilled. "He was ever so upset, the last time I spoke to him, about Dean leaving. He thought the world of his uncle, did Callum."

Finn thought of the self-deceptions with which that notion was loaded. But what right had he to judge. Maybe Cal had thought the world of him. He managed, "Dean seemed very supportive of Cal."

She nodded again. "He'll be devastated when I tell him. I can't bear it."

Finn walked the two miles home, shedding the weight of grief and poverty with every step. The Rapton estate, he thought, existed in its own social bubble, independent of and immune to the outside world. Or perhaps that wasn't the Rapton estate. Perhaps it was him. He stood in front of hundreds of kids every day and knew how different their lives were to his. It was the difference that money made, and class, and expectations, and he still did not know how to bridge that gap. Other than with education.

Cal's death was, for the most part, old news by the time school re-opened after the holiday. Those staff who, like Stephen, had been too far away from the beat of local drums, responded with an incredulity and accompanying volley of questions which Finn found both wearying and offensive. The eager picking over of the few known details seemed to him to be in poor taste and he could not bear to be in the staff room hearing it or worse, being plied for information himself. He kept to his classroom, or to Leigh's, avoiding even the society of Joss's office as he didn't feel, quite honestly, that he would be much company.

But he did need to speak to Stephen. Who listened, horrified, to a fuller version of events than Finn had given him on the phone when he'd returned from Italy on Sunday. "I've spoken to DS Whelan, this morning," Stephen told him. "He wants to come into assembly to ask for information."

"And he needs to be in an assembly to do that?"

"I think it's a good idea. Hammer home what's happened. What dangers can befall you if you stagger drunk through the streets in the middle of the night."

"Is that the line he's taking?"

"Apparently so. Though you'd imagine a gang beating him up for pleasure would do more damage."

"Unless Callum was mugged. He might have had money on him. His mobile." Finn stopped. He really didn't want to be drawn into this. "Have you noticed the atmosphere around school this morning?"

"Subdued." Stephen shook his head. "It takes the death of one of their own … How long will it be, I wonder, before the shock begins to wear off. Incidentally, something I've failed to grasp, why was Leigh Somers with you when you found Callum?"

Finn looked at him.

"Ah. *Oh*. I see. Well … that's good?"

"More than good," Finn replied, briefly unguarded. "So much more."

Leigh's form was more than subdued. Several of the girls were crying, several of the boys threatening retribution. But no one here was offering any new insights or information, no one had seen Cal since Friday afternoon in school. Dean had already gone, Leigh had gathered, his mother was working.

But unless Cal had fallen, injured himself, and that was still a possibility, someone, somewhere must know something.

"Todd?" He looked as withdrawn as Finn did. "You okay?"

Todd, his feet up on the empty chair beside his, a book he wasn't reading open on the desk, raised his eyes to hers. "I can't get my head round it."

"No. Me neither."

"Was it you that found him, miss? You and Mr Macallister?"

"Yes." Everyone knew this too. Most effective broadcasting service in the world, Rapton's grapevine.

"Must've been horrible."

"It was." She took a chance. "Did Cal say anything to you, that Friday? Any-thing about going to see Mr Macallister?"

"No. Mr Macallister said we could talk to him if we wanted to, and Cal said it jokingly – *we know where you live*. I thought he was joking." Todd considered. Was there a connection, that comment about pay-back time and turning up at Big Mac's place in the middle of the night and – what? Getting whacked? Passing out? He shook his head. Said aloud, "It doesn't make any sense."

"It doesn't," Leigh agreed. She smiled. "Goes for me too, you know. If you want to talk, I mean."

He looked at her, mock-reproachful. "Don't say that to me, miss. I might end up dead on your doorstep."

The sense of shock and sorrow pervaded the hall as though it were not an assembly they were attending but a memorial. Row after row of pupils entered in silence, sank cross-legged to the floor, waited quietly. Those who had known Cal were either genuinely shaken and upset or wise enough not to say otherwise, the younger children awed by the solemnity of their elders. Would Callum himself, Leigh wondered, have been taken aback by this stunned hush? Or would he have expected it as one of his loudly-claimed rights? No one had yet dared to express anything but regret that Callum Bywater had been taken from their lives. It surely would not be long before something inappropriate but more truthful was said. She hoped it would not be said just yet in Finn's presence.

"Good morning." Stephen stood before them, his light suntan jarring with the black suit he wore, with his sombre air. "I should be welcoming you back to school after the holiday as I did in September, as I always do, with words of encouragement for the term ahead. I should be talking to you again about striving to do your best, achieving your potential. About the highlights which this half of the term holds. Unfortunately, my message today is very different. As most of you already know, one of our Year 11 students, Callum Bywater, died last week … "

Somebody sobbed. Leigh held her breath waiting for somebody else to laugh, derisively or nervously, but it didn't happen. Presumably those who might have done so were already excluded. Last term the dissolution of the Focus Group had been every teacher's prayer yet today, with its ringleaders gone, it seemed a hollow victory. She glanced across at Finn, his face grim as he listened, his acute sense of responsibility both his failing and his strength. Had Cal been found somewhere else, by someone else, would he be bearing it as heavily as he was now? Or was that just Finn, did he always feel too keenly other people's burdens? She might barely have left his side for more than a week, she reminded herself, she might be falling in love with him, might instinctively trust him, but she did not yet know him very well.

DS Whelan, introduced to the pupils by Stephen, rose heavily from his seat and walked to the centre of the stage. "It's a terrible thing," he said, his voice in the receiving silence gruffer than Stephen's, his accent far broader, "when someone you know dies. Even if you didn't really know them, even if you didn't like them very much, it's a terrible thing. Callum Bywater had a life. A future. He doesn't have those things anymore, and it's my job to find out why. Now I don't know very much about how or why Callum died. It's not usually that quiet in the centre of Rapton of a Friday night. Someone must have seen him. Someone must have noticed him. He'd had a bit to drink, so he might have been staggering, making a nuisance of himself. But between about half past three on the Friday you broke up, and six the following morning, he seems to have become invisible. Of course he didn't, and you might have seen him, and because he was always around and you were used to seeing him, you didn't register it at the time. It's that sort of place, Rapton. Tight-knit. We all bump into each other all the time and think nothing of it. But the closer we can narrow down the time at which he really did disappear from view, the better chance we stand of finding out what happened. If you know anything at all, even if it doesn't sound very important, or you think it's silly, come and tell me, or one of the other police officers who will be in school today. Sometimes what seems like something daft can solve a case. Because in a couple of weeks or months, in a few years, if it's you wandering round town at night a bit the worse for wear, you'd want to think we'd been on to anyone who might do you harm and put them where they belong. Wouldn't you?"

The silence following DS Whelan's speech lasted long enough for Stephen to echo his message, for the Year 7s to begin leading back to their classrooms. Leigh heard the first susurrus of relief among her own form and had not the heart to shush them. "Come on, let's go." She stood, indicating their turn to leave.

"I'm gonna stay here, Miss. I wanna talk to them about Cal."

One after another, possibly with no information to give but all needing to play a part. They had found themselves on the edge of a drama and needed to stay there, to begin to assimilate it, to talk, to be together. She understood.

Todd was afraid he was losing it. Big-time. When Miss Somers had been nice to him in registration he'd felt his throat constrict. Tears pricking the back of his eyes by the time she'd said he could come and talk to her. What was the matter with him, that a kind teacher, who was always kind to everyone, not just him, nearly had him blubbing like a five year old just by being ... well, kind?

Other stuff too. Harder and harder to keep his patience with Sheryl. His chest hurt all the time, as if he were going to explode. Couldn't sleep much. Christie, his lifeline, was great to talk to late at night on MSN, but she wasn't *here*. Couldn't be here. He tried to recreate in his head the way she'd looked, half-naked beneath him on cushions on the terrace, entirely naked astride him in the sand, the elation he'd felt when he was with her, the way she'd held him to her tight when she was kissing him, like she was drinking his soul. Most nights he tried to recapture the way it had felt to come inside her, but it just wasn't the same going solo. It made him feel sad and desperate but then maybe that was what he was, sad and desperate.

And he thought he kept seeing Cal. Tell me if you saw him that night, DI Whelan had entreated them. What if I've seen him since? Todd thought. Do you want to know that too? Glimpsing him at the end of a corridor, haring off down the estate. Hearing the scornful laugh, the crowing 'I'm joining the army, me'. Never again. Todd would blink and he wasn't there anymore, his voice and his laughter silenced forever. We were at the same schools since we were five years old and yet we hardly knew each other, Todd thought. How can I miss him?

More than this, far more than the sum of hating Sheryl and longing for Christie and coming to terms with whatever it was that had befallen Cal, he knew something was fundamentally wrong. It kept him awake at nights and emotional and continually on edge and he couldn't, couldn't quite …

Well he could, actually. He knew exactly what the matter was, truth be told. One unbearably painful word. One syllable.
Mum.

The week tip-toed to a close. Though he could feel the shocked silence of the first day or two ebbing away, Stephen noticed it leaving in its wake an uneasy calm. Posters for the end of term talent show appeared on corridor walls. The football team beat the grammar school's team hollow. Lessons, he saw on a couple of impromptu tours of the school, seemed generally to be going well. No pupils hurled themselves cursing into corridors. No teacher was screaming for order. No one was sent to the isolation rooms, or to his office. Three children all week were placed in detention. The zero tolerance behaviour policy he and Finn had instigated the week before half-term was either paying off in spades, or – well, he knew the real reason. But if they could hang on to this atmosphere of peace long enough whilst still enforcing the zero tolerance, maybe, just maybe, they might have achieved something. Maybe some long-term good might come out of all this. Peace in our time, Stephen thought. If only.

"So how," Claudia asked him that evening as they sat in the kitchen with their glasses of wine, "are things working out with Finn? Have you got him on side?"

"I think so. I hope so. He's the sort you want on your side."

"Telling me." She grinned.

He cocked an eyebrow at her, got up to fetch and sort through the day's post. "Yes all right. He is taken now, you know."

"Oh really? By whom?"

"By Leigh Somers, our new English teacher, no less."

"They didn't waste any time, then. Is she worthy of him?"

"Worthy?" He laughed. "She's very nice."

"Hm." Claudia considered. "Why don't you invite them round for dinner? He's your new best friend and *we don't see anyone, Stephen.*"

"All right. I'll ask him. Before or after I've told him you find him attractive?"

She made a face at him, watched him discarding fliers and brown envelopes. "Nothing interesting?" she asked.

"Bills and bumf." He frowned at the final envelope, thick white and windowless, his name and address word-processed in an italic font. Turning it over, he slit it open, took out the letter it contained.

Claudia, alerted by his silence, was watching him. "What?" she said.

He shook his head. "I can't believe it."

"Good or bad?" she said warily.

He finished reading the letter, looked across at her. "It's from the committee for the new curriculum. They've asked me to chair one of the steering groups."

She still wasn't entirely sure. "That's … good, isn't it?"

"That's great." Finally, he smiled. "It's recognition, and a chance to make a difference, at some small level, and … and actually, exactly what I need." He sank down onto one of the barstools, disbelief and delight clear in his eyes. Claudia laughed, hugged him.

"Thank God. See, I told you. Didn't I tell you? What will it mean?"

"Lots of extra work."

"Champagne?"

He smiled. "We don't have any, do we?"

"Not in the fridge. So will you tell them all, at school?"

He considered, briefly. "Not yet. It doesn't seem appropriate to be announcing my good news to the whole staff."

Claudia let out her breath. "Why is it that your staff are so determined not to accept that their careers are bound up with yours? You'd think they'd want you to succeed, and therefore the school to succeed, so they could bask in the reflected glory. Or leave and get better jobs somewhere else because due to you they'd got something positive out of Rapton."

"You'd think," Stephen agreed. "I'd hoped they'd take the attitude that we're in it together, but they don't. I meant, though, that I'll keep a lid on it because feelings are running high about Callum Bywater and it would be heartless of me to be boasting about my own good fortune."

She shook her head. "Thugs like Callum Bywater don't deserve your sensitivity."

Stephen frowned. He understood her anger with his staff for being so righteous and self-centred, with the worst of the pupils for making his job such a difficult one, loved her for her loyalty. There were times when their feelings on the subject converged. His own astonishment at Callum's death had been complicated by a host of ripple effect considerations and reactions. Callum had been a threat, to other children, to the staff, to himself, and to Stephen, who didn't think he had ever actually wished Callum dead, but he had certainly wished him gone. In fact, when Stephen recalled how fervently he had recently wished the boy gone, he felt deeply uneasy. He had sent a message of genuine regret to Callum's mother, knowing the despair and grief he would feel should, God forbid, any such horror befall his own children. And then there was the question of repercussions for the school; Callum had died far enough away from the school grounds, long enough out of school hours, for there to be no question of care or responsibility. There was no doubt Rapton High was going to be a different place without him, but it was not an absence for which Stephen was going to have to defend himself professionally. Which was just as well, given this invitation to chair the New Curriculum Steering Group, an invitation whose flame was already kindling inside him, raising his spirits higher than they had been for a long, long time. At last, some hope and recognition and a sense of progression again which perhaps wasn't going to be ruined by his school being in chaos. He had no intention of being the first to say this – in fact, he was going to make damn sure the words never escaped his lips – but at times and in part, his feeling about the death of Callum Bywater was gratitude.

Another Monday down in the endless progression of Mondays, the weeks marching inevitably towards Christmas, towards Easter, towards exams and even after those there would be no freedom. He was trapped with Vince and Sheryl no matter how many A* - C grades he got. For how could you leave home when you were sixteen? Where did you go when there was nowhere to go? A shop doorway? A park bench? But it had begun to dawn on him, and it was the darkest dawn yet, that it wasn't freedom from home he needed. It was freedom from himself. Freedom from the grief and despair which, to tell the truth, had been welling inside him long before Cal had died.

"Todd!"

Todd turned. Zak, the little *Dr Who* fan he'd chaperoned home along the estate the night he'd had dinner at Cal's. "Hi, Zak." They walked through the school gates, out onto the road which led to the estate, Zak babbling about his holiday, his voice so excitable Todd could hardly keep up. Eventually he paused. He paused for such a long time Todd had to look down to make sure he was still there.

"Todd." The excitable quality had gone. Zak sounded now uncertain.

"Yeah."

"Can I give you something?"

Todd frowned. "Sure." What was he letting himself in for?

Zak stopped, hauled his bag from his shoulders. Unzipping it, he reached down into the depths of the main compartment, rummaging purposefully among books and pencil cases and *Dr Who* collectors' cards. Todd waited.

"Got it." He smiled, pulled out a mobile phone and handed it to Todd.

"Why are you giving me your mobile?"

"It's not mine. Mine's in here." He patted the mobile phone pocket on the strap of his bag. "It's that boy's. The boy who died."

Todd felt cold, from the back of his neck down through his body. "Cal's." He stared at the phone as though it might burn its shape into his hand.

"Yes."

"What are you doing with Cal's phone?"

"He dropped it." Zak heaved his bag back onto his back. "He was out here with it, and I was coming back from the shop and I saw him so I hid behind my dad's car. I watched him. He had all these bags with him and I could see what was in them, it was all cans of beer and stuff. I think he must've already had some, because he was stumbling about. He must've thought he put his phone back in his pocket but he missed or it fell out, you know 'cos of all the bags, and being drunk." He hesitated. "When he'd gone I saw the phone on the ground and I picked it up. I didn't know what to do with it."

"Why didn't you put it through the letter-box?"

"I wasn't sure which was his house." And even if he had been, Todd understood, nothing would have persuaded him to walk through Callum Bywater's gate and approach the front door, so great was his fear that monsters or Rottweilers or Callum himself might spring out to devour him.

"You should've given it to the police."

"I forgot all about it. I didn't come back to school till today. We were in Tenerife, I was just telling you." Zak looked anxious, as though he suddenly doubted Todd's willingness to help. "I thought maybe you'd know what to do with it."

Todd took a breath. "Yep. I do know. Thanks, Zak. You did the right thing."

Zak smiled, relieved. "I knew you'd know."

The house was empty. Todd dumped his shoes and his bag in the hall, partly because he was in a hurry, partly to wind Sheryl up, ran up to his room and shut the door. Sat down on his bed, Cal's phone in his hands. It was switched off, which was lucky, because otherwise the battery would be dead. He wondered had Zak, cautious as he was, switched it off for just that reason.

Todd switched it on. The little screen lit with a photo of Cal and Josh and Liam gurning like stupid kids. The battery was low, the reception not bad for round here. No new messages. Todd checked the Call Register. No Missed Calls or Received Calls since early that Friday evening. Nobody trying to get in touch with him then. Was he less popular than he'd liked to suggest? Had everyone already known he was dead? He selected Dialled Calls. The last one was a number. Others, before that, labelled Liam, Josh, Connor, Amy, Jodie.

Dean.

Todd stared at the name. Pressed Call. Waited, dry-mouthed.

The mobile phone you are calling is currently unavailable.

Thank God. What did he think he would have said?

Back to the last number. He checked the details, grew colder still. The date and the time meant this must be the call Cal had made minutes before Zak had retrieved the phone. Probably the last call Cal had made before he died.

He returned to the number. It was eleven digits, a landline, the code for this area. Again he pressed Call. Again he waited. Why was he doing this? He didn't know why he was doing this.

The phone at the other end of the line was ringing. He held his breath.

A woman's voice - *I'm sorry we're unable to take your call at the moment. If you'd like to leave a message for Stephen or Claudia, we'll get back to you as soon as we can.*

Todd stared at the phone. Well that was no help. Who the fuck were Stephen and Claudia? He turned the phone off, chucked it onto the chair beside his bed. From downstairs, he heard a door close. The snapping of Sheryl's high heels on the wooden floor. Her shriek of rage as she discovered his bag and his shoes at the foot of the stairs. He groaned, dropped back onto his bed, closing his eyes and muffling her with a pillow pulled hard across his head.

Finn's doorbell rang. He left his pile of marking – only night of the week he had the energy for it, Monday - and went to the intercom in the narrow opening bit of the room which was supposed to be the hall. "Yep?"

"Please sir – " Leigh's voice, doing some bizarre Oliver Twist out of Dick Van Dyke accent – "can you spare a room for the night?"

He smiled. "Sure. Only got the one bed though."

"Oh you're ever so kind, sir, really you are."

He pressed the catch release. Opened the door for her. "Thought you were going home after the show," he said as she appeared.

"Couldn't face it. Tired, driving in the dark. Anyway, I wanted to have sex."

"Oh good. With me?"

"Well, you know, as you're here."

He kissed her. "Drink?"

"Mm." She slipped out of her shoes and padded after him into the kitchen.

"How was the show?" She and Joss had taken a coachload of Year 11s to see *Blood Brothers* at Manchester's Opera House. Finn, prevented by meetings from going too, had found his evening empty without her.

"It was great. I love that play. I'm so glad we're doing it for GCSE."

"See," he waved a teaspoon at her, "you're a breath of fresh air in that English Department. No one gets enthusiastic about anything any more. Iona's too busy poring over the TES jobs pages; Penny doesn't want to know about anything she hasn't been teaching for twenty-five years already; Plug – sorry, Derek – is too busy swinging from apathy to terror to even think about what he's actually supposed to be teaching and Alan ... "

"How is Alan? Did you go to see him?"

"Yeah, straight after the middle managers meeting. Tea or coffee?"

"Don't care. Does he remember anything yet?"

"He does. He says he tripped, it was all his fault." He added unhappily, "Too late now, of course."

She went to him, having to stand on tip-toe now she was barefoot, reached up and kissed him, a long, slow, wiping-sadness-from-your-mind kiss. He held her there, one hand sliding down over her bum, squeezing hard. "Oh forget the drink," she murmured. "Let's just do the sex."

Afterwards, he kissed her again, gently this time, stroked a line from her throat to her navel. "I love it when you last a long time, when we spend hours just ... " She tweaked his nipple. "Though that's not to say quick and passionate doesn't have a lot going for it as well."

"It's always passionate. It's just a different kind of passion." His fingers dipped down into her, where she was still sensitive. "I missed you, tonight."

"I'm here."

"You should just move in." He was barely joking.

She smiled. "After three weeks?"

"It might be three weeks since we undressed each other for the first time. It's more than two months since we first met. That's long enough to know you've fallen in love." Her eyes widened. He paused. "Too much? Am I scaring you off?"

She kissed him.

He smiled. "Tell me. With words."

She cupped his cheek in her hand, drew her fingers back through his hair. "With words. Okay. Thank you. I love you too. You are the most sensitive, passionate, intelligent, capable, thigh-weakeningly attractive man I have ever met.

Shush." He was laughing. "And this should feel worryingly fast, but it doesn't, it feels right, and I really, really want it to work. So there you are. Happy now?"

"Very happy. You forgot insecure though."

"Ah yes. Deeply insecure."

He rolled her into his arms to cuddle her. It was later and she was almost asleep when he murmured, "Oh and by the way? Stephen's invited us to dinner."

"I'm withdrawing goodwill," Sheryl announced at breakfast the following morning.

Todd wanted to point out that you could hardly withdraw something you'd never held to begin with, but he was too busy searching through the ironing basket for his uniform. Sheryl nibbled her multi-grain toast as she watched him. "You won't find anything of yours in there."

He turned, feeling ridiculous already in his boxers and t-shirt in the middle of the kitchen. He had hoped to sneak down while she was in bed but clearly she had anticipated this moment and parked herself at the breakfast bar as a spectator to his humiliation.

"Is this because I left my shoes in the hall?"

"It's because you're old enough to be doing your own washing."

For as long as he could remember, there had been a system by which they all dumped their clothes in the laundry basket, one of them – Mum, or Vince, or Todd as he grew older - stuck them in the machine, took them out again, dried them and Mum had ironed them. Vince, during the years Todd had lived here alone with him, had never much bothered with ironing. Sheryl sent it all away in a basket, several baskets sometimes, to be ironed by somebody else.

He said, "So where is mine?"

"Probably still in the laundry basket where you left it."

He looked at her. "You washed yours and Vince's and not mine?"

"As I said. You're so keen to be off as soon as you can, never mind Vince might've liked a hand with the business, about time you started washing your own clothes."

She contradicted herself all the time, to suit her purpose. "Vince doesn't want me to join his business. I'd be crap at all that stuff. I want to study English Literature, for God's sake. Why didn't you tell me you weren't going to be doing my washing any more and then I would have done it myself?"

"Well." She examined the seeds in her toast. "If your mother had brought you up properly ... "

Her words sliced him like a blade. "She did bring me up properly! She brought me up to be part of a family who loved each other and looked after each other, which is something you know fuck all about!"

"Don't you dare," she said icily. "Don't you dare use that sort of language in my house."

He had dragged his trousers out of the wash basket and gone to school, slamming as many doors as possible en route, fearing he was going to stink his way through the day. First period was Form Tutorial, during which Miss Somers chatted to them, or distributed whatever PSHE work Mr Macallister had dreamed up this week, or let them do their homework. Today she was chatting. He watched her as she perched on the front desk, wondered how old she was. Twenty something? If she'd worked at other schools, twenty-seven, twenty-eight maybe? She had long wavy brown hair and big blue eyes and a really, really nice figure. He remembered Cal describing her as 'well fit'. He also remembered Cal telling him that she and Mr Macallister were shagging. Having watched them together, Todd didn't think Cal had been wrong about that either.

But trying to distract himself with ogling his form teacher wasn't working. His chest hurt again, and his throat felt sore, and his head was all sort of echoey like he was hearing things from the bottom of a swimming pool. The conversations around him flitted in and out of his brain, disjointed as though he were channel-hopping. Mr Macallister had come in and was showing a *Blood Brothers* CD to Miss Somers and she was smiling like it was something really special.

And then he heard someone say, "Fucking Cal Bywater, who's gonna miss him?"

He stiffened. It felt like the whole room had stiffened. Mr Macallister, looking pained, was about to speak.

But Todd got there first.

"He's dead, isn't he? You don't say bad stuff about dead people!"

The girl who had spoken, and he knew it was her, she was sitting right behind him, was someone Cal had teased mercilessly for the four and a bit years they'd been at Rapton. She was overweight, wore glasses, had virulent acne and a firm and loudly expressed belief in her own superior intelligence. Todd had always thought intellectual superiority was the only shield she had against people like Cal, but he didn't care about that now. She was staring at him, slack-jawed. They all were. He could hear his voice blundering on, loud and incoherent. "I know he gave you a hard time, but that was just Cal, wasn't it, he gave everyone a hard time because his whole fucking life was a hard time! It's all right for you, you can move on, get over it. He can't. He can't say, 'Yeah all right, I was tight, soz about that Kayleigh'. You don't ever say bad stuff about dead people because they can't answer back, they can't make it right. Once … " His chest began to heave. "Once someone's died they can't ever … " His voice broke. Miss Somers was touching his arm saying,

"Come on, Todd. Come outside."

He wanted to pull away from her, but he was crying, and he couldn't bear the whole class staring at him like he was some sort of freak-show.

Mr Macallister said gently, "Go on, Todd. Go and sit in my office. Give yourself chance to calm down a bit."

But he didn't. He went to sit with her in Mr Macallister's office, but he didn't calm down. He sobbed. Miss Somers pushed a box of tissues along the desk to him. Waited. Eventually his chest stopped heaving and he could breathe properly again, but the tears kept falling. He felt embarrassed but helpless, as if it were out of his control.

"What is it?" she said.

He shook his head.

"*Is* it about Callum?"

"Kind of. Partly." His voice sounded thick. "My mum. Died. A long time ago. But." He cried again.

She touched his shoulder gently. "Who is it you live with now?"

"My step-dad. And his wife." He wiped his nose on one of the tissues. "She hates me."

"Todd … "

"She actually does. We were all right, me and Vince, until he met her. Now it's like I don't belong there any more." He wiped his eyes hard with the heel of his hand. "My mum, who died, she was great, she was *really* great. We had this thing, she just *got* me. I didn't have to be sporty or tough or … cocky. I could just be me, and it was okay. I didn't have to be *grateful* all the time. And I really miss her. Which is stupid, because it's nearly four years since she died and I was all right. I was coping. But ever since Sheryl … She hates me 'cos Vince really loved my mum. She hates that Vince looks after me when I'm not even his kid. She hates me even being in the house. It's really hard, living like that. It wears you down till … " He glanced at Miss Somers and couldn't bear the compassion in her eyes. "I'm okay, miss." He drew in his breath, let it out again. "I'm all right."

"Maybe," she said tentatively, "you should talk to Vince."

Todd shook his head. "I'm fine. Honest. It's just I'm a bit weird around dying. They should put me away. I'm a nutter. Can I go and get a drink?"

"Of course." She was looking like she didn't know whether to believe him or not. He didn't blame her; his voice was still a bit shaky and he couldn't produce a convincing smile yet. Truth was, he'd scared himself. It used to be a lot easier than this to pretend he was normal.

"Where are we going?" Donna whined.

Spig looked back at her, stumbling over the cow pats and tussocks behind him in another pair of stupid shoes. Why couldn't she wear trainers, like everyone else on the planet? *"It's not far now."*

She scowled and he began to wonder had this really been a good idea. Maybe he should've kept it to himself. The trouble with trying to share stuff was who you tried to share it with. But he didn't want to share anything with anyone except Donna and this was the first time in his life he'd had anything worth sharing. He waited for her to catch up. *"Why don't you take your shoes off?"*

"Because I don't want to get shit and mud all over my feet."

He laughed. *"You won't, if you look where you're goin'. The grass's dry, it'll be all right."*

She looked at him sceptically.

"I'll carry you," he threatened.

"I'm takin' 'em off, leave me alone." She scrambled after him through the cow muck and the daisies.

"It could be worse," he called to her over his shoulder. *"We could be in school."*

Ten minutes later he stopped, knowing she'd been so busy scanning her path for dung she hadn't taken much notice where they were. Now she looked up, saw the drystone wall and clump of trees, and frowned.

"It's a shed."

"It's not a shed, it's a house. It just ... looks like a shed." He wasn't having her spoil it for him but she did have a point. *"Come on, come and look inside."*

"Inside?"

"It's all right, come on."

She followed, doubtfully. As they drew closer you could tell, to his relief, it was more than a shed. An old cottage, maybe. Stone walls, an old green wooden door, cracked windows, creepers everywhere. Like it had been empty for years and years. She leaned closer, curious now. Stig pushed at the door. It yielded heavily. Donna shivered and drew back. *"I'm not going in there."*

"Don't be daft."

He led the way, stepping confidently across the threshold. Inside was a single room, another door in the opposite wall. Above this rose a stone staircase, its treads steep and treacherously uneven. The floor, scattered with yellowing newspapers, was cold grey flagstone, an old electric fire with a plugless flex screwed in to the peeling plaster. Beneath the window squatted an armchair, its foam cushions nearly put through with use, a brown drop-leaf table against one wall next to a dining chair with a frayed seat. Spig walked across the newspapers, opened the door in the back wall to a room half the size of the first, with a big enamel sink, a few empty shelves and a rusted cooker. Off it, concealed by a jerkily sliding door, a sort of cupboard containing a toilet, a basin and a bath for dwarfs. Everything smelled of damp, the whole place was filthy. Donna, her expression a mix of disgust and fascination, looked towards the stairs. "What's up there?"

"Two rooms. Nothing in them." He was unsure what she was thinking. "I thought it'd be somewhere to come. When it's raining and that."

"What if somebody lives here?"

He looked at her.

"Like, in the summer and stuff."

"Oh yeah, it'll be someone's holiday home, this place."

"Or a tramp."

"Donna, nobody lives here. I've been keeping an eye on it. I don't even think anybody owns it. If they do, they've forgotten, haven't they? What d'you reckon? We could do it up."

"We could make it nicer," she agreed.

Spig whooped with triumph. "It'll be brilliant when we've cleaned it up a bit. We could bring some stuff from the home, cleaning stuff. A broom or something. I could nick a few things, make it nice. There's always loads of stuff in skips, isn't there, things people don't want. That wouldn't be nickin', would it? It'd just be like ... recycling."

"It would be something to do," she said wistfully.

"Yeah. When you're not seein' whatshisface." He paused.

He didn't want to say this but he sort of had to. He had to let her know anything she wanted to do was all right by him. "You could bring him here."

He saw the change in her eyes before she looked away, didn't know how to respond other than by making light of it. "Don't s'pose you'd want to bring him here, though, would you? Isn't he dead posh, your bloke?"

"He's got a mum and a dad and a house on the Old Road, if that's what you mean. He doesn't live in a home like us." She was annoyed. "But he's normal. He's not snobby or nothin'."

"No, I didn't mean ... "

"He'd probably help us. He's probably dead good at fixin' things." Her voice wavered. Spig frowned. He never used to know what to do when girls cried, but he'd seen Donna cry before, lots of times, and shutting up and listening usually worked.

She paused, trying to compose herself. "We sort of ... we had a bit of a row."

"Bastard. D'you want me to get him?"

She laughed, in spite of herself. "It weren't him, it were me. I said he were too good for me and he got dead narked."

"He doesn't think he's too good for you, then?"

"No, I told you, he's not like that." Her eyes filled this time. "It's just, he's got all these ideas and plans, all these things he wants to do."

"You've got ideas and plans and things you want to do." She had, more than anyone else he knew. It was one of the reasons lads liked her, her excitement for life. One of the reasons he liked her was when she wasn't feeling excited, she could tell him the truth. "Can't you do them with him?"

She shook her head. "It's not the same. We're not the same. I know there's gonna to be a time when he's not around anymore and it really hurts to think about, it hurts in here." She pressed her hand to her chest, her face crumpling. Spig said nothing. He wanted to find this posh bastard and take him apart just for existing. "Because when he's gone," Donna wept, "I'll have nothing."

He blurted - "You'll have me."

She looked at him, and he knew she understood exactly what he meant, and he had to pretend he meant something else again.

He cleared his throat. "And this place. Be a palace by then. What more could you want, your best mate and somewhere safe to stay?"

Her gaze travelled across the damp and flaking walls to the dirt encrusted window sill, tendrils of creeper twining in through the cracks, to the ceiling, a large chunk of it lying on the flags below, to the greasy, grubby armchair and the two-bar fire which was never going to heat anything. She swallowed.

"Okay."

He started to smile. "We're gonna do this?"

"Yeah why not?" She sniffed. Rallied. Smiled waterily at him across the room. "'Course we're gonna do it. You and me, Spig of the Dump. With bells on."

Nine

Kershaw's Building lay a five minute walk from the centre of Rapton on the Manchester Road, a long, straight litter strewn road heavy with traffic and populated with chippies and shabby newsagents, bookies and pubs. Another mile or two towards the city and there were second hand car dealerships, Indian take-aways, branches of Netto and Lidl. Vince kept saying he should move premises but Todd knew Kershaw's Building would sit at the Rapton end of the Manchester Road until Vince sold it on or closed it down. It was something to do with pride – being hard enough to establish and successfully run a business in the rougher part of town - and something to do with permanence. Both of these mattered a lot to Vince.

Todd entered the site through the main gate, skirting the path of an oncoming forklift truck, its driver raising a hand in greeting, past the workshops and the timber yard, past the warehouses packed with machinery and bags of sand and aggregates, with bricks and blocks, pipes, tools, tiles. Todd had always understood perfectly the attraction of building, of using your hands instead of your brain, seeing an end result for hours of labour. He'd even done a few basic jobs himself, under Vince's guidance. It just wasn't where his heart lay. He climbed the metal staircase up to the office, which was unlocked but empty, glancing at the naked breasts of Miss November as he opened the mini-fridge under the counter and took out a can of Red Bull. At the back of the room was a low, leather swivel chair Vince had once appropriated from a house clearance and he dropped down into it, resting his heels on a corner of a table, swivelling back and forth and observing the chaos.

Vince had never been keen on paperwork, which was why Sheryl had come into their lives in the first place. Having initially hired her to take on the administrative side of the business, within a few months she had also taken on Vince himself. Now her role was executed neatly and efficiently from her PC in the study at home – partly, Todd thought, because the barn conversion was a far more pleasing environment than the builder's yard, but also because as their marriage wore on Vince needed somewhere to escape to, and having her tucked quietly away in the hillside suited them both. To avoid her dropping in unannounced, he had begun taking all the paperwork home for her to deal with there, and his office had lapsed into the comforting masculine confusion it had always been. Todd had had his best talks with Vince in the jumbled warmth of this room. It was probably why Vince had summoned him here now.

After half an hour or so, by which time he was longing in spite of the Red Bull to sleep, the door blew open and was pushed shut. Vince walked to his desk, picked up a handful of papers, glanced over them, said "Bloody 'ell" and sat down. Glimpsed Todd's feet up on the table. "Oh, you're here, are you?" As if he hadn't texted in the middle of Todd's Maths lesson to demand it.

"Yeah," Todd responded.

"Could've done with you here at half-term, sorting all this bloody mess out for me."

"Thought that was Sheryl's job."

Vince flicked him a look. "Fancy a brew?"

"I'm fine, thanks."

Vince made himself a mug of tea, resumed his seat. "What's going on with you then, Todd?"

Todd shrugged.

"Only I've had a call from school. Nice woman. Said you'd had 'a bit of a meltdown' in class."

"Yeah. Sort of." He didn't blame Miss Somers. You couldn't have hulking great lads skriking their eyes out and not try to help. "Just felt a bit sort of ... low."

Vince surveyed him. "Is it owt to do with that lad who died?"

It would be so easy, Todd thought, to pretend it was. To blame it all on whatever it was that had happened to Cal. But he couldn't be so dishonest. "No."

Not the answer he'd been hoping for. Vince sighed. "Sheryl

... I know she can be difficult ... "

Todd said nothing. He picked up a hacksaw from jumble of tools in front of him and ran its narrow blade back and forth against the edge of the table.

Vince tried again. "Things can seem much worse than they are at your age. I remember when I was fifteen or sixteen, my dad used to get right up my nose. I thought he was a right tosser. It was only when I got older that - "

"Why," Todd interrupted, still sawing "are you telling me what you were like when you were my age? It's not going to be hereditary or anything, is it? We're nothing to do with each other."

Vince paused, stung. "That's a bit harsh – "

"It's true."

He lost patience. "Now look here, Todd. I've had enough of this attitude. I'm the closest thing you've got to a parent and all right, I might not be the dad you'd have wanted, but I'm all you've got. I've done my best since your mum died. You know that. I don't deserve you being shitty with me."

"And I don't deserve you being shitty with me." He sawed harder as his throat clogged again. "You *were* like a dad to me for a bit, and then you married her. Now it's all about what she wants. I don't matter any more. She wants to go on holiday without me, so that's what you're doing. Every time we have a row you take her side. After mum, I had this fragment of a family and now I don't even have that. I'm on my own."

Vince took a breath. "You're not on your own."

"I am."

"Todd will you put the bloody hacksaw down."

He threw it aside. "I'm on my own because everyone says, 'you're Vince Kershaw's lad', and I'm not." He was going to cry again. Shit. Fuck. He clenched his jaw hard.

Vince said quietly, "Well you are, in a way. Everything I've done for you, it's the same as I'd have done if you were my own lad. That's how I think of you. Not just as Eileen's lad, but as mine too. I have Sheryl to mind as well now, and I know she's not easy, but I don't think any less of you for it."

Silence.

Todd said unsteadily, "Sorry."

"Listen - "

Todd pushed up from the swivel chair. His skull was pounding. He couldn't talk about this anymore, said instead, "You've never heard of anyone called Stephen and Claudia, have you? Those two names together, like they were a couple?"

Vince was confused. "What? No."

"Right." He stood, head bowed for a minute, trying to gather some semblance of control. "It's nothing against you, Vince. It's not ... I don't ... " He stopped, his throat working. They told him at school he was bright and articulate, and yet he couldn't string a few words together when it mattered most. "Shit. Sorry."

"It's all right." Vince, full as Todd knew him to be of guilt and regret and exasperated sympathy, was at a loss. "It'll be all right, lad."

Todd winced. They were the only words of comfort Vince had ever been able to find. He couldn't remember a single time they'd been proved true.

Leigh settled her Year 7s into the auditorium-style seating she had created in her classroom during break, allowing her little tribe of actors time to prepare. They had been studying a modern version of *Pyramus and Thisbe*, each small group allotting parts, learning lines, collecting together costumes and props and now taking it in turns to perform their scenes. Leigh clasped a clipboard with details of the marks she had so far assigned each child on the basis of effort, team-work and behaviour, took her seat at the centre of the first row of chairs and called, "Ready?"

They trooped in, six eleven and twelve year old children, stood in front of the board to enact a story from Shakespeare with thick Lancashire accents and prepubescent sensibilities. Several times Leigh pressed her lips together to keep from laughing when she shouldn't. From the first she was bowled over by their seriousness, their capability, their evident hard work. And then came the scene with the Wall.

EXCLUDED

A child almost as tall as Leigh planted himself centre-stage, right arm extended, first finger and thumb forming an oval chink. On one side of him the smallest Year 7 boy Leigh had ever seen stood as high on tip-toe as he could manage and on the other a bulky sensible girl bent her knees to reach the hand. They chirruped and growled their lines. A chair squeaked. Someone giggled. The Wall stifled a sneeze. Then the little boy, still on pointe, offered his rosebud mouth to the chink and began to sing. It was James Blunt's *You Are Beautiful*, sung so appropriately beautifully and with such feeling the room stilled. Tears sprang to Leigh's eyes as she watched his face, pinched with concentration, listened to his clear, lilting voice. It was so rare and moving and surreal a moment after the last weeks of menace and violence, in this atmosphere of ebbing shock, she could scarcely believe it was happening. The child, having reached the end of the song and overcome his self-consciousness and the pain in his toes for as long as he possibly could, dropped down. Leigh led the standing ovation.

"And that," she said, "is why I'm a teacher."

Everyone laughed. Stephen, smiling, handed her a glass of wine. "I hope you were filming it."

"I should have been, shouldn't I? We could have used it as part of our promotional package for Open Evenings."

She was saying all the right things, Finn thought. Stephen loved anything which cast the school – and therefore himself - in a good light. But better still, in his eyes, Leigh was not saying these things to win Stephen's approval; she was saying them because she believed them. He gazed at her as she talked, her long hair rippling to her waist, her slender curves within her strapless, knee-length blue silk dress. Desire had been his instinctive response when he'd been admiring her from afar and it seemed taking her to bed most nights now served only to fan the flames. He was having to work hard at concentrating on anything else; if he let slip, for one moment, his focus on teaching or driving or whatever it was he was supposed to be doing, there she was. Naked, usually. Half-naked. Kissing him, her hand sliding down his groin. Not that he was deriving from it anything other than absolute pleasure but at the same time he understood how much more there was going on here than being achingly, insatiably consumed with lust. He loved that she was smart and positive and nobody's fool, that she was compassionate and sane and made him laugh. That he had to be with her if not all day, then at least part of every day. That it seemed, miraculously, that she wanted to be with him too. He half-smiled, watching her, wonder and pride and longing all fighting it out for first place.

"She is lovely," Claudia agreed, beside him.

He laughed, embarrassed. "I'm so transparent?"

"Oh yes." She smiled. "I wouldn't worry about it. It's very charming. Another drink?"

"I'm driving."

"Ah. Another soft drink?"

He went with her into the kitchen, which like all the rooms in the Lords' house seemed to be rolling acres of comfortable, expensively furnished space. In the vast hall, a central wooden staircase rose from the polished floor to a galleried landing. The drawing room's large stone fireplace was flanked by two enormous, tapestry covered couches, heavy crewel-work curtains screening out the dark evening, thick wool rugs spreading over cream carpet. Every brass, wooden and glass surface gleamed. In the kitchen low lights beneath the cherrywood wall units shone down on granite empty of the usual culinary detritus but displaying arranged bowls of fruit, selections of oils, a considerable collection of alcohol. From the Aga-style range the smell of cooking was tantalising. Finn laughed again. "This is an amazing house."

"Thank you. Mortgaged, I might add, to the hilt."

Yeah, mine's mortaged to the hilt, he thought. It doesn't look like this. Was this what the responsibility of headteachership bought you?

"We've been very lucky," Claudia went on. "Bought at the right times, sold at the right times. Anyone would have thought we knew what we were doing. Inherited at the right times too, sadly. When you lose people you love it's not what's upper-most in your mind, is it, the money?"

He looked sympathetic. "No."

She met his eyes. She was a glamorous woman, he thought. Bobbed wheat-blonde hair, cool grey eyes, her air of capable good-humour. Why was it, when there were clearly so many calm, sensible women in the world, he had once had a penchant for the fragile and the unstable? "Now then," she said. "A soft drink that doesn't make you gag."

Back in the drawing-room Leigh and Stephen were also discussing the house. What other subjects sprang so easily to mind? Finn wondered. Anarchy in the classrooms? The suspicious death of one of your pupils?

"How," Leigh was saying, gesturing towards the many framed photographs of two cherubic blonde children, "do you manage to have such a pristine and beautiful house when you also have a family?"

"Lucie and Henry are seven and nine now," Claudia explained, dismissive of any part she might play. "It was much more of an effort when they were smaller."

"Nonsense." Stephen grinned. "Claudia runs this house with military precision. It's like living with Baron Von Trapp. She blows a whistle, we all jump."

"Oh shut up," his wife replied, also grinning. "Excuse me, I need to go and dabble in the kitchen."

"Can I help?" Leigh asked

"Not at all. Not much to do." She departed, elegantly.

"Let me put some music on." Stephen moved with energy towards a cupboard which, it was revealed, contained an alphabetically arranged collection of CDs. "Who do you like?"

They exchanged glances. "Oh, we like everyone," Finn said.

"I always quite fancied Kirsty MacColl. Do you remember her, or is she before your time?"

"I remember her. She did *Fairytale of New York* with The Pogues," Leigh said.

"She did indeed." He slipped the CD into the machine. "Music from our youth, it never leaves us, does it?" It provided an unexplored and rich seam of conversation, and they mined it tirelessly until Claudia blew the metaphorical whistle which took them to the table.

It was not, Finn thought while he ate and drank, that he was seeing a different Stephen Lord this evening. Rather, it felt as though he were seeing the man behind the office. A relaxed, urbane, family man with a love of cricket and good wine and off-the-wall American television drama. A man he could like. A man who could be glimpsed, in flashes and if you were perceptive enough, sometimes at school. But the responsibility he insisted on bearing entirely alone had placed a barrier between him and his staff, his humanitarianism seen as a weakness so great he was regarded by them as a failure as a headteacher. It didn't have, Finn mused, to be the case.

" … have you taught before?" Leigh was asking as he zoned back into the conversation.

"Before Rapton, I was Deputy Head at St Thomas' in Halifax. Before that, Head of Department at Gilderdale High near Warrington, where I'd come in as Second in Department and before that … " Stephen paused, minimally. "Before *that*, I was a classroom teacher at the coal face of West Park."

"Really? You taught at West Park?"

"I did. It was not then the school it is today. Would that I could say the same of Rapton." He topped up Leigh's and Claudia's glasses.

"Rapton will get better," Finn predicted.

Claudia said drily, "When?"

Her husband cast her a glance.

"No really," she insisted. "I know I keep saying this, but you won't change my mind. The years you've put into that place. When is it ever going to get any better? The only way that will happen is if you swap its catchment area. Introduce an entry exam."

Stephen sighed.

Finn looked at her, bemused. He said, levity masking his reproof, "Are you saying the children of Rapton aren't worth educating?"

She matched his tone. "I'm saying education is a privilege that some of the inmates of Rapton don't deserve."

"It isn't a privilege. It's a right." Finn was appalled. Surely, being Stephen's wife, she didn't need this pointing out? "And those children who appear to be least deserving are actually those who need the education we provide in school the most, because God knows no one else in their lives will supply them with it."

Stephen was conciliatory. "It is a right, but it's one of the few of their rights in which they aren't interested. And as for making it better, there are no easy answers, are there? We need to have faith that under our governance things will improve or give up and go home."

"Or find a job in a better school," Claudia murmured.

"Surrender, you mean? Wash our hands of them?" Stephen shook his head. "You might as well quit teaching altogether."

"Now there's a thought," Finn agreed, deciding to be a good dinner guest and go with appeasement. "What would you do?"

Stephen had clearly thought about this. "Captain the England cricket team. Buy a chateau in France with its own vineyard."

"And Finn could travel there and write about it," Leigh joined in. "And I could renovate it for you."

"Really?" Claudia was interested. "You're into property development?"

The conversation changed course once more. Claudia urged them all to second helpings, emptying the white porcelain serving dishes ranged along the middle of the table, suggested a pause before dessert for which they were all, replete with generous portions of good food, thankful. Leigh helped to clear the table. Would have offered to help wash up, had she not spotted the dish-washer. "Is he still idealistic, Finn?" Claudia asked her as they stacked plates, scraped away sauce.

"He gets as fed up as anyone," Leigh admitted. "But yes, he believes in what he does."

"So does Stephen, unfortunately." She paused. "And how about you, are you settling in at Rapton?"

"Gradually. It's been a bit - challenging this term but … " she let the lid of the bin close, pushed the cupboard door to with her hip. "I don't want to tempt fate, but it feels as if we're over the worse of it."

"Because a teacher is in hospital and a boy has died?"

Leigh hesitated, suddenly discerning the current of bitterness running beneath her hostess' poise. How could you be married to the person most accountable for the appalling behaviour of his school's pupils and see the effect it was having on him, and not be angry? She wasn't sure how to respond. "Well – "

"I think," Claudia said, "it sounds like hell. I don't know how any of you bear it." She took a breath. "I can't say this to Stephen, not very often anyway, because it's not helpful and the last thing he needs is antagonism from me, but it seems to me that some of the pupils at that school are vicious little thugs who should be removed from society and save us all a lot of pain." She closed the door of the dish-washer with a bang. "Now. Dessert." She took a cake slice from a drawer and her hand, Leigh observed, was trembling.

Stephen too had noticed Finn watching Leigh. He and Claudia had been around Leigh's age when they had first met; he remembered very clearly looking at his wife as Finn was looking at Leigh tonight, wanted suddenly to say to him – *go for it, it's the most important thing in the world, loving someone who loves you.* But how deranged would that sound? Especially coming from him.

He had envied Finn in the past for his popularity with both staff and pupils and for the apparent ease with which he conducted all aspects of his life. He had, variously, envied his ability to inspire a class, that he always seemed to know instinctively the right thing to do, that his hair was dark and not prematurely grey. Tonight, and he had no doubt it was another depressing sign of incipient middle-age, he envied him being at the beginning of something. Not halfway through with a dozen doors closed to him, not tired and disillusioned and anchored by the consequences of his own mistakes.

He couldn't quite get a grip on why he should be feeling this, not now when school was relatively calm and academic progress was being made and his career might actually be on an upward trend again. Perhaps it was just, after the term they'd just had, that he was tired. Which really was another depressing sign of the onset of middle-age.

He cleared his throat to embark upon the proposition which had hit him like a blinding light a day or so ago. "I wanted to talk to you about something. What are your thoughts on next year?"

Finn looked intrigued. "Do you know more about my options than I do?"

"Well, Brian Wilson won't be coming back. I spoke to him this week, he's not risking another heart attack. We'll have a vacancy for a Deputy Head, which we'll have to advertise. If it goes internally, which I wouldn't mind and it might well, that will mean a vacancy for an Assistant Head."

"What are you saying?"

"That I'd like you to apply."

Finn was flattered, surprised. "I haven't done my NPQH."

"It needn't matter. You could do it in post. What do you think?"

"I … With what responsibility?"

"Negotiable. Finn. The staff like you, the children like you. You're a natural in areas I struggle with and the support you've given me this term has been tremendous. To be honest, I've never had the problems with communication and staff confidence that I have at Rapton at any other school. I suspect I'm not much of a team player, but it shows a lot more than I'd like it to. Which is where you come in. You have a talent with people which I should have, and it seems I don't."

Finn shook his head. "Don't take it so much to heart. It's been a god-awful term and things have come to a head, that's all."

"Well thank you." He paused. "Also, the committee for the New Curriculum has invited me to chair one of the steering groups. Obviously, I'm delighted, there're important initiatives involved, and it would be exciting for Rapton to be in on them from the beginning. But it'll mean further demands on my time, and I'll need to delegate rather more than I do."

"That's great news. Congratulations."

Stephen hammered the point home. "I'd like you on board."

"Thank you. Can I think about it?"

"I hope you will." Stephen smiled. "Another drink?"

"Please." Finn's humour was dry. "I need it."

The best thing, Spig realised, about acting like a dick at school was that when you didn't turn up to their lessons the teachers were so relieved they didn't bother finding out why. Didn't even bother reporting it, if you'd popped in to morning registration and then buggered off again. He wished he'd twigged this years ago. Would have saved everyone a lot of grief. Maybe if he'd had this place then, stuff to do that was real and meant something, maybe he wouldn't have acted like a dick at school in the first place.

He didn't know when he'd worked so hard. Clearing the place out hadn't been too bad. Bits of the windows had fallen off when he'd wrenched them open, but the house smelt better now. He'd swept up all the crap, nicked some disinfectant, cleaned it all up as best he could, an angry red rash on his hands to show for it. He'd had a go at filling in the holes with some plaster he'd found lurking in the shed at the home. It didn't look great but at least they weren't holes anymore. Sometimes it had got so late when he'd been working he hadn't bothered going back, slept here on an old mattress he'd heaved sweating through the fields one day and dropped with a thud in one of the upstairs rooms, where the damp wasn't so bad. He'd lit a few candles and listened to the radio and it had been quite cosy. No electricity, no water, but people lived without those, didn't they? In Africa and stuff?

And Donna came, whenever she could, trailing pots of paint and charity shop junk, curtains and cushions and bits of crap, a sheet and a threadbare purple and gold quilty thing for the mattress. She wore old clothes and tied back her hair and slapped paint onto the flaking walls and usually they had a laugh. Took it in turns to trek back to the shop for cans and crisps, for bottled water and lo-price bog roll. Not that the bog worked. They had to go in the grass and the nettles round the back of the house, creating their own stink. "We're marking our territory, like animals," he'd said, and she'd thrown a bog roll at him.

He sat on the bedroom floor trying to work out how to fix the old camping-stove he'd picked up outside a secondhand shop yesterday, Donna splashing paint across the opposite wall, spring sunshine lying in warm bars across the splintering floorboards. 'Right Said Fred' were playing on the radio and she was singing along, bopping her little bum in time to the music.

"'Deeply dippy 'bout the curves you got, deeply hot, hot for the curves you got ... oh my love, can't make head nor tail of passion ... '"

Spig wished she wouldn't sing about passion and wiggle her arse at him. He said, "Give it a rest, Don."

She laughed. "I'm a better singer than you, any day."

"That's not sayin' much, is it? You don't serenade him, do you? Your bloke?" Spig pronounced the final two words with contempt. He couldn't bear the thought of him, hated it whenever she talked about him, but it was like picking a scab, he couldn't resist.

She smiled in the stupid dopey way she did whenever he was mentioned. "He says I'm dippy."

"Nice of him." He prised a switch at the side of the stove too hard, broke it. "Dippy? What sort of wanky word's that?"

She glared at him. She'd spattered herself with paint as well as the wall and the glare didn't quite come off. "It's not wanky. It means, like, daft."

He pretended to be concentrating on the camping-stove. "Why's he callin' you daft, then?"

She paused. "'Cos of you," she said quietly. Not quietly enough.

"You what?"

"'Cos I got your name wrong."

He gave up all pretence of anything. "What you talkin' to him about me for?"

"I wasn't. He doesn't know who you are really. I was just saying you're me mate and I call you Spig, like 'Spig of the Dump' that we read at school when I were a kid. And he laughed."

He bridled. "He were laughin' at me?"

"At *me*. I hadn't remembered it right. It's not 'Spig of the

Dump', it's 'Stig'. That's why he said I were dippy. 'Cos it were one of me favourite books and I couldn't even get the name right." She stood back to look at the wall. *"I don't know if I like this colour. What do you think?"*

"It's fuckin' pink, Donna. What am I gonna like about it?"

She turned, the brush dripping spots of paint onto the floor. *"What's the matter with you? You've been like this all day."*

He said nothing. She rested the brush on the rim of the tin and went to sit next to him on the floor. *"Spig."*

"Stig, you mean."

"Nah, you'll always be Spig."

"Great."

"What is it?"

It was lots of things. A million things. He chose one. *"Me sister's pregnant."*

"Ha! You'll be an uncle."

"Shut up."

"It's all right though, isn't it? She's married and she's dead old."

He looked at her askance. *"She's nineteen and she's shacked up with some waster. It's not like roses round the door or nothin'."*

"Yeah, but ... " Donna drew her knees to her chest, rested her chin on them. *"It'll be nice though. When she has the baby. You don't have to be anything special then. Babies love you no matter who you are."*

He snorted. *"Dunno about dippy. You're fuckin' mental, you."*

"Shut up."

"And you've got paint on your nose."

She cuffed the back of his head.

"Oi!" He grabbed her arm, held onto it, noticed how his hand closed right around her bones, noticed the fine hairs, the delicacy of her wrist. It would take almost nothing to pull her close. To hold her to him.

Except if she yanked away he'd never be able to look at her again.

"Your turn," he said brusquely, releasing her. *"Fags and*

coke. Go."

Ten

It was a little after ten and Stephen was at his desk contemplating his future in education with renewed hope when Barbara rang from Reception. "DS Whelan's here to see you. Shall I bring him down?"

"Of course." Stephen crossed his office towards the door, met them on the threshold. "Good morning."

"Good morning," Whelan replied as Barbara melted away. "Sorry to disturb you, Mr Lord."

"Not at all. Come in." Recovering from his surprise, he stood aside. "What can I do for you?"

"It won't take long. Something's come to my attention. I just thought I'd see if you could shed any light."

Stephen gestured towards the chair on the visitor's side of his desk. "Please." He took his own seat, tried to read the detective's expression. Could not get past Official. "Are you any closer to knowing what happened to Callum? Were the children able to be of any help when you came into school?"

"Not as much as they'd have liked to have been. No serious leads, I'm afraid." Mike Whelan sat down. "But I'd like to know a bit more about your relationship with Callum Bywater."

Stephen frowned. "It was what you know it to have been. I was his headteacher, I'd known him since I came to the school when he was in Year 7. He had always been a difficult pupil, disruptive, aggressive. He resented me generally because I represented authority, and specifically because I was the end of the line when it came to discipline - if he'd made it as far as me it meant he was in serious trouble, with serious consequences. He didn't like that, facing consequences. He thought it was beneath him."

Whelan nodded. "And had there been serious consequences, for the trouble he was in?"

"He was looking at an exclusion, if he'd continued the way he was going. He was looking at more than that if Alan

Jackson had accused him of assault."

"So it would be fair to say that before he died, Callum might have been a bit wound up? A bit on edge?"

"Yes. It would be fair to say that. But wound up and on edge as a result of his own actions." Stephen frowned. "Aren't we going over old ground here? We had conversations similar to this the week Callum died."

"Similar, yes. But I have to be as sure as I can what happened to Callum that night, and there's something I need to follow up." DS Whelan paused. "Some new evidence has come to light."

It was the word 'evidence' that did it. Some pivotal change, Stephen under-stood, had occurred to swing him from being part of the scenery of Callum's life into the foreground. He said, "What evidence?"

"Callum Bywater's mobile phone has been handed in to us. And the last number he called before he died was yours."

Stephen blinked.

"Do you remember that call, Mr Lord?"

"I've never taken any call from Callum. Ever. Anywhere. You mean, my home number? How would he know what that is?"

"Would be one of my next questions."

Stephen's mind raced. "I don't know. We're ex-directory."

"Might there be a list, here somewhere, of the staff's home phone numbers?"

"Well there is, of course, Barbara – our bursar - has one in the office."

"And does she ever leave that office unattended?"

Stephen's shoulders sagged. "She does, yes. The list's pinned up on the wall behind her desk."

Whelan sighed. "I might advise you to take more precautions with your security, only it would seem a little late. However. Callum phoned you that night and you didn't speak to him?"

"We weren't at home," Stephen remembered. "What time was the call?"

"Just after six."

"We'd already left for the airport by then. We went to Italy at half-term, our flight was eight forty-five on the Friday night."

"And you left the house … ?"

"Six. No later because as I'm sure you know, you have to be at the airport two hours before European flights now." He frowned, thinking back. "I could ask Claudia, but I checked the messages, when we got home, as I always do. There was nothing from Callum."

"Not even just the sound of someone hanging up?"

"Perhaps. I don't remember. Lots of people do that, don't they?"

"They do." He shifted in his seat. "Mr Lord, why would Callum have wanted to talk to you?"

"I honestly don't know. In fact, he wouldn't have wanted to talk to me."

"Not even, perhaps, to find out whether Mr Jackson had remembered what had happened that day on the stairs?"

Stephen considered, but only briefly. "Not even then. Lads like Callum don't ring the headteacher at home to find out whether they're going to be punished for something they haven't done. They keep as far away as possible. We'd had a meeting, Callum and his uncle, and Finn Macallister and I. We'd talked about how to proceed. It seemed … resolved. As far as it could be." He shook his head. "It's something of a mystery."

"It is."

Stephen paused. "Is it possible that this information could remain confidential? It's just that I hate to think what the pupils would make of it."

"It'd put you in a difficult position, I understand." Whelan surveyed him. "I won't be telling anyone I shouldn't. Thank you, for your time, Mr Lord. That's all for the moment."

"No problem." Stephen stood up. "If there's anything else I can help with, let me know." After he'd shown Whelan to the door he remained there for a minute, staring down the empty carpeted corridor to Reception. It was time, he thought, that they all started leaving the death of Callum Bywater behind them.

"*'False face must hide what the false heart doth know.'*"

"Yes." Finn took a breath. "Well. Thank you, Whitney and – um – Giorgio. That was an interesting take on Act 1 Scene 7 of *Macbeth*." And a convincing argument for abandoning the teaching of Shakespeare to anyone with a CAT score of less than a hundred. Books were dropped to the desks, arms stretched, groans emitted.

"Shakespeare's well gay."

"Didn't understand a word of that. What were all that about nipples?"

"I hate Shakespeare, me. It's proper boring."

"Why d'they have to talk like that? Why can't they talk normal?"

Finn, screwing his own courage to the sticking-place, stood up, surveyed his class of cocky, street-wise fourteen year olds. "They talk like that because that was how people spoke in Elizabethan times. Not exactly like that, perhaps, but close enough. In another four hundred years, the way we speak and write now will probably just as incomprehensible to people as Shakespeare is to you – us, now. He didn't write it like that to annoy you."

Grunts, sighs, muttered curses.

"Essentially what's happening is Macbeth's having second thoughts about murdering Duncan and Lady Macbeth is telling him not to be such a wuss, okay? Opening speech, page nineteen. He's saying, it's better to get it over and done with …"

"So what's that about a poisoned chalice? I thought they stabbed him."

"He does stab him. That bit means if you teach crime , 'bloody instructions', to someone, or commit a crime, there's a chance that crime will be carried out against you. You're drinking the poison you handed to someone else."

"He's saying the same thing twice then."

"Well yes. Shakespeare does that."

"So is it like, 'what goes around comes around'?"

"Yes!" He could feel his jaw dropping. "Exactly. It's just like that."

"Or 'live by the sword, die by the sword'?"

"That too." Finn looked at them, impressed and taken aback. Someone cackled.

"See, sir, we're not that thick."

Their exodus, when the bell rang, was thunderous. The door banged shut behind them. Finn, appreciating the tailing into silence, piled the tattered copies of *Macbeth* onto a shelf, picked up a paper aeroplane from the floor and sailed it into the bin. Coffee, he thought. Leigh.

His door opened again. "Do you have a minute?" Stephen asked. "I know you're free next period."

"Sure."

He sat on a front desk, read Finn's notes on the whiteboard. "The Scottish Play and Year 9. A good combination?"

"Better than you might expect. Envy, greed, murder, ghosts. They love it."

Stephen smiled faintly. "It's murder and ghosts I've come to talk to you about."

Finn, quitting his half-hearted efforts at tidying, turned towards him. "Go on."

He paused. "At the risk of sounding callous, I want to try to minimise the effect of Callum's death on Year 11."

Finn considered. "I understand why, but I'm not sure you can. The shock's still there among the kids, even for those who disliked or maybe feared him. Especially for those – " he thought of Todd " – who'd grown up with him. They're all still reeling."

"Oh of course. Inevitably they'll feel the shock and the loss and I do think we've recognised that, even validated it, in school. But I'd also like to try to move on, refocus their attention. It's not as if their attention didn't need refocusing before Callum died."

"True," Finn conceded. "Though I don't think we're going to be able to draw a line under this for some time, at least not as long as the police investigation's on-going. If and when the truth of what happened ever emerges, and it comes to court, if it does, it could be months."

"But just because we're still dealing with the aftermath, it shouldn't mean the children should have to. We should be helping them by trying to maintain some level of normality."

"I wasn't aware we'd ever achieved a level of normality," Finn said wryly. "Yes, we could try. But you know, distracting them with the talent show and celebrating our sporting triumphs is only going to go so far. He'll still be there."

Stephen tried a smile. It didn't quite come off. "Banquo as played by Callum Bywater. The spectre at the feast."

Finn caught the shadow of despair in Stephen's voice, was suddenly aware, as he had been at his home on Saturday night, of him as a man perhaps not so very different from himself. "Are you all right?"

In that moment, the atmosphere between them changed, as if the genuine concern in his question had opened up a fatal chink in Stephen's defence. Finn watched as he pushed up from the desk, went to the window. Its view was a different angle on that from Finn's apartment, less panoramic at this first floor level, the enclosure of hills suffocating. He said, as though from a great distance, "Have you ever felt cursed?"

Finn thought of his marriage, of Carla's unstinting efforts to do him harm. "Yes, as a matter of fact."

"You spend years doing penance for a sin you didn't even know you were committing but you never truly get absolution. It's a black shadow at your heels for the rest of your life, you can't ever shake it off. Why is that? Our pupils complain tirelessly about what is and isn't fair and sometimes I want to shake them, tell them, *you haven't a clue, when it comes to what's fair, you've no idea what you're talking about*." He rubbed his eyes, sighed heavily. "Sorry. Sorry, Finn. You don't need to hear all this."

Finn thought that most people didn't drop hints if they didn't want them to be picked up, that they didn't look weary and disheartened if there wasn't something wrong. He said tentatively, "Why do you feel cursed?"

Stephen looked embarrassed. "Melodramatic of me. I apologise."

"Sometimes it's how it feels." He decided to trade a confidence of his own. "I felt cursed by my ex-wife."

"You have an ex-wife?"

"I don't know where she is now, how she is. Only that life with her became a certain kind of hell and there were times when I thought I must have offended the gods to have deserved it. It feels like melodrama because sometimes that's what it is."

Stephen nodded. "I did something stupid and reckless many years ago. Before Claudia, before I'd made any headway in teaching. And ... recently the outcome of what I did has come back to bite me." He stopped.

Finn, thinking of his own youthful propensity for acting like a prick, said, "Aren't you being too hard on yourself? We've all done something we don't think we deserve to be forgiven for."

Stephen was silent. He looked in the grey morning light much older than his years. "Anyway." His smile was thin. "Where were we? Year 11. Any suggestions?"

Finn regarded him steadily. What was going on here? This was not the Stephen of Saturday night, relaxed and spirits high, more or less offering him a job. Required to shift gear, he said carefully, "All right. It might not be my place to say this, but I mean it with the best intentions: while you're planning how to refocus Year 11, you might want to give some thought, short-term as well as long-term, to staff morale."

Stephen, rallying, looked surprised. "I'm aware it's an issue, but it's been made very clear to me that none of them is interested in anything I have to say. Everything I've suggested over the years has been met with so much rancorous cynicism I'd more or less given up."

Finn smiled. "What is it you keep telling us? Everyone deserves a second chance and we should never give up on anyone?"

"Never thought I'd be applying the Clean Slate Strategy to the staff." Stephen's smile was rueful. "Thanks. You're probably right. I'll give it some thought."

EXCLUDED

Looking out across the sea of assembled faces – adult ones, this time – Stephen wondered why it was that people went into teaching imagining that their day ended at half past three when the pupils' did and they could all go home immediately. He knew, from his years' experience of headship at Rapton and from the expressions of resentment that this was what many of his staff were thinking. He also knew that if he were to brook any sort of discussion of the matter, the word 'rights' would be thrown at him. He was heartily sick of people telling him what their rights were. Wouldn't the world be a better place, he thought, if we spoke not in terms of what our rights are, but in terms of what we have earned.

But as his gaze travelled from one to another, he realised that resentment and ill-humour were not written upon every face. Some were expectant, curious. One or two smiled. Stephen was surprised, almost caught off guard. Smiling in return, he raised his voice.

"Thank you for coming this afternoon, I'm sorry it was such short notice. I know you're all desperate to get off and I won't keep you long. There are two reasons I've called us all together. The first is that the police have now released Callum Bywater's body, and his funeral will take place next Friday. We will, of course, be sending representation from the school, that being myself and Finn. If anyone else would like to go, please let me know so we can arrange for your lessons to be covered. I'm sure a fair number of the children will also be going; it might be difficult to keep track of attendance on Friday, but these are … extenuating circumstances.

"The second thing I'd like to say is how grateful I am, in what has really been an extraordinarily difficult term, to you all for keeping things tight and pulling through the way you have. I walk around school now and things are more or less under control. I know immediately after the events of half term, the children were fairly quiet anyway, but they could have kicked off again and they haven't. The police presence in school was handled particularly well, I thought, and I am very thankful for the support you have given, to me, to each other, and to those children who were upset by Callum's death.

"What I'd like to propose is that we end the term on a slightly higher note, if we can. I know you used to have a Christmas do here, and that that's rather fallen by the wayside in recent years, and I'm not so sure that's a good thing. It's probably too late to try to book anywhere – though if anyone knows otherwise, please let me know – but we could at least have an evening here. Day after the talent show might be best. Something fairly low-key, perhaps, but I'm happy to provide drinks, food, music, if you're interested … ?" He held his breath, surveying his staff. A murmur of surprise and approval was rippling around them. Wider smiles, now. More of them. "I'll take that as a yes?" He was smiling too, feeling quite moved, quite ridiculously relieved. "Let me know, if you've any thoughts."

The outraged resentment of the staff room was quelled. Not substantially, just enough to make a difference. Leigh, flicking through the contents of her pigeon-hole, heard approbation cautiously expressed, cynicism quashed, muttered and grudging words of praise.

"Over two years, we've waited for him to do something for us."

"Do you think he's finally realised how everyone feels?"

"He'll need nominating, for Headteacher of the Year. He'll need us behind him. Could be he's just realised that."

"Could be he's making the effort at last."

Leigh chewed the inside of her cheek to keep quiet. Listened to a half dozen more comments and said, half to herself, "Could be he's had as shitty a term as we all have and he's just trying to do something nice. He's trying to keep things calm, to be more approachable and to come down harder on the kids, which you were all desperate for him to do. It seems to be working. Give the guy a fucking break."

Silence, at least among those within hearing range. They melted away, as if she had expressed sympathy with the British National Party or exposed a breast.

Except for Finn, unexpectedly beside her. "Way to go,

Leigh," he said, with humour.

She smiled. "It's just, he's trying so hard and still they'll only give him an inch."

"That's teachers for you. To be fair, it's staff anywhere for you. I think Stephen's handling this better than anyone would have expected and they don't quite know how to deal with it. Not used to admitting respect, this lot. What are you doing now?"

"Aren't we going for a drink? It's Friday night."

"Sure. But I was thinking, just you and me? There's this place I know, blazing log fires, great food. I'll drive."

"No, you always drive so I can drink. It's my turn."

He smiled, and she wanted him to lean in and kiss her. But not in the staff room, even with everyone else gone home, even though every single one of them knew. Pleasure deferred, she was having to learn, working beside him every day, was all the sweeter.

The night was chill, frost icing the pavements by the time they arrived at the pub, its windows lit with red lanterns, heavy brocade curtains draping the stone walls. Once a coach-house, it was now an inn comprised of a series of alcove rooms, at either end log fires roaring from enormous hearths, tea-light candles on scrubbed wood tables surrounded by a mismatch of chairs and settles. The food was, as Finn had promised, very good. The wine was even better. "Have some," he urged her, halfway through his fourth large goblet. "We'll get a taxi home, pick the car up in the morning. I don't want to be drunk on my own."

"Tough. I have lots of work to do tomorrow and I won't be able to do it with a hang-over." She smiled sweetly at him and he groaned, took another swallow anyway.

"How's Todd Kershaw?"

"Withdrawn." She frowned, wondering whether to voice her suspicions. "He can't sleep, he tells me, he's emotional. It sounds like depression."

He nodded, "You could be right. He worries me, he's always been so level-headed, so laid-back. I'm slurring my words, aren't I?"

"Just a bit." She smiled. "What are we going to do about him?"

"Be vigilant, I guess. Be prepared to take things further if we have to. I know Vince, his step-dad. He's a decent bloke. Brought Todd up since his mum died."

"Did you know Todd then?"

"Yeah, he was in Year 7. He was so self-contained when it happened, so fragile. Broke your heart to look at him. He isn't related by blood to anyone he lives with. Imagine that. Vince is all he has."

"Mm, he told me. But Vince has remarried and Todd thinks she hates him."

Finn gestured, helpless. "And he's sensitive and vulnerable and one of his friends has just died. No wonder he's depressed. But Todd knows we're here if he wants to talk, and maybe he'll come through this by himself. I remember what it's like to be his age, everything so intense, such a big deal, even the trivial stuff."

She leaned her cheek on her hand, watching him, his eyes bright, his face slightly flushed. "What were you like then?"

He smiled. "A pain in the arse, probably. My dad was – still is – such a strong role model, head of the family, capable, successful. He's a financial consultant, climbs and abseils, excels at all that macho outward bound stuff even now. And he's a good man. An honourable man. It seemed such a lot to live up to. So of course I did the predictable thing and rebelled. Acted cool and tough, pretended to be sorted, self-conscious and needy as hell underneath. I was always much more relaxed around girls – less to prove, I guess. And maybe that's why I always went for the flaky ones, I could be strong for once, instead of this emotional, sensitive arty type. It took me a long time to realise that I didn't have to become my dad. That I could be myself and still be … worthwhile."

Moved as she always was by how easily he shared his feelings, exposed to her his vulnerability, she stroked his wrist, wanting to climb onto his lap and kiss him, slide her hand inside his shirt. "Don't drink anymore."

"Why? Is it because I'm rambling? I know, I'm sorry. I

always ramble when I'm drunk."

She smiled. "It's not the rambling."

At twilight on Monday, Stephen was standing on the floor of the Arts Theatre, gazing with mild concern at a couple of Year 11 boys hanging off the lighting tower. "All right up there?"

One of them looked down at him. The other, precariously balanced as he adjusted the angle of one of the spotlights, gave an acknowledging grunt. "Fine thanks sir," the first boy said. "Just trying to get these lights sorted for Friday."

The words *risk assessment* and *health and safety issues* floated through Stephen's mind like leaves on a river. "Be careful up there, lads."

"Yes sir." Said as though to an equal and with weary good humour. Friday night was the school talent show, an event being organised with wit, flair and the occasional diva style tantrum by the BTEC Performing Arts students as part of their final grade. Stephen liked pupils who were passionate about a subject. They almost invariably displayed maturity, self-motivation, enthusiasm and a positive approach to life which would serve them well. It was the apathetic and disenfranchised ones who did themselves and others most damage. But surely, he thought, even the apathetic and disenfranchised must love something. Perhaps he might make it the theme for next term. Find Your Passion, Find Your Future. He smiled at its intrinsic cheesiness, its potential for parody. Was Harness better than Find? Focus Your Passion?

"Stephen." Geraldine, his deputy head responsible for Teaching and Learning, standing beside him clutching a sheaf of papers. Geraldine was rarely to be seen without a sheaf of papers. Pale and parlously thin with close cropped brown hair and deep-set eyes, she resembled nothing so much as a ferret in human form. Anally retentive about assessments, reports, grades and data cross-referencing, she was also a disaster in the classroom. Which was probably why, Stephen reflected, she had been drafted onto the senior management team in the first place.

"Geraldine."

"Year 11 autumn term grades."

"Yes."

"Ten per cent up on our predicted A* - C s."

He looked at her. "You've added it up wrong."

"I haven't. I treble checked it."

"Ten per cent up. *This* term of all terms?" He shook his head. "Why?"

"Some of the children must have been working."

"Don't be silly."

She smiled. She had an unexpectedly twinkly smile. Could ferrets twinkle? he wondered. "It's across all the departments."

"It's a bloody miracle." He thought of his first steering-group meeting at the beginning of next month, chairing a discussion on the new curriculum. Of the possibility of no longer being the lowest performing school in the valley. Of the splintering of the Focus Group and the thawing - by a degree or two - of his staff. Maybe there was a chance, a small chance, that he could snatch triumph from the jaws of disaster and this wouldn't be the worst year of his life after all. He smiled at the cliché, his smile shrinking, as it always did, when he thought of Callum Bywater.

"So are you doing anything for this talent show?" Leigh asked Todd at registration on Wednesday as the message informing her that tickets were now sold out flashed up on her laptop.

"Just presenting," he said, as though it were the smallest and most thankless of tasks. "I'm not much good at the tech stuff."

She looked at him, sitting on the desk in front of her own, his bag still on his back as though he had no real intention of staying. He had been calmer so far this week but it seemed to her to be a fragile calm and he wore it as a shield. She could see it in his eyes, in his deliberate interaction with his form mates, his resolute equanimity whenever she spoke to him. Her misgivings weighed heavily, but she had briefed his step-father and Finn and what else could she do.

He saw her looking, said quietly, "I'm all right, miss."

The bell rang. "Off you go!" Leigh called unnecessarily, as

everyone stirred, slouched out of the room. Todd stayed where he was. "Thanks," he murmured. "You know, for … listening and stuff."

"Any time. It's what I'm here for."

"It's not though, is it? You're here to take the register and give out letters and make sure we've all got our ties done up. Anything more is down to you. So thanks, you know, for being bothered."

"Mr Macallister's bothered too."

"I know. He's sound." He paused. "Are you going, on Friday?"

"To the show, or … ?"

He shook his head.

She understood how Callum's funeral might loom as a monolith in his path, eclipsing not just the sun but any way forward. She wasn't sure she understood why. Or how, afterwards, anything would have changed. She said, "No. I didn't know Cal very well, and I need to stay here." She hesitated. "It's going to be a difficult day."

"Yeah." He glanced away. "Sort of why I can't get too excited about this talent show." He pushed up from the table. "See you later, miss."

In the doorway he stopped, turned back to her. "You don't know anyone called Stephen, do you?"

"What, apart from the Head?"

He stared at her.

She was puzzled. The name Stephen Lord was everywhere. Television interviews, newspaper articles, embossed in red upon the school's headed paper. "You knew Mr Lord's name is Stephen?"

Of course he had known. He'd always known, somewhere deep in the recesses of his memory. He just hadn't made the connection. He felt slightly dizzy. "Is he married?"

"Yes."

He could barely form the words. "What's her name?"

Leigh hesitated. It wasn't information which was hers to give, and she might not, to any other pupil. But this was Todd.

"Claudia," she said.

- *Hey Todd. Whatcha doin?*
- *Lying on my bed, missing you*
- *Come here for Christmas or New Year parents say is ok*
- *Can't*
- *Can't or don't want?*
- *Can't bad stuff happenin not good company just now*

Almost instantly his mobile buzzed. He spent a while persuading Christie that no, really, he was fine and he hadn't meant to scare her and it was just a combination of missing her and Vince and Sheryl being crap as usual. Just the usual torments. He wished fervently he could be as honest talking to her as he could writing onto a computer screen but reassuring the anxious little voice on the other end of the phone won out. Besides, what could she do? What difference would it make telling her when she was fifty miles away and couldn't put her arms around him? When she didn't have the answers any more than he did?

Because this was weird stuff. Or maybe it wasn't. He didn't trust his own judgement anymore. He kept trying to organise what he thought he knew, or suspected, or had heard into some kind of sense, but it kept slipping away from him. Cal had said Dean was looking for someone, that coming into school had freaked him out. That Dean had hit him. That it was pay-back time. And now Cal was dead and the last person he'd phoned before he died was Mr Lord. What was that about? Why would you phone your headteacher when you were up to your neck in trouble with him? When you hated him and called him a wanker and took every opportunity to annoy him? Maybe he'd been in some other sort of trouble, maybe he'd been ringing Stephen Lord for help. Maybe all that talk about risks and being sure of the odds had backfired on him somehow and Mr Lord was the only person who could sort it out. Would you go to him, if you were in trouble? Todd himself might, but he couldn't imagine Cal doing it. His headteacher'd be a very desperate last resort. Wouldn't he?

And while Todd knew there was no predicting Dean, that violence was a form of currency in some people's lives, and Cal's was no exception, somehow Dean hitting him felt ... wrong. He could understand how coming into school might freak someone like Dean out, and maybe he'd just been looking for one of his mates from the old days and found him. Cal talked a load of bull half the time about shit-stirring and pay-backs and wanting to be minted.

But Cal was dead.

He sat on the edge of his bed, hearing the silence of the house grow suddenly eerie. It had been dark and empty when he'd come in from his rehearsal for the talent show, everyone there pissed off at him because he'd only been going through the motions, and he'd been either umbilically attached to his Ipod or talking to Christie ever since. It was now almost nine o'clock. Not unknown for no one else to be back at this time, but not usual either. He opened his door, looked out into airy blackness. Not a sound.

As he flicked the light switch the landing appeared before him - pine linen chest, book shelf, armchair no one ever sat in, as bland and tidy as it always was. He listened harder, but still from the great reaches of the floor below there was only darkness.

And then, something.

A door closing, maybe.

"Vince?"

No response. He couldn't do it. Couldn't form her name. Called again, "Vince?"

Shit. What was the matter with him? He crossed the landing, flipping switches as he went, flooding the silence with light and shadows. Descending the oak staircase into the hall, he saw that every door leading off it was shut. Had every door been shut when he'd come home? He couldn't remember. Neither could he bring himself to open any of them.

Jesus Christ Todd get a grip.

Another sound. A familiar, identifiable sound. The kettle boiling.

He pushed into the kitchen. Sheryl in her Barbie pink tracksuit, pouring water into her teapot-for-one. "Jesus," he said under his breath. Aloud – "How long have you been home?"

"About fifteen minutes."

"Why didn't you answer, when I called?"

"You weren't calling me."

He chose not to respond to that. Instead he opened the fridge, took from it a can of Dr Pepper. "Where's Vince?"

"You know where he is. He's in Pontefract on a job. Staying overnight."

"Don't they have their own builders in Pontefract?" He had been going to add - *when's he back?* but couldn't bear to want even the answer to a question from her. He took his can into the utility room, stood it on the counter while he knelt on the tiled floor to drag the clothes he had shoved earlier into the washing machine back out again. Sheryl came to lean in the doorway with her mug of tea.

"I hope you're not thinking of tumble-drying any of that tonight."

He sorted the drying stuff from the non-drying stuff and rammed the former back in. Shut the door, turned the dial. Said tightly, "I need it for tomorrow. I'm going to a funeral, remember?"

"You're a teenager. All your clothes are black. No need to keep me up half the night with that thing going."

He looked at her in disbelief. The tumble dryer was almost soporific in its gentle chugging and swishing and her room was on the other side of the house.

"About time you had a bit more consideration for the other people." She took a detour from her well-worn path. "Anyway, he was a nasty little shit from what I've heard. Only his mother'll be mourning him."

He clenched his jaw. I've been here before, he thought. I've stuck up for Cal and ended up skriking. Well not in front of her. He pushed to his feet, took a swig of his drink, walked past her out of the utility room, back into the kitchen.

Sheryl swivelled on her heel. "Good mates with him, were

you? One of his gang?"

Todd ignored her.

"Because that'd be a real turn-up for the books, wouldn't it? Little Mr Perfect showing his true colours? About time Vince saw the side you show me. Then he'd know what you're really like."

Something held too tight for far too long snapped, releasing him. He spun back to her. "Why don't you ever talk to me like this in front of him? Then he'd know what *you're* really like!"

"So tell him." She looked at him with a mixture of triumph and complacency. "When he comes home tomorrow, you go and tell him – 'Sheryl can't stand the sight of me'. See what he says."

Todd's memory flashed snapshot through the years he'd spent with Vince playing Dad, his blustering kindness, his awkward affection. Then he thought of now, and all the allowances Vince wanted him to make for Sheryl, the endless injustices he expected him to bear. The holiday from which he'd been so heartlessly excluded.

Sheryl was watching him. "You see, it's your word against mine. Who will he want to believe? Who will he want to put first?"

"Well I know it's a long shot," Todd said bitterly, "but maybe the person he's brought up for the last ten years."

She laughed. "He doesn't care about you. Why would he care about you? You don't belong here. You're just some stray animal he can't bring himself to dump at the roadside. He's too soft, is Vince. I keep telling him."

He caught his breath. "I've lived here with him a lot longer than you have. He treats me like I'm like his own son."

Sheryl was withering. "You're not like his own son. How could you be? It's not just that he doesn't know what you're really like. He doesn't know who you really are."

"Of course he does, he was married to my mum for seven years!" The words erupted from him like lava. "That's what this is really all about, isn't it? You can't stand the fact that she died and he really loved her, that he loved her a lot more than he loves you. He only married you because he was mad with wanting her back. He was so desperate he thought he could have what he had with her with someone else. That's all you are to him. Just a stand-in."

Her mouth twisted with pain and contempt. "I'm sick of hearing about your mother. It's about time someone told you the truth about her."

"Don't even mention her name!" Todd, having had enough, began walking away. "You don't know the first thing about her."

"I know she wasn't your mother."

He stopped. Everything, the whole world, stopped. He almost laughed. "What?"

It wouldn't have been so bad, he wouldn't have had to believe her, if she hadn't looked guilty, like this time even she knew she'd gone too far. She repeated, quietly but firmly, "She wasn't your real mother. She adopted you when you were a baby. Vince told me before we got married."

The cogs which turned his brain jammed. Anything that had until now kept him alive – strength, energy, blood – was draining rapidly out of him, seeping into the floor, leaving him trembling. "It's not true." Even his voice wouldn't work.

"It is true. Ask Vince. He should've told you. They both should."

The room was sliding, blurring. He stared, though he couldn't see her, couldn't see or hear or feel anything.

It couldn't be true.

He said hoarsely, "What did you mean, he doesn't know who I really am?"

"Your real parents. All a big mystery apparently. Right. I'm off to bed." She collected her mug of tea, car keys, handbag from the worktop. As she left he placed his hands flat on the surface of the island unit, leaning his weight upon them until his shoulders hunched and his head was bowed.

If it were true …

His throat felt tight, and sore.

It made everything a lie. Love and grief and childhood and every last thing he'd clung to as a certainty, a lie.

If it were true, a stray animal was exactly what he was.

EXCLUDED

"OI!"

Spig froze, but only for a split-second. Shoving the money into his jacket he legged it out of the shop, down the street, his heart pounding in his throat, feet barely touching the hot pavement. He'd made a stupid mistake; it hadn't been the half-blind old dodderer out of sight of the till but his young, bulky slap-head assistant. The same young, bulky slap-head assistant whose footsteps were now echoing close behind him, bellowing foul curses at the top of his voice as well as chasing him hell for leather through the streets, across the roads, down the alley, over the bollards at the entrance to the park. Spig could hardly breathe but he didn't dare stop, didn't dare look back.

And then he had no choice.

The full weight of his pursuer at his back sent him sprawling, his knees and chin crunching as they hit the gravel path. He was hauled onto his back before he could react, as he struggled another blow connecting with his eye socket, knocking his head back to the ground, hands grabbing inside his jacket for the money. Trying to sit up, to fight back, a hefty kick to his ribs brought an explosion of pain and he howled. The weight lifted from him, another couple of kicks delivered for good measure to his torso and kneecaps, and suddenly he was alone, lying curled in the empty park on a sunny morning, his head and his chest throbbing, spitting blood onto the path.

He rolled onto his knees, pushed slowly to his feet. The world spun and blacked around him and he waited for the moment to pass, for his vision in his good eye to clear, but his gut twisted and heaved and he vomited into the grass. Wiping his mouth with the back of his hand, finding it streaked with puke and blood, he stumbled back a step or two. One leg of his jeans was ripped open at the knee, a good three inches of skin missing, gravel deep in the wound. He wanted to vomit again. His eye hurt so much he could hardly keep it open. He limped to the brick toilet block, found its doors chained and padlocked. Swore though he wanted to cry. Where else? Where else could he go to clean up, hide away? Not the home, never any privacy there. Questions would be asked, judgements and sanctions meted out. His house, his and Donna's house, was too far away and without water. Only one place he could think of to go, though he couldn't think at all, words sticking in his brain, images fading before he knew what they were. One familiar place to go, and if he didn't know its dark corners and deserted passageways, who did?

He was luckier this time. These low-ceilinged, badly lit corridors which were always empty during lessons had not suddenly spawned gangs of kids bunking off or teachers on the warpath. He slunk along close to the wall, his body pounding and aching, his nerves tight as guitar strings. The boys' toilets in this decrepit building were rarely used, due soon to be knocked out and the remaining space used to house a computer suite. You'd need to do a lot more to it than that, he thought as he swung inside. Raze the whole fucking place to the ground.

No bright fluorescent lights in here. No shiny white tiles. A narrow strip of opaque window along the top of the room provided a murky light, the leaking basins stained with streaks of yellow beneath the taps, urinals and cubicles stinking of too much use and not enough bleach, of sweaty kids and bad plumbing. He approached the single mirror with trepidation, drew in his breath at the sight of his swollen eye, his bloodied nose and chin and lip. He tore off a strip of damp bog roll and held it under a juddering tap, wiped his face, which felt as though the skin had been flayed even where he wasn't bleeding. He bent to wipe his knee too, tried to pick out some of the gravel but it was too deeply embedded to get at with his fingers and made him want to retch. Staggering here from the park had knackered him, he wanted to crouch down in a warm corner and close his eyes. He could do that at the house. Lie quietly on the bust-up old mattress, pull Donna's quilt around him, block out the world. Except it was a long way to go, feeling like shit as he did. He wondered were his ribs broken. Could a good kicking from a slap-head's boot break your ribs? How fragile was he, exactly? He had to look away from his reflection. Too fucking fragile. That much was obvious.

Making his way gingerly back down the corridor, he heard the sound of a door clicking shut, footsteps somewhere behind him at the far end. He stopped. Waited. Nothing. Hobbled a bit further, finding he could use his injured leg more steadily now, move a little faster.

"You, boy!"

He caught his breath, halted without turning round, knowing he was about to get done for being out of a lesson, not wearing uniform, breathing. He waited for the footsteps and the voice – those of Bill Duffy, deputy head – to draw closer.

"Who is that? Turn round, lad!"

He turned, slowly, knowing he was in shadow.

"Hah." Duffy grunted, too far away still to understand there was anything wrong. "You. I might've known. Where should you be?"

He had no idea. "Dunno. Geography or summat."

"Where's your uniform?"

He shrugged. Something, some infinitesimal detail he hadn't even noticed himself, must have alerted Duffy because he paused, came another half dozen yards down the corridor. Spig didn't move. There was no point. Duffy was a PE teacher.

The authority drained from his voice and his expression. Spig felt uncomfortable. People didn't often look at him with anything other than annoyance or contempt. "What's happened to you?"

"Got beaten up, on the way to school."

"Why?"

He shrugged again. Duffy gazed at him. "You need looking after."

The words almost felled him. It was what he wanted, what he needed, more than anything. He began, involuntarily and humiliatingly, to cry.

"Come on." The teacher touched his shoulder. "Come with me. Let's get you cleaned up."

He sat on a spongey orange chair outside Duffy's office, tears and snot joining the blood and vomit now. It was warmer up here, brighter, but he was on view for the staff to see as they passed with messages, mail, mugs of tea. Someone made one for him, put it down on the low circular wooden table beside him. The head's assistant hoved into his line of vision with a first aid box. Spig sipped the tea, which was too hot, wiped his nose with a tissue from the box he'd been given. Heard, from behind the half-ajar door of his office, Duffy on the phone .

" ... might need to go to Casualty, best if you picked him up ... he won't say ... can't have young lads assaulted in broad daylight ... have a word with the police ... "

When he emerged, a few minutes later, from his conversation with the head of the children's home, Bill Duffy found nothing but a mug of tea and a few scrunched up, blood-stained tissues.

If he told himself he was feeling better all the time, it might start to be true. He'd pocketed some change lying on the table before he left, dragged himself up to the main road and caught a bus to the edge of town, ignoring the stares of the bus driver and the few other passengers, hopped out again a mile or so away from the fields which would lead to his house.

He spent the remaining money he'd swiped on a large plastic bottle of Sprite and a couple of bags of crisps. The bottle grew heavier as he toiled past the big houses along the country road, their windows watching him as he struggled by, their empty gardens full of flowers, velvet green lawns sprayed by sprinklers. Some of the drops caught him as he passed and the moisture on his face felt like luxury. He had to keep stopping, have a rest and a drink. It took him twice as long as usual to reach the fields, to haul himself over the drystone wall. He remembered Donna the first time, stumbling in her high heels as he was stumbling now.

It was midday by the time he fell through the door, which was good because Donna had said she'd come this afternoon, so it gave him a few hours to recover before she got here. His leg was agony with the effort of crossing the fields, and no longer having the energy to remain on his feet, he negotiated the stairs on his backside, crawled on one knee to the mattress and collapsed onto it. Closed his eyes. Every bit of him throbbed and ached. He understood completely how if you were really seriously wounded you might just lie down to die.

Hours later. He could tell by the angle of the bars of sun through the window, he'd sat here so many days watching the progression of their journey across the floorboards. Having drunk the whole bottle of Sprite, he needed desperately now to piss. Rolling onto his hands and knees, attempting to stand, he realised his knee had stiffened up, that his ribs if not broken were going to be black with bruises. He swore, limped to the top of the stairs, crashed down most of them into the living-room below, and wondered where Donna was. It had to be three-thirty, four o'clock. She should have been here long ago.

Peeing in the nettles behind the house, wiping his hands on the seat of his jeans, he heard in the distant air a sound, a kind of gulping, strangulated mewling. Imagining an animal, someone's cat perhaps, trapped somewhere, he followed the sound round to the front of the house.

And found Donna, shambling and sobbing across the moor towards him.

"What's happened?" He dragged further across the grass towards her. Seeing him, she stumbled on until they were only a few feet apart. She looked like she'd been crying a long time. "What's the matter?"

She shook her head, unable to speak.

"Come here." Awkwardly he drew her to him, put his arms around her. He'd only ever done this before in play while she giggled and shouted, pulling away. It felt weird, sort of too grown-up, doing it now. She leaned her forehead against his collar bone and wept, holding nothing back. "Come on." He didn't know what to do. "Let's go in."

He had nothing to give her. She sat on the mattress where a few minutes ago he'd been sleeping, her knees drawn up to her chest, her head on her folded arms. He stood above her, uncertain. Nothing to eat, nothing to drink, certainly nothing to say. In the end he went for - "You gonna tell me or what?"

She looked up at him, her eyes wet and swollen, her mouth swollen. "What happened to you?"

"Some bastard I was tryin' to rob."

"Looks bad."

"I'm all right." Which he was, compared with her. He sat down beside her and she caught a glimpse of his knee.

"Jesus, Spig, that's really horrible. You need to put some stuff on that."

"Right, I'll check out our emergency medical kit, shall I?" He tried a smile. She couldn't return it. *"Tell me, Don. What's happened? Is it your bloke?"*

Tears welled again. *"He's dumped me."*

He didn't know which was greater, his rage or his relief. *"D'you want me to kill him?"*

She stared at him.

"Joking. You know I'm joking, right?"

"It's not funny." Her face crumpled again. *"It's the end of my life and you think it's funny?"*

"No, I didn't mean ... " Shit. *"It's not the end of your life, don't be stupid."*

"What would you know? What do you know about anything?"

Stung, he inched away. His heart was pounding. *"What'd he dump you for, then?"*

"I don't know. He said we were too different and he wasn't good for me and it wasn't working and ... I don't know."

"Load of fucking bollocks." He'd been making excuses, Spig understood. Spouting any old rubbish to get rid of her. Bastard. His anger simmered. *"Where's he live?"*

"Shut up, Spig. He's not gonna change his mind about wanting me if you beat him up, is he? You can't force someone to love you."

"I know that," he said bitterly. Added, *"You love him?"*

"'Course I love him, or we wouldn't have ... I wouldn't ... " She was crying again. He didn't think he could stand it. *"I thought he was special. I thought we'd be together for ages. But you know what's worse? He made me think I was special too. An' I'm not. I'm just some stupid little tart who'll never be good enough for someone like him."*

"Don't say that." He was furious. *"Don't you ever say that."*

She sobbed.

"Donna." He slipped his arm around her again. "Donna, come on. Stop it. He's not worth it."

"He is, he is worth it." She wiped her nose on her hand. "It's me that's not worth it. He's lovely. He were dead upset."

Spig, gritting his teeth, decided arguing this was pointless. Instead he began slowly stroking her hair, hoping to calm her, to remind her that he was there for her even if he didn't know anything. She sat, still sniffing and whimpering, but more softly now, and he thought the rhythm of the stroking was beginning to soothe her as it was beginning to soothe him. She leaned against him, her head resting on his shoulder, her shoulder pressed to the less painful side of his ribcage, her hip and thigh alongside his. He almost forgot his own wounds; the rise and fall of her chest, the sound of their breathing, seemed so peaceful.

He kissed her.

He hadn't meant to. It was just so nice, sitting close to her like that, and he wanted her to know he cared even if no one else did, and he'd never been much good at saying things with words, so he'd kissed the top of her forehead, where her hair sprang dark from its parting.

She stilled.

Emboldened, he kissed her again. The tip of her nose, this time. He hadn't kissed anyone for a long time and she was soft, and smelled sort of hot and salty from the tears.

She said, uncertainly, "Spig."

"S'all right." He inched nearer, feeling the ache in his body, pain and longing entwined.

She swallowed. "Just a cuddle, yeah?"

"Yeah, 'course."

She lifted her arm around him, feeling him wince as she hugged him, feeling him hug her too. After a moment he drew back, and she was on the point of being relieved and comfortable with him again when his mouth opened against hers and his hand clumsily cupped the little pad of her breast.

"What you doin'?" She was pulling violently away, slapping at him, her voice shrill with indignation, as though he had

forced her down on the mattress and wrenched her legs apart.

"I was only ... "

"Takin' advantage."

"No! Fucking hell, Donna. What d'you take me for?"

"Is that what this is?" She was on her feet, glaring down at him. "This place? Your little knockin'-shop? I thought we were mates. I thought I could trust you!"

"You can *trust me."*

"What, feelin' me up 'cos I'm upset? You've never wanted to be mates with me, you've always just wanted to get in me knickers."

Her words hurt more than any amount of punches to his face, kicks to his ribs. "If all I wanted was to shag you I'd've done it by now. All this time we've been on our own here. I'd've pretended like he did. Made up a load of crap to make you think you were special. Like he did. But it's not what I want. Not all I want."

But she was beyond reason. Had been, he was realising far too late, beyond reason long before she'd shown up here. "Don't talk about him! You don't know anything about him!"

"I know he's dumped you. I know I'm still here."

"How many times?" she cried. "How many fuckin' times, Spig? I don't want you. I don't love you."

He ducked his head, as though she were brandishing a physical weapon. She stopped, hearing the echo of her own words in the silence.

"Ah shit. I didn't mean ... "

"Didn't you." He hoisted himself up, pushed past her to the stairs, two at a time even on his dodgy leg, his heart like a rock inside him. She followed, slipping on the treads, grabbing for the handrail.

"Spig ... "

"Fuck off Donna." He kept going, gritting his teeth hard to keep back his tears, through the living-room, out of the door, across the empty fields.

No matter how much she shrieked his name that wasn't his name. No looking back.

Eleven

The church had been built two hundred years ago so high into the hillside that from its arched doorway the view was of the opposite moors, of distant sheep and clusters of trees and long abandoned quarries. The road bisecting the valley, the small town commerce and streets of Rapton, lying so far below, vanished from sight. It was – symbolically, Finn thought - a steep and winding climb. In the worst winter weather those determined to worship left their cars at the bottom of the hill and made the ascent on foot rather than risk so treacherous a drive. On this grey late November morning the wind whipped his hair, drops of rain spattering before he'd so much as locked the car. The pathetic fallacy, pulling out all the stops for Cal Bywater's funeral.

The sound of a dozen other car doors slamming, Stephen, Penny, half a dozen other members of staff who'd known Callum as long as he had and cared enough to come. Pupils driven here by their parents. Pupils who'd battled up the crumbling tarmac path. Todd Kershaw, looking sombre and withdrawn. Josh Ferris and Liam Clough, pale and cowed. Ex-pupils, friends, neighbours, extended family. Everyone, even the kids, in black. He'd overheard a conversation at school – *'I ain't got nuffin' black.' 'You'll 'ave to borrow summat then, won't you? It's, like, a mark of respect, innit?'* And the hearse, taking the gradient so slowly it seemed impossible it didn't roll backwards. He saw the children's faces as the vehicle approached, the further sobering, the stepping away. Finn joined the others near the porch, meeting Stephen's eyes through the crowd, seeing an already tearful Penny take a handkerchief from her bag. The hearse drew to a halt, Cal's name worked in white carnations alongside the coffin. Julie Bywater, her face bearing the marks of a composure she had clearly only recently gained and struggled to maintain. With her a short, stocky man of jaundiced complexion who might – or might not - be Callum's father. And, barely a footstep behind them, as grim and tightly wound as Finn remembered him, her brother Dean.

The last time he'd been to a funeral he'd been twelve years old. At home in the days after she'd died he'd lain on his bed crying, listening to the harsh choking sound of Vince weeping in another room. But the moment he'd stepped into the church he had become dry-eyed with terror. Standing in the front pew beside Vince, he had been transfixed by the coffin, his hands holding the hymn sheet shaking so much he couldn't read the words. Vince had laid his paw on his shoulder, gently prised the paper from between his fingers. "It's all right, Todd." So he had stood, staring at the long wooden box beneath its posy of lilies, the swell of the organ drowning out the words of a hymn he didn't know, speechless with fear and surrounded by strangers.

Almost four years on and the vicar, an old guy who if he'd any idea who Cal was contrived to put a euphemistic gloss on it, was talking about heaven. Todd would have been surprised to learn that anyone here seriously believed Cal had gone to heaven. Personally, he didn't believe in heaven at all. Death was sleep, as far as he could see, The End, and everything else just so much bullshit. Did it actually make anyone feel better? Cal's mum, did she feel better about her son being dead because some old bloke she'd never met before was rambling on about a god she probably didn't believe in? Or was she going to choose to believe, because if she deluded herself long and hard enough, it might just give her some comfort?

Todd swallowed. He had to hold on really tight here. Such rage and pain simmering inside him, he could tip either way.

Finn heard but could not allow himself to engage with the words spoken about Cal, for he knew if he did, if he indulged in remembering the boy he had known, he was already so precariously balanced on an emotional brink he would lose it completely. And whilst if you couldn't lose it at a funeral, where could you, he was hemmed in by Stephen and Penny, by the pupils thronged around him. He didn't want to feel

Cal's death in front of them. One day, he knew, he would be attending the funeral of someone he loved so much he had no choice about feeling their loss, and this ceremony then would be only one small part of a great chasm of grief. Today it was an ordeal which if he concentrated he could steer himself through. He clenched his jaw, grateful to be seated so far back he had no view of the coffin in which Cal's body lay, grateful for the luxury of being able to distance himself.

Listening to the vicar's verbal portrait of Callum, Stephen realised that for all his talk about turning potential criminals into young men of substance, he had never truly thought of Cal as anything but an affliction. Had he ever spoken with him at length on any other subject than his own bad behaviour? Had he ever conferred upon him praise or responsibility? He tried to remember trophies and commendation awards in assemblies, merit certificates, competition prizes; to his chagrin he didn't think Cal Bywater's name had ever appeared on any and he was ashamed of his hypocrisy.

The music playing in the few moments they were instructed to take to remember Cal was *Ghetto Gospel* by 2Pac. On the surface, Todd thought, there was not a lot Cal had had in common with gangs of black streetkids in East Harlem, but the sense of hopelessness and alienation had to be the same wherever you were. And it was a song Cal had liked a lot. And the line 'peace to this young warrior' struck a painful chord. Todd blinked. If he stopped analysing long enough to give himself up to the music he'd crack, and with the rest of the Focus Group lining the pew in front of him, that wasn't something he was going to let happen. He thought instead of how the incongruity of a murdered black American rapping about street violence and tolerance in this insular Lancashire valley church was something Cal might have appreciated. That it might have made him laugh.

At first it seemed the music had punctured the mood: on the short walk up the hillside to the graveyard people fell into step with one another; murmurs of conversation carried by the wind; a palpable lifting of the stern sorrow which had bowed heads and hearts. Todd stood back a while, letting the small crowd of mourners flow past until he was able to make up the rear. He wanted to be an observer not a participant in this next stage of the ceremony, for he knew already that he could not listen to another minute of *in the midst of life we are in death*, of *holy and merciful saviours* and *souls departed*. He knew there was something obscene about standing beside Cal's yawning grave and he would not do it.

So he hung back, watching the rows of black figures lining the graveside, shivering inside his thin jacket, his fists clenched in his pockets. The wind lifted hair and hats and billowed the vicar's surplice, rain spattering fitfully from a leaden sky. He looked away.

"Todd."

The voice was low, so close he started. Dean had reached him without making a sound. Todd, glancing at him through the mists of his own misery, saw the deeper lines grief had cut into Dean's face and his heart thudded. "Hi," he said, inadequately.

"Y'all right?"

"Mm."

They stood together among an outer circle of worn headstones, watching the ritual take place. He felt unnerved by Dean's presence, remembering how Cal had been with him, that they'd just forged some sort of ... bond. Dean had meant something to Cal, Todd had understood that, however loathe Cal might have been to admit it. He said, "I'm sorry."

"Me too." Dean cleared his throat, gave it a minute. "I got a missed call on my mobile from Cal, after he was dead. You wouldn't know anything about that, would you?"

Todd was silent. He didn't see any point in being other than completely truthful. "It was me. Someone – a kid, from school – found Cal's phone after he'd ... died, and gave it to me. I handed it in to the police. I thought it was the right thing to do."

"But first you tried my number."

"I don't know why. I was a bit – messed up."

Dean regarded him for a moment. "Anything else?"

Todd shook his head.

We therefore commit his body to the ground

"You know what Cal died of?" Dean said. He didn't wait for a response. "Subdural haematoma. That's like, a brain haemorrhage. Someone hit him, or he fell, might have been hours before he died. Nobody knows." He paused. "So help me out here if you can, Todd. If there's anything else you know. Because I want to find out exactly what happened to Cal. I owe him that."

earth to earth

Todd squirmed. "His last call. I checked that too."

ashes to ashes

"And?"

dust to dust

"It was weird. It was to Stephen Lord. Our headteacher."

in sure and certain hope of resurrection to eternal life, through our Lord Jesus Christ.

Dean nodded. His expression had not changed. "Was it now."

Finn stood with Stephen and Penny at a short but respectful distance from the grave and the Bywater clan dark at its brim. Listening to the service, observing its bizarre and familiar rituals, he knew that although he didn't believe in a single word he felt a powerful need to believe in something.

Penny murmured, "Such an upsetting day."

He nodded.

"It's affected me so much I can't tell you." She dabbed again at her cheeks with a tissue from her pocket. "I haven't been able to sleep thinking about poor Callum."

Finn tried to remember when Lady Penelope had ever been in the same room as poor Callum. Couldn't recall a moment.

"I shan't be able to go back and teach again today. I shouldn't be surprised if I have to go home. It's made me quite ill, all this."

Finn and Stephen exchanged a glance. As the ceremony drew to a close she excused herself, slipping away with surprising agility before either of them could persuade her otherwise. They stood aside, allowing others to tread the damp and grassy path back down towards the church before them, behaving as gentlemen, needing to allow themselves some small space between the laying to rest of one child and the management of a thousand others.

"Well." Stephen let out his breath. No need, Finn knew, to comment further; they both knew how dispirited they felt. "That could have been worse."

Finn agreed. "The kids behaved remarkably well."

"They did. Though it would be cynical of me to mention it to them, implying that even in such a situation as this I'd expect them not to." He hesitated. "Time to move on now, do you think? Without appearing insensitive?"

Finn nodded. "Time to move on."

Todd slunk through the activity of Kershaw's Building and up into the office. Had the place been quiet, no doubt someone would have spotted him, creeping across the yard among the forklifts frozen like sleeping monsters, tip-toeing past the piles of sandbags and multi-fibre floor boarding. This morning, brick lorries pulling out of the gates, men humping materials, loading vans, his arrival went unnoticed. He swung through the office door, plucked a can of Red Bull from the mini-fridge, as he always did. Changed his mind before opening it and swapped it for a can of Carling. He yanked at the ring-pull and swallowed long and hard. Wiped his mouth with the back of his hand, sank down in the leather swivel chair, and began.

To his surprise, nothing was locked. Not a cabinet, not a drawer. The files on the computer were password protected but he'd known that password a long time and he didn't think anything he was looking for would be hidden away there. Kneeling on the floor, he tugged at the bottom right hand drawer of the desk only for it to wheel smoothly out, its rows of suspension files neatly labelled in Sheryl's precise handwriting. He riffled through the files one by one, all Vince's business paperwork – orders, invoices, guarantees, insurance, bank statements. It would be easy, he thought, to squirrel something away in here. Hide it among decade old papers you were never going to look at again. Unless of course there was another file, efficiently and heartlessly labelled The Truth About Todd.

Anger rose sour in him until it constricted his throat, pricked at his eyelids. He lifted out one file after another, shuffling through them fast, dates and balances changing in front of his eyes like cartoon flick drawings at the corner of a page, dumping them down, onto the next.

And nothing.

Or not here, anyway.

Sitting back on his heels, he stared at the shelves high on the wall opposite him which housed computer manuals and box files, material samples and promotional leaflets. Each shelf was full from deepest recess to front lip. But then how much room was his identity going to take up? He pulled out a stool to stand on and began removing the contents of the top shelf, bundling them into his arms at first then giving up, letting them tumble to the floor. Sheaves of papers fell and scattered, boxes dropped or crashed. He cleared every last sheet, each item, knowing how easily a letter, a photograph, an official form could be missed. When he was satisfied the shelf held no secrets he shoved its wares back crumpled and chaotic, moved onto the next. He'd been cautious to begin with, taken care to open and close doors and drawers noiselessly on their hinges and runners, to leave papers and files as he had found them. He had carried his despair locked inside him as he always did. Now, standing at the centre of this maelstrom, he was breathing hard, his chest rising and falling and he kept having to blink tears from his eyes. How could there be nothing?

Footsteps on the metal staircase outside. He knew it was Vince from their weight, from the way the door banged shut, from the way he was whistling *Always Look On The Bright Side of Life* from Monty Python's *Life of Brian*. He counted – five, four, three, two, one …

"Todd. What the bloody 'ell are you doing, lad?"

"Looking for something."

Vince gazed at him bewildered, standing on the stool amid a

surrounding welter of pamphlets and instruction booklets, roof tiles and plumbers' samples, looking miserable and manic and lost all at the same time. "I can see that. Did you find it?"

"No."

"What were you looking for?"

"Proof." He muttered it, stepping down from the stool, the debris crackling beneath his bare feet. "You've not spoken to Sheryl then?"

"No, I'm just back from Pontefract." Vince looked at him with sympathy. "Was it the funeral? Terrible things, funerals."

"No it wasn't the fucking funeral!" He burst into tears.

Vince took a step towards him, hand outstretched, "Eh, lad …"

Todd jerked away. "I'm not your lad." His voice cracked. "But I wasn't hers either, was I? Why didn't she ever tell me? Why didn't *you* tell me? How could you tell *Sheryl* and not me?"

Vince, collapsed by understanding, lowered his bulk into the leather swivel chair, his face heavy with regret. "Sheryl."

"Yeah. Fucking Sheryl."

"Oh Todd. I'm sorry. I am sorry. We should've told you. I should've told you. But you were Eileen's son, you know. Don't doubt that. She couldn't have loved you more."

Todd wept.

"She adopted you when you were a few months old, years before I met her. Couldn't have children herself, you see. But she were that proud of you. You know that." He paused. "All I know is your real mum had died. None of the details, just that. It used to upset Eileen sometimes, to think she'd gained from another woman's death. But it wasn't something we talked about much. You were hers. That was all that mattered."

"Did she not think that one day I'd want to know? That I had a right to know?"

"She did, of course she did. She knew she should've done it when you were small, that she were asking for trouble in the long-run, but she kept putting it off and putting it off. And the older you got, the harder it were going to be. Then she took ill, but we didn't know she were going to go so quick, we thought

224

she still had months. When she were back home from hospital, we were going to sort a lot of stuff out. But she never came back home."

Todd said nothing. He didn't want to think about that just now.

"You were ours. Maybe you were so much ours we didn't give a lot of thought to who else's you'd been." Vince paused, said gently, "It's not really important, you know, who you were. It's who you are now that counts. If where you come from was all that mattered, no one'd ever make anything of their lives unless it'd been handed to them on a plate when they were born. It's where you're going that's important. What you choose to do with your life. What you make of it."

"But it means everything's a lie," Todd said desperately. "Everything I believed about myself."

"Like what? That you had a mum who loved the bones of you? She did."

"She loved me so much she lied to me all my life? Because she did, Vince. Not telling me was lying to me. I've got this picture of her in my head, that I've always had, but it's like it wasn't real, nothing was real, because it was all based on something that wasn't true. Even my name. I don't even know what my name is."

Vince hauled himself out of the chair, stepped heavily to the low shelving at the back of the office where the safe was hidden. Todd waited, scrubbed at his eyes with his sleeve.

"There you go." Vince placed a small brown envelope on the desk in front of him. "It's all there was. It's all we know, you were left at a hospital in a sort of carry-cot, and that was tucked into your blanket with you."

Todd stared at him. "This is … ?"

"Well we never knew for sure. But we always thought it must have been from your mum."

His mouth had dried and his heart was thumping. The envelope lay an inch from his hand and he couldn't touch it.

"Shall I give you a bit of space?" Vince said.

He nodded.

"I'm down in the yard if you want me."

His eyes had filled with tears again. For a minute or two after Vince had left him alone he could only stare at the envelope, paralysed with disbelief and fear and excitement. Eventually, his fingers shaking, he picked it up and opened the unsealed flap, drew out a piece of lined paper torn from a spiralbound pad. The handwriting was large and unjoined.

This is Todd
Please look after him

His tears fell. It was really his name. The name he'd been given when he was born.
Something else. Two passport size photos from a booth. A girl with curly brown hair and a shy smile, looking through the camera right at him. His gut twisted so sharply he drew in his breath, for he had seen this photo, or one from the same sequence, a few weeks ago. In the dust on a dresser top, among a motley collection of personal possessions: a silver necklace; playing cards; a vodka bottle; heavy metal CDs.
Belonging to Dean.

He had been away for what felt like a lifetime, though in truth it was only from the close of one warm, sunny Spring through to the rain and squalling winds of the beginning of the next. And although it was short of a year, he felt confused as he strode past the big houses with their blankets of soaking wet lawns and their shrubs dripping with buds and raindrops, by how little everything had changed. How the place he had left as a boy looked exactly the same when he was no longer a boy at all.

It had been easy, to begin with. He'd been so fired up with rage and pain and hurt he hadn't cared. The nights had been short and warm, sleeping rough had been a grim sort of pleasure. Desperate to put as much distance between himself and Donna and the whole fucking mess of his life, he'd caught a bus into the city, nicked a load of money from an unattended kiosk on the station and jumped onto the first train he came to before anyone noticed and summoned security. He hadn't a clue where the train was going but he'd been prepared, with his newly acquired wealth, to buy a ticket to the end of the line. As it turned out no conductor ever appeared, and he'd drunk most of a half bottle of vodka he'd also filched then woken several hours later in a seaside town he'd never heard of. He stood, bewildered, on the deserted platform. Either he'd become very stupid in his sleep or all the signs were written in another language. Stumbling out of the station into the twilight, he realised he could smell the sea and hear gulls and for the first time in a day which had begun with a beating, his heart had lifted a little.

He'd slept on the beach nearly the whole summer. He was loathe to squander his money on a B&B because a bruised and bloody kid on his own would arouse suspicion and who knew where his next stash of cash was coming from and anyway, they were bound to be full this time of year. He'd cleaned himself up in public toilets, bought a toothbrush and some antiseptic stuff and plasters from a branch of Boots in the town which looked like it belonged in the nineteen-fifties. Gradually he'd got his bearings. It had dawned on him he was somewhere in Wales, that there might be summer jobs to be had even for someone with no address or National Insurance number or even a change of clothes. Grudgingly he bought another set of underwear, a couple of t-shirts and a pair of jeans which were cheap and looked like shit but at least they weren't ripped at the knee with his blood all over them. He bought a sleeping-bag as well, and then he started to get nervous because a lot of his money was gone and he didn't know if he had the guts to steal on a regular basis. He'd get beaten up again, arrested, and then what? And then to his astonishment someone gave him a job.

It wasn't much, just collecting money from the kids at the go-kart track, issuing tickets, keeping an eye on them to make sure they didn't kill themselves falling out the go-karts. Ron, the feller that ran it, had been let down, he said, by his university student nephew who'd decided to spend his summer travelling round India instead, and Ron'd seen him hanging about, bored and homeless but never any trouble. Taken pity on him, most likely, but he didn't care. Couldn't afford to care. He did as he was told, was nice to the kids, respectful to their parents, turned himself into a good and honest worker. Ron let him open up in the morning, bought him cups of tea and chips for his lunch from the café on the beach. Paid him a bit more. The days and weeks developed a rhythm. A kind of peace. He thought a lot about Donna, and one afternoon he went to the tattoo artist on the sea-front and had him ink a little D and a symbol of bird's wings into the tanned skin at the top of his shoulder. He might not ever see her again but now she'd kind of always be with him. It made him feel a little bit better.

And then the summer was over, and with it what he'd begun to think of as his new life. After the madness of the August Bank Holiday, the prom and the beaches emptied, the seasonal, tourist-focused shops closed down, the heat withdrew from the air, dusk fell sooner and darker. Ron said with regret he had no more work for him, with affectionate concern that he was a good lad and he needed to take care of himself. He knew someone, an HGV driver going as far as Chester, if that was any use. He'd nodded and mumbled his thanks, hitched a ride with HGV Man and found himself hours later abandoned at a motorway service station, a miscellany of belongings in his rucksack and nowhere to go.

He figured a big city would be a good place to be in the winter. Though he distrusted cities he knew there would be casual work, shelters, empty buildings to squat in. So he'd hitched again, landed somewhere else with an impenetrable accent but at least he could read the signs. He was scared here, though, uptight and on his guard the whole time. Ron'd told him about homeless shelters, how they had them in all the big cities, and he'd looked one up in a phone book in the library, which he'd noted was somewhere else warm and safe to stay, then headed out there. The people running it had been kind in a detached sort of way, said he could stay a maximum of five nights, shown him a bed he could sleep on, given him a hot drink and some toast. They tried to give him advice too, about benefits and work and half-way houses but it was as if he couldn't hear them. Their mouths kept moving but nothing they said made any sense to him. During the day he harassed market stall holders and blokes on building sites for work, swiped what he could when he could without getting caught. He hung out in pubs, hoping to hear someone saying they needed a job doing. For a couple of weeks he collected glasses in a backstreet bar and then one night there'd been a fight in which someone was killed and he hadn't felt much like going back. He did some labouring on an inner-city dump that was going to be a new shopping and leisure complex, but that petered out too as the weather worsened. By now he'd found a squat to hole up in, but a load of junkies and alcoholic tramps lived there too, shouting and mumbling and shambling around, and he hardly dared sleep at night. But he understood how they got that way.

And then one evening, sitting depressed and numb in the corner of a pub, minding his own business, this bloke had come over to him. He'd looked all right and he was dead friendly and polite, and he'd said was he after a job? It was easy money as it turned out, picking up little packages from one address and delivering them to another. They'd even given him an A-Z so he could find his way about. He caught buses and local trains but mostly he walked, got to know his way around pretty quickly. He had to go to some really rough places and he realised that what he was doing was probably so dodgy he was better off not knowing what was in the packages, but it was something to do and it stopped him thinking too much. If he thought, he got really scared, and ashamed, and he felt jittery all the time and couldn't concentrate. Blocking stuff out really helped.

Until the night of the guns.

He'd made his last delivery after midnight, arrived back at the bar where they did their business to find the gang slouched alone in the middle of a lock-in, hard drinking but not quite drunk. He'd collected his danger money from his boss, when the door crashed open and someone was shouting something and someone else swore and instinctively, without having seen much of anything, he whisked out the back door into the alley. He stood trembling violently on the path, his heart stopping every time the gunshots exploded. No more shouting. He vomited against the wall into the litter. After a long time he crept back inside, lifted back the curtain concealing the back door. His boss and his two side-kicks were dead, blood and bullet holes obliterating their faces.

It was then he'd decided to come home.

So here he was, trudging back up the same hill with its posh houses and its footpath across the fields. He didn't know whether the home had reported his absence, whether anyone had bothered looking for him. Whether his little house on the moors had been razed to the ground or bought by developers. But there it was, he could see it already, a blur of white amongst the trees. To his overwhelming relief it looked just the same. He thought of all the places he'd slept, and stayed rigidly awake, these last ten months. They made this run-down shack he'd never quite managed to do much with seem like luxury.

He moved faster, gaining ground across the wet grass, eager to be somewhere safe and dry and alone, where there were no guns or knives, no users or pushers, no reason to be afraid. He pushed the door at the same time he flicked the catch, a trick he'd invented to make it difficult for anyone who didn't know it to get in. They could always kick the whole things down, of course, which probably wouldn't take much but it did kind of give the impression the door was locked.

Except today it really was locked. Or bolted, as the resistance seemed to come from above and below.

He frowned, tried again. It wouldn't give. He cursed – and glimpsed a face he knew at the window. Heard a cry, her voice piercing his heart.

The door was flung open. Shock large on Donna's face. "I thought you were dead."

"Why would you think I was dead?"

"You disappeared." She stepped back to let him in. "Where've you been?"

He could not begin to explain. Didn't need to, just yet, for she reached up and hugged him, tight. "I thought I'd never see you again."

He could have wept. Instead he hugged back, just as tight, letting his body fuse into hers. Let relief and gratitude pour through him. Promised himself he would never, ever let her down again.

Heard a disorienting sound from somewhere else in the room.

On the floor in front of the fire that had never worked was a rectangular turquoise box, plastic turquoise handles hanging down either side, at one end a hood lined with an alphabet print. And suddenly, flung up above the rim, a tiny clenched hand.

Twelve

The classroom nearest the Arts Theatre had been set aside for rails of costumes, props, musical instruments, drink cartons and boxes of crisps. Its double doors which opened out onto the yard and had been propped wide to take delivery of a set of amps and a drum kit were now pushed shut against the winter evening. The buzz, Leigh thought as she dashed hither and thither, was intoxicating. She had always loved the atmosphere surrounding a show, and whilst never much interested in performing herself, enjoyed experiencing the thrill vicariously by providing backstage or front of house support, holding rehearsals, directing now and then. When she had offered her services this time, the BTEC pupils had said regretfully that they were supposed to run the whole shebang themselves, then one of them had checked and discovered that they were allowed to recruit on the understanding that they accounted for it in their evaluation. Leigh, recruited as general dogsbody, fetched and carried for the acts, calmed nerves, soothed fraying tempers, pinned costumes. Twenty minutes before curtain up, she stood in the Green Room classroom with thirty excited and nervous or affectedly nonchalant pupils, fixing the hair of a Year 9 girl who was part of the Cell Block Tango dance group when someone cried, "Where the *fuck* is Todd?"

Leigh looked up. The irate girl demanding an answer was Sophie Cottesmore, prima donna extraordinaire and Todd's co-presenter for the evening, beautiful in her strapless fuschia gown, her blonde hair a masterpiece of artfully cascading curls, heavily mascaraed eyes wide with terror.

"Why?" Leigh said stupidly. "Isn't he here?"

Sophie sank woefully down onto a nearby table. "He was supposed to be at the dress rehearsal this afternoon and he didn't come to that. No one's seen him since Cal's funeral and he's not answering his mobile."

Leigh finished French plaiting the dancer's hair, hoping it didn't show in her face that she was worried. "I'll see what I can find out."

"I can't present it all by myself!" Sophie wailed.

"Of course you can. You might have to." She crossed the corridor into the darkened Arts Theatre, the audience comprised largely of family and fellow pupils already filling the tiered rows of seating, and out into the foyer, where Stephen and Finn were on reception duty. She drew Finn aside. "Todd isn't here."

"I'd heard."

"How did he seem, this morning?"

"As we all did. I didn't speak to him." He squeezed her arm. "Don't worry. He'll be here soon. He won't let people down."

She hesitated. "I think you're underestimating – "

"I'm not. I'm hoping for the best. Which is all I can do, short of going out there with a torch and a loudhailer." He smiled, reassuring, quelling his own doubts.

Leigh said nothing, looked towards Stephen meeting and greeting, his public mask very firmly in place. Having spent time in his company out of school she could see, as she knew Finn now could, a clear distinction between the man and the role, could understand the connection between them. He was ambitious, sure, but he was also shrewd and thoughtful, a kind and decent man, and humanitarian to such an extreme it had become his fatal flaw. And if you had to have a fatal flaw, what better?

Finn, watching her, said, "Are you needed backstage?"

"Yes. I'll watch from the wings. Catch you at the interval." She slipped back through the shadows of the theatre, into the corridor. One of the bands, an unlikely bunch of Year 11 boys with hair to their elbows and t-shirts you could camp in sauntered past her with their guitars, the rest of their equipment already in place behind the curtain. Leigh stood aside for them. "Break a leg."

"Yeah thanks, miss."

"Respect."

She grinned, dipped back into the classroom where Sophie Cottesmore was having her eye make-up repaired by an honoured Year 7 child with a less than steady hand. Sophie's eyes were red with tears of frustration. "He's still not here! I could kill him."

"All you need to do," Leigh said, "is introduce the acts."

"But we'd rehearsed all our ad-libs."

Leigh smiled. "You will shine, Sophie. But then I suspect you know that."

"Good evening."

The members of the band, sitting at drums and keyboard, waiting with their guitars, listened with amused resignation to Mr Lord's Welcome speech. Sophie took deep breaths with her mike switched off, the warmth and susurrus of the audience making her stomach flutter. In truth she knew that Todd's absence would make her the star of the evening, that because he was – she had reluctantly to admit – fit and quick-witted and naturally charming he could steal her thunder without trying. Whatever emergency had detained him tonight, she was glad of it.

And then there he was. Emerging from the backstage darkness, wearing cool jeans and a tight white t-shirt, a black waistcoat slung casually over the top, his hair lightly gelled. "You fucking bastard," she said as he stepped up beside her.

He cocked an eyebrow. "Love you too."

Mr Lord shut up. The curtains parted. Todd and Sophie stepped forward to tumultuous applause. Todd waited for it to die down, said into his mike, "We'd like to dedicate this evening's performance to the memory of Cal Bywater."

He was hardly aware of any of it. Not the fantastically good acts nor the excruciatingly bad ones, not the deafening crash of Viper doing Meatloaf out of Bon Jovi or the sweet tones of Emily Pope singing *Kiss Me* by Sixpence None The Richer. He remained oblivious to stand-up routines, dancers and improv which wasn't. He did remember his script for as long as he needed it, standing staring out into the dark of the audience, the stage lights bright and hot, Sophie preening and simpering beside him. He must have been functioning on auto, which was a bit scary, his mouth opening and saying the right words, stretching itself into a smile, covering for Sophie when she cocked up. For inside he was cold and numb and he felt like he was somebody else.

Which actually he was.

His mum was a pretty, dark-haired teenage girl in an old and creased picture from a photo booth. No one, not even Vince, knew who she was or what had happened to her. *Maybe you were so much ours we didn't give a lot of thought to who else's you'd been.* They hadn't wanted to know, hadn't asked the questions.

His dad was ... and here was where it all fell apart. Why he felt sick and sweaty and like he wasn't really there. The person he'd believed himself to be, all these years, did not compute with his mother having been hardly more than a child and his father ...

His father having been Dean Bywater.

The moment the curtain closed at the beginning of the interval Sophie's Oscar nominee smile vanished and she flounced off to bitch about him to her mates. Todd couldn't have cared less. He walked carefully out into the corridor, through the classroom where everyone was bubbling or lamenting, swigging from illicit bottles of Wicked and cans of beer, through the double doors to the yard. In the pelting rain he took out his mobile, into which before he'd handed over Cal's phone he had keyed Dean's number (and why, why had he done that then?), and pressed Call. It was ringing. He closed his eyes as he shivered.

The mobile phone you are calling is currently unavailable.

He slammed his fist against brick. Texted fast.

need 2 c u todd

Leigh collected her two inches of warm white wine as she passed through the crowded foyer in search of Finn. En route Jasmine, one of the girls from her English class, intercepted her. "What d'you think, miss?"

"It's very good," she smiled. "I'm really enjoying it."

"That band were proper mint. And Todd Kershaw! I never

noticed him much before, but he's *well* fit, i'n't he?"

Leigh laughed. "What do you want me to say? I'm his form teacher."

"He is though. Has he got a girlfriend?"

"I don't know. If he has, I don't think it's anyone in school."

Finn was at her side. Jasmine looked from one to the other, said, "Ah! You two!" and teetered away as though she wasn't used to wearing her own shoes.

Finn smiled. "Us two what? See, he got here then, I said he would."

Leigh looked at him. Is it just me? she thought. Am I the only one who can see there's something wrong with Todd? Or am I overreacting?

"What?" Finn said, reading her eyes and taking her hand into his despite being surrounded by pupils and parents and governors.

"Nothing." Maybe Todd was just nervous tonight. Nervous and depressed as he had been for weeks and maybe the shadow of something darker was nothing more than her own imaginings. She would talk to him later. Seek him out at the after-show party to which Stephen had finally acquiesced. Tell him someone thought him fit. She felt the warmth of Finn's hand around her own and pressed lightly. He smiled.

Dean stood with his back against the dark wall of The Tunnel, the pounding beat of music vibrating through the brick. Rain puddled the tarmac at his feet, plastered his hair to his skull. He took out his phone and switched it back on, since Julie had made him promise to be available to her at any time, and he didn't renege on his promises. Not any more.

His phone, which he had killed for the few minutes he had been standing in the deepest of shadows outside the Arts Theatre doors, beeped instantly. He read Todd's text. Considered. He had his own suspicions about Todd, which a month or so back had seemed like lunacy. Now he no longer knew what lunacy was. He only knew that if he hadn't come back, Cal would still be alive, and his responsibility for his death flayed his heart and his conscience until he wanted to crawl away and die himself.

But first he had business to attend to.

He hesitated over Reply. Closed his phone and stuck it back in his pocket. Pulled up his collar and shut his eyes against the rain.

" … most of all, how *proud* I am of our young people tonight, not only of our winner, Emily, but also of everyone who took part, whether on stage or behind it. And I think we owe a particularly big thanks to our hosts this evening, Sophie and Todd … "

The applause, the whooping and whistling and stamping threatened for a moment to spiral out of control. Sophie beamed and twirled prettily in the spotlight. Todd looked embarrassed. Stephen's closing remarks, almost but not quite drowned out, concerned further thanks, and hope to see you again, and safe journey home. The stage lights dimmed, house lights suddenly and cruelly full on.

The Arts Theatre emptied.

Leigh, collecting paper towels from the girls' toilets to deal with spilt drinks in the Green Room, halted at the sound of someone next door in the boys' throwing up. She walked round into the doorway. "Are you all right?" she called.

Another retch into the pan.

She crossed the threshold. "Hello?"

He came out, red-eyed, wiping his mouth.

"Oh Todd."

He shook his head. "Don't ask me. Don't ask me if I'm all right."

A thought occurred to her. "Have you taken something?"

"No." Added, with bitter irony, "Just high on life."

She gazed at him. Wanted to put her arms around him and give him a hug. Didn't dare.

"Don't be nice to me, miss."

"All right." She tried to think of something supportive to say that wouldn't reduce him to tears. "You should go home."

"I will. I am. I'm going now."

"Okay for a lift?"
He nodded.

Part of Stephen's bargain over the after-show party had been that clearing-up took place as well as chilling-out. Costumes were bundled into holdalls, instuments carried out into vans and parents' cars. Leigh helped to sweep empty crisp packets and cartons into bin-bags, Finn to haul away flats and stage weights. Stephen stayed talking and smiling for much longer than his face muscles could manage without complaint, then sought refuge in the emptying theatre. The boys up in the sound and lighting box were playing Razorlight and Snow Patrol over the sound system, a few kids shuffling and bobbing, most just hanging out, packing up. He slipped into a seat at the back, wanting to be anonymously present, to take a few minutes. Weeks ago he would not have believed the school could pull off an event as civilised and successful as this had been, a reflection not on the nice, focussed kids who'd managed it, but on the school's morale as a whole. On his own state of mind. It was simultaneously unsettling and cheering, the speed with which everything could change.

"What an amazing evening." Leigh took the seat beside his.

He smiled. Leigh Somers was fast becoming one of his favourite members of staff. He found her perceptive, intelligent, grounded and immensely attractive. That Finn Macallister was entirely captivated by her was no surprise to him at all. "It was, wasn't it? It's heartening to know, after the term we've had, that we're capable of it."

"Dedicating it to Cal was a nice touch."

"Simple yet sincere," Stephen agreed. "Trust Todd."

Leigh said nothing.

Half an hour later, Finn stood alone in the centre of the deserted theatre, eerily silent now the sound and lighting boys had gone and the party was over, only one row of house lights glowing dimly in the dark. Leigh picked up her jacket from a seat, walked slowly towards him. "Time to go?"

"Yeah. Stephen says he'll lock up. I've said our goodbyes."

"It's been a great evening," she reflected as they walked to his car.

"Yeah, but a fucking weird day. I'm knackered."

"Do you want me to drive?"

"My car? Do I want you to drive *my* car?"

"Oh shut up. I'm a good driver."

"I know." He kissed her forehead. "I'm fine. Let's just go."

She made tea while he showered, slid a Jack Johnson CD into the player, undressed and pulled on his bathrobe. He returned, towel knotted at his waist, to find her sitting cross-legged in the middle of his bed sipping her tea. "Better?" she asked.

"Much."

"It'll be shifting that scenery. You have to be careful at your age."

"I'm thirty-four!"

"I know. Getting on." She dodged the pillow he chucked at her. "What's the towel about? Shy, all of a sudden?"

"Cold, all of a sudden." His telephone rang. He groaned. They listened to it without moving.

"Might be important," Leigh said.

He reached across the bed to pick up, lay back. "Hi." She watched his face. "Claudia," he mouthed to her. Frowned. Said into the receiver, "I left him locking up … I didn't realise it was that late. An hour ago." He listened. "Maybe … " Sighed inaudibly. "Sure. But ring me if he gets to you in the next ten minutes or so. Okay. No problem. Speak to you soon." He hung up. "Shit. Stephen's not back and he's not answering his mobile. She wants me to check he's not still at school."

Leigh understood his reluctance. But. "If it were me asking for help … "

"I know." He got up, began pulling his clothes back on.

"Do you want me to come?"

"No. You," he told her, "stay right where you are."

The school gates stood open, Stephen's car still in the car park where he'd left it six hours earlier. For the third time that day Finn parked beside him, slammed his door. The foyer was still lit, its door ajar. He pulled it wider, crossed the shining tiled floor, called "Stephen?" into the Arts Theatre, where the house lights still burned their pale yellow glow. No reply. He walked down the echoing corridor towards Stephen's office. Its door was locked as it had been all evening. He called again. Still nothing.

Something spooky about an empty school at night. Shadows at the end of long and silent corridors, impenetrable dark at the top of the stairs, the absence of voices, footfall, doors banging, only the subtlest trace of emotion in the air, the way they said ghosthunters' equipment picked up the electrical imprint of the past in stone.

Stop it, he told himself.

Only some of the places they had used appeared to be lit. The toilets were locked and in darkness, as was the office where they'd left the cash raised this evening and the remaining boxes of wine. Had he begun closing down and only got so far? Why was his car still here? Why wasn't he answering his phone? What could happen to a healthy forty-something man in an empty school? What kind of accident could you have? What kind of heart attack or stroke or –

He knew before he stepped into the classroom. Before he heard the wire coat hangers jangling on the empty rail, the flapping corners of notices on the wall, all disturbed by the wind blowing in through the open double doors to the yard. His instinct was to close them and he began to make his way down the aisle between the rows of tables and chairs then glimpsed something so terrible he had drawn in his breath before his brain registered and made sense of what it was. For there, crumpled awkwardly at the foot of those doors and soaked with blood from the deep dark wound beneath his ribs, was Stephen.

Thirteen

"Stephen?" Finn was on his knees beside him. "Jesus Christ. *Stephen*. Can you hear me?" He was slumped unconscious against the door, his skin clammy, breathing harsh, his shirt, his lap, the floor beneath him a deep, wet red. Finn cursed again. There was nothing with which to staunch the flow. Shrugging out of his jacket, he pulled his shirt off over his head, bunched it, pressed hard against the wound. "It's okay." He barely recognised his own voice. "You're gonna be okay. We'll get some help." *Fuck.* How long had he lain here? Long enough for the pool of blood in which he was kneeling to have spread so wide. But hardly more than an hour since he and Leigh had left. Who had done this to him?

And then the laboured gurgle of his breathing stopped.

Finn sought his pulse. Nothing. Dragged him down to lie on his back, tilted his head, lifted his chin. Still not a sign of breath. No time to panic but shit, how did you do CPR on someone with a hole in their chest? Pinching Stephen's nostrils closed, he blew into his mouth.

And somewhere outside, the sound of sirens.

Clattering in the hall, the quick soft thud of footfall behind him in the room. A hand on his shoulder, gently urging him back. "What's his name?"

"Stephen."

"Stephen. Can you hear me?"

The paramedics took over with swift, professional calm. Finn stood up to give them room, backing helplessly into a table. One of them, performing chest compressions, glanced over at him as the other continued with rescue breaths. None of it, as far as Finn could see, making any difference. "How long ago did you find him?"

"Just a minute or two. Is he … will he … "

That they gave no answer was confirmation enough. This is not real, he thought desperately. This cannot be happening.

"Was it you called the ambulance?"

"No." He was shivering, bare-chested, his bloodied shirt discarded on the floor.

"Somebody with you?"

"There's no one with me." It hadn't struck him until then. His thoughts whirled. "I don't know who called the ambulance."

Needing some air, he staggered outside to sit against the bonnet of his car, staring at the blue lights flashing in the dark, at the paramedics in their green and yellow uniforms, the SOCO team in their spacesuits. The crackle of police radios punctuated the rainy night. He hadn't realised he was shaking until he tried to phone Leigh and was unable to hold his mobile steady.

"What's happening?" She was shrill with worry. "Are you all right?"

His throat constricted. "There's been … " He could barely speak. "I found Stephen."

Silence. After a moment she said, waveringly, "And?"

"He's been attacked. Stabbed." Silence again from her end. He closed his eyes. "He's dead." He heard her intake of breath. "The police're here, ambulance. I'll need to give statements … "

"Finn." Her voice cracked. "Come home."

"I will."

"Mr Macallister?" DS Whelan coming across the car park towards him.

Finn, his mobile still in his hand, looked at him and was barely able to register who he was.

Whelan regarded him. "Are you all right, sir?"

"I don't know." The truth, but it didn't sound anywhere near good enough. He didn't realise he was sufficiently white-faced and hollow-eyed for the question to be redundant.

"I'm sorry," Whelan said. "I know you and Stephen Lord were friends as well as colleagues."

Finn swallowed, nausea rolling in his belly. It was all over. The burgeoning friendship, the growing respect and trust, the promise of team-work. No more of that. No husband for Claudia. No father now for Lucie and Henry. "I have to tell

Claudia."

"Don't worry, we're taking care of that. What happened tonight, do you know?"

He explained, briefly and brokenly. Whelan's questions were few. "Do you want me to come and make a statement?"

Whelan shook his head. "You need to go home. We'll deal with all that in the morning."

He nodded. The foyer doors opened, paramedics wheeling the covered stretcher through the cordon and towards the ambulance. Mike Whelan watched as distress began to melt the shock in Finn's face. "Are you going to be all right to drive?"

"I'm fine." Far from the truth, but he could not bear to wait around for someone else to take him.

Leigh, ready to draw him into her arms as he stepped through the door, caught her breath. Pale and wild and rain-swept, he wore nothing beneath his jacket. The knees of his jeans were soaked, his fingers smeared with blood. "Oh my God."

He said unsteadily, "Give me a minute." He walked past her into the bathroom, dumped his jacket, kicked off his shoes, unzipped his jeans. Leigh fetched him some clean clothes.

"What happened?"

"I found him on the floor by the doors to the yard. Blood everywhere, no one else around. I was too late." He looked at her, tears standing in his eyes. Leigh began to cry. "Why did I let him lock up on his own? What would it have cost me to wait?"

"Don't," she told him. "How could any of it be your fault?"

"But maybe I could've prevented it, you know? Just by being there."

"And maybe you'd have been killed too!"

He stared at her, reached to embrace her and saw the blood still staining his trembling hands. Whispered, "Oh Jesus, Leigh."

She held him as his tears fell.

The doorbell rang. Finn swallowed, wiped his eyes. A DC

Hitchen at the other end of the intercom. "Can I have a quick word, Mr Macallister? It won't take long."

"Sure."

Hitchen – fifties, local, shrewd-eyed – came up, shook Finn's hand. "Just to introduce myself, really. Let you know CID are involved, brief you on procedure."

Finn nodded. He wasn't capable, Leigh thought, of doing much else. She stood in the kitchen making tea, listening to Hitchen's low voice, glancing now and then at Finn and struggling with her own composure. A few hours ago she had been sitting beside Stephen in the dim, anticlimactic emptiness of the Arts Theatre, watching the kids hanging around, clearing up, congratulating themselves on the evening's success. She could hear Snow Patrol's *Chasing Cars*, see the relief in Stephen's smile, the sincerity in his eyes. It was not possible, she thought, that an hour or so later he was dead. When she thought of knife crimes she thought of inner cities, rival gangs, drugs, racial tension. Her tears streamed. She heard DC Hitchen saying, "So if you and Miss Somers would come down to the station tomorrow ... "

"Of course," Finn replied.

"And in the meantime, if I could take the rest of your clothes?"

Finn fetched them, handed them over. When Hitchen had gone she hugged Finn to her, took his hand and led him gently to bed.

They lay awake, staring into the shadows of the ceiling. Finn, almost afraid to voice the thought, said, "What if they think I'm involved?"

She turned her head to look at his profile in the dark. "You are involved. We both are. But they know you didn't kill him."

"Do they? I was first on the scene, his blood all over me."

"Finn, don't."

He was silent.

She added, "I can't stop thinking about Claudia."

"No. Me neither." He paused. "You know who else I can't stop thinking about?"

"Yes." She was watching him. "Cal."

"Two deaths. Two deaths within a month and I found them both. I'm sure the police'll draw that to my attention tomorrow. Because it's weird, isn't it? It's suspicious."

"It's weird but it's explicable. Cal came to talk to you and died before he could. Claudia called you because she knew you'd been at school with Stephen and yours was the only number she had. Cal's more than likely to have been whacked by someone he'd annoyed. He annoyed enough people. And maybe tonight thieves were hanging round outside school knowing there'd be the takings from the show. It's happened before, you know that, laptops have gone, petty cash."

"And Stephen got in the way?"

"Tell me it doesn't make sense."

He rubbed his eyes. "Come here."

She rolled closer. "I love you."

He held her tight. "And I love you." Added, after a long moment, "But thieves, thuggish kids with knives, do they stab someone and leave them for dead and then call for an ambulance?"

The interview room was grey and cold, its single fluorescent strip barely supplying any light, the table small and stained, the seating hard. Someone brought her tea steaming in a polystyrene cup, a couple of Rich Tea biscuits on a plate. Claudia noted the tape recorder on the desk between them. "You're going to be taping me?"

"It's a murder enquiry, Mrs Lord. It's procedure."

She didn't comment. She felt she was inhabiting a parallel world in which the bizarre and cruel and impossible held governance. They had told her last night that Stephen was dead, which could not be true. That they needed to interview her, which was plainly ridiculous. That they were conducting a murder enquiry, which left her puzzled. She had stood, early this morning, beside her husband's body in the hospital mortuary and felt as though she were a character in a play. Yet some distant, cocooned part of her understood the truth perfectly. She listened while they named who was present and what day it was. Her mind was wandering. She didn't know what the matter was with her.

" ... and clearly any information you can give us to help find whoever did this will be invaluable."

She looked at the police officer whose name she could not remember and wondered whether he thought her behaviour odd. But then he had, presumably, years of experience of interrogating the violently bereaved and, also presumably, they all responded differently. It didn't necessarily mean anything. "What would you like to know?"

"Recent background, to begin with. Had anything in your husband's life changed, in the last few months? Had he changed?"

"Well yes, but for the better. He'd had a horrible beginning to the term, dealing with appalling behaviour, the death of one of the pupils – but you'll know about that – and then suddenly everything seemed to get better. He was asked to chair a steering group, which he regarded as an honour, school seemed to settle down, results were up. Staff relations were improving. He was happier than he had been in a long time."

"And at home?"

She looked him in the eye. "We were fine. We'd always been fine."

"Tell me about what you know of last night."

"I don't know anything. He stayed in school helping prepare for the show, rang me to say he'd be home at about eleven. When he wasn't, I called his mobile to see if he'd been delayed and there was no reply. So I called Finn Macallister."

"You were worried?"

"Yes."

"But you didn't call the police?"

"It wasn't that sort of worried. I thought perhaps the car had broken down. Or ... there were a few parents, of pupils Stephen had excluded, who had been threatening towards him. I thought as the school was open to the public last night, some of them might be there. That if he'd been cornered by one of them Finn would be able to help."

"Do you know which pupils these were?"

"*I* don't, no. Finn will."

"What sort of threats did they make?"

She said wearily, "Oh the usual, I expect. You know the mentality of people round here better than I do."

"Physical threats?"

"I believe so, yes."

The police officer – Phelan? Wheeler? - gazed at her as though he were weighing her up. A headache was beginning above her right eye and she wanted to go home. She said, "I'm sorry, I don't understand is why you're still sitting here speaking to me. I need to go home." She rubbed her right temple with the heel of her hand. "I need to be with my children. They've been with my parents since last night and they don't know what's happened."

"Of course. I'm sorry. Just one last thing. Does the name Todd Kershaw mean any-thing to you?"

She sighed. "No. I've never heard of him."

The temperature had plummeted after last night's rain, leaving patches of pale blue sky and a watery sun edging through the clouds. She noticed this as she hurried down the steps outside the police station, the light in her eyes, glinting off the cars and the plate glass of the showroom on the opposite side of the road. A tall, dark-haired man was walking purpose-fully towards her, a woman at his side. "Claudia." She was confused. He must know her from somewhere. "Claudia. I'm so sorry."

Her consciousness slammed back in, but no words came with it. She let Finn embrace her. She said tightly, "Thank you, for going to him last night."

He shook his head. He looked, she thought, tired and upset. "I should never have left in the first place."

"Did he say … anything?"

"No. I'm sorry. He was already unconscious by the time I got there."

The woman, whom she recognised now as Leigh, hugged her too. "I can't believe it. It's so awful. If there's anything at all we can do, anything you need … "

"Thank you." They both seemed so distressed, so desperate to help that she tried to think of something to appease them. "I suppose there're his things, in his office. His personal belongings."

Finn nodded. "I'll box them up for you. Unless you want to come in … "

Claudia looked at him. "I don't ever intend setting foot in that school again."

She tried to drive away without putting the car in gear, forgot to use the handbrake whilst queueing on the hill out of Rapton and almost rolled back into the bus behind. Angry with herself, she strained at concentration, announcing out loud potential hazards, traffic light changes, mirror-signal-manoeuvre as she used to do when she was seventeen and had first passed her test. But focussing so intensely on the mechanics of driving seemed to mean that something else had to slip out of control, for she discovered twice that she had taken a wrong turn on this oh so tediously familiar route from Rapton to home, was steering carefully along a country lane she did not recognise, or entering the fringes of an industrial mill town miles from where she ought to be. Unnerved, she turned the car around, following the lane or the dual carriageway back to the point at which she had drifted. Gritted her teeth and drove on.

More than an hour after she had encountered Finn and Leigh, she pulled up in the side-street behind the delicatessen in the small town which was home, in her favourite row of up-market shops and bars and small expensive restaurants. The area had been pedestrianised years ago, its central paving home to extravagant flower tubs and ironwork benches during the summer, a French market at Christmas. The town had a zero tolerance order against drinking alcohol outside and was to everyone's relief policed on a regular basis. Claudia had always felt safe here.

She entered the dimmed interior of the deli, picking up a wire basket from the tray near the door. Lucie and Henry loved the chocolate animals they sold here and she dropped two into her basket as a treat, a crocodile with iced scales and a rather surprised owl. Dinner on Saturday nights, whether they had guests or not, was always special and she lingered around the wines, eventually selecting a French red and a Californian white, chose three pots of different kinds of olives, some home-made garlic mayonnaise, a round of ripe camembert. There was some fruit at home, she seemed to remember, which would do for dessert, but failing that she took a lemon torte from the chiller cabinet. She always judged whether she had finished shopping by the weight of the basket on her arm rather than by the number and price of its contents, and just now it felt satisfyingly heavy. She opened the door, hearing its familiar musical chime as she stepped into the cold sunshine.

"Claudia?" Marissa, who owned the deli and was one of Claudia's closest friends, had followed her out.

Claudia looked at her expectantly.

Marissa indicated the weighty basket full of unpaid-for goods which was cutting a red welt into Claudia's forearm. "Are you all right?"

"Oh! I'm so sorry. I must have been miles away … " She stopped abruptly, staring at the ingredients for a special Saturday night dinner for Stephen and herself. And then everything seemed to stop: the cogs in her brain; the pumping of her heart; her ability to breathe.

"Claudia, what's wrong?"

"No, I'm fine, really. It's just, Stephen was murdered last night."

She saw the horror in her friend's eyes and at the same moment clasped her hands over her mouth to contain her own howling scream.

Finn sat in the same cold, grey room in which Claudia had been interviewed, his head in his hands, the boiling tea in its polystyrene cup sending wisps of steam into the air. He thought of Leigh, being spoken to simultaneously in another room, of Claudia's vacant eyes, the deadness of her voice. Of feeling guilty and appalled and ashamed of having any feelings at all. The door opened and he straightened up. Whelan, with another officer Finn hadn't seen before.

"Finlay Macallister, DI Patrick." Patrick nodded. He was

fiftyish, close-cropped grey hair, the face of a benign brickie rather than a senior police officer. They sat. Whelan said, "How're you feeling this morning?"

He gestured, helpless. Watched Whelan do the stuff with the tape, announce their attendance. Finn rubbed his eyes, reached for the tea.

"How long have you been teaching at Rapton?" Mike Whelan asked him amicably.

"Five years."

"No illusions, then?"

Finn acknowledged the wry humour. "I never did have. I was a pupil at the grammar, so I've always known Rapton by reputation and by truth."

"Ah. A local boy."

"Kind of." He sketched in his background, understanding the form. Relax them with the innocent questions, watch them like a hawk with the tricky ones. "But I've been happy at Rapton. I hope I've done some good work. Built up good relationships with the kids."

"And that's important to you?"

"Sure. I think it's partly – mostly – what teaching's about."

"And the staff?"

"The staff too."

"You'd got to know Stephen Lord quite well?"

"Recently, yes."

"What did you think of him?"

"I liked him. A lot. It's a huge loss, personally and professionally."

"Tell us," Patrick said, "what happened last night."

He described the evening. The talent show, the party afterwards. Stephen's offer to lock up. "I was knackered," Finn said. "I just wanted to go home. I wish to God I'd stayed."

"When you left," Whelan said, "was there anyone else around? Any other cars?"

"There was nothing that struck me as odd. But the school had been full of people all evening. And as I said, I was tired. I might not have noticed if there were."

"So you went home?"

"I did. We did, Leigh and I. And then around midnight, Claudia rang." He detailed her concern, his drive back to school, the minute by minute journey from getting out of his car and trawling the empty corridors to finding Stephen.

"But you didn't make the emergency call?"

"I didn't have time. I was trying to … " He stopped, thinking of his vain attempts to prevent Stephen from bleeding to death, to resuscitate him. Of how for those few minutes he'd genuinely believed it possible.

"Trying to … ?"

He shrugged at the hopelessness of it all. "Save him." He still couldn't absorb the words. "I was thinking last night, who does that? Who stabs someone to death then calls for assistance? Is that more likely to happen if it's a personal rather than a random attack?"

Whelan nodded. "Exactly. But you're looking at it from the point of view of expecting it to make sense, which is what I tended to do when I first joined the force. Sometimes nothing about a crime makes any sense at all. Which is why anything you can tell us, however bizarre it seems, might be crucial."

"Do you know of anyone … " Patrick hesitated, as though considering how to phrase it " … anyone who might have wished Stephen harm?"

"Not that kind of harm. Sure, there were people who were pissed off with him - kids he'd excluded, parents of kids he'd excluded, staff with axes to grind. There was a boy, Josh Ferris, who was excluded for terrorising a Year 7 girl with a knife. I know his mother came in to complain to Stephen. But no, of course I don't know of any one who'd have actually wanted to kill him. People don't, do they, in the real world?"

Patrick gestured. "Unfortunately they do. Also, though, things have a tendency to escalate. Most murders aren't premeditated. Especially where knives are involved. So we'll be talking to anyone who harboured even the smallest grudge against Stephen Lord." He paused. "I understand it was you that found the body of Callum Bywater?"

"Yes."

"Quite unusual, finding two bodies in as many months."

"It is for me," Finn said with feeling.

"Do you think that could be at all relevant?"

"I don't know. Obviously there's a connection between Stephen and Cal through the school. Between me and Stephen and Cal through the school."

"Is there any other connection between the three of you?"

Finn had been backwards and forwards with this all night. "No."

"We have to explore all possible avenues, Mr Macallister, that's all." Patrick added unexpectedly, "What do you know of a lad called Todd Kershaw?"

Midday and barely twenty minutes into her interview and Leigh felt drained and hollow eyed. It felt, to be fair, less like a police interview than a conversation and for that at least she was grateful. DC Hitchen, who'd come to Finn's apartment last night, and DC Miller, a woman of around Leigh's own age, spoke to her with sympathy and concern. As though they understood how it felt for your colleague to be murdered. Quite possibly they did. DC Miller said, "How long have you known Mr Macallister?"

"Since September, when I first came to the school."

"And you've been together … ?"

"Since half-term." A few weeks. She felt as though she had known him forever.

"Did you spend yesterday evening together?"

"Not really. I was helping out back-stage. I saw him briefly before the show started, and during the interval, and afterwards of course."

"Did you both get on well with Stephen Lord?"

"Very well, yes. We were becoming friends."

Hitchen took over. "Leigh, were you and Finn the last people to leave the school last night?"

"Yes, as far as I was aware."

"Did you speak to Stephen before you left?"

"No. He told Finn he'd lock up."

"You left the school at … ?"

"Elevenish. We went back to Finn's apartment. He had a shower, I made tea, put some music on … and then Claudia rang."

"And Finn left straightaway?"

"He did. He phoned me about forty minutes later to tell me Stephen was dead." She swallowed.

There was a silence. She looked at them both and was filled with a sudden sense of foreboding. "Leigh … " Hitchen cleared his throat. "What can you tell us about Todd Kershaw?"

She frowned. "He's a boy in my form. He's an A* student, presented the talent show last night, and he's a bit … unhappy at the moment. Why?"

DC Miller looked anxious. "It seems he's gone missing."

She'd gone a bit funny, had Donna, after she'd had the baby. He watched his sister Julie with her baby, snivelling little scrote that it was, and he didn't see a lot of change. True, Julie had a council flat where her bloke, while being a waste of space, popped in now and again. Donna didn't have anyone except him, or anywhere to go except the children's home where social workers and care workers and health visitors were on her back the whole time. She had to escape from them, she'd explained, so she came here for hours on end, running from other people telling her what to do. He'd thought she were mad, the day he'd turned up to find her squatting in their shack with a baby in a carry cot. That there was a baby at all had freaked him out, and then thinking of her having to go through all those months on her own, being pregnant and scared and lonely. Giving birth, in pain and scared and lonely. "Where's its dad?" he'd demanded that first day, like after leaving her on her own all this time thinking he were dead he had any right to demand anything.

"Well he's not here," she'd said coldly. "And he's not 'it'. He's called Todd."

The baby called Todd had looked right up into his eyes from the carry cot, waved its little fist at him. "How old is he?"

"Four weeks."

He said softly, "Fuckin' hell, Donna."

"I know." She paused. "He's just beautiful, isn't he?"

He nodded. "What happened?"

"Me and his dad split up, but you know that. You disappeared. I found out I were pregnant. As soon as it started showing all kinds of shit happened. Authorities and that. They made me register him but I wouldn't give his dad's name. It's my business, isn't it? It's not about him. It's about me and Todd. I just want to be on my own with him. But I can't do this on my own. It's really hard, Spig." She'd shut up then because she was starting to cry. He put his arm round her.

"You don't have to."

It should have worked. He'd wanted it so much to work. They'd talked about him getting a job and somewhere proper to live or maybe renting this place, if they could find out who it really did belong to, so it would be all legal and everything. But Donna, who he'd always thought of as flaky, got flakier. He watched Julie, docile and calm like a sow with its piglet – the squalling Callum he'd never much taken to – and compared her with Donna, on edge and tearful and moody to the point of unnerving him. Julie wasn't bright, he'd always known that, but she was capable and practical and nothing much fazed her. Donna, on the other hand, who had been all right at school, who liked reading and had all sorts of dreams and plans for her future, somehow couldn't hack normal life anymore. She didn't seem to look after herself as well as she looked after the baby, and if he offered to take him so she could have a bath or go shopping or something she shouted at him for accusing her of being an unfit mother. He nearly gave up, but he liked Todd, who was no trouble. When he'd smiled at him for the first time last week he'd nearly broken his heart.

The trouble was, there were no jobs, and no college would take him with his pitiful lack of qualifications even if they weren't already full. He'd fallen back into the life he'd resorted to when he was away: odd jobs, labouring, nicking stuff. He did a bit of running for Julie's bloke but it was in Moss Side and he was scared shitless by memories of the Night of the Guns. Couple of weeks back he'd done a burglary down the road – lifting a VCR so crap he'd had to give it away – and been arrested and charged, then up in court today and released on bail with a curfew and a criminal record. He'd traipsed back to the shack, to find the baby in his carry cot on the floor again and Donna gabbling hysterically that she had a plan.

"What plan?"

He stood truculently in the middle of the living room, watching her dart back and forth shoving things into bags. All the baby's stuff that she kept here, no matter how many times he told her it weren't hygienic, her bits of clothes and make-up, the bottled water they drank and washed with. A book she'd been reading. The mirror with the shells stuck round the frame. It was like, he realised suddenly, she wasn't coming back. "Donna you're making me fuckin' nervous. What's goin' on?"

"I'm goin' to meet him."

"Who?"

"Someone who's gonna help me."

"I'm helpin' you."

She stopped. She was kneeling on the floor trying to wrench closed the zip of a holdall she'd packed to bursting. Said, accusingly, "Where were you today?"

He told her. His court appearance, the bail and curfew shit. He tried telling her it wasn't fair, they were picking on him when he'd hardly done anything, it was only a stupid VCR that didn't work anyway, but his words sounded pathetic and self-pitying even to his own ears and he shut up.

Donna shook her head. "That's you helpin' me, is it?"

"I was tryin' to get us some dosh."

"Well now it's my turn. I can't trust you, Spig. You go missing for months when I need you and then you turn up again like nothin's happened. You make me promises and you end up in court. I can't rely on you. You're useless."

He couldn't have hit out at her even if he'd wanted to. There was the baby, for a start. And then, she was right. He was fuckin' useless. He said dully, "Will you stop callin' me Spig?"

"Sorry."

"So what you gonna do?"

"The thing is," she said quietly, "I'm useless too. My baby means everything to me, I love him so much it's like it hurts. But how am I gonna bring him up properly? I'm like you, I've got no money and nowhere to live and no chances of getting a job. I can't look after him." She was crying. "I'm not staying at the home, I'm not bringing him up there. I don't want him to have a life like ours."

He was horrified. "You can look after him. We can. We'll start again."

She pushed to her feet. "It's too late. We're no good for Todd, you an' me. But ... there's someone who is."

He stared at her in disbelief. "You're gonna give him

away?"

"No of course I'm not gonna give him away! What d'you take me for? I'm gonna ask him for some money. A lot of money."

"And he'll just give it to you, will he?"

"Yes. He will." She dragged the bags together in the middle of the room, beside the carry cot and the sleeping baby. *"I'm gonna need some help."*

"Why will he give you money, Donna?"

"With the bags and that, I can't carry it all on my own."

"Donna."

"Because he feels fuckin' responsible, all right?" She hissed it so as not to wake the baby. *"Now are you gonna help me or not?"*

The journey was almost impossibly hard. She managed the carry cot, which wasn't heavy but kept banging against her legs, and a holdall packed tight with baby stuff over her shoulder. He lugged all the bags, one on each shoulder, one in each hand. He kept having to stop, they were so heavy, sliding and chafing against his collar bones, wrenching his wrists and elbows from their sockets. She said it was okay, they had plenty of time, but he felt her impatience like a current, dragging him remorselessly into deeper waters. They staggered laden across fields and through streets, knees buckling until they paused barely long enough to catch their breath, pressing on over the waste ground until they reached the motorway embankment, their feet slipping and stumbling over the grass. Twice Donna almost fell and he'd gasped, shouted her name, knowing the chances of surviving rolling down this hill into speeding traffic, the carry cot tumbling after her.

And then they reached the bridge.

"Here we are." She placed the carry cot carefully down on a piece of flattish grass in the shadow of the bushes, let her holdall drop to the ground. He followed suit.

"Here we are, where?"

"We're meeting on the bridge. He should be here soon. You stay here with Todd and the stuff."

"Why are you meetin' him here?"

"Because it's private."

"Because it's private and he can make a fast getaway?"

She glared at him. "You don't know."

"No, too right I don't fuckin' know. I don't know what the fuck you think you're doin' or why you think it's gonna work."

The baby stirred. They exchanged glances. He stirred again, mewling a little. Donna was panicked. "It's time for his feed. There's a couple of bottles in the bag. I made them up before I came. They'll still be all right."

He stared at her. "Me?"

"You've fed him before."

Not on the side of a motorway, in the dark and the wind and the spitting rain.

"Please." She looked desperate.

"All right." He bent down to the carry cot, lifted the baby out. Holding him against his chest with one arm, he unzipped the holdall and rooted round for a bottle of Ostermilk. Scooped it out and sat down on the damp grass. "All right." He snapped the lid off the bottle. "But you tell me. What makes you think this bloke's gonna give you money? If he gave a toss about you we wouldn't be here now."

She ignored that last bit. "Like I said, he feels responsible."

"What makes you think that? He's not been near you, has he? What makes you think he feels responsible for the baby?"

She was scanning the carriageway, the opposite end of the bridge. "Not the baby. I haven't told him about the baby. It's me. I was fifteen, wasn't I, when we did it."

He tipped the bottle, letting the teat fill with milk, the baby's arms and legs wiggling in anticipation. "So?"

"So he was twenty-six."

He shook his head, fearful. "Donna, what you doin'? This ain't gonna work. You're sixteen now. How're you gonna prove anything?"

"I won't need to prove anything! He'll have to help me!"

"You're not thinkin' straight!"

"I am, I am. I've got it all worked out."

The baby began to suck. He cradled him close, holding the

bottle. Looked up at her. "Plenty of blokes shag girls who're underage. They don't hang you for it."

She was still surveying the road, traffic passing fast beneath the orange lamps, impossible to tell one car from another. Her heart was racing with them. "This is different."

"Different how?"

"He's a teacher. It'd be big trouble for him, if anyone found out. Shit, he's there. On the bridge, I can see him. Spig ... "

He was reeling, said automatically, "I'm not called Spig anymore. Donna, why haven't you told him about the baby?"

"Right. I'm gonna go. I won't be long." She looked back at him. "Dean? Look after Todd for me."

Fourteen

Todd had stumbled from the stage, through the bubbling euphoria and grabbing hands, past Sophie, all sweetness now and pouting when he disentangled himself from her arms, past the too-cool-to-emote band members and his own very relieved BTEC Performing Arts crew in whom there was now a clear and powerful need to party. Escaping down a still deserted corridor and out into the yard, he'd tried Dean again. Still no reply. Maybe his phone was switched off. Maybe he couldn't get a signal. Todd, leaning back against the wet brick of the wall, had stared up into a dark and cloudy sky.

Playing through his mind on a never-ending loop was his evening at Cal's. Dean frying eggs and sausage in the grimy kitchen, Cal effing and blinding and generally behaving like a pillock. Dean saying, *have we met before?* and *is your family local?* and asking about his mum. He had known. Todd remembered Cal's throwaway introduction to him, Dean's brief, intense and dawning gaze. He had known.

And said nothing.

Why? Because he thought Todd was playing happy families with Vince and Sheryl? Because it was all too long ago and far too complicated? Because the last thing anyone in their right mind would want was to acknowledge Todd as their son?

Or was it because of the girl his mother? What had happened to her? Why had she died? How? He took the photograph, crumpled still further now, from his pocket and stared at her. His hair was darker and straighter than hers had been, but maybe there was something around the eyes, the shape of his jaw. She looked, in the photo, to be around the same age he was now. And she had died.

Raindrops were falling on her. He slipped her back into his pocket, wiped his face with his bare forearm. Shit. What was he going to say if someone caught him out here crying? And it wasn't exactly helping him find Dean. Swallowing hard, he walked back into school, into the classroom where everyone was changing, drinking, chilling out. Music played so loud he couldn't tell what it was, almost drowning out the hysteria of the girls, the shouting and tuneless singing of the lads. Unnoticed, Todd discovered a half-bottle of vodka secreted away behind the boxes of crisps and cans of Sprite and, uncaring whose it was or whose mouth had been around it before his, swigged long and deep.

The alcohol hit his bloodstream and his stomach instantly. The sensation was so distracting he took another large gulp, the liquid he couldn't take in dribbling from the corners of his mouth down his chin. The room blurred comfortably. He took another.

Ten minutes later he was chucking up.

Miss Somers was there when he came out of the cubicle. "Oh Todd."

"Don't ask me. Don't ask me if I'm all right."

"Have you taken something?"

"No. Just high on life."

She continued to gaze at him. He knew that if she said one nice, sympathetic, caring thing he would break down and sob. It was a likely scenario, it had happened before. And he was tempted, he was so tempted.

He said, thinking of his need to find Dean which would go out the window if she stuck around much longer, "Don't be nice to me, miss."

"All right." She was reluctant, he could tell, but she didn't want to push. "You should go home."

"I will. I am. I'm going now."

"Okay for a lift?"

He nodded. When she'd gone he'd washed his face, taken a deep breath. Stepped back out into the night. People were leaving already, cars queueing to pull out of the gates, their taillights bright and blurry in the rain. Girls who weren't staying for the party sheltering and shivering beneath their umbrellas. Parents loading their boots with costumes and props. Todd hung in the shadows, watching. From the Arts Theatre he could hear the distant notes of Snow Patrol and his heart ached as he listened, willing everything, including himself – especially himself – to shrivel up and blow away. A tremendous shudder passed through him, head to foot like lightening.

And there he was, Dean. Disappearing into The Tunnel.

"Everyone gone?" Stephen asked. He and Finn surveyed the residual damage in the Green Room; nothing half an hour with a vacuum cleaner and a lost property box wouldn't sort out.

"Yeah, all quiet out there."

Stephen smiled. "I think we've turned a corner, you know. Possibly more by luck than judgement – and I wouldn't admit that to anyone else – we've handled something right and the kids are on board and after the term we've just had we get a night like tonight."

Finn agreed. "The feeling tonight is something we could do with bottling. What about making a DVD of all the filming we do at these events over the year, and maybe more general footage around school, putting a music track on it, and giving a copy to the Year 11s when they leave?"

Stephen grinned. "Selling a copy to the Year 11s when they leave? It's a good idea." It wasn't going to do, he thought, to let on to the rest of his staff that Finn Macallister was fast becoming his right-hand man. He knew very well he had some excellent teachers in his employ, but they weren't all necessarily nice people. The consensus of liking and respect for Finn could quite easily become eroded by envy and resentment and that wasn't going to do anyone any good. He'd have to be careful how he played it. He said cautiously, "Have you had chance to give any thought to what we discussed the other night, about the Assistant Headship?"

"I have," Finn admitted. "I'm very flattered, and it would be a great opportunity, and if the situation arises, then yes I will be interested."

Stephen's relief was visible. "Which is exactly what I wanted to hear. Can I have it in writing in case you change your mind?"

Finn smiled. "You have my word. You can trust me."

Stephen looked at him, said with sincerity, "I wish I felt that about more people. You get off now, if you want, Finn. I'll lock up."

"You sure?" Finn smiled.

"Yeah. Thanks for your help tonight. See you on Monday."

After Finn had gone he checked the building, extinguishing lights and locking the toilets, the cash office and the cleaners' cupboard, ensuring doors he hadn't intended to be used hadn't magically unlocked themselves during the course of the evening, that no child still waiting for a lift was in danger of being incarcerated for the weekend. Many people, he knew, found the school an eerie place at night but Stephen thought the empty corridors restful after the daytime rampaging of a thousand teenagers. It allowed him to take ownership again, to take control. To remind himself that it was, in the final analysis, his school.

He returned towards the Green Room, its more glamorous identity for the evening stripped away as the children had left, and raised his hand to the bank of light switches on the wall to the right of the door. Saw, as he did so, a figure sitting on one of the tables towards the rear of the room, in front of the yard doors. Instinctively he froze, then understood.

"Dean Bywater."

Dean frowned. "You don't sound surprised."

Stephen let the corridor exit swing closed behind him, came further into the middle of the room. "I suppose," he acknowledged, "I've been expecting you."

He strolled to a table a couple of yards back from Dean's, sitting against it to take a non-confrontational stance, giving them both space. He hadn't been teaching more than twenty years for nothing. The assumption of a calm, reasonable demeanour, echoing it deliberately in his body language, were just tricks of the trade. He said, "This is about Cal. I'm sorry. I did find the service this morning very moving."

Dean's eyes were shielded with hostility. "You can be as civilised as you like. This ain't gonna be a friendly discussion." He took from his inside pocket a six inch flick knife. Laid it on the table between them. "I don't wanna use it. It's just there to concentrate your mind."

Stephen swallowed. "All right."

"Now. You tell me what happened."

Stephen was silent for a moment. He could see no way out of this other than the truth, which he had a feeling Dean Bywater might recognise when he heard it. "What happened," he began, "is that late that Friday afternoon, when the school was quiet and everyone had gone home, Cal came to my office and accused me of rape."

Dean sighed, understanding immediately. "Oh fucking hell."

"Was my reaction too. He explained that seventeen years ago I assaulted and raped a teenage girl. That she was a pupil at the school where I was a teacher. That he was going to get me sacked and ruin my life." Stephen paused. "He was also keen to let me know that the source of this information was you."

Dean, entirely wrong-footed, shook his head. "It's not what I told him."

"I didn't think it could have been, since it's not true."

"He was jumping to conclusions."

"Yes. Why?"

"Because I didn't tell it right. I just fed him enough to get him off my back. *Fuck*ing hell."

Stephen watched him, dry-mouthed. Oh Jesus. Intent on keeping Dean focussed on Callum he said, "I told him it wasn't true. Naturally, he didn't believe me. Uncle Dean wouldn't lie, apparently. He was so pleased with himself. So bloody *sure*. He mentioned money. Ten grand to keep quiet."

Dean laughed in disbelief. This just got better. "He didn't lack for ambition, did he?"

Stephen paused. "He said he'd give me half-term to think it over. I said nothing would change, I wasn't giving him a penny, and that was more or less it." He was censoring fast. Dean didn't need to know that he'd told Callum he'd never give him the reference the army would need, that he'd promised permanent exclusion, that Callum had then been incoherent with rage. "He accused and threatened me a bit more and in the end he left. It was the last time I saw him. I didn't hit him. I certainly didn't kill him. To be honest, I was so shaken by what he'd said I could hardly think straight. It's never been my first response to use my fists."

Dean said, "But he still could've ruined you, whether he'd blackmailed you or gone to the police. How could you prove it weren't true? And while police and lawyers were runnin' round trying to sort it out, you'd have been suspended, wouldn't you? Reinstated afterwards maybe, but mud sticks."

"Yes," Stephen said bleakly. "I know."

"So whether it was true or not wasn't really that important, was it? Keeping Cal quiet was."

"When Callum died, I was on a plane flying to Italy. I wasn't, if you'll forgive the expression though it is literally true, on the planet."

Dean nodded. "He didn't die like that," he snapped his fingers, "though, did he? Someone hit him, and he got pissed, and when his brain started bleeding he was in no fit state to do anything about it."

"I know. I am so sorry. Genuinely. I'm a father myself, I know how - "

Dean snorted. "When you found out he was dead it must have seemed like a fucking miracle."

Stephen said nothing.

Dean picked up the knife, began turning it from point to end and back again on the table. Stephen watched him.

"So what are you going to do?"

Dean looked thoughtful. "See, I want to believe you. Part of me does believe you. I've not got any illusions about Cal. I know he could be an evil little sod. But he was my sister's kid. And if I hadn't told him what I told him ... " He stopped abruptly. His throat was working. "But I couldn't keep my mouth shut. I'd looked at you in your office that day and I knew who you were. Nearly sixteen years and your hair was a different colour, but I knew. It freaked me out. All these years later, and I think I'm doin' the right thing by Cal, and there you are. Like fate, or summat."

Stephen was washed with heat, then cold. He said unsteadily, "I'm sorry, you've lost me."

Dean, still playing with the knife, looked across at him. "No

I haven't. 'Cos it wasn't rape, I know that. But you still shagged a fifteen year old girl when you were old enough to know better."

Stephen flinched.

"Now that don't bother me that much," Dean's voice was unsteady, his tone grimmer still, "'cos she really liked you, and you made her happy for a bit. And we've all done stuff we shouldn't have when it comes to women. But she pretty much died at your hands, didn't she?"

He didn't see her until he was more than halfway across the bridge, the slight figure waiting on the embankment, saw her spot him and wave excitedly as she skittered towards him. "Hi!"

"Donna." He kept a distance between them, was grateful she didn't attempt to cross it. "Why here? This is a really weird place to meet."

"Well I thought it was far enough away from the home so no one'd see me, and we could just get in the car and go."

"The home?"

"The children's home, where I live."

His heart sank. This just got worse and worse. More and more unnerving. He couldn't believe he'd found her engagingly giddy the night they'd met, that he'd missed in his own drunkenness and despair what was now so humiliatingly obvious. "Go where?"

"Anywhere. I've got all my ... stuff." She gestured vaguely towards a clump of trees a couple of yards away on this side of the bridge. Hesitated. "It's just ... I really ... I thought you might lend me some money."

He'd stared at her, uncomprehending. "Money?"

"We could drive to a cashpoint."

"How much money?"

"I don't know. I thought maybe a couple of thousand to start with?"

His head whirled. She was asking entirely without guile, as though it were house-keeping. Or – he shuddered – pocket money. "I can't get a couple of thousand out of a cashpoint!"

"Haven't you got it?"

"No, actually. I'm a teacher."

"What about your mum and dad? You could say it was for – I don't know. A new car or something."

"I could lie to them?" She gazed up at him beseechingly, her face without a touch of make-up. She looked like the child she was. "Like you lied to me? You told me you were eighteen." And even then he'd felt a bit uneasy, there were girls in the sixth form at his school who were eighteen.

"I wouldn't have got into the nightclub if I hadn't said I was eighteen. Stephen, please. Please. I really really need the money."

"What for? For yourself?"

"And ... someone else."

He'd stared at her. "You want me to extort thousands of pounds from my parents for you to give to someone else? Donna." He pushed his hands into his hair. "Have you any idea what this could do to me, if anyone found out?"

Her eyes had filled with tears. "You're not gonna do it, are you? You're gonna let me down just like everyone else."

"Donna. Listen. I can't just – "

"You can though," she said bitterly. "I've always had to rely on people who've got nothin', people who're in a worse mess than me. No surprise they've let me down. But you ... you're someone. And you have to."

"I don't have to. I'm not going to compound one stupid mistake with another. Oh God. Donna. I'm sorry. I didn't mean it like that. Christ! What the fuck are you doing?" His voice rose in horror, for what she was doing was climbing over the railing of the bridge.

"This," she announced breathlessly, the metal handrail slippery in the rain, "is how much I need the money. Takin' me seriously now, are you? You think it's gonna look bad for you if people find out you slept with a fifteen year old? What's it gonna look like if she's dead?"

"Donna please. Please climb back over. I'm sorry, I'm sorry. Only please, let me help, give me your hand ... "

"Leave me alone!" she shrieked, and in raising her hand to

slap his away, she let go.

For a moment there was silence.
And then, car horns. Smashing glass, screaming.
Stephen stared in terror at the mangled mess of the car and the broken body, the spillage of windscreen and brain matter across the carriageway. He didn't see, yards away on the embankment, the boy holding the baby.

The silence of the empty school was a palpable force around them. Stephen could feel it weighing in on him, bowing him down. He said, "Yes, she pretty much died at my hands. Yes, it has haunted me ever since. All for the sake of one night. But if I could give ten years of my life to change that single moment, don't you think I would?"

Dean tested the tip of the knife against his finger. "I just know," he said, "that I would give ten years of mine. What d'you mean, for the sake of one night?"

"One night. One Saturday night at the end of August. I'd been at something of a low point for a while. My mother was very ill, my girlfriend of three years had just left me for someone else. I needed some sort of escape. I went to a club. Donna was there. I was pissed and depressed and she was pretty and … " Horribly inappropriate to use the words 'up for it' " … keen. We had a few drinks, we danced. I took her to bed. In fact, she took me."

Dean frowned. "But she told me … she made a whole relationship out of one night?"

A whole relationship? Stephen was equally bemused. "She was lonely, wasn't she? And a bit … "

"Barmy." He couldn't think about this now, about poor Donna weaving first love from a one-night stand.

Stephen frowned. "Wait. How do you know all this?"

"I was there." He put the knife down again. "I saw you. I wasn't a lot further away from you than I am now. I was her friend. I was there that night, standing on the embankment with Donna's bags. Holding her baby."

Stephen stared at him. "What?"

"Donna's baby. She didn't tell you? She had a baby, couple of months before she died. You know who that baby's turned out to be? Todd Kershaw."

"*What*?" His head was spinning. "*Todd* is Donna's?"

"Yep. Though he's been adopted and step-fathered since."

Which meant … which had to mean … how many weeks … he couldn't calculate. Not enough, though. He felt sure. Not nearly enough. "How do you know all this?"

"Made it my business to find out."

"Does Todd know?"

"He might, he's been texting me every ten minutes."

The clatter outside had them both on their feet. "Hello!" Stephen called.

Nothing. But somewhere, outside, the slap of footsteps.

Dean paused at the double doors, saw they stood a few inches ajar. "You wanna find out who was listenin' to all that? You stay inside, I'll take the yard."

The corridors were as still and as deserted as he had left them. Stephen checked the dark and cavernous Arts Theatre, ghosts of tonight's audience filling the tiered seating, phantoms of the acts whispers across the stage. He could hear nothing but his own heartbeat. While they'd talked the menace had gone out of Dean's voice, but he was unpredictable, still looking for someone to blame. Had there been someone out there just now, listening to every appalling, damning thing he had said? Or the wind, providing Dean with an opportunity to disappear? He felt weak, as though the blood had emptied from his veins. Dear God. Pivotal moments on which his life hung: a dark and wet night nearly sixteen years since, and now this. How they caught you unawares before they killed you.

For the second time that night he stepped into the Green Room classroom to find someone he knew. This time, someone he knew considerably better than he knew Dean Bywater.

"Todd." He tried to sound only normally concerned. "I thought you'd gone home long ago."

Todd shook his head. He was standing near the yard doors, half in shadow. "I've been here the whole time." His voice was hoarse, his eyes red and swollen as if he'd been crying a while. Stephen had no doubt he had heard every word.

"Todd ... "

"So ... " He swallowed, tried to sound aggressive. "You shagged my mum."

"Yes."

"When she was fifteen."

"I didn't know she was fifteen."

The boy's face contorted. "How did she die? Exactly?"

Stephen took a breath. "It was an accident. A horrendous, shocking accident. She fell from the motorway bridge. We were arguing, she wanted to scare me. She let go and lost her balance. I tried to help her - " He stopped, helpless. No amount of attempting to justify his actions was going to make any difference. "I'm sorry, Todd. I'm so sorry. Believe me, there isn't a day that's gone by that I haven't blamed myself. I've always known I did a terrible thing, that I was partly responsible. Always felt I've been paying for it."

"How?" he cried. "How have *you* paid for it?" He shook his head again helplessly. "I thought Dean was my dad."

"Maybe he is."

"No. He said - 'Holding her baby', 'Donna had a baby'. He didn't say 'our baby'. He didn't say 'my son'." He was weeping, stumbling over the words.

Stephen's gaze had fallen to the table on which Dean had been sitting. To the empty space where his knife had lain. He was certain Dean had not taken it with him when he left to check the yard.

"Todd, where's the knife?"

For the first time he looked at the boy properly, from the ravages of his emotions in his face to what he now realised was not the design but a smear of red along the hem of his white t-shirt. A smear which formed a deeper streak trailing down the leg of his jeans. Dripping from the gash in his left wrist. In the other hand, he just caught a glint of it in the shadow, was a blade.

Stephen was cold. "Oh Christ. Todd. Put it down."

"Leave me alone." He swung away.

Stephen crossed the room towards him in seconds. The knife was in his left hand now, a thin line of blood appearing horribly quickly down his right wrist. "Give me the knife. That's not the answer."

"What the fuck would you know about answers?" He was beyond anyone's control, including his own. "I don't want this. I don't want my mum smashed to pieces on a motorway because of you! I don't want you to be my dad!"

"I'm not. I can't be." In his panic and his guilt everything Stephen had ever learned about confronting an unstable person wielding a weapon deserted him. He grabbed for Todd's hand, intending to hurt him enough to loosen his grasp, as desperate and determined and blinded by emotion as if he were his own son. Todd tried to whip back. Stephen yanked hard and in a fatal misjudgment of speed and direction pulled the boy's wrist, slithery with blood, hard towards him.

Todd stared in disbelief. The front of Stephen's shirt was blossoming crimson yet the knife was still in his hand.

A moment's silence.

Stephen staggered back against the frame of the door, looked with horror into Todd's eyes. "We're both going to need some help here."

He nodded.

"You've got your phone?"

He could scarcely move, make a sound.

"You go. I'm all right. I'll just wait here." His skin was already ashen. His legs folded beneath him and he sank to slump against the cold glass of the door.

Dean found him reeling across the car park as if he were drunk to the gills. "Todd!" He stared at him through the dark as he walked towards him. "That you?"

Todd wheeled round. "Dean."

"What the fuck … " Dean drew level, read the dazed shock in his face. Saw the blood braceleting his wrists. "Jesus fucking Christ. What did you go and do that for?" He gripped Todd by the shoulder, marched him towards his car, opened the passenger door, shoved him inside. "Right." He got in behind the wheel. "Where's Stephen? Did you see him?"

Todd looked at him, glassy-eyed.

Dean wondered how much blood he'd lost. How much did it take? "Well?"

He whispered. "He's in the classroom."

"In the classroom?"

He nodded.

"Okay." There was something he didn't like about this but Todd's wounds didn't look like he could waste any time deciding what it was. "Put your hands on your head. Keep them there. Let's get you to a hospital." He started the engine, took the turn out of the school grounds at speed, tyres screeching. "You're stupid, you know that? Nothing's worth that. Nothing." He'd been driving a few minutes before it occurred to him. "What did you use?"

Todd could not reply.

"Was it my knife?"

He grunted.

"Where is it now?"

Todd tried to force his brain to make connections. "I don't know. I think I lost it."

"Brilliant," Dean said savagely. He didn't know where he was going. Which hospitals had A&E units these days? He didn't have a clue. "Did you talk to Stephen?"

Todd struggled to remove his phone from his pocket. The screen bleeped and died. "It's out of battery."

"Great. You don't need to text me now. I'm here."

"No. He said I should get some help."

"Who said?"

"Stephen."

"For you? We're getting you help. That's what we're doing. That's why I'm driving through the night like a fucking madman not even knowing where the hospitals are."

"Not for me. For him."

I knew it. Dean found he could not swallow. *I fucking knew it.* "What?"

"Only, I think he might be dead."

Dean pulled over. "Right. Hands back on your head. Now.

Tell me, quick."

He did. He didn't cry, but the words were mostly in the wrong order and at times his voice was so faint Dean could hardly hear him. His face was too pale, sheened with sweat. Dean took out his own phone, dialled 999.

And saw ahead, shining among the fold and dips of the valley, the lights of salvation.

It was fucking surreal, he thought, wandering the aisles of a 24 hour supermarket, a suicidal teenage boy bleeding in his car, a man he'd pretended he were capable of knifing himself an hour ago possibly already dead. The bright lights, piped music and cheery 3 for 2 offers made him feel he'd stepped into some bizarre other world. As though blood and death and past secrets were normality, and this only a stylised cartoon fantasy. He found the cold remedies, vitamins and painkillers aisle, loaded antiseptic wipes and lotions, dressings, a couple of first-aid packs and some sleeping pills for good measure into his wire basket. He was pretty sure he looked suspicious, but then he always looked suspicious. If they had him on security footage, so be it. Sorting Todd was his priority.

Back at the car Todd didn't look any better, but he was still conscious. Dean frowned at him. "Todd. Are you with me?"

"Mm."

"I've bought some stuff. Just gonna fix your wrists up. Might hurt." He ripped open a pack of sterile dressing, held it firm against Todd's bloodied wrist, bound it with tape. "Other one."

Todd held out his left arm, like a small child. Dean repeated the treatment, wiped at the remaining blood with one antiseptic wipe after another, was left with a lapful of dark pink tissues like petals. Finally he reached onto the back seat for his old jacket, wrapped it around Todd's shoulders. "Something we need to be sure of, Todd."

He drove back towards the school, parked high up on the back road, out of sight. Todd didn't look like he was capable of putting one foot in front of the other but he said it anyway - "Listen. You don't get out the car. You don't make a sound. Right?"

Todd stared at him.

"Right?"

He blinked.

"Okay then." Dean stepped out, trod carefully down the hill, keeping to the shadows. An ambulance stood in the yard, its rear doors open. Opposite it was a marked police car, two other cars, a small van. He could hear from where he stood the crackle of radios, see the cordons of police tape, a figure he recognised as Finn Macallister sitting against the bonnet of one of the cars, someone else who had to be a police officer walking towards him. Another minute and the doors of the school were opened, a stretcher wheeled out, the body upon it entirely covered. Dean's heart sank.

He pretended to himself there were options he could legitimately reject. Not Julie's. First place they'd look. Not Todd's home. There was only one other place he knew.

He parked at the top of the drive. Todd, less alarmingly out of it by now, peered through the windscreen. "Where are we?"

Dean sighed. "Home. Once upon a time."

It was partly furnished, the water and electricity connected. Still intended to appear as though it were possible, even desirable, to live there. Dean smashed a window in the kitchen door, flicked the lock and they were in. Todd looked at him. "You used to live here?"

"Didn't look like this then." He paused. This might be his only chance to say all this, even if the lad was exhausted and too badly hurt to be able to take it all in. He deserved to know. He filled the kettle, switched it on. "Me and your mum. It was a wreck. We thought we could live here. It was somewhere safe, private, for us to go."

Todd sank down into the rocking chair near the stove. "You really were her friend?"

"Yeah."

"But you're not my dad?"

"I wish I was. I wished it then and I wish it now." He busied himself with making tea, so Todd couldn't read the emotion in his eyes. "She asked me to look after you. When she died I took you to a hospital. I didn't know what else to do. Put a note in your basket with a couple of photos of her."

"That was you?"

"I wanted to do more. Kept tabs on you for a bit. Found out you'd been adopted, thought you'd be all right. We had a crap life, me and your mum. No hope, no way out. Least, we didn't think so. Look at me now. Still got a crap life."

Todd hesitated. "What was she like?"

Dean thought of her, as he allowed himself to think of her now and then, not too much, just a flash of how she had been before everything went wrong, for both of them. "She was lovely. Bit daft. But kind, nice. She liked animals, wanted to work for a vet. She liked readin', and getting dressed up and goin' out … "

Todd gazed up at him. "And she liked you."

"Well. I dunno. We were the same." He handed him a mug of tea. "How're you feelin'?"

"Tired." He paused.

"You should ring home."

Todd shook his head. "They won't notice I'm gone."

Dean doubted this. "There's a load of shit to deal with tomorrow, Todd. I'm gonna try and sort it for you. But you need to get some sleep. There's some sleeping pills on the side there. Take a couple. Beds upstairs. No one's gonna find us tonight."

Todd paused before attempting the stairs. "Cal said you were looking for someone."

"Yeah. I was. Bastard I blamed for Donna. It was useless. She thought the sun shone out of him but all she ever told me was he lived on the Old Road. It's not a lot to go on. I gave up. And then … "

"And then I killed him."

Dean wanted to be able to say no, you didn't. No, it was my fault. Instead he rubbed his eyes, hard, for he could barely bring himself to look at Todd, knackered and ill and broken with guilt. His voice when he spoke was hoarse. "Get some sleep."

Dean sat alone in the darkness. He could walk away from this. He could disappear tonight, return to Scotland. How long before the police were looking for him too? Probably they already were. But Todd's fingerprints would be on that knife. Todd's blood had dripped across the yard.

He rested his elbows on the table and his face in his hands. When had this started? With Cal's death? With the kitten in the bag? With a highly-strung girl sixteen years ago? Was all of it his fault? Or had he just stepped in at the wrong moments right down the line? The kitten thing, for a start. Gang of thugs behaving like idiots in the school yard, the domino effect of more stupid behaviour, exclusions, knee-jerk reactions … and there he'd been, giving Cal the ammunition which had blown up in his face. Take him out of the equation and where would Cal be now? He remembered the conversation word for word.

"It's not what I did," he'd said. "It's what I know."

Cal had looked unimpressed. "So what d'you know?"

Dean slung his bag in the car, leaned back against the door. "About that headteacher of yours. Stephen Lord."

Cal narrowed his eyes at him, trying to work out whether he was being fobbed off, like how the fuck would Dean know anything about Stephen Lord? "Yeah? What about him?"

He'd paused. "If I tell you, you keep your gob shut, understand? It's in the past, let it stay there."

Cal had snorted, sat down on the wall outside his house, still torn between scepticism and interest. "'Course."

Dean had taken a breath. "When I was about your age, livin' in that kids' home up the road, I had this friend. A girl. She were me best mate. She … got pregnant. I went away, came back, and … she'd had a kid."

"Right." Cal stared at him, still waiting for him to get to the point. "So?"

"I saw who he was. Bloke who got her pregnant. Knew I'd never forget his face."

"And?"

"Saw him again this afternoon."

Cal shook his head, not up for solving riddles. You could see, Dean thought, his brain struggling to make sense of the gaps he'd left because he couldn't bring himself to fill them in. Cal said, after a minute and in slack-jawed disbelief, "Stephen Lord?"

"Yeah." Dean wished he'd never started this, wished he'd kept his trap shut.

"Fuckin' hell." The news sank in. Cal grinned. "Stephen Lord, eh?"

"What have I told you? You keep schtum."

"Yeah all right. But I don't get it. Birds have it off with someone, they get pregnant. Happens all the time. And this is like, sixteen, seventeen years ago, why're you still so pissed off about it?"

Dean reined in his temper. "She needed his help and he wouldn't give it. She was just a kid herself."

Cal frowned at him. "A kid? How old was she?"

"Fifteen."

Cal looked like he couldn't get his head round it. "What fifteen year old girl'd shag that tosser?"

"Sixteen years ago, Cal. He didn't look like he does now."

"Yeah, but he were always a tosser, right?"

Dean said nothing. Cal watched him. "What happened to her?"

Just say the words. It happened. Say it. "She died. Just after she'd had the baby."

"He was a teacher, he shafted a fifteen year old girl who had his kid and died?"

"Yeah." Dean exhaled. It might help to explain, tell the story properly. Only he couldn't go there. "'Bout the size of it."

"And that's why you're pissing off?"

"Can't live with it. Can't stick around here, knowing who he is, where he is, without doing somethin' about it." He caught the expression in Cal's eyes. "She were me only mate. I thought a lot of her. I never really got over her, Cal. But I'm not goin' back inside for him."

Cal looked at him. "If you thought so much of her, why didn't you help her? 'Cos it's all very well blaming the bloke what shagged her, but she'd have been relying on you wouldn't she? If you were such great mates."

Dean felt winded. "I tried. But I were only sixteen meself – "

"So fuckin' what? Don't matter how old you are, you can still stand up for someone." He looked at Dean with disgust. "It's a long time ago. You've got me and me mum to look after now. Why are you pissin' off and leavin' us over summat that happened all them years ago?"

Dean said nothing.

"It ain't fair." Cal's voice was tight with emotion. "It's not right, what you're doin'." "You can't deal with what happened in the past and you haven't got the guts to stand up to Lord. You are a fuckin' coward and you know it and that's what you can't live with."

"And that's who you want to stick around, is it? A fucking coward? If that's what you think of me Callum, what's the point?"

"Don't put this on me," Callum retorted. "Not my fault. Who're you thinking of here, Dean? Dead people? Some bloke who doesn't know you exist? Me? Me mum? The only person you're thinkin' of is you, you selfish bastard."

"Yeah you're right." He'd been bone-weary suddenly. "You're right. I'm a fucking coward and a selfish bastard. See you, Cal." He'd opened the car door and slid inside, started the engine. As he pulled away he'd heard the door of his sister's house slam hard.

He'd regretted it as soon as he was away, heading north. As soon as it was out of his mouth. He'd promised Julie. Promised Cal. But what was a promise worth to someone who hated you? Cal was a kid, hitting out because he didn't know how else to react, Dean understood that. He'd done it himself often enough. But he was right. Cal'd cut to the heart of it and it hurt. He hadn't stood by Donna. He hadn't helped her. He was just as fucking guilty as the bloke on the bridge. What right did he have to think he could teach Cal anything?

And now. Coming back for his funeral. Wanting to batter the truth about Cal's death out of Stephen Lord and instead getting him killed. Getting a vulnerable boy into the kind of trouble he might never recover from. And not just any vulnerable boy.

Donna's boy.

EXCLUDED

He remembered his flight through the night with Todd in the carry cot, horror streaming in his veins. Remembered scribbling the note in the hospital car park, tearing a couple of photos from the strip Donna had once given him, slipping them down the side of the blankets. He'd thought the baby would be safe, in a hospital. Somewhere warm and clean, where people would look after him properly. And then he'd disappeared again, and his life had spiralled out of control once more, sending him back into squats and homelessness and petty crime which had ceased to be petty, ending with a prison sentence for an armed robbery in which he had been only peripherally and reluctantly involved.

Then spewed him out onto the streets of Rapton. And now two more people were dead.

Yet because of his actions all those years ago, Todd had been saved. He was clever, he talked posh, he wanted to go to university. He lived in a big house with people who fed and clothed him. Did that count as getting something right?

But he'd fucked it up again, hadn't he. For tonight this clever, well-spoken, nice young man with plans and a future had tried to top himself. Tonight he had been involved in someone else's death. The same person who was responsible for Donna dying. It ought to be fate, some sort of divine justice, yet somehow it wasn't. For fate didn't account for the supreme talent of Dean Bywater for wrecking everyone else's life. He had been there. Every time.

He scrubbed his face with his hands. All-time low. That was what this was. There had to be some way to make it right. Forever.

"Dean? Look after Todd for me."

Fifteen

It had grown cold overnight, the fields shining white with frost in the pale dawn. In a few weeks it would be Christmas, the first Christmas he hadn't spent inside for seven years. It ought to feel like something to celebrate. Dean could not imagine a time when there would be any point or meaning to celebrating anything. His whole life had been an endless solitary tunnelling without ever reaching the light; only ever a series of wrong turns which seemed to take him further underground, deeper into darkness. His turn would come, he had once believed. One day he would be out there on the surface with everyone else, when the sun would shine on him too and the prize of ordinary happiness would be his for the taking. He didn't believe it anymore.

He had not slept. Sitting upright on the foam sofa in the stage-set of a living-room, he had felt his body jerk now and then through the night and realised he'd fallen briefly into sleep. Every so often he'd hauled himself up the stairs to check Todd was still breathing, the anxious parent to the newborn. Now, at first light, he'd washed and made himself some tea with the bags from the cupboard and the milk he'd had the foresight to pick up along with last night's medical supplies, stood clutching the mug and looking out across the frosty fields. It was really the simplest and smallest of lies. Every other detail he could describe exactly as it had happened. Playing these over in his mind reassured him. From his arrival back in Rapton at the beginning of September, his involvement with Cal and his flight to Scotland, to his grief and anger at his nephew's death. He could take them through every minute of yesterday and not have to lie about a single thing.

Until that final, flashpoint moment.

One of the items which the house's owners had not left behind to dizzy potential buyers with the illusion of comfortable living was a television. Dean left quietly through the kitchen door, tramped round to the front where he'd left the car, sat inside its icy shell and switched on. Searching the radio stations for local news he hit upon classical music from the BBC, the inane babble of Century FM and a discussion of farming in the Ukranian steppe. Opera, some nineteen-seventies pop, a preview of the days' sport. He'd got so impatient he almost missed it, had to twizzle the dial back to find it again, the solemn female voice pronouncing names he knew.

" … murder last night of Stephen Lord, head of Rapton Community High School in East Lancashire. Mr Lord, who had been stabbed to death, was found in a classroom by one of his colleagues following an evening of entertainment at the school. Fiona York has the details … "

Dean listened for another minute then snapped the radio off. He knew the details. Every last one of them. The point was, it was now public knowledge. Would the vanishing of Todd also be public knowledge? Would the police even be looking for him yet? How many teenage boys spent the night at a mate's without bothering to tell their parents? How much fuss would Vince Kershaw be making? Dean suspected it wouldn't be until they'd analysed the blood samples from the floor that anyone'd start getting seriously worried.

And where would Todd be by then?

It was the only factor he couldn't control. Todd himself. He knew that if he explained to the boy exactly what he was intending to do, Todd would have something to say about it, something which would land them in even worse trouble than they were already in and the promise he had made Donna all those years ago would be broken for good. On the other hand, if he didn't tell him …

He got out of the car and went back inside the house. Todd was still asleep, on the single bed in the tiny blue painted room clearly meant to be viewed as a nursery. Dean stood, gazing down at him. His cheeks were flushed, his breathing fast and shallow. He needed a wash and some food and – ideally – proper medical attention. Ordinarily Dean wouldn't want to leave him alone, but what was the alternative? He didn't know what to do with the boy. Drop him back at Vince's? Deliver him to the police? Todd needed to know what truth he was going to be telling. What could he do, leave a note for him which could incriminate them both?

Or trust, to Todd's intelligence and everyone else's assumptions? Who was anyone going to believe more capable of killing - accidentally or otherwise - a surly, homeless ex-con with the murder weapon, the motive and a criminal history stretching back two decades, or a pleasant and popular young lad from a good home and with a history of nothing but kindness and decency?

Dean switched on his phone, its charge full, signal on two bars and left it on the little fake pine table beside the bed. He hesitated, touched his fingers briefly and gently to the boy's forehead, and left.

Leigh felt disoriented as she left the police station, so burdened by the reality and the ripple effects of Stephen's death and now the news of Todd's disappearance she couldn't quite assimilate the sight of Christmas decorations, of Saturday morning shoppers, ordinary life. Finn was waiting for her on the low stone wall separating the station forecourt from the pave-ment, rose to meet her as she came towards him. "How was it?"

"All right." She hugged him. "They were very nice."

He nodded. "They tell you about Todd?"

"Mm."

He squeezed her hand. "Maybe he was out celebrating last night, got drunk, dossed at a friend's."

"He didn't look as if he felt much like celebrating to me."

Finn sighed. He had slept only fitfully during the night, his dreams of Stephen vivid and horrific, waking damp with sweat and a pounding heart to remember this was the nightmare. Learning this morning than Todd had been reported missing was more than he could bear. "Do you know what I think we should do? We should drive out somewhere, Wycoller or Downham maybe, somewhere quiet and beautiful, have a pub lunch, walk by the river."

"You want to escape."

"Yeah." He was rueful. "Does that make me shallow?"

"No."

He heard the reservation in her voice. "But?"

"No, I think it's a good idea. I just ... I want to feel I've done something to help Todd."

He held her gaze. She had become his conscience. "Such as?"

"I don't know."

"Leigh, you know, what are the chances? He's probably fine, holed up and hung-over somewhere."

"And what if he's not? How will you live with yourself Finn, if he's not?"

He took a breath. He had fought enough. "All right. We'll go to see Vince. Todd might have turned up by now, might have rung home."

She nodded, reassured. "You know where he lives?"

"I grew up around here. I know where everyone lives."

They walked, hand-in-hand, to his car. He paused with the key in the lock, his attention caught by something she couldn't place. "What?"

He straightened, watching the man crossing the forecourt a few yards ahead of them. Leigh frowned. He was in his thirties, she guessed, had a dirty blond skinhead, was wearing stained jeans, a battered biker jacket and an expression of rigid determination. Alone with him in a dark street, she would have been uneasy.

To her surprise Finn walked over to him. "Dean?"

The man called Dean stopped in his tracks, bewildered.

"Finn Macallister." Finn held out his hand. "We met at school back in October? I was Cal's Head of Year."

Leigh watched. The contrast between the two men – Finn's longish dark hair and open demeanour, the casually hip way he dressed – was so striking they might have been of different races. Different species.

Dean took the hand offered to him. "Yeah ... I remember."

"I didn't get chance to speak to you yesterday. Just wanted to say how sorry I am, about Cal."

He looked taken aback. "Thanks. That's good of you."

"I'd known him since he first came to Rapton. We started there the same year. I won't deny we had a few run-ins," he smiled, "but I always had hope, you know, for Cal."

"That's more than most people," Dean admitted. He paused. "I've just … " he gestured towards the shining glass walls of the police station, " … got business to do."

"We all have," Finn agreed, "today."

"So," Leigh murmured as they watched Dean push open the door to the station. "That's Dean Bywater."

"Yeah. I'd've thought he'd have come to see me, you know. In the circumstances."

"Maybe he will yet. How is it you know him again?"

"We met recently in Stephen's office to discuss Cal. He was at Rapton when I was at the grammar school. I only knew him by repute back then. Although, I did go out for a while with a girl who was friends with him. She was very sweet and she thought a lot of him so he can't have been all bad. She had this weird nickname for him. What was it?" He couldn't remember.

Leigh said, "Okay. Vince Kershaw's house?"

Finn considered. "Saturday morning. Let's try him at the yard."

Todd woke with a start. Several things registered at once, all of them equally unnerving. He had no idea where he was. His wrists throbbed. He'd peed himself. Groaning, he swung to sit up, discovering a headache sledgehammering into his brain as the memories of last night sledgehammered his heart. Shivering, he shuffled naked and stiff-limbed out onto the narrow landing, found a tiny bathroom where he emptied what was left in his bladder. Catching sight of his reflection he drew in his breath. He wouldn't have recognised himself. His skin was pale and waxy, his eyes bloodshot, their lids pink and swollen, his hair sticking up in strange tufts. Maybe this was how you looked when you stopped being a normal person. Once you'd killed someone and tried to kill yourself, you were hardly going to look like you did before, when all you'd been worried about were spots and coursework and how to keep your step-mother off your back. He remembered crying a lot last night. This morning he felt only drained, as if there were nothing of himself left.

Clumsily he washed the pee from his legs and his groin, patted himself with a soft pink towel hanging at the side of the basin. At the top of the stairs he croaked, "Dean!" Even his voice wouldn't work. He tried again, and in the silence of this strange little house surely Dean would have heard him. Back in the child's lilac blue bedroom he found his clothes. He didn't recall undressing before he'd fallen asleep, prayed Dean hadn't done it for him, but his gratitude that his jeans and t-shirt weren't urine soaked was replaced with dismay at the stink of body odour and vomit, the dried streaks and smears of blood. He checked the wardrobes in this room and the next. They were empty. He had no choice but to dress himself in the threads of his own despair.

He picked up the mobile phone next to the bed. Dean's, presumably. Did he not think he needed it? Where was he? Why had he abandoned him here? Cautiously he descended the stairs, looked into the empty living-room and kitchen, sat down at the table with the phone. Dean had said something about having a load of shit to deal with. Was that where he was, dealing with shit? *I'm gonna try and sort it for you.* What had he meant? How was he going to sort it? How much confidence did he have in Dean sorting anything? Except Dean had rescued him last night. Bandaged his wrists. Found him somewhere to stay. Saved his life.

Shit.

He had to swallow hard, his headache reverberating like endless bombs inside his skull. The dressings around his wrists were bloody but dry. Tentatively he picked at the tape binding his left wrist, peeled it back, part of the dressing coming away with it. Steeling himself, he lifted away the stiff red pad. His stomach heaved. The vertical slashes looked deep, unhealed, the skin around them red and swollen, some nasty white stuff in there which probably shouldn't be. He saw, suddenly, instead of his own wounds, the deep red gash in Stephen

Lord's chest, his blood pumping out over his shirt, his look of disbelief. *It was an accident.* Would anyone ever believe him? The knife had been in his hand.

He picked up the phone. Dialled. *Please help me. Please help me.*

"Hello?" Sheryl said.

His heart plummeted. "Is Vince there?"

"Todd?" He could say nothing. "Todd, is that you?"

"Mm."

"Where are you?" she squawked.

"I don't know."

"What do you mean, you don't know? Have you any idea the state Vince is in? He's worried sick about you, you selfish little shit. You want to get back here now and explain yourself."

"I ... "

"He's given you everything and you've caused nothing but trouble for him. You're not even his. I wouldn't ... "

Todd closed his eyes and switched her off.

*

"I wanted to talk to Stephen Lord." Dean watched their faces, DS Whelan's and DI Patrick's, now he'd finally got their attention. It was depressing how long it had taken to get past the desk sergeant and the DC and the people who made the fucking tea. Busy, he'd been told. Murder investigation. He might have heard, it had been all over the morning's news. He had taken a deep breath and explained who he was again, with some force. He knew more about it than they might imagine and he wasn't confessing twice. Senior officers and a tape recorder or nothing.

They had seemed, when he'd finally got to them, mildly surprised that someone with his record was here of his own free will. As if they'd been expecting to drag him in handcuffed after an operation lasting several days and a manhunt covering three counties. Maybe he'd spoiled their fun. They weren't happy about him waiving his right to a solicitor either. But their faces, as they listened, were grave and he was too intent on convincing them of his sincerity to arse around with smart remarks.

"I wanted to talk to Stephen Lord. He was the last person Cal phoned before he died. Which struck me as a bit funny. Why would a lad like Cal be ringing his headteacher? I'd heard, at Cal's funeral, some of the kids talking about this do that were on at the school last night and I thought there was an odds-on chance Stephen Lord'd be there. That it'd be a good place to catch him in private, have a bit of a chat. I hung about, and when everyone else had gone, I waited for him in one of the classrooms. We had a conversation."

"About what?"

"About Cal, mostly. About Stephen." He paused. "Did you find the knife?"

"We did."

"It's mine. It'll have my fingerprints all over it."

Whelan frowned. "This ... conversation you had. Would you describe it as heated?"

"No. In fact, it were quite civilised."

"You had a civilised conversation with Stephen Lord concerning your nephew's death, and then you stabbed him and left him to die?"

"Yeah."

Patrick looked at him for a long moment. "Is it me, or are we lacking a few details here?"

"No," Dean agreed. "That's just the bones of it. We're lacking a lot of details."

"Would you care to fill them in?"

Dean paused. It was harder than he'd anticipated, telling someone else's story. Why, when he was doing this to save the boy, did revealing fragments of the truth feel so much like a betrayal? He said, "Do you know a lad called Todd Kershaw?"

Finn used the Customers Only car park outside Kershaw's Building, took Leigh's hand as they passed through the entrance, dodging brick lorries and forklifts. "It's something of an empire, this, isn't it?" she said, impressed.

"It is. He's a real success story, Vince Kershaw. And a good man."

"Salt of the earth?"

"God. Did I sound that patronising?"

"No. I'm teasing you."

"Sorry." He looked wry. "Bit slow on humour today."

She squeezed his hand, indicated the iron staircase leading up to the offices. "Best bet, d'you think?"

They climbed the creaking treads, knocked and waited. No answer. Finn pushed the door open to find a large man sitting behind a small desk, his florid complexion lined with worry. "Vince Kershaw?" Finn entered, Leigh at his heels.

Vince looked up at him. "Mr Macallister, isn't it?"

"It is. This is Leigh Somers, Todd's form teacher. We wondered whether you'd heard anything from Todd?"

He said heavily, "I've not seen him since yesterday afternoon. You'll have seen him since I have."

"He hasn't phoned?"

He shook his head. "I keep telling myself I'm being daft, that there's nowt to worry about. But then the news this morning. Terrible shock. It can't be anything to do with Todd, can it?"

Neither Finn or Leigh could think of anything both honest and comforting to say. She glanced round at the mess of paperwork, the dumped tools and materials, the Page 3 calendar on the wall. Miss December, with her Santa hat, her air-head smile and improbable breasts.

Vince said, "How was he, last night?"

"He did a fantastic job of presenting the show," Finn told him.

"Aye. I can imagine that. But he wasn't himself."

"No," Leigh concurred. "He wasn't. He was … upset. But he's been upset for a long time, hasn't he?"

Vince looked unhappy. "Yesterday, though, that were down to me." He looked at them both. "He's always been a bit emotional. Sensitive. Worse since he became a teenager, of course. I think his mate dying just made things worse, I don't think it were anything to do with him really. Just sort of churned him up even more." He sighed, the anxiety creeping back into his eyes. "What it is, Eileen, my first wife, she adopted him when he was a baby. He didn't know. We never told him. Then the other night Sheryl, my wife, lets the cat out the bag and ... he was in here yesterday after the funeral. Right upset, he were. I couldn't help. I've never known anything about his birth mum. All I've got, all I've ever had apart from his birth certificate, were one note and a couple of pictures." He rose from behind his desk, lumbered out towards the back of the room. Leigh and Finn exchanged a glance.

"There you go." He handed the open envelope to Leigh. "Looks like he's taken one of the pictures with him. Don't know why I'm showing it to you, mind." She took out the note, read it and passed it to Finn. Studied the photograph for a moment – a girl of fifteen or sixteen, curly brown hair, big dark eyes, sensual mouth. This too she passed to Finn.

"She's Todd's mum?"

Vince nodded. "He were even more upset after seeing those. I don't know why. Maybe it brought it home to him. And she were only young."

"What happened to her?"

"She were killed, in an accident. That's how he came to be adopted. I've done my best, you know, to give him a stable home, bring him up right."

"Oh, of course," Leigh said, filled with enormous sympathy for this fearful, kind bear of a man.

"When ... " Finn cleared his throat. "When was Todd born?"

"Nineteen ninety-two. Twenty-sixth of February. Can I give you my mobile number, and the house number? If you hear anything, will you let me know?"

Leigh scribbled down her number and Finn's too. "Same goes for us. Have you talked to anyone else from school? Do they know anything?"

Vince shook his head. "I haven't spoken to anyone who saw him after about half past ten, eleven o'clock last night. It's like he just vanished into thin air. I just keep thinking, what if he saw what happened to that headteacher? What if whoever killed him turned on Todd?"

Clattering back down the iron staircase, Leigh thought that

she had come here in the spirit of rallying the troops and was now only further depressed. Vince's fears ran deep in her too. No gang of drunken or stoned yobs intent on robbing the school would let Todd go free after killing Stephen. She turned to Finn as they climbed into his car. "Let's do it. Let's go for that lunch and that walk you were talking about."

He shook his head. She touched his arm, knowing that he was still living the horror of finding Stephen, that he worried for Todd too. "I just want to go home."

Todd hadn't lived in Rapton all his life for nothing. Stumbling out of the cottage and down the tarmacked drive, through the five-bar gates and out onto the road of rich men's houses, he realised where he was. The exclusive end of Rapton. It would take him half an hour, from here, to walk to school. Twenty minutes one way to the centre of town. Twenty minutes in the other direction to home.

Except he wasn't going home again. Ever.

And twenty minutes, in his present state, would be out of the question. It wasn't just that he didn't look so good, what with the smell and the blood and his face looking like Mr Hyde's when for nearly sixteen years he'd been Dr Jeckyll. It was more that he couldn't actually walk properly.

If he was going to be really honest with himself, he couldn't actually breathe properly. It was like he kept having to breathe really fast. He couldn't control it and it was scaring him. He half expected a path to open up before him, people parting like the Red Sea to let him through, but there was hardly anyone around and when there was, they weren't looking at him. Maybe he wasn't as conspicuous as he thought, with his *Dawn of the Dead* clothes and his bandaged wrists. His bandaged wrists that hurt like hell and looked even redder and more swollen than they had an hour or so ago. He hadn't dared lift back the dressings again and peer underneath.

Eventually reaching a major road which branched east towards school and west towards Vince and Sheryl's house, he plunged on south, which was good because it meant going downhill. It would be easier, he told himself. He stood swaying on the kerb, nervous at having to negotiate the traffic. He didn't trust himself to make it to the opposite side without crumbling. Somewhere, in his distant consciousness, he knew there were far greater dangers to face than a few cars, but he couldn't go there. It was too bleak, too frightening, and he was, he realised, too ill.

He kept shivering. It was December and he was on the streets in a t-shirt, but it didn't feel like that kind of shivering. It felt inside him somehow. He wanted to sit down, wrap his arms around his knees, bury his head. He wanted what he had wanted last night, except then it had felt like teetering on the brink of madness and now he just felt sunk at the bottom of the pit.

Fuck you, Dean. It could all have been over by now. Why did you have to help me?

There was a park, halfway down this incline which would lead him through the little council estate and then out into town. Lots of bushes, in the park. He could sit down on the soil in the middle of them and no one would know he was there, he wouldn't frighten the little kids or anything, wouldn't alarm the old people or attract the attention of anyone likely to beat him up. It might be warm, in the bushes, and he could rest for a bit. He halted at the entrance, seeing the children on the swings and climbing frames, the old guy walking his dog, the teenagers – ordinary teenagers, not psycho ones – sitting on a bench, laughing at each other. It looked to him like the real world and he wanted to cry again. Someone had said to him once, something like - *if you want to talk, come and find me*. He tried to remember the exact words, the context, but it was like trying to remember a dream, melting away as soon as he came close. And he knew – instinctively, because the process of thinking anything was beyond him now – that finding him was what he must do.

"All right."

They were back, the big boys. Whelan and Patrick. Dean squinted up at them from his seat at the table in the cold and dingy interview room. He was knackered and uptight and desperate. Probably just the way they liked their suspects. "All right. So you were there, at the school. Your fingerprints are on everything."

Dean gestured – what did I tell you?

"But we've been to the house. Todd's not there."

Dean sat back. "Fucking hell. Where's he gone?"

"Believe me, we're looking."

"He was there. You'll find his prints and stuff."

"Oh, I'm sure we will. We found a lot else besides. But we need to find Todd himself. He'll probably need medical attention."

"Yeah," he conceded. "He will."

"So then." Patrick frowned, as though wading through the finer details of Dean's testimony had been a labour so arduous and time-consuming he was no longer capable of cogent thought. "You're telling us that in trying to wrestle your knife from Todd Kershaw you accidentally stabbed Stephen Lord."

"*Yeah*. How hard is that to understand?"

"It's not hard to understand at all. In fact, given what we know – and I'm not saying there isn't more evidence to uncover once we get test results back, but given what we do know, it seems the most likely and reasonable explanation."

Dean sagged. "Thank Christ for that."

"It's just … " DI Patrick considered. "And I can't say why. It's just a suspicion. It should make complete and absolute sense. And it does. So why is it, Dean, that I don't believe you?"

Having abandoned the drive, the lunch, the walk by the river, they returned instead to his apartment. Finn, numb with shock since their meeting with Vince, went to make a drink, sent water spraying from the tap against the tiles, dropped a cup smashing into two jagged halves. "*Fuck!*"

Leigh, watching him, took off her coat, hung it over the back of the sofa. "You okay?"

He shook his head.

She went to him. "Tell me."

He swallowed.

She stroked his arm. "Finn. He'll be all right."

He could not speak.

After a minute - "That girl, in the photograph. It was her." He couldn't quite believe the words. "The girl I was telling you about this morning. Dean's friend."

"The girl in the photo was Dean's friend?"

He nodded.

"Dean's friend that you went out with?"

"Donna Sullivan." He swallowed again, distraught. "She was fifteen and I was eighteen. She thought it was huge, that age gap."

Leigh gazed at him. He could read her understanding in her eyes.

"She was so sweet," he recalled shakily. "So sexy. We had such a great time together. But I was going away to university. I thought, better to say goodbye now than hurt her later when … " He stopped.

Leigh said carefully, "When was this, exactly?"

He had been working it out. "Nineteen ninety-one. January till June." He looked stricken. "I didn't know she'd died. I wasn't around. No one really knew we were seeing each other, I never took her home, we spent all our time alone together. They'd have had no reason to tell me."

"You didn't know she'd had a baby?"

He shook his head.

She drew him to her, held him for a long moment. "Come here." She led him to the sofa, sat down with him still holding her hand. "So," she said bravely. "Todd could be yours?"

He wiped his eyes with his free hand. Said, after a second, "Yes. He could be. Yes, I think he is."

"Okay. Did Donna … "

"Sleep around?" He shook his head. His face creased, remembering her as she had been, knowing now what had happened to her. "She wasn't like that, she was nice, very loyal. She … "

"Loved you?"

"Mm."

"And you loved her?"

"Kind of. Yeah, I loved her. Just not enough." His throat ached. "I feel so guilty."

"But you couldn't have known."

"Why didn't she *tell* me?"

"When did you leave her?"

"In ... June. Before ... she might not've known she was pregnant. After I'd done my A levels I went away for the summer and then ... " He ran his hands through his hair. "Jesus. Leigh. If I'd known, if ... All this time, I could've ... " He paused, his thoughts crowded with memories. "There was this house, she and Dean hid out in, this ramshackle cottage. We'd go there sometimes. We were just kids, you know? It was *Spig*," he remembered suddenly. "She meant Stig, of the Dump. But she called him Spig." He rubbed his eyes, his nerves strung taut, thinking of Todd, who was his. Who was missing. "I can't believe it's true."

"But you know it is."

"I do." He looked bleak. "What's happened to him, Leigh? Where is he?"

She squeezed his hand.

"I've got to find him."

"Do you want me to ... ?"

"Sort of have to do this by myself." He read her face. "I love you." Held her tight for a moment, kissed her forehead. "Please be here when I get back."

"Of course I will." She hugged back, just as hard. "I love you."

He pulled on his jacket as he left, checking his car keys in his pocket, took the concrete stairs instead of the lift. He couldn't begin to unravel the knot of emotion pulling tight inside him, to unfold the map of his past and chart Todd's existence within it. The need just to find him was so insistent there was neither room nor energy for anything else.

He emerged onto the ground floor, crossed the stone and chrome foyer, went out through the security door to the top of the steps. A yard or so away, beneath the tall brick archways, between the tubs of winter plants, the river running alongside metallic in the fading afternoon sun, sat a boy.

Finn's legs buckled as he stumbled down the remaining steps. "*Todd*. Todd, are you all right?" He crouched down beside him. Todd looked feverish though he was shivering, breathing too rapidly but breathing all the same. Finn flipped open his phone, made the emergency call, took in the bloodstained clothes, the badly bandaged wrists, his flooding relief replaced by fear.

"What's happened to you?" His voice cracked.

"I didn't know," Todd panted, "which was your flat. I was just gonna … sit here … and wait."

"Shh. It's all right." He squeezed the boy's shoulder, his throat so tight he could barely speak himself. "Thank God you came here."

"You said … if I needed anything … to come and find you. Sort of … need some help now."

Finn's tears spilled. "It's all right. It's going to be okay, Todd. I'm here."

Her beautiful home had become a house of death. Claudia had taken to retreating to the kitchen, entrusting the children to the care of her shocked and deeply sorrowful parents, or to Stephen's parents, whose grief was almost more than she could bear. Most nights she shared her bed with Lucie and Henry. Most days they clung to her. Every single one of them broken by his loss.

She stared at the black granite surface of the island unit. No more drinking a glass of wine with him here after a long day, no more laughter or therapeutic rants about work, no more mutual support or sharing the responsibilities and joys of the children. No more being loved, however well or badly she behaved. No one to look after her, no one to keep her warm. No more anything. Ever. She had screamed, as the truth had hit her, out there in public in front of Marissa's shop, but she had not yet cried. It seemed his loss was too great for tears.

For as long as she had known him, just shy of fifteen years, Stephen had talked with feeling of atonement. He had behaved with restraint and decency in all areas of his life, had been so concerned with integrity and justice. Perhaps it was only appropriate then, that it was through her own abandonment of these that she had lost him. Perhaps not literally. Perhaps there would turn out, after all, to be no connection between what she had done to Callum Bywater and the reason her husband now lay dead. Perhaps her silence on the subject had not caused her world to shatter.

He had turned up at the house late that afternoon, the hideous Callum, when she was packing for their trip to Italy and her parents, having collected the children from school, had taken them out for tea. He'd come oozing in through the kitchen door as she was sorting the laundry she'd brought in from the washing-line. His face ugly with malice, he'd bragged that he knew exactly what Stephen had done, shocked her with his twisted version of the truth. He was not to have known that Stephen had confessed to her long before they married his all too human error of judgement regarding Donna

Sullivan, the ensuing tragedy and his terrible guilt. She had never been entirely sure she'd persuaded him that one appalling accident did not need to taint his life. The prospect of Stephen, his career and their life together being ruined by one vicious little thug had been unbearable. Having listened for far too long to his threats, his sneers and his foul language, she had told him that what he thought he knew was nonsense and if he did not leave, immediately, she would call the police. He had laughed, being of the opinion that the police would be more interested in what he had to say than what she did, and when she had turned away to call his bluff he had grabbed her from behind, her throat hard against the crook of his arm. She had flailed, dragged backwards by him across the kitchen floor, her hip hitting the corner of the island unit, fought with her elbows and her heels, struggling with all her strength to tear out of his grasp before he choked her. And then she had grabbed for the handle of her Le Creuset omelette pan and cracked the back of his head with it.

The moment at which she managed this they were in front of the French windows. She'd jerked, dropping the pan, pushing at him as she wrenched herself free. Sending him through the open door and sailing down the set of concrete steps onto the lawn below.

For a moment he had lain there, blank-eyed and unmoving. Retching and panting hard she had stared down at him. To her astonishment he looked, as he sat up, his face icing white, as frightened as she felt. "Fucking bitch," he'd hissed, staggering to his feet, swaying a moment before he'd run.

She had thought it was over but then he had telephoned while Stephen was packing their luggage into the car shortly before they left for the airport, so drunk he could hardly speak, promising to go to Finn Macallister and tell him everything. She had slammed down the receiver. When she had later learned of his death she had felt sick and afraid and as though justice had been done.

But now, but now. The life she had tried to protect was lost to her for good. It was atonement enough. No need to embark upon the sordid business of admitting anything, of depriving

Lucie and Henry of both their parents. She would live with her guilt, for she would not lose them too.

She opened one of Stephen's favourite bottles of wine, poured two inches of it into a chalice shaped glass. Set it on the granite worktop, imagined the door opening, Stephen coming home, smiling, sighing, hitching up onto a bar stool and telling her about his day. Stephen meeting her eyes over the children's heads in mutual amusement or pride. Taking Lucie onto his lap to clumsily brush her hair. Discussing with Henry the finer points of the championship league. Stephen engrossed in American TV, trying to read classic novels, laughing, holding her, falling asleep. The memories rolled from her like water on glass.

It was going to be a long time before she could cry.

*